AUSCHWITZ

Also by Angela Morgan Cutler

The Letter

AUSCHWITZ

Angela Morgan Cutler

GALILEO PUBLISHERS
Cambridge

Third edition

Copyright © 2016 by Angela Morgan Cutler
Jacket design by Nuno Associates

ISBN-13: 978-1-903385-50-0

Galileo Publishers
16 Woodlands Road, Great Shelford, Cambridge
CB22 5LW, UK
www. galileopublishing.co.uk
galileopublishers@gmail.com

135798642

I cannot light the fire, I do not know the prayer, I can no longer find the spot in the forest, I cannot even tell the story any longer. All I know how to do is to say that I no longer know how to tell this story. And this should be enough.

Jean-François Lyotard

Today, as I began to address this page, the poem kept wiping
itself out as I wrote, until all that was left were the words

Toward the page of dedication.

1st Dedication: sign of respect or affection. Origin: ME: from L. dedicat-dedicare 'to
devote or consecrate.' I check the thesaurus: Dedication: devotion, commitment,
inscription, zeal, loyalty, adherence, into hallowing …Ask: Will any of this do?

Begin again: The place of dedication is a page of intimacy [obvious enough]; what
can and cannot be spoken; who can and cannot be acknowledged; what can and
cannot be named nor declared; the page is a palimpsest.

We are both inside but outside the book, aside-the-writing; after-writing, for the
writer isn't it that the dedication's not penned, finalised often until it's all over … *I
have finished the book!* The writer cries. I haven't yet begun, you hear yourself reply,
on this page of before-and-after.

The page of dedication declares itself as the place of family and friendship, of loss …
In gratitude … I am indebted to you … I remember you … With love, my love. For
those who are absent or have passed away, I cannot bring you back but maybe inside
the shelter of the book you can live a while come rest a while.

I tread carefully here, I barely speak … Come now. For this moment held between us
the book is of no concern to me. Shh. Not yet. Wait! This page where life and writing
are not so easily separated, *I am not advocating a merger here*, she says. Here one word,
one name, the smaller the better, as few words as possible could fill us, invite us
close, invite the eye toward a clue given: This is nothing to do with me, the writer
says, this page is yours, who ever heard of this page written *To me*. This page that
addresses all of us, whispers what is shared between our common love and thanks.

My pen down,
where am I now: you, me, together again. How many times have I done this,
put my eye close to the page of dedication before the book threatens to obliterate all
that one holds dear in a name
so carefully pressed into the white page
where you wrote
Your turn now
a line you gave me
where I forgot the poem and found the dedication
where I was not joking but am laughing,
not to be cruel or unkind, but with the joy of what
and who cannot be erased, here
toward the place of dedication
from the outside - in

For
Ian
Sarah
Luke, Seth & Max
(and the characters they are)

For
Mary
(and where it all began with *Kate's speech* ...)

In memory of
Raymond

Elise
Wilhelm and Ella Engelhart
who are not forgotten

This line begins my words to you. A line that won't be stilled. A line that resists, escapes all beginning. A line scribbled violently out, is rewritten, rearranged, lost again. A line that stretches out across the page and into another country, vanishes again. That won't do, can't ever do. Lines coming into motion with the motion of the book, with the commotion of the bus. We are on the bus to Auschwitz, isn't that what I'd said? We are on the bus to Auschwitz hidden among a line of people restless to find their seats, fighting to find their seats, a line of heads sit now settle so quickly divide, two by two, pattern themselves into the rhythm of the engine, the promised departure; mesmerised by the lines of the road that soon move us forward into the lines of the book.

When we leave for Auschwitz, it's July - as if it matters. It's July when my son presents me with a new notebook, written inside: *For your birthday, Mummy, for Ashwitch*. The same notebook that I persist in carrying everywhere - as, if this book were to find its opening lines, it would no doubt begin in Poland on a bus to Auschwitz. A child's gesture inside the empty notebook inside an oversized polished Polish handbag. A notebook of hand-made paper covered with dried rose petals, sentimental to the last.

When we visit Auschwitz it is the 22nd of July. I do not go there alone. En my husband is with me, my children Seth and Max. A year ago, almost, En had brought his mother Elise here to Poland. They'd come alone. A type of pilgrimage En had called it. They'd found the village where her father had lived as a boy. They'd searched for her grandmother's grave, but to no avail. They'd learned how to tell a female grave from a male's, how to read the Hebrew inscriptions. At home, in his absence, I'd slept badly. It was one of our hottest summers - as they like to say - as they did say: It's exceptional heat. But that's another story, another year gone by, heat repeats itself and this time we all leave for Poland together.

Auschwitz.

This is where we are. Look.

We are sitting on a stone step, my eldest son and I, my back pressed into a wooden hut and we are shading ourselves in its shadow. It's the 22nd of July, just five days before his thirteenth birthday. He is lying between my open legs and his head is resting in the crook of my left arm and he's asking me when we can leave. My other son is walking around more and more rooms with my husband En, because here in Auschwitz there are many rooms. Rooms categorised with maps and information, relevant documentation, plans, according to people, nationality, gender, task, and I've already seen enough. Instead, I rest a while and am fanning my eldest son with a small Auschwitz guidebook. He keeps asking me the obvious question ... Why does it have to be so hot? I feel no need to answer; instead, I continue to cool him as best I can - I even find myself rocking him slightly - not that he normally allows this at his age but he is tired and he has forgotten himself and by forgetting himself he's allowing himself to remember the way that our bodies can tangle together and for a moment he's remembering that forgotten rhythm we'd make - way back, for now, he's closing his eyes and when I see he is relaxed I follow his gesture. I close my eyes. I fall into a memory, a fleeting image I had of a tree growing out of my son's head. Yes - absurd, the weight of his head in my arm; on my hand his sweat that is making his hair curl: the image of the tree. I say to him - my eyes still closed, trusting his are too - Remember that dream I had of you, of this head, this very one, sprouting a pine tree filled with lights and baubles ... yes, it was so beautiful, your head and the small tree worn on the top like an elaborate hat. We laugh and when I open my eyes everything is as it was: his staring eyes, the unbearable heat, the aspens still in place, the grass cut, the buildings clean and tidy and we are in Auschwitz, that today, for now, is neat and orderly. That much I can say.

If the book you were not expecting comes crawling to you in person begging to be written, Moinous says, do you refuse it? If the book comes wearing my mother's face and smile, do you say ... Don't believe a word of it!

No, instead ...

I hold my leg before it like a shy horse, not sure whether to kick or run. Admit that when the book comes calling me awake, it looks so different to what I'd expected - and what had I expected. I even notice that it's finished, ha! but I don't know how to greet it. As far as I know I haven't even begun this book and I see it already named. Yes, if the book comes to me in its binding, in its gift-wrap, its dust jacket and lettering, its colour almost visible, what should I do? Shh. *Deny the book*. LOOK. *No, try not to look*. My eyes cross as it opens, flicks me through ninety-nine pages, still, hundreds more, when I'd expected a tiny book, an abandoned book. Hear my meagre defence that I have no glasses on ... I'm half-asleep, unwashed, my breath stinks, I'm not ready for you. I'm covering my ears to a book demanding that I recognise the lines. Look, damn it ... Are these your children? ... Is this your husband En? ... You are writing to Moinous ... Are you not?

I say nothing, nothing.

Tell me what you found there in Auschwitz, C. says. Her voice gentle, familiar, trusted. Yes, tell me this as if I am seven years old and very wise. Think about the form, Moinous says. Which only makes me think of winners and losers, of turf accountants, of horses jumping huge fences, horses disappearing into the sky as if their hooves were winged. Think writing, Moinous says. My constant bleating indecision of: Who am I writing this for? Who am I addressing with my befores and afters ... Angela, you are writing it for me, Moinous says. Dear Moinous. Tell me the reverse of the story that circles the pond [the pond comes later]. Shoes and selections, that's what I'd said. Cooking pots and wedding rings; straw; smoke and abandoned cots; use footnotes if you will.

And in the process of writing I search, re-search, search again, the subject again. Auschwitz. I find other people's stories are everywhere. Some in unrepeatable prose, some made into books and diaries, TV series, films and documents, more and more stories everywhere. Some I feel unable to repeat, many found by accident: children's stories, anniversary stories, journals, dates underlined in scratchy red ink, so many letters crossed through, censored, unread kisses, unheard last lines, hurried letters, letters lost or found too late, it's never too late they say, shy rhymes, x-rayed stories. So many poems, even musical scores - yes, even Auschwitz the musical. So many stories told in so many ways. So how to find a way to write more, to say that there is nothing else to say? - and what a cliché that's become. This gets you nowhere, only more and more stories that give me no clues, no direction, no blueprint, no - this way forward, no - start here please, no map.

Auschwitz. I am trying to get used to saying it, writing it down, I am trying to get used to the word on the page. Auschwitz. Auschwitz. Auschwitz. But each time I say it I avert my eyes. Keep saying it, Moinous says. *Again.* Auschwitz. *Again.* Auschwitz. Auschwitz. Auschwitz. The word that disgusts, frightens me, makes me feel ashamed, angry ... no. I don't even know what it makes me feel ... Bewildered.
     Auschwitz.
     I turn away.

Maybe this time a different sound is needed, the sound containing the sound of laughter, even here, we agree, especially here, yes, if we lose laughter then we lose everything ... I hear Moinous say as he always does ... *Laughter is very philosophical ... Of course, laughter, tears, in the end all comes out the same.*
H.C. writes, *I think about the book all the time and the book thinks of me. And this is how it continues, the book and me: we never leave the other's thoughts.*
     Instead, there's only fragility. Unformed pages, everything still to come, still to be found. There's just Angela here at Auschwitz, for four maybe five short hours with her two sons and with En her husband. That's all I know: what Angela saw, or rather didn't see when she visited Auschwitz. And you're right, Moinous: maybe you are right and I am not being direct enough, not yet, I am not even able to write down the name of this place without wanting to as you had: XXXXXXXXX it through, when the name is all that's left. Instead, look, I find myself writing the Polish Oświęcim, that's how I'd started then restarted, with the name Oświęcim,
We are on the bus to Oświęcim.

NO

start again ...

say it

We are on the bus to Auschwitz.

A   u   s   c   h   w   i   t   z

Auschwitz,Auschwitz,Auschwitz,Auschwitz,Auschwitz,Auschwitz,Auschwit
z,Auschwitz,Auschwitz,Auschwitz,Auschwitz,Auschwitz,Auschwitz,Auschw
itz,Auschwitz,Auschwitz,Auschwitz,Auschwitz,Auschwitz,Auschwitz,Ausch
witz,Auschwitz,Auschwitz,Auschwitz,Auschwitz,Auschwitz,Auschwitz,Ausc
hwitz,Auschwitz,Auschwitz,Auschwitz,Auschwitz,Auschwitz,Auschwitz,Au
schwitz,Auschwitz,Auschwitz,Auschwitz,Auschwitz,Auschwitz,Auschwitz,A
uschwitz,Auschwitz,Auschwitz,Auschwitz,Auschwitz,Auschwitz,Auschwitz,Au
schwitz,Auschwitz,Auschwitz,Auschwitz,Auschwitz,Auschwitz,Auschwitz,Ausc
hwitz,Auschwitz,Auschwitz,Auschwitz,Auschwitz,Auschwitz,Auschwitz,Ausch
witz,Auschwitz,Auschwitz,Auschwitz,Auschwitz,Auschwitz,Auschwitz,Auschw
itz,Auschwitz,Auschwitz,Auschwitz,Auschwitz,Auschwitz,Auschwitz,Auschwit
z,Auschwitz,Auschwitz,Auschwitz,Auschwitz,Auschwitz,Auschwitz,Auschwitz,
Auschwitz,Auschwitz,Auschwitz,Auschwitz,Auschwitz,Auschwitz,Auschwit
z,Auschwitz,Auschwitz,Auschwitz,Auschwitz,Auschwitz,Auschwitz,Auschw
itz,Auschwitz,Auschwitz,Auschwitz,Auschwitz,Auschwitz,Auschwitz,Ausch
witz,Auschwitz,Auschwitz,Auschwitz,Auschwitz,Auschwitz,Auschwitz,Ausc
hwitz,Auschwitz,Auschwitz,Auschwitz,Auschwitz,Auschwitz,Auschwitz,Au
schwitz,Auschwitz,Auschwitz,Auschwitz,Auschwitz,Auschwitz,Auschwitz,A
uschwitz,Auschwitz,Auschwitz,Auschwitz,Auschwitz,Auschwitz,Auschwitz,Au
schwitz,Auschwitz,Auschwitz,Auschwitz,Auschwitz,Auschwitz,Auschwitz,Ausc
hwitz,Auschwitz,Auschwitz,Auschwitz,Auschwitz,Auschwitz,Auschwitz,Ausch
witz,Auschwitz,Auschwitz,Auschwitz,Auschwitz,Auschwitz,Auschwitz,Auschw
itz,Auschwitz,Auschwitz,Auschwitz,Auschwitz,Auschwitz,Auschwitz,Auschwit
z,Auschwitz,Auschwitz,Auschwitz,Auschwitz,Auschwitz,Auschwitz,Auschwitz,
Auschwitz,Auschwitz,Auschwitz,Auschwitz,Auschwitz,Auschwitz,Auschwit
z,Auschwitz,Auschwitz,Auschwitz,Auschwitz,Auschwitz,Auschwitz,Auschw
itz,Auschwitz,Auschwitz,Auschwitz,Auschwitz,Auschwitz,Auschwitz,Ausch
witz,Auschwitz,Auschwitz,Auschwitz,Auschwitz,Auschwitz,Auschwitz,Ausc
hwitz,Auschwitz,Auschwitz,Auschwitz,Auschwitz,Auschwitz,Auschwitz,Au
schwitz,Auschwitz,Auschwitz,Auschwitz,Auschwitz,Auschwitz,Auschwitz,A
uschwitz,Auschwitz,Auschwitz,Auschwitz,Auschwitz,Auschwitz,Auschwitz,Au
schwitz,Auschwitz,Auschwitz,Auschwitz,Auschwitz,Auschwitz,Auschwitz,Ausc
hwitz,Auschwitz,Auschwitz,Auschwitz,Auschwitz,Auschwitz,Auschwitz,Ausch
witz,Auschwitz,Auschwitz,Auschwitz,Auschwitz,Auschwitz,Auschwitz,Auschw
itz,Auschwitz,Auschwitz,Auschwitz,Auschwitz,Auschwitz,Auschwitz,Auschwit
z,Auschwitz,Auschwitz,Auschwitz,Auschwitz,Auschwitz,Auschwitz,Auschwitz,
Auschwitz,Auschwitz,Auschwitz,Auschwitz,Auschwitz,Auschwitz,Auschwit
z,Auschwitz,Auschwitz,Auschwitz,Auschwitz,Auschwitz,Auschwitz,Auschw
itz,Auschwitz,Auschwitz,Auschwitz,Auschwitz,Auschwitz,Auschwitz,Ausch
witz,Auschwitz,Auschwitz,Auschwitz,Auschwitz,Auschwitz,Auschwitz,Ausc
hwitz,Auschwitz,Auschwitz,Auschwitz,Auschwitz,Auschwitz,Auschwitz,Au
schwitz,Auschwitz,Auschwitz,Auschwitz,Auschwitz,Auschwitz,Auschwitz,A
uschwitz,Auschwitz,Auschwitz,Auschwitz,Auschwitz,Auschwitz,Auschwitz,Au

schwitz,Auschwitz,Auschwitz,Auschwitz,Auschwitz,Auschwitz,Auschwitz,Ausc
Look at that, Auschwitz. Wallpaper, knitting, gift wrap. The book's cover. Maybe
there's the clue. It's on the diagonal. The zigzag of embroidery. It takes courage,
that word, it takes time and patience and practice or otherwise spit it out, spit
it away from one body to another - no, too harsh; feel your tongue move inside
as you try to speak, do nothing to resist, tell yourself this time you must neither
respond nor pull back, you just stand there, your head held, heart open, the word
kissed out of your mouth, nine letters taken from you, into the other too soon.

I have no wish to sensationalise, sentimentalise, sterilise.

If you write this to me C. says, write as if I am CLUELESS
If you write this Feldman says, his question being not only, *How can one write after
Auschwitz* [and is that on or in] *but how can one eat one's lunch after Auschwitz?*

If you write this, Feldman says, *do NOT let it be said fearfully Certainly NOT
despairingly Therefore NOT painfully
NOT for godsake starvingly
NOT weepingly
NOT resignedly
NOT, please, horribly, hideously, moribundly.*

Try again …

We are waiting for the bus to Auschwitz. I did not come here alone. It's an
ordinary enough bus. The destination seems something that should not be
spoken yet people call it out and very loudly: the bus to Auschwitz leaves in
fifteen minutes, stand 38b. The bus to Auschwitz that has the Polish OŚWIĘCIM
written on the front. I am making it up, that part about the number of the bus;
no longer recalling such details. I don't know why but I had not expected to see
the destination enlarged with such blatant authority, eight bold illuminated red
letters that cause me to falter before boarding, relieved in a way that it didn't
spell out *Auschwitz*, yet either way when we'd earlier paid for our tickets, the
woman behind her reinforced screen, her oh-so-powerful microphone tuned full
to blasting, ensured that our destination was amplified across a waiting room
filled with people. It's breakfast time, people are going to work, we are going to
Auschwitz. *Where?* She'd shouted leaning into her mouthpiece… *Where?*
    When we get on the bus I slowly come to realise, that we are the only ones
headed that way. I mean, there are plenty of people on the bus, it's almost full,
but its not hard to work out that we are most likely the only tourists headed for
Auschwitz … until, just as the bus is about to depart, two young American women
arrive, call from the front, Does anyone here speak English? Shrill birds… and I
know I have to respond. IS THIS THE BUS TO AUSCHWITZ? … they wail.

I wait, hope that someone else will soon deal with their request. Shut them up. Sit them down. Stop them looking as if they recognise the English language in our faces. No-one says a thing. And after expecting even the local bus to contain a larger percentage of others with the same destination, I hesitate to reveal ours, especially to declare it with the needed volume my reluctant voice requires to reach the affirmation of my own language forced out of me in order to shut up the wretched sound of this word that goes on and along the aisle of a bus, a local one at that. Repeat, we are not on a guided tour as if in our decision to make our own way there, alone as it were, we'd imagined ourselves as a different kind of tourist, a different kind of voyeur; our misguided pride carried inside this distinction, surely shared with others before and after the event, the fact that we did not rely on a guide at any point not fully realising that this slightly smug decision made us stand out more than ever on a bus where others are simply caught up in their day to day, probably with no concern for our curiosity, the men carry newspapers, the women have their baskets of eggs, they have stopped off at the market on the way here. Bags bulge with clothes and cabbages, fruit of every kind. With my eye on the basket I see myself already covet the egg, wanting to take one in my hand, wish on the egg that instead of going to Auschwitz, I too was headed for some other stop where nothing would now satisfy more than to break bread, to take an egg in my hand, to say: now I have everything.

And as I sit, my nose pressed to the window of the bus, the more detours it makes around the greetings and partings of locals, the more of a visitor I feel than ever. One of the Americans on the bus fidgets with her hair, gets up and down in the seat, scarves on and off; the other examines her face in a small compact, changes her clothes, leaves me to cuss at their wiles, to wish they would stop drawing so much attention to themselves, becoming ourselves ... Their preening stops as everyone becomes distracted by a woman carrying her daughter onto the bus. Hair for now abandoned, compacts away, all eyes straight as a mother carries her teenager from a collapsible plastic blue wheel chair that looks piss-stained; the child's hair tied in different coloured ribbons too young for her face. I nervously spill water over my skirt that turns a even deeper shade of blue-green. The man to my left turns to the sound of my apology ... and to whom. If I imagine he stares, it's because I have made the wrong decision today of all days with my clothes. That such a strong colour must be in bad taste; that I, who always insist on wearing black, today impulsively decided on a turquoise skirt as if some colour were needed - as if it matters that I'd prepared this morning, asking, what clothing could be appropriate for such a visit, saying: Look at me, dressing for Auschwitz. The bus already moving off again, passes tenement blocks where children play on tricycles, or small houses where chickens are free to roam the yards, garages where men gather and even their talk smells of car oil. What did I expect? The smell of wood-smoke, a sudden stench and stretch of forest. The sun is high and running for it. Our children asking too loudly ... When are we there, Mum? This I'd imagined and of course am thinking the same, wanting to get there but worried of what we'll feel when we do.

Auschwitz.

And who hasn't done this: anticipated everything on the way there, composed a whole book while staring out at the expected woods thinning and thickening, trees forming sentences, hours of sentences which are aborted before they find a home on my page, the empty notebook I feel unable to take from my bag. The bus moves us on, holds us in the suspense, follows every village, every bus stop. I had not imagined the ordinary life around here just going about its business. Small shops, the odd factory and garage; geese in the road pursue the children who pattern the dirt, fall from their bicycles; the telephone calls being made, the gossip told at street corners; cement being mixed on the road side, women hug their hips, washing hung, woods come and go, the houses come and go, the awnings rolled up or down, the occasional sign indicates we are in the right direction; road-works delay, more children are carried on and off the bus, a couple argue, a man folds up his newspaper kisses his girlfriend good-bye, his tongue in her throat, the children wave from the pavement where the man's spit forces the dog into a piss that rolls a can back and forth, back and forth, man, dog, spit, piss, kiss; words form themselves only to blur with the speed before my eye, words gather themselves in the mouth only to be swallowed erased and forgotten. Impossible, the way the woods know everything.

And for sure, unsure - tentative, we'll hesitate on arrival as the driver translates, turns, shouts again, that word again ... Snatched conversations ... *It's my first time here ... Could be the last!* Yes, surely on arrival, as arrive we must, as arrive we do; at last I can say, hear someone say, think someone said, this could be it, must be ... Auschwitz. The word turns in the driver's mouth, turns his body, turns over in our heads, the body straightens of its own accord, a vacant expression, an attention, a look of concentration, call it what you will, we find ourselves standing up and down to his: *Here. Come. Move.* We only repeat: *Auschwitz? Auschwitz,* he says, impatience, now, third - *fourth* time around his beckoning turns the direction into a command, turns the two American women into parroting, rising, their hair falls with their question again: *Auschwitz?* they shout out, knowing the answer, jump up, almost the click of heels. We leave the bus: shall we leave the bus? Follow the two American women out, nod in agreement, make the small walk along the aisle that seems to elongate as the locals wait for us to disembark. The uneasy walk from the back to the front of the bus. Uneasy that these other people have to wait for the minutes it takes us to collect ourselves properly into motion, each seat a new expression, another face, two-by-two, each row four eyes stare up at us as we pass by, imagining ... Stop that, I tell myself, pulling at my child's arm. His resistance makes me wonder if they both resent that we have brought them here today, the children, the locals on the bus; if this detour only reminds them of a place they'd prefer to forget, dragged here on this daily business when they are simply on their way home or out for the day or taking their children to school, last stragglers. I also consider that no-one any longer cares. I mean, maybe no-one else is thinking anything about this place, maybe as usual it's just me writing, making things up, even as I walk the length of the bus am I looking for a narrative where there is none; am in danger of sounding no better than one of those cheap journalists I so despise, the ones who report from other people's countries in hushed tones with a look of misplaced concern that no-one asks them for. Whatever sentences I form continue to collapse on arrival, no better than the piss-stained wheelchair at the front of the bus. I try to think about my own bus trips at home, as if I can in any way compare this, myself sitting there on the bus on the way back from my local supermarket. Let's say I am sitting with my daughter - if I had one, that is - for a moment I'll make one up, my daughter, my country, here we are sitting on our local bus, asking: how does it feel to be sitting here with my child, my bags of shopping tucked between our feet while the tourists stop off at the local death camp that was; cameras, bags, back-packs, notebooks covered in pink petals, pens and flasks and tears to the ready. This leads me nowhere only outside, only down the dusty bus steps and into the sun where we stand a while, watch a while, final looks, no-one waves, not us, nor the hint of a tongue poked from the child closest to the window, don't make me laugh, just final looks we accept and return as the bus forms its final turn in the dust, as we turn to mark our arrival, watch the two other tourists rush ahead, leave us, they, eager to get inside, still fixing their hair, making the final decision over clothes. We still flounder, too sure of where we are - where we are not. The temporary relief of arrival tinged with the solitude of the what-now, of abandon; to be or not be on the bus, run after the bus, change our minds, the sudden stifling heat as the bus disappears from view replaced by Seth's voice, deeper than remembered, an upswing breaking on ...

Mum ... Where are we going?

We are here, my love.

This can't be it.

Is this where they shot them?

No, darling Max: it's a field. Well, maybe ... well, I don't know. But no, it's over there ... the camp, it's over there. Through those gates and trees, I expect.

It's peaceful for a moment, En says. No people for a moment, just the four of us together in a circle.

Should I put on my glasses now, Mum? I don't mind, Max says. Remember you read last night in that book you were given ... it said we wouldn't get into Auschwitz unless we were thirteen, remember we said I'd wear my glasses 'cos I'm only eleven ... if they ask I'll lie. You said I should wear my glasses. Seth said they make me look older.

They do. He should put them on.

What should I do, Mum, if they ask me if I'm a boy or a girl, Max says. My hair is long: they'll think I'm a girl. It happens all the time: people call me your daughter. Remember, Mum? What would your lovely daughter like?

You are my daughter … Anyway, I probably got mixed up, misread. Forget it love. Forget it.

He'll pass for a girl, Seth says. An older girl. Girls look older and always get let into places more easily.

We're having the same conversation as we did last night, En says. I can't believe they won't let you in.

I'll call myself Christine. Remember, Mum? It's my favourite girl's name: Christine.

Forget it all, I say. It's okay. I'm sure we'll get in. Call yourself Max... Max!

What if I have to lie about my birthday too? Seth says. I'm not officially thirteen until the 27th of July and today is only the 22nd Mum. I might forget. What if they ask and I forget? What day of the week was the 22nd? When I was supposed to be born? What day? What if they ask? And my hair's too short for a girl's. I don't look anything like a girl.

Oh, my god. Just say nothing, En says. It doesn't matter. Mum just got mixed up. Just be yourselves. Just say nothing … I don't know.

Know what?

If this is it.

But you've been before. Don't you recognise any of it?

No. Well, maybe … Oh, I don't know, it just all looks so different. Maybe we came in by a different entrance last time … Last time we came by car, Mr what's-his-name, drove my mum and me a completely different way. It just looks all wrong.

Mr Les?

That's it ... Les, Des. Something like that.

...and the sun ...
A voice interrupts, startles, passing us by: a man of god, the glint of his dog collar affirming just that. As he reads to his wife, he strides along, the book he holds springs to and from his face; beside him, his wife, possibly his sister; pompous enough - his voice louder, drowning out, that is - possibly his mother trailing behind them, her hips wobble and for sure sweat beneath tight floral polyester, her swollen feet squashed into sturdy brown heels, one nylon sock visible where her dress is pulled up by her limp that causes her to lean slightly to the right as she tries to keep up with the reverend's pace, the force of quotation: *The sun had to be biting in this scene, he'd said, because time is against us ... and the sun here ...*

The sun, like me, the sun has its best spectacles on. Get it, Mum? To make it look older, so it's let in. I think that's a lie, Mum ...

Shh ...

What he's saying, Mum, that man - about the sun. He's a vicar, look at his collar.

Don't point!

He's saying something about the Reverend Fleet, someone like him in that book and the sun? ...But there was snow here, remember, Mum. Those pictures you showed me of the snow and there was snow all over everything in Auschwitz ... And people froze and that's just as bad isn't it, Mum?

Hush now, Max.

The sun here is meant to make you suffer ...

Told you Mum, told you.

To think is to suffer, Moinous always said, again, again.

I can't shake off his words ... The Reverend Fleet ... We need to suffer when we visit such a place, he'd said. The eye squints, the lid forced half-open, a finger points up. The mother's limp gets more pronounced as she nods in rhythm behind the Reverend's verses ... *to somehow touch, feel the suffering of those who would find no resting place here.*

What's he on about ... Mum?

Shh, that's enough Max, HE'LL HEAR YOU.

I need to go pee, Mum, and quick. I need to go eat and pee.

And it's gone, all the worry over getting in, all the calculations over age and gender and spectacles on or off: all of it forgotten. There are only my child's words mixed up with the Reverend's, my son and a stranger talking one over the other, with no heed of our common language, of our proximity, of our following him on and in, as we enter through various gateways opening out into huge expanses of car parks and buses and other people suddenly everywhere, in small groups, in large colourful parties, backs humped with bags and maps, small cooking pots and packed lunches, animated calls that push us all forward, hands held and parted inside unwieldy lines spreading and spilling all sense of direction; the Reverend's words fade, part us once and for all with the contrast and repetition of my son's request, the familiarity of Seth's voice returning ...

Look. Over there. There's a shop and a woman with snacks. Snacks at Auschwitz.

Now there's only the choice of which chocolate bar and fizzy drink, no longer the fuss of calculating age but the right amount of Polish change. No longer a question of glasses, but a question of toilets, do they have them, an agreement that they must.

Everyone's gone, a woman says over the sudden odour of coffee. Chocolate licked from small fingers ... It's the films, she says ... they distort, pre-empt everything, they make you think you know this place and the first thing you notice is that the scale's all wrong.

Yes, when we leave the bus that brought us here, walk the short distance inside, enter beneath the words we have seen so many times before - *Work Shall Set You Free ... ARBEIT MACHT FREI* - there it is: we pass beneath, what happens, nothing happens; not now, look up; look into; already finding yourself agreeing with a stranger that the scale here is all wrong.

But before we enter, wait! go back. Just for a moment rewind, falter, run back, before we get to the infamous sign and gateway that marks the inside out, there is a shop selling cigarettes. Yes, there are postcards and over scented lilies we don't purchase. There's the smell of good ground coffee and shrill voices, and the florist's buxom over-baked breasts well-dressed and she's happy in her work, I can say, she's humming a tune I hold onto. Nothing works. No amount of repetition all day, the same small tune will go unnamed. There's us sitting in the small canteen and my son is asking for a sandwich. What did I expect? And there's a line of bus drivers outside, sitting on benches smoking their un-tipped cigarettes. Most sit alone. One has his face turned to the sun and he's smiling as if in memory of the Reverend Fleet's words. There are flushed toilets, we pee in white-tiled luxury, pay in small zloty coins.

The swishing mop of the toilet attendant, whiff of disinfectant spray of sickening chemical flowers fills the air, we all sneeze in turn, more coins given up, a map offered.

Mapping Auschwitz.

Our feet follow paths, unwritten lines, later the rails ... stone sleeper stone sleeper stone.

Look, here I am at Auschwitz. Here now but this can only ever be after the event. Look, here I am already. Already collecting. My head to the ground, En's laughing at me chasing a small grey feather for Moinous, digging in the path for some small stones some clue, yes, here I am already collecting small mementoes for Moinous as I said I would, asking myself if as a child I was short-changed on tragedy. Instead I came here mixed up with mission to please, say please; please find me something to say. Carry my notebook, write something down, find a quiet corner. En telling me this is where he left the stones last year, look, almost a year to the day he came here with his mother Elise. This is where I left the stones, he's saying, the ones you gave me to bring here. And he's pointing and I find myself bending down just beside the gate - beneath the *Work Shall Set You Free* - we look into the line of stone separating the electric fences and I touch the fence because I know I can. The children make a gesture to copy me, but don't complete it. I touch the wire again to show them it's okay, but none-the-less tentatively. I cannot lie. I do lie. I am not confident in anything here. Despite En's enthusiastic pointing I do not recognise the stones.

I collected small things for you, that's what I'll write to Moinous, of course I will. I'll write later from a small internet café. I collected small souvenirs for you: flowers - to keep them alive I crush water with water, the weight of a gallon bottle dries the flowers; a feather, not crushed, stroked, nothing more unusual than a common pigeon's; bark from the ash tree, nothing much but as you know there is nothing there. And whoever thought of planting an ash tree outside a crematorium?

There's a man over there, he's sitting in Auschwitz on the grass, close by, and he's telling someone that he's hoping to find the perfect line. He's saying, I am writing hoping to find the perfect line. I can hear the sound of pens scratching across paper, other people are writing out their lines and I am the only one who is not writing anything down. Not copying, drawing, photographing, videoing. Yes, among them I can hear a man say, I haven't found my line yet, but when I find it I will know it instantly, when it comes, my line, I'll know it for sure.

I am sitting with one of my sons and it's so hot and I carry handsome paper, the weave of rag still visible on the page. I carry what I can, paper, pen, water, children. I spend four or five hours here trying to write, too ashamed to write in the time we are here all I do is learn to spell the word Auschwitz, I sit on a stone step with nothing to write but I at least learn how to spell the name that was changed from its Polish Oświęcim. The name that refused to burn. A name that should be misspelled, Moinous will say: yes, it should be misspelled every time - it's an irritation to spell it, to remember how to spell it correctly.

Asking: what would you carry here apart from stones and cameras and empty books, the promise of words, what to bring here to this place if I could carry more? An offering of straw, I'll huff and I'll puff … A huge hunger and absence and a book to come, dear book. Each book, he said - I can't recall who said what now, but some such writer or other had said that - each book contains a clock. Yes, the book - and maybe she/he should have said - the writer too. A second heart and hand held me trembling. Words race to get out, eager, vulnerable beat. Not wanting the burden of time between us, the clock kept its own erratic time, sixty years passed by, time I don't yet know how to listen to here in Auschwitz, but I see that writing is patience, writing is love, writing is fearlessness, to make yourself partially deaf to the doubt that mocks, that laughs out loud, whispers: STOP. All the clocks stopped here. All the time stilled in Auschwitz.

What would you carry here to Auschwitz, apart from stones and stares and absence, he'd asked, if you could? What would you like to bring here? It's not a trick question, En had said, spontaneously enough: If your book were a meal, what type of meal would it be? A meze. Yes, maybe that's what I'd bring here, a meze of food. Hors d'oeuvres. More than that. More than appetisers. Food from all over Europe. Hummus. Sweet pickles. Oily fish. My book is not vegetarian. Lamb roasted with chilli, salt beef with mustard, smokey aubergine, spinach, yogurt and every kind of nut, horseradish, spiced peppers, don't forget the fish, soured cream, herrings, black peppercorns break open on your tongue; there's even a little liver to start and don't forget the bread: black rye, unleavened, caraway, pumpkin, the braided challah; bread torn open; a wad pushed deep into the soil as a gift. The bread sustains. As does the lemon and the egg. To take them in my hands, to hold them. The patience of the egg. The beauty of the lemon. But no soup here, not now, that is all that's missing, thin ugly soup is now denied. No rotten potatoes. Instead, I hold my skirt up to carry tomatoes eaten like apples, oranges chased over the ground. Here bite into pineapple. Place a pomegranate beside a grapefruit. Food with no hierarchy. No, this-comes-before-that. Eat up, I'd say, eat, eat, dip, graze, smear, spread, swallow, glug, I do not own a measuring cup. I have no scales here. No sword. There's only instinct and excess. There's only poppy-seed, purim cake, marzipan rich with dates, there are fresh strawberries, blueberries, sour apple strudel, coarse rice pudding with nutmeg; here we will have our cake and eat it, here we'll fetch the dessert; we'll carry the crème caramel, carefully, so carefully, we'll polish and pit the plums, we'll spread out the cheese, good strong blues, moulds that you feel in the sides of your jaw, a kick that salivates. What's at the heart: what's available, everything's available. Heavy in colour, needed herbs, the stink and juice of garlic, bitter syrups poured into the darkest tips and corners, to hell with order, to finish, a leaf of sage, plenty of goat's cheese, red onion - not that sort of tear. Fists dipped in honey. Everything's allowed. There are no restrictions, not here, not now, no more; we'll save the candles, we can say: we love the rituals, the tradition of pure white cloth spread out by hands soothing out all creases, a pattern of white tiny cross stitch at the centre and at each edge, the simplest pleasure of the cloth like the blank page the anticipation of words and guests, digressions, flowers, fine china bowls and plates, porcelain, nothing's matching, difference is allowed. No-one starves here, no-one's asking for more because there's more than enough, all you can carry and eat and lay down here over trestle tables that wind the length of the place, the cloth flapping on the breeze, held between knees, laughter, conversation, all you could bring here, all the baskets filled, each suitcase brimming with food, each pram and carry-cot overflows, and a book, a bread book shared and broken with the hands inside a day, a day held inside a night, a night that doesn't end.

Do I choose the book or does the book choose me [too romantic a notion - watch yourself here]. This is always how you begin ... he said, scene-infested. And then the real work begins. The real work is saying yes to this. Saying yes to this name, to this book. But still I don't look, still I don't look the name nor the book in the eye, instead shame keeps my eye on myself and I know it.

From: Moinous@aol.com
Sent: 6th, April 2004 8.30pm
To: angelamorgancutler@ntlworld.com
Subject: Poland

Amazing - July 16th - you leave for Poland - that historic day, the day the Jews were rounded up by the French Police in Paris 1942. The day my mother pushed me into the closet on the landing of our third floor apartment while she and my father and two sisters were bundled off to the trains to Auschwitz.
July 16th
Perfect

Tonight is first night of passover and we are going to the Kleins [you know, our Buffalo friends who moved here] for a traditional passover feast

matzo ball soup
brisket of beef
kookles
etc.

tell En to explain

but no prayers or anything like that - we are all atheists - jews are the best atheists in the world

too bad about Lublin. En and you would have liked Jurek - I don't know anyone in Krakow [the science-fiction writer Stanislav Lem used to live there and in 1981 I interviewed him once - but he moved to Switzerland.] krakow is the only Polish city which was not demolished during the war - it's quite interesting

There is a big square there with four churches - the square is called SUKENICK [yes, same name as my friend, the writer, Ron Sukenick]. In the middle of the square they have little stalls - Jewish merchants used to sell cloth there - and Sukenick, I believe, in Polish means merchant of cloth - one lovely May day with Jurek we were sitting on a bench talking when a young lady walked by with a cute puppy - we asked her what her puppy's name was [she spoke a little english - the girl, not the puppy] and she said SAMUEL BECKETT - I told her I also had a dog [I did at that time] called SAMUEL BECKETT THE FIRST [a sweet gentle somewhat paranoid Dalmatian] so I asked her why Sam Beckett and she said that a few days ago she saw a play by Beckett and she was so overwhelmed she called her dog after him. I told Beckett that when I saw him in Paris after that trip and he said - I should have been a dog. I also told Sam what Jurek and I saw when we arrived in Krakow by train from Warsaw - we arrived the day some guy tried to shoot the Pope - remember - and on the Sukenick square 200,000 Poles [all the women in white all the men in black] were on their knees praying for the Pope - the four churches had set up a platform in front of the church and the priests were conducting mass. It was quite a spectacle. We took pictures. We walked through the crowd from the train station that is near to the Writers' Union building [where we were staying] - a beautiful 15th century building [the room was great but the toilet rather primitive]. Try and visit that building. Next to the writers' union building was a theatre [damn I forget the name] a very avant-garde theatre - we saw a play in Polish - I didn't understand a damn thing but it was fascinating because in the play not only were there actors but they used mannequins and the mannequins were the bureaucrats whom the actors would execute - it was very politically daring - but then in 1981 when I arrived in Poland it was during the great movement of Solidarity [it was beautiful].

Auschwitz is not far from Krakow [there is a bus - though Jurek and I took a taxi to go there] It's the most ugly place in the world. And Treblinka even worse. We were there, Jurek and I, on a Sunday so all the offices were closed so I couldn't look at the archives to see if my parents' and sisters' name were inscribed, but what I did is pick up four pebbles from the ground which I still have. I keep them in a little box.

I wanted to go to the town where my Father was born to look at the archives - the name of the town is Siedlec - it's on the border of Poland and Russia - but I was told that Siedlec was totally demolished during the war and there were no more documents. So it goes.

Anyway, Poland is a curious country and in spite of its sordid history concerning the camps, the Poles are interesting people and Krakow is a great city. One of the few that were not totally demolished. It was inevitable that Auschwitz would turn into a tourist attraction. But It should be a most interesting and revealing trip.

The one friend I had there [a great translator] is dying of cancer. I always called him Raskonikov because he looked like a character out of a Dostoevski novel - I have been to Poland four times.
Look how talkative you made me this evening. Moinous xx

In a message dated 7th of April 2004 7:43:35 AM angelamorgancutler@ntlworld.com writes:

Amazing the coincidence with both the date and the dog's name.

You asked me yesterday about En's mother - and I did tell you this way back - but I know we have talked so much since - that it is easy to forget.

En's mother Elise [like your Erica] came from Vienna. En's mother was sent by her parents to Paris from Vienna in 1938 at the age of 18 and her brother Fritz [or Freddy, as he became known] who was 2 years younger, left some time after her. [Although every time this story is told, it changes and recently I was told that Elise came to England to stay with a family here when she was 18 and that when Freddy followed he was 14.] Freddy now lives in Canada. En's grandfather was from Kolbuszowa in Poland and his grandmother moved from Budapest to Vienna when she was little. His great-grandfather was called Balthazar - great name. They lived near the centre of Vienna in Kostlergasse, which is between Gumpendorserstrasse and the Naschmarkt, near the Apollo Cinema and Esterhazy Park. When En's mother came to London she joined the communist party where she met his father, Bill. En's father was in the army for 21 years and had joined the communist party in India during the war. He had to get out of the army in the end because of his politics, and went back to farming. Yes En [a little like you slaving on the farm when you fled Paris] was brought up on a farm - although I don't know if he took advantage of the cows like the old farmer in your book, but for a Jew he is very fond of pigs. [In fact, with the first reparation En's mother received following the war from the Austrian government, they bought a huge rather lethargic white boar called Adam. Yes, the reparation she received for being Jewish was converted into a steady litter of pigs. End of pig digression.]

His parents were always dragging poor En around on anti-war and anti-fascist marches and political rallies. He recalls being with his father, when En was very little, and his father and his father's friends left him in the middle of the road while they tried to turn over the car of the British fascist Oswald Mosley - another time his father carried En onto the platform where some fascists were addressing a crowd and shouted out - Are you telling me my son, this boy, has no right to live in Britain? En was very embarrassed and as it turns out, he'd prefer not to live here anyway … but yes, of course, that was not the point.

When En first made this trip to Auschwitz with his mother Elise, they began by flying to Warsaw then going on to Poznan - Wroclaw - Auschwitz and Krakow. Elise's father was from Poland and some of her relatives ended up in Auschwitz, although her parents were shot in a forest on the edge of Minsk - this was before the time of the gas chambers.

We will stay in Krakow. There is of course the absurdity of Auschwitz becoming part of the tour itinerary, along with castles [bouncy or otherwise] the salt mines and city centre architecture. Auschwitz differentiated in the tour guide as a *visit* rather than *sightseeing,* despite, no doubt, the obligatory Auschwitz gift shop.

Last time En went, they hired a guide, Mr Les, who drove them to Kolbuszowa, which is 100 miles east of Krakow about a two-hour drive. Kolbuszowa is where En's grandfather Wilhelm was born and lived before he left and moved to Vienna. His grandfather had lived in Kolbuszowa with his first wife and their son Charles. We tracked Charles down a few years back and met him [and two of his four sons] in Chicago. He died shortly after this. Sadly, he never got to meet En's mum; they were in many ways alike, in appearance and their very optimistic temperament.

En's grandfather left his first wife in Poland when Charles was 3 years old - nobody knows why - or if their first marriage had been arranged [or even legally dissolved] - arranged marriages were more common then in some Jewish communities. In Vienna he met and married Elise's mother, Ella, who was originally from Budapest. Charles later escaped with his mother to Belgium when the war broke out. Although he could not remember his father, he did help his father's brothers escape a concentration camp by saying the Engelharts were wanted by the Vichy and he was to take them immediately. Charles had fake papers and they believed him and released his uncles. They all escaped via Casablanca. When things became difficult in Vienna, it was said that En's grandfather wanted his wife and him to go to Belgium to escape but Elise's mother Ella wouldn't go because her husband's ex-wife was there. This strange human twist meant instead that they lost their lives.

En recently found a book written about Kolbuszowa. He made a few contacts to try and find out if there are any Engelharts still there or known of. A man did write back who was born the same year as his mother. He said that he didn't know of an Engelhart but he had written a book about the place ["A Jewish Boyhood in Poland: Remembering Kolbuszowa" by Norman Salsitz]. Salsitz stayed in Kolbuszowa during the war until they put him in a labour camp, yet he managed to smuggle out thousands of photographs of the town and its people that he hid in the roof space of a building. He later went back and helped demolish the labour camp. His wife also escaped by pretending she was a Pole and worked for the Nazis as a secretary. She prevented Krakow being blown up. When they realised they were losing the war the Nazis fled Krakow, wired the city with explosives and left instructions for her to destroy it, but she tipped off the Polish Resistance and the city was saved. She was later interrogated by her future husband, Salsitz [by then one of the first Polish officers to liberate Krakow] who thought she was a Nazi. She likewise did not completely trust him, and for a while was too afraid to reveal her Jewish identity. Just before the war there were 2,000 Jews and 2,000 Catholics living lives that were more integrated than in the larger cities. Out of the 2,000 Jews from Kolbuszowa only 9 returned after the war and then 2 of them were killed by Poles. As En and Elise drove into Kolbuszowa they noticed that the emblem on the town sign still had two hands shaking, with a crusader cross and the Jewish star. Mr Les said that as far as he knew it was unique in Poland to have the Star of David on a town crest. The main square had all the original buildings but with new shop fronts and cell phone shops instead of candle makers, etc. They spent about an hour in the pre-war Jewish cemetery [now very overgrown with trees and bushes] outside town looking for his mother's grandmother's grave but Mr Les' hebrew was a bit rusty and so they only found a grave that they thought might have been hers but they could not be sure.

Andor, En's mother's uncle, escaped Auschwitz and several other camps but I am not sure where, so many things we never asked him or discussed - it all somehow felt taboo. He later joined the French Resistance. I knew him for a few years before he died. He was full of conneries. He had a shop in the London Silver Vaults packed with jewellery but sadly he didn't leave us any diamonds.

Ax

From: Moinous@aol.com Sent: 7th of April 2004 9.30am
To: Angela
Subject: Poland

Diamonds are for BOURGEOIS

I'll be in Bochum Germany in November - check this one on your Europe map - not as exotic as Vienna but Bochum is where I'll be for a festival of the jews in the arts or something like that -
Moinous x

In a message dated 7th of April 2004 6:43:35 PM
angelamorgancutler@ntlworld.com writes:

For sure that's what people say when they haven't got any diamonds.

Ok I'll look it up, Bochum -

I just read the story you sent. Well, I read it in the toilet. I confess that am not normally one for reading in the toilet - isn't that a man thing - but it was the only place to get a minute's peace - also a man's thing. Having an outside LOO that is all so very British - yes - ours is where the cat sleeps and is full of paint and junk. It's dark and atmospheric with just a little light to read by - even in this temperature - it may make a perfect writing room.

I went back to a piece of writing called *Ashes* which I began in En's absence last year, when he went to Poland. It was inspired by several things, one being a bird I had to dispose of, I'll tell you about that another time; a friend burning her diaries and notebooks and sending me some miniature images of this and two small packets of ashes: a small selection of what remained of the books. Remember I sent one to you and the customs boys thinking it was an illegal substance, opened it - when you received it - eventually, it was covered in yellow tape! Also the small section I sent you ages ago, something that touched me very much when I came across it, a small piece by a survivor named Irka Anis who wrote - that one night in the middle of January 1945, she and several other female prisoners were ordered to work for three days removing about 6,000 huge urns containing ashes from a crematorium at Birkenau; the ashes were loaded onto trucks and removed from the camp just before the Nazis fled. The contents of many such urns were also tipped into nearby rivers.
I don't know - It's currently going in all directions - as is my way, it lunges from thing to thing - it might be awful - *imagination dead imagine*. I found Anis' words, as I am still drawn to reading what others have written on the subject of the holocaust but there is still no clue or knowing how to proceed. I do not feel it is an option to make myself into a character so called [as if my I is not one big fake come fiction anyway] but I am less inclined to speak through another's mouth, like some ventriloquist artist, to name myself Ada or Cornelia. Even though I admit I am fond of these other names!

For now there's just a few dozen pages beginning -

We have not yet properly begun to discuss the disposal of our bodies -

I'll send what I have soon - for now got to go, between Ashes, painting the bedroom blue.
Axx

From: Moinous@aol.com
Date: 7th April 2004 9.56 pm
To: angelamorgancutler@ntlworld.com
Subject: Re: these days

Angela - when you say MY ASHES it scares me - smells of mortality
- Could you give me more than just the number of pages - can I read it
- why am I here - are you censuring me from your words -

digressions - good - life is but a series of digressions - in other words not
linear but sinuous - The first creative writing prof I had at columbia university
- his name was Owens - he said to us at the first day of class - if you write
something and then you say - what a terrific piece what a great piece - destroy
it immediately - only keep the pieces to which you say this piece is shit awful
disgusting terrible -

Amazing E and I were discussing this very matter the other day while driving
to the casino - the disposal of our bodies - for me easy - burn the fucking thing
- reduce it to ashes - and dump the ashes in a sand trap on the golf course
where I suffered perhaps the most in my life trying to get the fucking little ball
out of the bunker - E wants something more romantic - she wants to have her
ashes thrown into the ocean where it seems they were destined - did I tell you
the story of E and the sinking of the Athenia - yes E and her parents and her
brother left Vienna in 1938 - she was only 6 - two days before Kristallnacht
- they spent a year in London - then the day war was declared sailed for
America - E's story is quite something too - I will tell you someday -

Moinous x

Dream #45622

I am in a Polish ghetto trying to find En but have been put in
charge of caring for my friend's elderly mother. Mother wants
to lie down and sleep and I am worried that if I let the old lady
sleep she will die so I keep talking sweet things to her and
walk her around. The place is full of muck and we are cold.
Mother's coat is damp. The place is full of market stalls run by
fat wealthy businessmen and I am looking at the stalls to busy
myself and take mother's mind off the cold, to take my mind
off the fact that I cannot find En. My friend shouts to me to
help her. She asks me to look after her toy stall. The toys are
made out of newspaper, wire, little cogs and springs, tiny and
intricate. I call back that I am busy with her mother and have
to keep her walking no matter what. My friend begins swearing
in another language, shouting obscenities, spitting at me. I
say - Please let's not fight - not now - I have to keep mother in
motion. We pass by the toy stall and come upon a stall where a

man is sitting. He's reading a large newspaper. Wears a monocle and a pinstriped suit. He's normally in uniform but it's his day off. I see a cabinet full of red glass. Rose coloured, very pale and beautiful wine goblets. I squat down in the muck and look closer, peep at the man who is still reading his paper. I open the front of the cabinet carefully so's not to alarm him, take out a glass and turn it in my hand, recognise it as my own mother's stolen glass. As I am about to slip it into my coat - just one glass - I see his monocle drop. He pushes his face to mine and says - Don't even speak - I do not want to hear what you are daring to think. And he takes the glass from me and places it back into the cabinet. He locks it away and goes back to his paper. Mother has wandered. She begins crying. Her shoes are falling apart. Don't worry, I tell her - catching her up - tomorrow I will make you a new pair from wool and cardboard - like this - look at my booties, I say proudly, trying to cheer her up, but when I hold up my leg to show her my boots, they've have gone.

Hair & Tears

I am in Auschwitz, walking from room to room, from photograph to photograph, passing the displays before me: in this case, hundreds of round almost rimless spectacles that have become twisted together. Somehow when I first see them - me, with my bad eyesight - the tangle of black wires look more like a mass of pubic hair. I recoil from saying this but can't deny that this is what comes to mind as I stand before them. Further along, a heap of artificial limbs. It is a large display, hands and legs in motion, some painted white or brown, some a hideous shade of deep pink, a few metal feet bound with soiled bandages, all caught in unfinished gestures. It looks like a car crash. The empty baskets still look new; the familiar buckled suitcases painted with oversized names that have become so symbolic of this museum, I wonder how I am to respond to these, and to the chewed-over toothbrushes, the baby chupetas, the mountain of cooking pots, and to the empty gas cans now before me. I say to En ... I don't know what I am supposed to be feeling ...

They look pleasing enough, these objects, these gas cans - and don't get me wrong, I mean aesthetically pleasing - as objects, as a field of muted colours, as displays, but admitting this to myself also unsettles me; the way they have been arranged so carefully in their glass cases, again looking like so many art installations that somehow got to us first, that maybe appropriated the real thing, and what does real thing mean any more when the look of them only keeps returning me to art objects. The subtle shifts in colour, the way the gas cans are stacked. Someone behind me is taking a photograph, it again makes me wonder if I should be taking a photograph. I can see that there is something so beautiful in the arrangement of colours, the shapes the tins make, the way metal rusts, letters fade or in some cases are retained, Gas. 500g, visible here and there; each tin labelled with a tiny skull and crossbones, almost a child's drawing, almost comical the way the small black skulls are laughing. I wonder what impression the cans make on the man behind and what his motivation is for taking the photograph. I hear him finish and wonder if I was also taken in his image, his looking capturing mine - Woman with Zyklon-B cans.

Should I take just one photograph? Yes, maybe this is the one I should take, maybe when you take one photograph here it then gets easier to take another and another. But then I ask myself why and what will I do with such a photograph, where will I keep it, how will I show it to others, and what will I say when and if I do ... Here are the gas cans. Look at the serrated edges and how they vary, how you can sense the fear, the excitement, the urgency of the person opening the can by the type of jagged ring outlasting, some making marks of panic, rushing to get it open, others more methodical, more considered uniform marks. Each empty can witness to the individual who said nothing but left his trace, his mood and temperament that day, bitten into metal. And what of the opener, I mean, can opener takes on a whole new meaning, yet floods my mouth with a childhood memory of tinned peaches, Sunday tea, father making bread and butter and tinned fruit at a time like this.

Moinous will say, Those displays did little for me. He'll say, The whole place is a circus … It's all sixty years too late. The woman who will return to Auschwitz after sixty years, who will bring her grandchild to share her story with him, shocked by the bus loads of people … Look at all these people here … now, she'll say … why are there so many people? It's like a market here. En telling me that his mother, Elise, walked out of here last year, saying she had to get out because she thought she saw their family name Engelhart written on one of the suitcases. It was not he says, but at the time she believed that's what she saw; will continue to tell us that the name was there right enough, and neither of us will feel the need to disagree.

I'm climbing the stairs, I am before a window of hair at Auschwitz, Moinous will later say … Maybe my mother's hair is in there.

I'm not thinking of a book - not yet, if someone overhears me saying I am looking for a way to write a book here, especially among all this hair, a book of shorn hair, I will deny it, I will say, what are you thinking, I will say, be quiet. Shh. Instead I'll recall the doll I'd disowned as a child, yes, way back, remember the doll, the one I'd lost, forgot, a momentary lapse, someone finding her, carrying her back to me, asking, Is she yours? Her nakedness, her green eyes and especially her dirt-matted hair causing me to deny her … I'll go on then with the thought of Moinous saying later, They used the hair, my mother's hair, my sisters' hair no doubt, for stuffing mattresses, for weaving blankets, for socks, for wigs, for dolls … laugh, he'll say - it's so absurd. He'll send me a small passage from a book he'll find … I am translating from the French, he'll say, a novel by Ourednik. Listen to this.

From the moment they got off the train on the way to the gas chambers it took ten minutes for the men to get there and fifteen minutes for the women because the women's hair was longer and thicker and it took longer for their hair to be cut and their head to be shaved.

Of course it's the stink I get first before sight, before I turn the corner there is the stench and I am glad of it. Glad of a definite smell. At last, at first a surprising smell, before I identify it warm in my nose, my hand to my nose. Something tangible, something that hits my senses, something that makes my hand react ahead of me, before I see what I have done, before I feel the shame that my hand is held to my nose before the window of hair at Auschwitz. Before I register and understand the smell as mothballs. Of course. Lowering my hand that seems suddenly too overt. Here before a window of hair that seems to turn grey as I move before it, changes colour as I stare in at the braids that have been carefully laid at the front. And I wonder who arranged this hair and what kind of aesthetic decisions they made. What person or persons spent days, maybe weeks in there, wading knee deep through all that loose hair. This is the real thing I tell myself, the real hair. Not just hair bought in for an exhibition or collected over years from any old barbers' sweepings. No one has posted these locks, or have they? Hair all over the house. Plaits found in a box hidden in a sock drawer, hair bound around utensils, found inside books, inside a mother's handbag, in with the bric-a-brac, inside pockets, even under the bed. Sack-fulls transported, counted, sorted, priced.

I walk back and forth in front of the window of hair, wondering if it may be more respectful to bury the whole lot. To bury what belonged to the body, what was taken, to give all of this a decent burial. Seeing my own great-grandmother, my grandmother and mother congregating in our front room. Three generations of hair being parted and wet with perm lotion. It was my job to pass the slim blue curlers and the small papers that looked like Rizlas; sometimes they let me apply the lotion. The black sections of my mother's hair held up. The startling white of her scalp. All of us searching out mother's tiny bald spot where she was burned as a child. My eyes and nose smarting on ammonia.

It's the gas, En says, answering my unasked question ... It changes
the colour, greys the hair ...

And so, now what? Walk back and forth, back and forth in front of the window of hair. It's one of the largest windows, it's also one of the deepest display cases. A wall-full, a small room-full of hair. En and me moving back and forth on the other side of the glass like a couple of the restless cats we'll see at the Krakow zoo the following day.

It is then that I leave the room. Change rooms and walk into a woman probably my age, her blonde hair messed up, uncared-for hair. It's her hair I notice and will remember clearly, and that she is with child and maybe a husband, who can tell who he is to her, the man walking some small distance away, caught up in his own gaze, turned away from her so he cannot yet know that she is crying, he cannot know that I am watchful on his behalf, how her tears now blur her vision, that she and I touch one another's hands as we swap rooms, accidentally, but enough contact to momentarily cause us to grasp the others' fingers, almost a reflex, as if our meeting, our collision, her tears, gives us the brief sensation that we are both about to fall; neither of us knowing what to say, if to say; in what language any stuttering between us could take place. As we reclaim our hands, too brusque for sure, maybe without realising, she begins using her blonde hair to wipe away her tears, she is crying and I am dry, she has snot running down her nose and I am staring unsparingly at her, she looks through me, only eager to get by.

And it makes me wonder about my lack of tears, no, not just that I was lacking but that until I saw the woman, found her crying before me, I had forgotten tears; Auschwitz had seemed a place so beyond tears; this in turn lead me back to a piece I had read in Ron Sukenick's novel, about his visit with Moinous to an old Gestapo headquarters in Berlin now exhibiting many photographs of the Holocaust, one more heartbreaking than the next ... he'd said. Moinous pointing out a young German woman to him, a young woman looking at the photographs and in tears. Ron writes ...

And I'll realize, not just then but at some time in the still unspecified future, remembering this, that it's a reaction it never occurred to me to have, tears, that it always seemed to me a response too simple, for that enormity, almost a diminishment or even an insult simply to cry, while remembering at some subsequent time that young woman for that moment reduced to her tears it will come to me it's probably the only reaction simple enough to be adequate. Even though it's not adequate ...

And in the same way I will later continue to think about the woman I saw in tears, about the momentary confusion I felt at seeing her, I will continue to ask, are tears adequate, and if so, where were mine. Yes for some time after our visit to Auschwitz I will mull over my absence of tears, my lack of words. I also find that when you take on such a project as the Holocaust - *project*, another inept word - people begin to tell you their own personal Holocaust stories, their anecdotes, their hearsay; my kitchen becomes a kind of confessional, and as people pass over these small tales, with their own personal slant and examination, I find it is the book that is distracting my listening, the way I have of always writing quietly to myself, of sawing myself up in two, so that instead of being in the moment with people - I mean wanting to be there, trying to appear so - yet always some part of me off and writing, plagiarising and fictionalising, digressions meandering me farther away from the point I was trying to get to regarding the tears, or my lack of them so far. An example being, about a month or so after our return from Auschwitz, a neighbour visits, and by then I have begun the first pages of the book - well, at this stage, I am only writing in my notebook to say there is nothing to say about my visit to Auschwitz, and so day after day my notebook gradually fills and I realise that in not writing the book, I am writing the book. In saying no to the book, pages and pages are now making themselves known. Anyway, when my neighbour arrives, and he is at the moment always in tears as he has quite recently lost his wife, lost, yes, and it occurs to me while writing this lost word, that when I was nursing, yes, during those distant days of my work as a psychiatric nurse, I often had to ring people up and be the one to tell them that their relative had died, that phone call forcing the choice upon me, the choice of anything but the DEAD word ... She's passed on. She's passed over. She's gone to a better place. Slipped away - as if she's a burglar, a thief, an adulteress, a conjurer, as if she's already away and laughing at us. We've lost her. You've lost her. She's laid out. Resting. At peace now. Dead. She's dead. Yes, maybe dead was finally the only word that would do.

But to get back.

My neighbour has recently lost his wife and so I am now used to him sitting with me, sitting across the kitchen table in tears - not me, I am the one again without tears, the dry one - finding ourselves so quickly talking about Auschwitz, talking about the book. Ha - to even call it a book seems too presumptuous a thing, like calling a field of weeds a garden, but to go on ... My neighbour asks me if I have been to the Holocaust museum in Paris? Which I haven't. He says it has a wall of pebbles, one inserted into the wall for every Jew that was killed, or was it for every Parisian Jew? If I am truthful, I cannot remember exactly what he said; if he said - There are also smalls piles of rubble on the floor, dust taken from every concentration camp, well, maybe just the main camps. At the Paris museum ... he says ... There you cry ... You can't help it, everyone cries there. And so again I am confronted by my own lack of tears, finding myself facing him, wanting to tell him ... I did not cry at Auschwitz. I did not. But I cannot disagree, cannot say this, it somehow seems disrespectful to his own response to speak at all, to wonder quietly to myself - Who was crying at the time, when the streets were lined with Jews and others taken away, when they were all being herded into trucks, who was crying? But I fear the sound of my own pomposity, the height of the horse I am in danger of climbing and no doubt toppling from. I say nothing. We sit across the table and there is for now only our silence before the other, only his recalled tears in the Parisian museum reinforcing the delicacy of the subject, the taboo of the subject, the sudden stillness of the hour.

Soon all the witnesses will be dead, he says.

Maybe we are all missing people

From: angelamorgancutler@ntlworld.com
Date: Sat, 23 Oct 2004 9:32:56 +0000
To: Moinous@aol.com
Subject: Re: 668.12x

Moinous - so - yes here I am writing to you again - I am such a pushover
or was it that the two days passed in one night's sleep

I decided to stay home today while En, Luke [my stepson] and the boys
have gone to see En's mother Elise - and so I made an excuse to Elise
and said I had to catch up with some work - which is true - but also
that I have to catch up with the book - the book I am avoiding - well
that occupies my head most
days - yes, all day I think about Auschwitz and then I think what a
thing - how can one spend the whole day thinking and reading about this
- book after book - like the one I found by Guber - the one I told you
about - the one I am a quarter of the way through - and it is good -
and most of it reinforces the thing I circle around and know - as if I
read to look for clues or affirmation - some pat on the hand - as if I
cannot do this alone - when the more I read the more I keep looking and
searching … and for what - when maybe the point
is that there is nothing to unturn - there is nothing that hasn't been
said already and isn't that the whole point the whole sorry cliché to
say that there is nothing to see nor find nor reveal - *only millions of
unfinished moments* as you said once - Guber's whole book [*Poetry After
Auschwitz*] - like so many - propelled into being with Adorno's infamous
statement *to attempt to write poetry after Auschwitz is barbaric* and
Guber says - *No - to not find a way to write poetry after Auschwitz is
barbaric* - and so she gives examples of those who have told the story of
remembering what one never knew - this is her subtext and yes - *Poetry
- she says - is the only form that can work - as it is fragmented and
pre-narrative working through images without closure or explanation -
poetry is the only thing that can begin to reflect the incomprehensible
memory* - but then Heaney goes onto say … *no poetry ever stopped a tank*
- Ardono's statement now so overused - or is it maybe the very line
that he knew would goad us on.

And there are no conclusions to be found here - *It is the act of writing
- Agamben says - that language is taking place - that matters -*

Yes - and I know how irritated you get by me quoting this and that -
but the hardest part is trying not to erase everything and end up with
what Sarah says is - *possible nihilism that takes me back to Adorno's
barbarism* - or am I as someone in Guber's book suggests just *consuming
trauma -*

How do I find myself in someone else's story when I have no story no
memories of my own - what is left for me but to find an/other's to leach
myself to - suck on its titty as if it were my own - *growing up haunted*
- making myself what someone called a *proxy witness -*
[Agamben] - *this is why those who assert the unsayability of Auschwitz
today should be more cautious in their statements. If they mean to say
that Auschwitz was a unique event in the face of which the witness must
in some way submit his every word to the test of an impossibility of*

speaking, they are right. But if, joining uniqueness to unsayability, they transform Auschwitz into a reality absolutely separated from language, if they break the tie between an impossibility and a possibility of speaking […] then they unconsciously repeat the Nazi's gesture; they are in secret solidarity […] Their silence threatens to repeat […] events too monstrous to be believed.

So the remnants of Auschwitz - the witnesses - are neither the dead nor the survivors, neither the drowned nor the saved. They are what remains between them.

And hasn't this also been cried out ad infinitum - that soon all the witnesses will be dead and who then will speak of this subject - if the subject is dying with the last of the victims - and have we even begun to address Auschwitz - could we. When the nearest I can get to a witness [yourself in-and excluded] is Elise's uncle - who before he died, chose silence - in Elise's case - her lack of story, cut off when she was given her 1.5 generation status - a survivor of - *a child of* - *the label of the Jew she didn't see herself as* -

And if I could ask you, her, others, what should I ask - What did you say recently - *There are some stories that cannot be told. Should not be told. Only those who died in the camps have a right to tell what happened. But of course they cannot. Those who were there and survived - Primo Levy, Paul Celan, Jean Amery, and so many others - have a right to tell their story. The rest of us, marginal survivors, children of the Holocaust as we have been labelled, can only appropriate these stories, and to do so is a form of arrogance. But we must do it anyway … my role as a survivor here or over there, in the cities, the countries, in the books I write or will write, my responsibility is to give back some dignity to what has been humiliated by the Unforgivable Enormity … of the Twentieth Century.*
    I am trying to invent a language appropriate for my experiences. A way of telling what I have lived without tumbling into the imposture of realism and the banality of sentimentality. The Holocaust was an obscenity. One cannot write about it with Belles-Lettres. One must invent an obscene language. A language that implicates the reader rather than pacifies the reader.

Moinous, last night, at a friend's opening show - on the wall of one room projected are two pages of an open notebook - on the right hand side a huge cream page and on the left the same - Rabab's right hand on the right-hand page writing in english - her hand moves quickly occasionally faltering or rather concentrating on the word to come - she is not copying anything - her hand is in the act of writing - she is not visible but the hand becomes her - I recognise the words - she has read them to me before - as I witness her remembering I remember her lines: *I am trying to translate the word for bridge - I am asked to draw a map of the world* she writes - *I am asked to draw in my country* - on the left-hand page her hand struggles to translate what she is writing on the other side in english - she writes awkwardly almost painfully from right to left in her native Arabic - the words are pleasing but her gestures to translate to remember to write in the other direction and in her other language is a child's hand a child's memory - the Arabic writing is large, looks more like doodles - the crossing out is frustrated - messy - the right is moving ahead with ease - too quickly too confidently to be caught -

I try and remember the word for watermelon she writes …

I cannot remember the word for dust …

Since I began the book everyone has been sending me words of encouragement - yes - postcards - snippets from newspapers - I even receive small gifts and words of encouragement as if I am sickening for something - a poem sent to me in the post - for instance - Anne Frank Huis by the poet laureate - my neighbour telling me the story over the same lunch - of Anne Frank's house - *Everyone's been* - he says - *everyone was talking on the way in - people lined up - ate snacks around the small Dutch street in the heat - And on the way into Anne Frank's hide-y-hole - as we are only let in a few at a time - we squeezed behind the bookcase and on the way in everyone's talking and on the way out everyone is silent - yes - you must go - he says - you must see it -*

You are not a tourist here you'd said to me Moinous, in terms of the writing that is, literally how else but to go there and look... yes, just the other day you said this again, have said this so many times before - We are all implicated one way or another -

Feldman has nothing but a fine excess of scorn for laureates fattening themselves on words of wisdom about and after Auschwitz. *As these banqueting 'godlings' up on a 'noble dais' in 'hog heaven splat down their pearls on us... '*

And amn't I my friend always sure to be pointing in the wrong direction over this -

Sarah's initial reaction:

Maybe some subjects are too sacred to be touched - but many calls later we have shifted on to how can you NOT write this - attempt to - you have begun - when you are not writing you are surely still writing -

And Moinous - I know that you will soon wake and it has been so long since I have written to you like this - about this - among our daily pell mell babble...
Angela

From: Moinous@aol.com
Date: Sat, 23 Oct 2004 11:32:56 EDT
To: angelamorgancutler@ntlworld.com
Subject: Re: 668.12x

exactly angela

you cannot write about Auschwitz in a normal organized controlled way - it has to be a mess - the writing must be as obscene as Auschwitz was/is

one does not write about what Auschwitz WAS - unless one was there - one writes about what Auschwitz IS now you standing there before that window of hair - and of course digressing from it into other hair –

into my mother's hair which perhaps was there in that grey pile

the mess

yes Auschwitz was a mess
this is my first reaction

but listen

in the midst of all that horror one must not lose one's sense of humor - or rather one's sense of cynicism [en would say] when writing about Auschwitz but remember what you are writing is

ANGELA AT AUSCHWITZ - and not somebody's else visit to Auschwitz

I was there and I never wrote about it

I could only write about Dachau

and of course digressions

Auschwitz cannot be written directly - one must make circles around it

what you said before about not crying when the Jews and others were being rounded up

I was there in the place des vosges in 1942 and no one was crying - not me - I was just looking with wonderment and incomprehension

From: Moinous@aol.com
Date: Sat, 23 Oct 2004 11:48:14 EDT
To: angelamorgancutler@ntlworld.com
Subject: Re: 668.12x or 5,000 words -

oh have I known that frustration when writing what I had to write but maybe you don't need to say that - maybe that is implicit - an important part of your project [let's call it that for lack of a better word for now] is in fact the frustration over the inability to write it - but not in the sense that it cannot be written because it is unwrittable or unspeakable [bullshit] but because it is not easy to write yes, we were all and are still implicated in this undertaking
yes we are undertakers of that horrible affair

From: Moinous@aol.com
Date: Sat, 23 Oct 2004 12:07:03 EDT
To: angelamorgancutler@ntlworld.com
Subject: Re: 668.12x or 5,000 words -

we are all thieves - I am the worse one - I was not there - but I know
about the ashes and I am not ash-amed

From: Moinous@aol.com
Date: Sat, 23 Oct 2004 12:07:14 EDT
To: angelamorgancutler@ntlworld.com
Subject: Re: 668.12x or 5,000 words –

I am a fake survivor

From: Moinous@aol.com
Date: Sat, 23 Oct 2004 12:11:00 EDT
To: angelamorgancutler@ntlworld.com
Subject: Re: 668.12x or 5,000 words -

this Feldman that Guber is quoting is he the same Feldman whose line I
used as an epigraph in To Whom?

And all we shall know of apocalypse is not the shattering that follows but
brittleness before, the high mindlessness, the quips

From: Moinous@aol.com
Date: Sat, 23 Oct 2004 1:18:00 EDT
To: angelamorgancutler@ntlworld.com
Subject: Re: 668.12x or 5,000 words -

Did I send you the piece I wrote about the word that is so important in my work
- the chut - the shh my mother left me - I can't remember -
The piece is called *CHUT - GODOT IS COMING*
Well here's a small section from this - in relation to what you were saying
about the idea of guilt - and asking about my good relations in Germany -

DEBRIS & DESIGN OF THE HOLOCAUST
2. Chut : Godot Is Coming

[...]
But when was it that it was decided that I should become a writer?
When I was ten years old, twenty years old, or when I published my first novel,
my first real book, at the age of forty-one. I mean the book that began to tell
the story I had in me, the novel entitled Double or Nothing.

For as I have written somewhere in one of my novels: My life is my story. But,
my story is also my life.
Well, I know exactly when the decision was made that I would be a writer. I
know the exact date and time when the muse whispered to me. It was decided
at 5:30 in the morning on July 16, 1942. On that day, at
5:30 in the morning, I was given the first word of my story.
That first word was Chut. Yes, spoken in French.

I was born in Paris, France, in 1928. May 15. I was born a Taurus, which means one who lives in the world with his feet firmly on the ground and his head in the clouds. But if this is my official date of birth, it was not until July 16, 1942, that my life and my story really began.

On that day, known in France as the infamous Jour de la Grande Rafle, more than twelve thousand people [who had been declared stateless by the Vichy Government and forced to wear a yellow star bearing the inscription Juif] were arrested and sent to the Nazi death camps.

That day, my father, mother, and two sisters were also arrested and deported to Auschwitz where they died in the gas chambers. There are records of this.

I escaped and survived because my mother hid me in a closet when the Gestapo and the French Police were going up the stairs to our apartment. I consider that traumatic day of July 16, 1942, to be my real birth-date, for that day I was given an excess of life.

And that day, I was also given the first word of my story. That first word was chut. The last word I heard from my mother as she shut the door of the closet, and left with the Police. That day, my mother gave me a gift. The first word of the story that I would write.

After that, the story unfolded by itself. It was simply a matter of finding the right words, the right aggregate of words, as Samuel Beckett would say, that would follow that Chut and bring the story to its conclusion. Or rather, to its final resolution.

That Chut was the last word I heard from my mother. The only word I remember of all the words she spoke to me before that Chut. It took me a long time to understand the exact meaning of that word.

[…]

I often played with the word Chut. I imposed all kinds of symbolic and metaphorical meaning on it. But that Chut remained silent. […] After all chut implies silence. Like an idiot, like a novice, for years I failed to understand what my mother meant by leaving that word with me.

With that Chut my mother was saying to me: Raymond, it is in silence that you will survive. Silence will be your companion, just as absence will be with you when you no longer hear the sound of my voice. But someday, you will have to make that silence speak.

That's what my mother meant with her final Chut. I am certain of that now. A Chut spoken so low that it was barely audible from behind the door in my closet, barely emerging out of silence before falling again into silence as soon as it was uttered.

It took me a long time to recognize the meaning of silence. A silence that became synonymous with absence.

It took a long time for me to be able to articulate what I thought was the meaning of my mother's last word to me.

[...]
Last July 16th marked the 60th year of that Chut. In order to bring the story out of this silence, I had to invent a language for myself. The language of my fiction.

[...]

Well, the Germans have understood that Chut. They have understood the silence and the absence inscribed in my work. That is to say, what I cannot tell, what refused to let itself be told.

The Germans have understood because they know exactly what is missing from my story. The unspeakable. The unnamable. It's easy for them to fill the holes in my stories, the gaps, the precipices, the void, the silence, the absence. They know the story. It is part of their history.

[...]

Not in the sense that the Germans have pity on me because of what I tell in my stories, true or false, factual or fictional, since, as I have so often repeated ad nauseam, I make no distinction between what happened to me and what I imagine happened to me, no distinction between memory and imagination.

That is not what I want from the Germans. Certainly not their pity. Nor am I interested in their guilt. Those who feel guilty for their past suffer from romantic agony.

The real reason the Germans [...] understand my story is because I make them laugh. Agreed, it is a rather muffled laughter. But my laughter, the sad laughter of my writing, makes the Germans laugh. And that is good, because in laughing, they understand that the only way to survive, even if you have a sordid history and a sordid past behind you, is to laugh. To laugh the laugh that laughs at the laugh.

[...]

And so while laughing with me, not at me, but with me, the Germans and I are reconciled in order to continue to survive, as best we can, on this fucked up planet of ours.
coda

In a message dated: 9th of July 2004 11.22.07 am angelamorgancutler@ ntlworld.com writes:
FW: look

```
Moinous, LOOK -

Uzytkownik angela morgan cutler napsia?:

Isn't this fabulous - translates as - in a message dated - in Polish -
yes - I want all our words translated into Polish - much more visually
satisfying - yes - Moinous while you are gallivanting around on buses
- I am having an e-relation - you could say a bit on the side in Polish
with Simon who is renting the apartment to us in Krakow - Simon and me
write small messages every day and yesterday I said - Simon - I am sorry
for so many questions - but I have to know - as I can't live without
camomile tea - what is the Polish word for camomile?
and it is: rumianek

now isn't that just darling
What next …
Axx
```

In a message dated 9th of July 2004 10:56:11 pm moinous@aol.com writes:
9th July 2004 - 10.56pm Re: FW: look
I knew it …
And I understand camomile is made from horse manure -

In a message dated: 10th of July 2004 11.03.07 am angelamorgancut- ler@ntlworld.com writes:
FW: look - 9th July 2004 - 4.48pm Re: Simon says

```
Simon moves out while we move into his Polish apartment - in fact -
Simon comes to Britain while we go to Poland - that's how we get his
house - and we get cared for by - hang on - Gosia - but she doesn't live
in she just does the laundry …
how bojoius
```

what else?

From: angelamorgancutler@ntlworld.com
Date: 10th July 2004 6.10pm
To: Moinous@aol.com
Subject: Re: I am back

oh I see you guys are doing one of those Xchange of places like that british
novelist [shit I forgot his name] wrote about - or maybe it's the other guy who
died - malcolm bradbury - david lodge - now I remember
it's dangerous to xchange lodging - you never know what you will find
under the bed

So Gosia is going to have an intimate look at your smalls -

no - not my smalls - my bigs -
and it's not an Xchange - I have no idea where simon is going and Gosia
only washes sheets -

what else

right now nothing

the solution

to what?

you must take a crash course in french when you come back from Poland

impossible - unless maybe one sentence a day - but make them clean
sentences - but how will I know how to pronounce as I can't hear you
speak - I'm sure Polish is easier

no - try not to learn any Polish it will affect your learning French
I thought the boys were not going to Poland but mum was taking care of them

NO I told you they are coming with us - you never listen

In Poland buy yourself some jewellery - that brown stone stuff - I forget how
you call it -

you mean Amber - I hate jewellery -

don't buy Polish books they are unreadable - but if you find a copy of the
Polish Smiles [title in polish - usmiechy na placu waszyngtona] in a bookstore
grab it
Does the apartment in Poland comes with a computer?

I'm not sure

By the way when are you leaving?

WHEN DO WE LEAVE - we go on the 16th THE !^TH - that historic day of
yours - and no doubt you will keep asking and saying the sam-same thing
until we go -

an historical date july 16th as you know -

yes I know - a strange coincidence - but then you know me and coincidences
- that's how the writing gets onto the page -
And I have no idea what a birdie is - not really

From: Moinous@aol.com
Date: 11th July 2004 9.09pm
To: angelamorgancutler@ntlworld.com
Subject: Re: Re: another day

Angela -
I'm in a horrible mood today
when I come out of it I will explain birdie in full detail be patient
I shall recover
this is a temporary condition
the problem is to know how long temporariness is
do you have a way of measuring it?
terrible dream last night

it took place in Poland somebody wanted to kill me

lucky for me I woke up on time

 oui

the only excuse I can furnish - if an excuse is appropriate - is that I don't know
why but I came back from that fresno reading totally depressed - feeling totally
out of place out of time out of sink [sic]
I think it has to do with the writing - I cannot get the new novel going - I am
feeling like I should maybe give up writing - what's the point -
I am not kidding

I sit here in my beautiful study trying to find the words and the only words
that come are the old words I have written and which are not dormant - so I
play around trying to revive them by taking them out of the dead files - I have
printed over 500 pages of such dead words - the

more loose shoes and dirty socks - and I tell you they stink though I should
tell you this -
listen

this morning I got a letter from a women historian who lives in Montflanquin
and who is writing a book about the jews who took refuge in that part of the
country during the war
and she asks me some questions

but most interesting - she found my name in some old archives of the region
that gives the name of displaced children who in november
1942 were supposed to be sent to the united states - and of course
never made it as it is told in Return to Manure.
remember that part angela from Return to Manure
This is what happened.

During the early years of the German Occupation, the Swiss Red Cross tried to rescue the children who had been left behind when their parents were deported. The children hidden in closets or abandoned in train stations. The displaced children, as they were called. There were notices passed around from town to town, and from church to church, telling people what to do if they knew of such children.

One Sunday, after mass, the priest of Concordat motioned me to come and talk to him. Josette and the old man [from the farm where I hid and slaved as a boy] were already outside of the church. He showed me this notice that said that children who were without their parents should report to the Red Cross in Villeneuve-sur-Lot for a medical examination, and if they passed this examination they would be sent to Marseille where a ship from the Red Cross would take them to America. Imagine, a ship to AMERICA.

The notice did not say Jewish children. Just children. But I wonder now if the priest of Concordat suspected that I was Jewish and was trying to help me.

I did not go to Marseille. Or did I. I cannot recall. I think I was too scared to ask the old man to let me go to Villeneuve-sur-Lot even for one day for the medical examination. I'm sure he would have said no anyway.
But perhaps if I had gone, and passed the medical examination the Red Cross would have arranged for me to go to Marseille, and then to America for the rest of the war. How different my life might have been.

The Red Cross had gathered hundreds of those children in a football stadium in Marseille. Some very young, and some my age. The children were fed and dressed with new clothes, and they were told that a white ship with a big red cross on the side was going to take them to America where Jewish families would take care of them until the end of the war. Until their own families returned.

I could have been there. If I had been in that stadium in Marseille I would not only have been fed and given new clothes, but during the night before we were to board the boat, it rained so hard that the people of Marseille brought rain clothes for the children.

Somebody gave me a long black raincoat made of plastic with metal buckles. It was so long it reached all the way down to my feet. I have never forgotten that raincoat. So I must have been there.

The ship was supposed to leave early in the morning. There were more than four hundred children in that stadium. We all had a tag tied with a string around our necks with our names on it. In case, I suppose, some of the children would forget who they were when they arrived in America. It was raining hard that night, and it was cold as the children huddled close together in that open stadium, but the ladies from the Red Cross had explained what would happen in the morning, how we would be put on that white boat that would take us to America. So, though we were all anxious, at the same time we were happy to go away to America.

*During that night, the Allied Forces in North Africa landed in Italy. Immediately,
the Germans invaded the rest of the French free zone, and the Red Cross
ship left Marseille without the children.*

*This happened in November 1942. I don't remember the exact date, but that's
the day the Germans invaded the rest of Vichy France. After that a lot of
those hiding in Southern France were caught and sent to the death camps.*

*Me, because I was one of the older children, I was told to go back to where I
came from. So I walked the twenty kilometres from Villeneuve- sur-Lot back
to the farm. That's how I missed my first chance to go to America. Lucky I had
a second chance.*
Anyway - it suddenly makes my book seem relevant
OK - what now
love mxx

**From: angelamorgancutler@ntlworld.com
Date: 12th July 2004 7.44pm
To: Moinous@aol.com
Subject: Re: I am back**

Yes, I remember that story very well and that finally you couldn't
remember if you were making it up -
- I'm not clear. Did this happen, [you say,] or did you make this up.
You've told us that story before, [E says to you,] but we were never
sure if you were inventing it or not. And each time it was a different
version. Last time you told that story, the medical examination was to
take place in Montauban, and you went there by bus because it was far
from the farm. Now you say it was in Villeneuve, and you walked.

- To tell you the truth, [you tell Erica] I don't know myself if it
really happened, or if I wished it had happened when the priest of
Concordat showed me that notice. All the details of where to go and what
to do were specified in the notice.

Anyway - to change the subject for a moment - look what your horror-
scope said yesterday
You may be feeling frustrated as you wish to complete projects but
cannot due to forces beyond your control. Things may seem to be swirling
around you when you just want to take the time to get organized. Don't
worry, a project will come together soon if you approach it one step at
a time. A good outlet for you would be meditation.
You see
go meditate
go walk
relax
and all will come right
Amazing the woman finding your name in that list - so do you think
now you did go to Villeneuve-Sur-Lot? I wonder what happened to the
raincoat?
Ax

From: angelamorgancutler@ntlworld.com
Date: 9th August 2004 11.52pm
To: Moinous@aol.com
Subject: Re: gravity boots

I am having a screwy day today - En is hanging upside-down in the
garden - not a reverse form of suicide - rather his bad back. A kind
of makeshift traction. Years of working on his father's farm he says.

Claire wrote that she showed your book - Voice in the Closet - to a
woman she just met - an actress who has some part in Claire's play -
the woman is Jewish and lost family in the war - maybe grandparents I
don't know - she began reading your little book at Claire's apartment
and then all of a sudden gets
up and says - oh I have to go I can't take it - and she leaves just like
that in a big rush - you see the effect you have -

oh well - I make people suffer -
Tell En that hanging upside-down will make the blood rush to his head and
make him more of a cynic than ever - jews are famous for their bad backs

To change the subject radically - or maybe not -
En got some photocopied papers yesterday morning from his sister - she
had been to Vienna recently with his mother and they had been given a CD
and papers with all the names of the Jews who were deported from Vienna
- [the now available on CD - rather tragicomic] so Anne - En's sister -
sent him copies of papers with their grandparents names on - Elise had
known for some time that her parents were taken to Minsk but not dates
of deportation or execution - the date of their deportation was given as
20/5/1942 - the date of their death 26/5/1942 so [obviously] from that
we can assume it must have taken them six days to get from Vienna to
Minsk as it was indicated that they were killed on arrival - They found
out that En's mum's aunt was also deported 3 weeks later and killed 6
days after embarkation - the papers included records of the farm where
they were taken: Maly Trostenets - 15,000 Jews were taken to that camp
alone - trains arriving in Minsk always between 4 and 7a.m. - then the
8 carriages were unloaded and a few people selected for work on the farm
but most were to be killed - valuables - clothing - etc. removed. The
victims were then taken into the forest and shot - later they diverted
the trains along a branch line into the forest where the farm was
located and all were killed either in one of the 3 gas vans they used
from May '42 or more typically people were shoot into pits - one of
En's cousins also had family killed there - his 2nd cousin's uncles on
his father's side - From 9,000 Austrian Jews deported to that camp only
17 are known to have survived - It had a little more detail and names
of who did what and a bad copy of a photograph of part of the building
- all the usual carefully written recordings - It was very strange to
hold copies of the unexpected papers - to see the handwriting - well
it was the first time I have ever seen En moved by it - suddenly these
words these forms with some person's scrawly handwriting and signatures
and stamps and dates made it very real - sorry but it was just such an
unexpected moment early yesterday morning between the cooked breakfast
and the washing up - you know -

I also have to admit that last night I dreamt about nazis all night - En had found some website that was dedicated to those who dreamt of the Shoah - well those people who had no connection with the holocaust yet since childhood had regular very vivid dreams that they were either involved in the war and had died or been killed in one of the camps - and as a result of reincarnation had been dreaming of their so-called previous life - many of the dreams were documented and for sure I found this all very distasteful and wouldn't read it - Having said that - I then realised [almost hypocritically] that as a result of writing to you and writing this book and the pages of stories I have sifted through - I too am now regularly dreaming - what you might call - my own holocaust dreams - [not - I must say - with any feeling of reincarnation] but maybe this is not so surprising when all day I am thinking of little else - neither does it help that every evening this week En's been reading about Kolbuszowa in Poland where his grandfather lived - our light bedtime reading - for instance - before they deported all the Jews from Kolbuszowa - the Poles were killing the people in Pogroms - hanging - shooting - one day they shot about 10 or more men and then came back the next day to the ghetto and demanded the money from the remaining Jews for the used bullets! - As a result for nights now I've been dreaming a recurring dream in blue.

Dream #07477

We are in a city. It is familiar and I am happy to be back. I enjoy showing it to the children who have never been here before. The city is dark. We can see our breath before us and as we walk and laugh together, the city is lit up like a Christmas tree. We are shuffled into an empty house by some friends who tell us it is still not safe for us to be out in the streets. I recognise the house as my old childhood home. I am so happy to be back in it, even though it is emptied out and stark. The walls are blue-grey and the floorboards are dirty beneath our feet. They creak every time we move over them. There is a big dresser in the living room that is now bare. I remember it used to be filled with every kind of plate and dish. The door is open on the right side of the dresser. The glass is covered in a frenzy of fingerprints. I go close to see how many different prints I can recognise. As I do, I hear En in the other room, separated from us, as officers and soldiers climb the wooden stairs. I remember William singing Up the Wooden Ladder as he'd shoo us off to bed. The officer's uniform is seductively blue-grey and matches the walls. I want to touch the cloth. As if reading my mind he asks, Do you want to touch the cloth? I think he must be erect beneath the good quality cloth of his trouser. We smile warmly at one another. I smile because I am worried, not because I want to. Behind me I can hear my children chatting. They sound happy. I can feel them just behind my body. I notice the shine of the officer's pin glint on his collar, I smile again. I am wearing a thick black turtleneck jumper high at my neck. As I begin to turn away my head, I see him reach into his collar. His hand flaps before me like a wing. I feel his bullet enter the back of my head. My slow fall to the floor. I think he should have killed the children first so I will know they had a safe death.

From: Moinous@aol.com
Sent: August 10th 2004 10:45 am
To: angelamorgancutler@ntlworld.com
Subject: Poland

the jewish thing

we are all jews one way or another - the holocaust was a universal affair in which all of humanity was implicated - I am such a bad jew
- I know nothing about jewish stuff - except that it was decided that I should become visibly jewish by wearing a yellow star -
that dream of yours I seem to have dreamt a number of times what is a jewish dream
does it wear a yellow star

but you say it was blue maybe next time they'll make us wear blue stars

Last Night's Dream in Loose Shoes - is somewhat similar
and so is the Blue Room [another dream]
I also have many such papers - So it goes - Next topic the world -
the world is so fucked up these days - I propose that you and I leave
the world behind and concentrate on our rapport [shit I have to find a
 better word] our relations -
I'm fed [no pun intended] up with the world
I'm leaving
you want to come pack lightly
Mxx

The Photograph

Whether or not the subject is already dead every photograph is this catastrophe.
Roland Barthes

There's a long old corridor in one of the buildings, I forget which one. It's the building that has all the photographs lined up on either side - well, all the rooms have photographs in their different ways, but these are the official photographs - I mean the photographs the Nazis took when people were ... what's the word ... *processed* - you know, on arrival. Lines of portraits, of individuals with the clichéd shaved heads and stripy prison garb. En told me that to begin with they took photographs when people arrived to make it official, orderly; to begin with systems were everything, and photography of course played an important role and so, as you go in, there are the women to the left and the men to the right. And at the very end of this aisle of portraits, there are two doors - and she's there. She's right there ... Look, on the wall over there, where the two doorways meet. There's her photograph nearest to the doorway ... I'm confusing you. Try again ... not the right ...but nearer to the left, on the left by the door, that's her face. Right there.

And is there any point to such questions as: why her and not the woman over there? Why this one and not that one? Why have I suddenly stopped before her photograph, this particular one?

I picked her out, is that it? Not really ... I mean, I didn't think about it - I just stopped. En and me, just for a while caught up in our own ways of looking, moving in and out of focus, have become separated, like a dance to and from, then comes the dance back and forth before the image that keeps asking for both my distance and proximity, neither one nor the other will do. The children have also wandered away, I don't know where, maybe they are momentarily outside, or in another room, because here in Auschwitz there are more than enough rooms. And here I am alone for a moment loosing myself in looking, in the trying to look, in the comings and goings of trying hard to find something to see.

I don't mention this to En. Her face that is, that I stop before her photograph. En has wandered ahead and he is staring up at a handsome enough man who has the same surname as his mother's cousin: Kerpel. He will tell me later that he'd noticed him last time, almost a year to the day when he'd stood with his Mother Elise staring up at the same photograph of the man. When he'd photographed the photograph of Kerpel - how ridiculous, a photograph of a photograph but what else is there to do here - but the negative blurred, worse, that particular slide was blank. I'll no doubt ask him to try again but he won't and neither will I offer to retake it for him.

For now, I don't think En notices that he's wandering ahead and that I've stopped awhile before the photograph of a woman who is probably the same age as me. And I will not tell En about her: not now, not until the time of writing which will be many months later. But I do whisper this to you, I mean to you in the photograph facing me with a less shy expression than the one I return; talking to myself, to your face, as if I know you, because I tell myself I must in some way know something of you otherwise what stopped me, when surely all that is too simple a notion.

And here I am already telling you that my simple gesture of hesitation in front of you is making me uneasy. Maybe the body deciding ahead of me, is that it? The body deciding of its own accord, the mind just the hum of the engine, I heard that somewhere, the mind just the hum of the engine, some way off. The way I stop in front of you neither a decision and of course a decision, when I had passed so many other faces, women to the left, men to the right, rows and rows of faces, too many to look at, obvious enough, and me just walking and wandering, asking, should I stop, and if so, when; how to look at each one of these faces that surely, each one, needs attention, deserves to be seen.

But here more than anywhere I have to decide on my own protocols of looking. Here inside such an absence of people, still the eye saturates with the command … Look … Look, why come to Auschwitz but to learn how to look, to forget how to look, realise you know nothing of looking, learn how to look all over again, scan, read, search, take in, investigate, consider, attempt to find, rely on, hope, make sure, claim, exclaim, look down one's nose at, look you in the eye, directly, without showing, without embarrassment or fear, with or without shame or anger, with or without doubt, look lively, look after, take care of the one you're looking at, look sad, happy, look to it, look back, look like you're suffering, look down, look in, look on, make a visit or call-by, watch without getting involved, watch by getting over involved, look no further, take great notice, have a great deal of respect for, looking.

And is that why some take a guide who will huddle them into groups, who they'll pay well enough, to advise them how to look, when to look, if to look; the guide dividing up the time comfortably into bite-size sections, easing their guilt of having no idea of the length looking should take, easing the awkward silence of looking alone, with a guiding incessant jabbering and hand-holding reassurance and informed authority that eases their conscience, no doubt, denies the awkward breaks and autonomy that may require uneasy unstable thinking time. But no, as much as I am not sure how to do this alone, neither do I want the guide, the over amplified mistress of anecdote and numerous tongues; isn't my looking so crooked such a private concern?

And I wonder about Moinous, when he came here, had he looked through each one of these photographs for his family, or did he pass them all by? Wanting to recognise and find them, wanting to not. And I know I will want to ask him and will not in any way ask him what kind of looking would that require, what kind of not wanting to look might that take. And who would admit to boredom here? Who would admit to closing their eyes?

I select you, is that it? Like the small selection I'll come to find in a book. I'll digress before you, is that it? What else is there between your face and mine?

Your face, before which I dare not think of, let alone speak the word: us. Should I instead tell you of the book, the one I am trying to write, of the ones I have read, will never read, as this place more than many entices language out of people, yes, despite the claims of the nothing to say, yes, despite the calls of the nothing to be done, there are more than enough books written on this place. And for now does it matter what this comes before that, here the order of things, is just the order of things, what comes now what comes later, I tell you, here order is everything, order is of no concern. All you need to know for now is that I'm here in Auschwitz and I find myself standing before your photograph, I'm alone with you for a moment and in my own way you could say I have made a selection. To Select, *carefully choose as being the best or most suitable. Select for or against survival* … or so it says in the big book of words. Ask … What is so careful in the speed of a glance, all this before one thought: I find you and what do I find in you in just one look; does the shame of selection always go both ways; the shame of the chosen; the shame of the person staring upon another that in some way touches something unsayable in you, me: our sudden shameful intimacy. I choose you.

And so I find myself standing before your face and telling you of the student. Yes, the student I found pressed into a book I read. He was an Italian, that much I remember. And the student was blushing before the SS guard. His face flushed pink, that tiny moment that touched and stayed with me … During the march from Buchenwald to Dachau the SS shot anyone who slowed the march. Antelme recounts the Italian student turning pink when instructed to move out of line selected by the SS officer, at his command that the student should come here. He flushes pink - - *pink everywhere* he says - - *And* [the officer] *having found him he looked no further. He didn't ask himself: why him, instead of someone else? And the Italian, having understood it was really him, accepted his chance selection. He didn't wonder why me, instead of someone else?* The intimacy of the haphazardly chosen - - *he and no one else* […] *this flush, this shame.*

Continue on with the thought, if it's not far too easy, that I recognised you … because … there's something of the here and now about you? Isn't that what I'm saying? That you somehow look as if you don't belong to this row of faces, and then what is that saying of the others beside you, of the ones I did not see or stop before or choose. Is it that you belong to a different time, as if there is something contemporary about your image? Too inept a word. But for sure I am looking into your face and you're my age. I am standing before *you* and not *her, you* and not *him* … Because … Because … Maybe you are a mother, but I cannot tell and I wonder about this, and the photograph looks contemporary, *said already*; because I simply recognise something in you … *SAID!* … Yes, that said, that the kind of thing people say all the time; others add their two-penneth come tuppence worth: Most likely a question of identification? Well, maybe narcissism's alive and well and I'm waiting for the echo in you. No, you look nothing like me. Or is it simply … *WHAT?* … That when I entered this hall of photographs, I felt I should stop and look at someone, anyone? *Was it simply time to stop?* Don't say that! Maybe it's no more than the tale of the flushed man, his pink face, the shame of body betraying something of the *haphazard* in me, in you, as simple as a smile between us, smiles at a time like this … And what point is there in analysis, in asking: is there any difference in the one who chooses to look upon to remember you or to kill you?

And as I stand here facing you for these few moments; all these photographs presented here, some smile, they managed that much, maybe more by instinct and habit, fear, the sheer madness of it all, it reminds me of the *Sunny Smiles*. And maybe you know nothing of this - as far as I know it was a British thing, a distasteful enough name and concept. I had completely forgotten about those small books of faces we'd get forced into buying as children … And I admit also to having completely forgotten, until now, that it was the church folk who would come round the doors with them, always the church ladies selling you an African baby. Me, as always, not knowing how to say no. Always feeling I had to agree to those faces flickering before mine. Now such a book, such a selection, would be inconceivable in the thirty-five years that have passed. Or maybe now there are swifter electronic choices. Make your decision they'd say, Be quick! There were always many more doors to call on. Always feeling more guilt over the ones I didn't choose. Most made their choice on looks, there was little else to go on, those children with biggest water-filled eyes, smiles of course persuaded out of them, and cute please-have-me pouts. Often I'd try and go in the other direction mostly on purpose, mostly as a way of tricking myself into going in the other direction as if some bad luck would come and cuss me if I went for the obvious look. Because once you'd chosen you'd own the child: they'd tell you that, the church ladies. And there you were with your selection, other kids comparing little 'uns in the playground, judging you on what you'd picked, and that's how it went on in those days. Mamma's buying me a black baby, but I never felt easy with these chosen ones, with her name and my signature there on the dotted line, paid for week by week, in photograph only, she's yours all the same.

Move on, I tell myself, I've been standing before this photograph of your face for too long, as if I am claiming something of friendship between us when you can neither see nor hear me, you, who return my gaze, cannot return my gaze, your face is looking into the eye and lens of the person who photographed you some sixty years back, your face both dead and alive, either way about to die, another assumption, when I have no idea of your fate. Either way, by now surely you would no longer be here - if you'd survived, I mean - either way, you are both here and no longer, not in any way here.

And I want to write down your name but worry I have already taken enough from you. I ask, would you want to be seen like this - shaved of hair, numbered? Should you be here on display at all? I never reach a conclusion for how could I. And what will I take with me from here, from this place, from this woman's face. I have still not taken one photograph or written down one word while others around me scribble, sketch, photograph, video and discuss with a fidelity that maybe I lack; still unable to take the notebook from my bag, hidden, empty in the knowledge that the book I whisper quietly to you, to myself in Auschwitz, will never be the book I'll later write, anything I write on the way here will be too quickly forgotten, anything I say before your photograph is to be lost the minute I turn away from you. And I see that you are looking at me well enough when it is me that can't see for the looking.

And now I have stopped before you, how to proceed, how to decide if to move off again, to stay, to pass by? How much time is respectable before a stranger's face? Instead, I find myself doing what I said I wouldn't: I approach you further, move close enough to see your name; tell you that I will later regret not writing it down. Although I am carrying my spectacles in my bag like the notebook they never get taken out. Deciding when I came here that this was not a place for clear vision, too much clarity scares the hell out of me, especially when things feel beyond translation; beyond the eye, I need the reassurance and the distance of the out-of-focus, the way that pushes me to rely on other senses. Nonetheless, I step forward just enough so I can read your name. It looks Polish, maybe. It is in fact three names. I think about writing them on my hand. I try to pronounce them quietly, but fail. I tell you instead that I will find you when I get home, that there must be records, archives of these very photographs. I haven't even left your side yet and already I am at home planning to try to find you again, at a respectable distance, is that it? To see if I can find out something about you when I get safely home. And all this ridiculous monologue, as I know I will not retain one name, especially not three, spectacles or otherwise, your name is not easily pronounced, therefore not easily retained. I write nothing down, not here, not a number, nor a name. And when I get home I will not be able to find you. I already know that all we have is a few moments together, no more.

And if you are nervous - I assume you must be - how else, here? - you're not looking nervous, or if you are you're not showing it, you're not smiling out of fear: not yet. You're doing something I recognise with your expression. I don't feel the need to explain, sure that I have taken quite enough of you I hear myself say … We could have been friends. I can't believe I'm saying this, that I even thought it, of course I did: We could have been friends, maybe that's what stopped me … What complete schmaltz. Well, maybe we could have, maybe this moment has made us just that, the intimacy of selection, in that way that friends find you in the most unlikely of places and times. To you in the photograph, that's the kind of thing I might say if I were to pause a while, to look a while, to imagine you a while. There you are. Anyone could have picked you; for sure others had before me. Simple. That fucking simple.

I don't bother to look at their faces she says. A woman behind me now, her shrill voice moving me on. The way he'd said sugar is never sweet, sugar for me is always violent … her tight old mouth on me only tries to see what I'm staring at so carefully, and she's preaching at her friend … There are simply too many faces she says, and you can't see it all, and who bothered in the end …

And at the point when maybe we'd only just begun, it's her reflection mixed with mine that finalises what fragments of time we have left, that obliterates your image with hers and her words that won't stop; as abruptly as I'd approached I move away again, no warning, no good-byes simply move on to the next room...

Because here, there are more than enough rooms. Rose light on the floor. Look at that, who ever thought of that. New rose-coloured glass inserted into the old window-frames. The flush of pink over the story, a blush held in glass. This is the type of afterthought we are dealing with, the type of misplaced aesthetics. One narrative weaves its way into the next. Concentrate: there's the clue. There's a square of pink light deepening at the centre of an empty room, on the bare wooden floor and here I am crouching beside it, turning my hand this way and that, my hand turning deep pink as though it were just my eyes' imaginings.

From: Moinous@aol.com
Sent: 28th January 2003 12.19am
To: angelamorgancutler@ntlworld.com
Subject: merde

OK Angela the notion of shit - wordshit Sam called it in *Texts for Nothing* - holds a central place here in all we have so far written and will no doubt go on to write -

let me tell you first how shit became so important for me - you may have already gathered the story from the little pieces I have scattered all over - but I will tell you again what happened in the closet -

one day when we meet again maybe I can take you to Montrouge so you can see the house and if we can get inside - the closet –

first let me tell you [tell en to listen] what happened at 5:30 a.m. on July 16th 1942

moinous is 14 years old now

the gestapo and the french police are coming up the stairs to the third floor where moinous, his father his mother and his sisters Sarah and Jacqueline, live in a one-room apartment with a little kitchen - the sisters sleep on a lit cage in the kitchen Moinous on a cot in the large room father and mother behind a curtain in the same room - 5:30 in the morning in Montrouge - as the Gestapo and French police come up the stairs they shout - Federman - troisieme etage - somebody shouts in the staircase - quickly the mother awakens the children takes the boy by the arm - he's only wearing his little [soiled] slip - grabs his summer shorts and shirt [but forgets the espadrilles] and pushes the boy inside a little closet on the landing and as she closes the door she says - chut - in french - that much of the story you already know - I won't drag on telling you how long the boy stayed and how finally when he came out he discovered that he had been given an excess of life - what happened in the closet - the boy had to take a shit [I know you know this already] and feeling guilty he wrapped the shit in an old newspaper and when he finally came out of the closet the next night he held the package of shit in his hands still feeling its warmth [such a good shit it was] and climbed a little ladder that led to the skylight lifted it and placed his package on the roof

that's basically the shit story that has been told and retold - what may not have been told Angela is that the first thing the boy did when he got back to Montrouge [he was 17 then] is to go up to the top of the stairs and look on the roof for his package of shit

that symbolic package Angela that contained - well no need to spell it out

it marked the scatological beginning of Moinous' life

Moinous started his life in shit up to his neck, one could say - and has been trying to extricate himself since then - in vain - it seems - but you know what Angela - one gets used to shit —

End of the shit digression -

FROM: angelamorgancutler@ntlworld.com
Date: Friday, 1st february 2003 11:40:39 - 0500
To: moinous@aol.com
Subject: the coincidence of madness and the parcel of shit

And this week, Moinous, has indeed been a week of coincidences that in turn completely changed the tone of the writing I was planning to send you - well, in that I wanted to talk to you more about the ten years or more I worked in those large psychiatric hospitals, those bins as they were called - I wanted to tell you of my response to what you'd sent me re: the parcel of shit and your beginnings from your closet and also my response to that 20-page unpunctuated sentence you wrote - your book - *Voice in the Closet* - and how listening to the recording of that text triggered off a memory of the experience I had working as a psychiatric nurse - one response triggering off another and so on in turn until the writing unfolded in a completely different way - and all that made me consider the effect coincidence has played in bringing not just this piece of writing into being but maybe all my writing into being - yes the digression that carries the work along and the part coincidence has now played in enabling me to speak about madness - the question of how to speak of things that are often unspeakable - to find the right language to convey what is unavowable - which is what you did with your book - Closet - but I will go back to that some other time -

for now I wanted to stay with your Voice

Yes - I am listening to the recording of your book [*The Voice in the Closet*] - I put on the headphones - I am cleaning the house - it's a Friday evening and we are expecting friends for the weekend - the house smells of polish - smells good - the food is prepared - the rooms are full of fresh flowers and I am listening to your voice so defiantly alive - a voice that is telling me how it escaped death - how having looked into the mouth of death this voice is more alive than ever - and in the madness of the situation - the story of the 13-year-old boy [well, here the age I note keeps changing - sometimes you say 14-year-old boy - sometimes 13, 15, even once I read that you were 12?] hurriedly shoved and hidden away in the closet on the 3rd floor landing of their apartment - the morning of the great round-up of the Jews from Paris - you are shoved into a closet by your mother while the Nazis take her your father and two sisters away to be killed at Auschwitz - out of the unspeakable madness of that situation 16th of July 1942 came that voice - a voice that finds its resurrection - *I was reborn naked out of the closet* you say - *in that July morning I was again given life* - yes we find our first unexpected breath in the most unlikely of places - that carries us for a whole book - we find our oxygen - we take a deep breath that sustains us enough to write a whole book - a book that is a scream that is music

57

that is unstoppable relentless mad laughter running between the lines -

And in that Voice - in that small endless stream of words in that one unpunctuated sentence in those repeated squares of text that small book that lasts for just twenty pages - I also find the small gesture - the wrapped-up piece of shit that becomes a language of its own - and I wanted to talk to you about the connections that made for me - the involuntary memory it evoked that I had quite forgotten - but first I read the retelling of your words by the Old Man in *The Twofold Vibration* -

He - the boy you were - hidden away from his killers in the closet has to go to the toilet but cannot yet leave his hiding place so he forced to shit his fear into a newspaper -

Yes and in response to this parcel - the imaginative quality of this parcel of shit - I recalled Roudinesco's book on Lacan and what I found interesting in her book was also the small wrapped-up parcel of shit - do you know that book? You could smell the stink of vinegar when you read the opening lines - from the gossip about Lacan - the tattle about him and Sylvia Bataille to the stories of his family who were vinegar merchants - yes sometimes you read a book - of course forgetting most of it - but one part stands out - one small snippet from thousands of pages finds a place inside you - and out of the book what was retained was the opening story of the vinegar and tucked away in thousands of words - was Blanche - hidden away in the psychiatric hospital where Lacan worked - Blanche admitted into his care with her delusions - Blanche wrapping up her shit - keeping it in a little purse or container or something - all prettied up with beads - well that's how I recall her - I'll go find the section - hang on - it reads like an extraordinary piece of prose - yes and in many ways the language of madness in the case studies he wrote up read like many surrealist texts - at the time Lacan wrote and worked in the hospitals he was also mixing with surrealist artists and writers many of whom were against the incarceration of the mentally ill into asylums - regarding their language as *sublime involuntary poetry - madness close to truth, reason to unreason [...] coherence to delirium.*

She [Blanche] *sees herself as a four-headed monster with green eyes. What made her realise this is that her blood is scented. In high temperatures her skin goes hard and turns into metal, then she is covered with pearls and sprouts pieces of jewellery. Her genitals are quite unique: she has a pistil like a flower. Her brain is four times as powerful as other people's brains, and her ovaries are tougher. She's the only woman in the world who doesn't need to wash [...] The patient admits to some very strange habits. She makes broth with her menstrual blood: 'I drink some every day; it's very nourishing.' She arrived at the hospital with two hermetically sealed bottles: one contained urine and the other stools, and both were wrapped in weirdly embroidered cloths.*

Weirdly embroidered cloths - what an image that made in me - what stitching - what material - what choice -

In the same way - it was the small package of shit that struck me in your work - that I was not expecting - that took me back to Blanche -

to the days I worked as a psychiatric nurse - yours a different situation
of course to Blanche's but then in the same way a poetic gesture a poetic
language found in the wrapping and repetition of that shit in your work -
the abject speaks what is unspeakable - *too absurd and obscene to be told* -
speaks the madness of that day in July - the gesture of wrapping articulates
everything that cannot be understood or spoken by the boy - both Blanche
and your Closet taking me back to a forgotten memory of a woman I nursed
in London - a Jewish woman who had also escaped Auschwitz but in different
circumstances - ending up in a small hospital room where she also wrapped up
her stools - hiding the small parcels in her room - she hoarded everything
her body produced so that the stink became unbearable and we would then have
to find the bundles and clear them out - but she would scream and cry and
hang onto those valuable little parcels - yes - I had quite forgotten Esther

Axx

From: angelamorgancutler@ntlworld.com
Date: 15th July 2004 3.03pm
To: Moinous@aol.com
Subject: Re: the rich

Are you going out with the million air tonight -

I know no millionaires only you who are close to the rich - me I am a
chicken in a chicken house with no money but still words are free of a
fashion - well, in many ways shackled - will you [virtually] miss me when
I go to Poland

I miss you permanently since you are never here in the flesh

my house is in chaos and I haven't even started packing but for an hour
or two as En and me are going to relax have lunch and a bottle of wine -
yes - we go to Poland in 11 hrs - 2am we leave the house for London -

I started missing you yesterday - I always start missing people I love several days
in advance just to get a head start and really get into the thick of missingness by
the second day of absence re-the pronoun - maybe you should only ever address
me as you

back on the 1st of august - max's b'day -
my love to you Axx

From: Moinous@aol.com
Date: 15th July 2004 7.17am
To: angelamorgancutler@ntlworld.com
Subject: Re: the rich

what day of the week is august 1st - I want to make sure I shave and take a
shower that day to greet you -
xxxm

I won't be able to send this message to you, Moinous. This is for now just a note to myself - by the way of your silent ear, while we are stuck here in Warsaw airport, have a two-hour delay for our transfer to Krakow. The toilets' stink and the rows of plastic seats make me feel we are waiting to see a doctor who will surely only give us bad news. The small waiting room has the familiarity of all places [lost souls] in transit; the sound of soap operas on the various TVs translate into the same high drama, emotions vary little, affairs and heartache make the same overacted sound and posturing regardless of the country or accent; there's also an unfamiliarity that cannot be located nor properly touched but has a sharpness, a lucidity that charms some part of me. Sam's: *I have an ocean to drink, there's an ocean then.*

I was thinking about the coincidences of ash - I mean all I had written a year ago almost to the day, when En and his mother came here to Poland, to Auschwitz. That week, a friend, B, had [by coincidence] burnt all her notebooks and her diaries. And it had both startled and satisfied me, the images she'd sent me of the burning, the parcel of dust words she'd sent; her enflamed words parting under the lens; what proceeded to be burnt, words unfurling into an enormous red rose releasing the smell of secrets. All the sentences I'd written that week that went nowhere: *evening darkens, she pushes him under her skirts, later carries him across a field made of ash. ... En carrying three, no four stones to the murder site in my absence, dark blue stones we collected from the dust.*

Pain conceals itself in a stone Ronell wrote... *What does it mean to learn that a stone is speaking? [...] the stone, finally begins to speak. The place of petrification, one of the two pebbles established within the colon, opens [...] like a mouthpiece for which he has become the receiver. [...] The ghost in the weed garden was petrified into this stone [...] Pain conceals itself in the stone [...] - for the stone not only speaks out but awaits the opening of a listening mouth that could suck in this pain and swallow it - it is one of Beckett's sucking stones. It plays with fire [...] reducing the stone [...] threaten[ing] to turn the calm into splintering white ashes.*
You see, I was sitting reading her words - B's words, that is, this time last year, her scorched words, rather, the letter and tiny photographs she'd sent me explaining what the small parcel of ash contained - when her burnt words reformed into birds. Birds have always followed me, found their way into me, the birds outside my window reforming themselves as I read. Yes a few days after En had left for Poland, last year, yes, almost a year ago, a gull appeared. A gull tapping at my door. I almost took him inside. I wanted to take him inside. I rang someone I said … *There's a gull tapping at my door I don't know what to do, he won't fly.* Ah a *juvenile* she said, as if I should know, as if I should know that it's normal to get pushed from a nest or that I should carry an umbrella if he approaches. *Carry an umbrella,* she'd said, *a hat, a flag, any old head shelter, that way you won't get attacked from above by its guardian,* reassuring me that he'd of course take flight in a day or so.

But too soon he was flattened out on the road, the bird, that same week.

I was sitting at my window, I may have been writing to you, a message to someone, when I looked up drawn to the commotion, to a small gathering, nothing grand, just three maybe four people but enough to distract. I found him there that morning other birds swooping down to him, the odd car drove around, I could barely hear what people said as they stood over his body, stared down at the squashed bird, his head only just recognisable. People formed a circle, it was almost pagan: the anonymous pouring of a salt ring around his body, a single wing rose and fell in the breeze, flies settled in the salt, dehydrated and died alongside the bird; but I'll try and continue with what we had in common that week with what I wanted to share with you. The gathering of people around the gull's body made me realise: short of death, how short of ritual we are; take a look at what we will become - featherless, few changes; the landscape still half-lit billowed with smoke; things still burned at their normal speed; you only had to move and you'd sweat in the heat. Some people don't like the wind as if it's an omen, an ominous language, all that to come, all that considered, there were times when an old can was enough, when an odd kettle and old rusty container was enough to fill me with levity, when we'd follow the ash fields one beside the other.

I carried an umbrella like she'd said, like she'd warned me. I carried an umbrella like a Victorian bourgeois to keep the sun from my skin, the birds from my head. I carried everything in advance, swallowing all in advance, her words, that week, B's words blown to the night; the now-dead bird, not simply dead but squashed flattened inside me, imprinted in me the guilt that I should have taken him in.

I scraped up the gull. It was July. He, she, who can know, had begun to smell in the afternoon sun. I scraped the remains from the road with En's oversized shovel, one his father gave him: what a history of defence. The scraping made a hideous noise. I was afraid of being seen. I worked late, waiting for the evening's conspiracy; made a small fire in the garden and burnt the body with some prunings, admitting quietly to myself that the bird was the nearest thing I had come to a kind of crooked satisfaction those past days; our encounter - the bird and I, my need to dispose of his body, who else - left me with, or rather, began those very lines … *We have not yet properly begun to discuss the disposal of our bodies*

Yes the sound of his bird's body cracking, the ash collected on my tongue, mingling with my hair, the quiet impregnation of cloth mixing up the greenery with the odd plume escaping, all this made me realise how short of ritual we are, how short of good decent gestures, as there in the ashes I found a scrap that refused to burn.

Wednesday 21st of July 2004

It feels like I'm in the past tense.
I scribble down the Polish words from the Krakow apartment wall that have been translated.

Pozar: fire

Ratunek: help - rescue - salvation

The Polish flies are large and green and land on my page as I try and write a few lines to you Moinous. As I sit here at a large open window looking out over the city, at the billboards, the truck drivers, a woman feeding stray cats with bread, I realise I cannot remember anything we'd said when we were on a bus going to Montrouge, when we were in Paris, only that I'd asked you: Is it hard to go back? Is it hard to go back to where your family lived and where you last saw them or rather heard them descend the stairs while you hid? Is it hard to show me your old home, the school you went to? And you barked almost, NO. Well maybe not that you barked, more that you were so definitive in your NO. Almost too sure and final and I wanted to say, Should I believe you? I feel nothing, you'd said. Not any more. I decided I must believe you. En's relative once said that he never understood how his parents could so easily, so it seemed, return to Vienna after the war and many times since, as tourists. He used to look at them, looking for clues of their unrest, but saw none. When his mother was dying he sat close to her and said, Is there anything you want to tell me mother, you know, knowing what you went through, with the war and all? Tell you? she said, What is there to tell you. And she died.

Tiny moments.

Losing track of the dates to come.

I wake searching dreams, heat, darkness.

Here in Poland we eat
fried sheep's cheese
chicken livers
cabbage

I want to tell you a story.
Of the monks
who see no-one.
Especially women - in case of distraction, I'm told that only 12 days a year are women allowed into the monastery. I want to tell you of the Krakow hermitage, of the Camaldolite monks who live inside the vast Bielany forest - a favourite picnic destination. The hermitage atop Srebrna Gora [Silver mountain]. Of the mummified bodies of their ancestors that are kept in four-sided crypts. Of the monks who bury their ancestors for eighty years. How the crypt walls are then opened, the body placed in consecrated ground, but the skulls kept by the monks. I wonder which monk gets to keep whose skull. Do they have a say, with each other, a choice? I wonder what they whisper to these old boneheads in their half-sleep. I wonder what stories and secrets the bonehead returns.

I wanted to tell you of the Zakopane Salt Mines. Of the Guided Tour. Of the two hours of salt we endured. 200 zloties to descend by the way of the 394 steps. They don't mention this until you pay. We're standing in a small enclosed space. Herded in. Packed tightly against strangers. As our guide talks I try and feel the gentle motion of us falling deep underground. He is humourless enough, the guide, and the only one among us who is allowed a hard hat and a torch. I expect when he opens the door that we will be at our starting depth of 64 metres. Instead we haven't moved at all. We are after all not descending in a lift; imagined motion where there was none, we have yet to walk the tight spiral of 394 steps. At the bottom Max whispers that he needs to find the toilet. NOW. En shyly asks the guide already suspecting his answer, there is no way back only 2 hours of tunnels and salt rooms 400 metres thick. There are no salt toilets only us lingering behind the crowd of people in our PARTY hoping to find a suitable sculpture, a salt king queen or my lord that maybe my child can discreetly relieve himself upon. I taste salt on my fingers as instructed rub them across the withered paw or nose of a sculpted creature now almost obliterated from too much mauling. We are told when we can and cannot touch. We remember the horses blinded by darkness. We gaze into the lake where people drowned, we listen to opera over dark water plagued by ghosts, played out as a light show, swirling about our heads. Peer into other corners where bodies were burnt or exploded. This time told not to touch, I taste the black salt that gives most things here the appearance of dull concrete. I'd expected white sparkling walls, glittering rooms. Finally the open chapels and the crystal salt chandeliers satisfy a little. I taste more and more salt and follow strangers through tunnels and realize we are all most likely bound to die of thirst. I think only of the lifts to exit - at last - at last. We skip the shop and the obligatory salt gifts the illuminated rock-lamps and key rings - the oversized canteen with salted dumplings - we again queue for the lifts that are also hidden from view like the steps that brought us here. Now at a depth of 125 metres we gladly make our ascent. Six of us pressed and shoved hurriedly into a tiny crude cage. The metal doors slammed shut. Two strangers and the four of us pressed together. The lift begins with the lights being cut, lights flicker on and off as we speed through layers of salt. Nervous laughter in the dark as an illuminated mouth and oversized teeth turn for seconds into a stranger's breath in my ear. Hurtling speed. Fingers caught in my hair. Apologies and jokes in the dark. A man in a uniform finally releasing us too slowly from the cage. Keeping us in line with a stick, much shouting and pointing: We must sit over there and not move until everyone is up. We wait. I see the door to leave is open. Trees. Sun. Nobody moves. We follow him in a neat procession. He turns every now and then and shouts at us, of course we cannot understand what he says but fully get the message to keep in line. He is pushing a woman back behind him again with his stick. We follow him neatly, obediently to the gate.

Herring
Fried Fish
Chicken Livers
Fried Cabbage
Goulash
Stuffed Dumplings
Beef in Horseradish Sauce
Spinach
Purim Cake
Coffee
Tomorrow Auschwitz.

I'm learning how to spell Auschwitz.

From: Moinous@aol.com
Sent: 16th July 2004 4.55pm
To: angelamorgancutler@ntlworld.com
Subject: Re: bye then

popolsky popolska djancouilla

glad that you could send a few words

have a good time but don't whatever you decide - don't - don't even consider doing it - it would be fatal worse than that - think of En - one of these days he may have to reveal his identity by dropping down his pants - I speak from experience - I had to do that once in a train station and was I ashamed not of my dimension but of my nakedness my skin was so white that's because I was so undernourished then but whatever don't I implore you don't do it - don't stay in Poland - Polish computers are so bad you wouldn't be able to connect with the outside world and imagine how sad depressed lonely homesick paranoid schizo you would become and the boys back in the foreign country crying night and day while jumping up and down on the bed in their parents' room having a pillow fight and all the feathers flying all over the place and the boys laughing while crying because mum decided to stay in Poland - you see the consequences - the tragedy that looms ahead - and worse over there in Poland they would have to change your names - it's the custom - Polish names must have at least one c two z's three a's and one k in it - so you would become anczekala kutzca - do you realize what that would mean for the rest of your life - I shall await anxiously your decision for it will determine the course of the rest of my life -
M

From: Moinous@aol.com
Sent: 20th July 2004 4.28pm
To: angelamorgancutler@ntlworld.com
Subject: Re: exile in Poland

so happy to get even a few garbbbbbbled words from you

auschwitz

yes - you can light a candle for my family

but better yet - as I did - pick up four pebbles from the ground and bring them back –

it's the most ugly place in the world - unless since the day I was there in 1981 they have made it more hygienic

ah jewish food - what's your favourite?

is En having a good time too

me sort of feeling blah here nothing happening

I lost money at the casino yesterday

that's about all

in other words I MISS YOU TERRIBLY - I feel you far away
xxxxM

From: angelamorgancutler@ntlworld.com
Date: 2004/07/17 Sat AM 10:26:24 GMT
To: Moinous@aol.com
Subject: Re: bye

this is my thgird go I have moved now but we have no internet at the
apartment and I am not sure if these aer getting through
on the market stalls they are selling small jewish figures made of sood
i meann wood - playing violins and wearing their Hassidic garb -

if this has got through 3 times you can compare the differences and if
not then you won't know
Ax

From: Moinous@aol.com
Sent: 18th July 2004 8.30pm
To: angelamorgancutler@ntlworld.com
Subject: Re: bye

angela ron is dying he's in a coma on his way towards the big hole - I am sad
but told julia to tell ron that I'll join him soon and over there together we'll go
on fighting the battles

your Polish is adorable - it's starting to sound like Javanese - not always easy
to decipher but from the tone of it one gets the sense that you're having a
good time over there - don't worry about the heat it's good for you makes your
blood boil - makes blood sausage - have you tried them by the way we french
call them boudin I love them but I am digressing
I'm trying not to feel sad - to take my mind off Ron and all –

what now

more loose shoes & smelly socks is finished - today I'll count the pages I'll
have to do it by hand because I didn't want the pages to be numbered in this
book I want the book to be one long sentence with all kinds of deviations in it

65

you know shifts of fonts shift of size shift of color shift of punctuation shifts of typographie you know what I call the deviations of writing

I had fun putting it together the pieces are piled in a box one on top of the other in the order they came out of the file in my computer

and here it is - the longest sentence I have ever written and of course it shifts here and there from english into french or french into English - the only place where a reader can pause a moment is when the reader arrives at one of the titles given in bold capital letters for the purpose of giving the reader a pause if necessary before proceeding with the reading of the longest sentence I have ever written I'll try to count how many words there are in that sentence

send more poglish xxxm

The Shoe

And where did she think she was going in such shoes ... coming all this way in white stilettos ... for god's sake. In the end it's just a room ... it's just a forest ... it's just a shoe among a million other shoes ... a window of shoes ... a way of walking preserved, squashed-in ... it's the absence of a foot ... his voice beside me. En's saying ... *What I do, as there are so many shoes here, is I find one and I imagine the foot that it held, and I work out from there, like this one ... like the white stiletto at the front ... I see the foot and then the leg and that's how I bring that person back, just for a moment ...*

And just for a moment I am saying ... *You would choose that one ...* momentarily jealous of a dead woman's shoe. Jealous of his way of looking, of his imagining another woman's foot and leg pressed inside his head, onto his eye, a dead woman's shoe, worn down, just a white stiletto, unremarkable. Pretty.

I have no right to think or say these things ... Don't speak of this she said.

And as we stand before the white stiletto, En's hand pressed hard on the glass window, I think about the day people first chose these shoes, first wore them, blisters, excitement. Heels sinking into the grass. I think of new tight shoes, brand new occasions; of covering his mouth with mine. But En has his head turned away, he's still looking at the shoe. He's saying, *The shoes are usually the last things people throw away when people lose a loved one, it's the shoes they often cling on too, that resembles them most, that they'd need most if somehow they were to come back, that's the hope, that they'll come back and need their shoes again.*

And if I find his mouth, now, if I do, will he be shy; pull back a little in surprise; expectant, is he waiting for me to find his mouth, maybe a peck on the cheek would do better, I mean, here of all places, at a time like this, a small kiss on the forehead perhaps, the lips after all, tenderly, softly, if only to show that his way of looking has touched me, yes, after all, his way of seeing and wondering has touched something in me, something I could not find alone.

I would have kissed you, I tell him, here in Auschwitz, here before this window of stolen, abandoned shoes, if I'd have known, thought, acted upon, I would have kissed you here of all places where there should be, must have been, kisses, where everything we see here has already been and gone when we have already spent a life time together, imagine we know everything of the other, can know nothing of these others.

Dream #65633

I am in Paris and I have arranged to meet En. I have on an open dark coat and beneath the coat is a jacket, layers of elegant clothes. I see that my blouse looks lime green in the morning light. Is beautifully made, sewn by hand. I remove the layers of clothes down to the blouse that I notice has a section cut away exposing my breasts. I am not unduly surprised. Except after some time of walking around like this I say to a woman waiting with me at the roadside, Do you think it is OK to expose my chest like this. Yes she says, you look very nice, why shouldn't you. As I continue on, I look down and I notice great black hairs now sprouting from my chest and arms. I say to a passer-by, Look. I have to get rid of all this hair or I will look like a man. He takes me to find a barber but the barber tells me he has no way of cutting such strong hairs that are now covering the whole section of my chest. I sit outside on the barber's steps, wondering what to do. I meet a young man. He has wild black hair. He sits with me and begins tuning up a silver cello he is carrying. I say to him, Maybe you can teach me to play mine some day. He laughs. When he turns his head I notice he has a patch behind his ear that is completely bare. The more hair I grow the more he loses. I think I should go before he becomes completely bald. I am afraid to tell him so I apologise and make my excuses and leave swiftly. I continue on my way to meet En. I will tell him about the hair and the cello player, the silver instrument. When I again remember my chest is now completely covered in a pelt of hair, I feel suddenly ashamed. I notice a man staring at me as I pick up a newspaper from the floor. I will use it to cover my chest. I realise the paper is the Jewish Chronicle and it is full of photographs of Jewish graves. The paper is written in Hebrew. I wrap it around my body and tie it securely with a piece of string that I find in a bin. I am to meet En in a few minutes. I walk with my arms held up in the air so that I do not obscure the photographs.

Dream #17547

I am awake. Well, I tell myself I must be. A woman's voice has woken me. I remember we had been to visit Auschwitz, En, the children and me. I want to tell her about this but it is hard to properly locate her voice. I heard her speak, yet maybe the voice I heard is my own, surely just the mind sparking up as if the TV has been left on and was talking to me as I woke. I try and call out to En, to wake him, but the words refuse, common enough, lines, questions all stuck in the throat, and nothing will pass the gag.

G. enters the room. I ask him what he is doing here so late at night. He tells me it's almost dawn.

I see we are on a stage-set that is an exact replica of the

bedroom En and I are sleeping in, in Poland. I see that on the TV, which is screwed to the wall, the woman I thought I heard wake me up is staring down from screen, blinking at me. I can't be sure if the woman can see me or not.

G. says, I never wondered before how many different voices can a body hold … I mean, it's a revelation to me that others hear so many voices speaking at them all day and night, voices coming at them from the inside of their heads, from the face in the window, from the refrigerator, from the toilet bowl, from the washing machine, or just in bed in the dark, from an unwritten book … No, don't get me wrong, he said, it's not madness, well maybe here and there, who can know, it's just the voices are in all of us, surely? … Maybe it's a question of how you handle them, how you respond to them, he said, how you handle them and them you.

L. enters the room, or rather the scene.

I wasn't expecting you, I say to her.

It's almost dawn, she says … I heard the word voice. I entered because I thought that was a cue and I wanted to tell you that I'd once heard a voice that interrupted my digging … Yes, Once, L says, way back now, I had been digging and digging, it was new to me, earth, the outdoors. I was learning to love the feel of muck, I was digging and making small trenches with an hb pencil. I'd planted tiny seedlings, the shoots were so green, so delicate they moved me to speak to them, to give them some words of encouragement. I worked with pencil and mostly with my hands. I no longer cared if I had soil over my mouth and in my hair, all that mattered was that I was close to the earth, that I could feel my knees make imprints in the soil, the growing shoots in which I could feel a small tremor of time present and time that was yet to come. I wanted to grow potatoes, so with a larger stick I made another row next to the one where I'd planted the tiny seedlings. I placed the small spuds with running eyes into the soil. And this was when the voice came to me, with the promise of those first potatoes, a voice kept interrupting.

Was it your voice you heard?

No …

She seemed sure enough.

I just went back to my digging, went on, trying not to listen, trying to cover everything up … but the potatoes began giving me messages, they were saying I was to make an even bigger trench and bury myself alive, to water myself in … Maybe I was feeling guilty, she says … about the potatoes, about burying them like that.

I wasn't expecting any of you. I wasn't to know you were coming tonight.

It's dawn G. says. Don't you remember?

Remember what?

Remember that you were sitting like this in the dark once. You were just sitting like this - there in the dark, not in bed, as you are now, but in a chair. It was then, as it is now, 3.30 a.m. and the birds just about to start, the first one just on the edge of coaxing or was it irritating the others into song, you never knew when the first one would again set everything into motion, always everyone slept while you sat there alone waiting for that first trusted bird. You were sitting facing a door, you said that your back was to the day-room - that's what you and they called it - where you'd worked, those enormous corridors and dormitories filled with breath and snoring, the smell of stale cloth, feet and the passing of the night's gas - behind the door, the dormitories faced you where the others slept on. And someone must have tiptoed and put their hands gently on your shoulders, tiptoed, night-gowned, in bare stockings not properly rolled nor gartered only tanned stockings loose around her ankles; she just placed her hands gently so's not to shock you into turning. She was firm enough - well, you supposed the person to be a she, as the hands felt small for a man's and you felt the ends of nails - and you did not turn as if you knew that's what she wanted, for your composure, for your stillness to promise that you would not turn to look at her, that you would just let her hold you, neither did you in any way speak.

I'm going to make a sandwich L. says, do you mind if I use your kitchen?

Is there a kitchen? I mean, if this is a replica bedroom is there a replica kitchen and city, is there anything outside this room?

Maybe I'll just exit for a moment L. says, I'll think of something.

The screen is flickering. Pans out. I see that the woman with her children beside her on the screen are running through a wood. There are dogs in pursuit, the woman and her children are fleeing, being hunted down.

What can I know of this, I say to G., seeing someone like this. What do I know of running. I have no idea.

L. returns, interrupts the scene. She is chewing on a crust and a pickle. Don't ask about the kitchen, she says, stop worrying about what is real and what isn't. She takes G.'s hand. We all look up at the screen.

Once I asked someone like her, tell me how do I look in your dreams. But people never tell you what you need to know, not really, not the details, maybe they don't know themselves, how to get beyond bland descriptions that mean nothing, so little can be mustered, I mean we live with people sometimes all our lives and when we try to describe them all we are left with are abstractions, red wiry hair, kind eyes, large thumbs, anecdotes, the eye is not the place of memory. That's all she said: the eye is not the place of memory. Yes, forget all that, I say, forget sleep. What do I know of running for your life like that. And how can I recall this scene, the children beside her, when look at me just lying down here on this bed and not in any way moving, my knees pulled up to my chest, asking myself what can I know of fear, of the smell of dogs. When's the last time I ran like that and in woods, and of course here in Poland there are more than enough woods. And if I say to En, yes, if I were to wake him early, soon, tell him of this, of you, of the woman on the screen; say nothing, instead what if I were to take him to a wood and command: Chase me, but like you mean it! As if he could or *would*, as if it wouldn't all be too much a game, a luxury item, as if I wouldn't be too ashamed to even ask if we could borrow the neighbour's dog, he's mean enough, all teeth 'n' shit, fart and drool. If I were to say, Let's see what's possible when he forgets it's play - the dog, not En, or maybe him too, how else. None of it will do, I say.

What's your name? I'm sure I ask, want to ask the woman on the screen, as if she can hear, as if she can listen.

It's getting light G. says, Soon the clock tower will sound, we've a simulated one, just like the one in Krakow. You won't tell the difference, just wait. Four strikes. Pink light. The bugle. The birds just starting their opening address.

No-one's answered with a name, I say.

No-one's answered with a name because no one asked the question, L. says.

Often the question arrives too late, G. adds, often the question is too quiet to be heard.

Isn't that a bit corny, G., a little too cliched for its own good ... And what comes next? ... Is anything written down ... I mean, are there any guidelines, any instructions between us on how to proceed, how to talk about this woman on the screen, how to talk about what she is showing us, what we are witnessing here. There on those papers you are holding, is there anything written down - or were you ad-libbing?

You catch on quick, G. says, page 3 ... What comes next? you ask, hear yourself ask, What's been written down? That's what's written down.

She had on a summer's dress, L. says. That's the next line. The woman on the screen. She had on a summer's dress. She was running. En is still asleep to your right. Next we all turn our heads to check. It says so here, we turn to En, then back to her face on the screen. That's next L. says. Listen … The woman had two children, only a year held those two boys together and apart. The dogs in pursuit were choking themselves on longing. You find it distasteful, that this scene keeps rewinding, men in uniform are in pursuit, and you can hear her breath everywhere in the room, and it is obscene. In this scene you keep denying, quietly to yourself, that we are in the room with you. You keep telling yourself you must still be asleep. You are dreaming-awake, surely. You are calling out to En who is asleep-dreaming for sure, you are still trying to wake him, but the sound will not be heard. You repeat constantly that you are making us all up. It's written in - I'm not making this up - page 4. The bedroom scene, your denial is written in.

Continue … it says

[G. continues]

You sit up in bed, try to move closer to the screen, yes, you **stand up** it says [bold lower case]. **UP** [Bold, capitals]. Put your face close to the TV screen. The TV is on the wall, the bed is unstable, look it's written in … page 4 - the sheets are bunched up, making the bed difficult to walk on. You are both trying to wake En and worried that you'll walk on him. Worried how he'll react when he sees how many people are in your bedroom. That he may not understand that you are in a replica of the room, one you thought you were asleep in, in Poland; all you know of the outside is what she shows you on the screen; all you can see is that she is in a wood, possibly in Poland. One wood looks much like another. Your apology that you have no idea how to run, how she felt. How could anyone know that. Look, you repeat the apology to her ad infinitum. That's written here, look, you press your face close to hers on the screen and say sorry to her, in the way sometimes people say thank you after every small detail or gesture or utterance, you keep repeating how sorry you are, how sorry.

Go on …

[L. continues]

You have to steady yourself on the bed, to find her face, her grainy mouth dissipating the closer you get to the screen. Inside the screen, the scene pans out more and more, her noises of panic make you wrestle with the remote, search for the volume control, and surely if you found it, you'd feel unable to mute her voice still ahead of the men in uniform who are following, whistling, the contradiction of the cloth the beautiful colour of eucalyptus, leaves flash their underside, there's a slight breeze that she won't have time to notice, she is constantly turning her head back and forth, the childrens' necks twist backwards to check how close they are to one another, to the ones in pursuit; feet pick a forward direction where there is NO SUCH DIRECTION. Only the noise of their six feet hitting the ground, some way back, the thump of other's feet in a pattern, sometimes out of synch ... Voices behind them laugh wildly, hold their pace back a little. For now the ones behind want only the chase, they want only to laugh at her ridiculous movements, knowing she had no notion how to run.

[Go on ...]

Instead she flings herself ahead, the dogs a little in front of the ones in pursuit, are held back on the leash, dogs have to know they are dogs

Little wood 1

Little wood 3

You tried to keep up ...

Continue ...

[G. continues]

You tried to keep up.

It was hot. The throat would not be slackened. The hands cut, turned ankles, smells heat up, slipping on leaves, on shit, on vines, tripping one another up, branches cut the eye, whip the face, blood in the mouth tastes warm, never seen herself this way before, the children shouting, *Get up, mother* ... that sound carried, amplified everywhere screaming, two different woods merge through two different names called together in two different languages, Touch the trees - her son shouts - *touch each one mother,* they were touching one another when they could. One son's too quiet ... one who normally never stops talking, runs ahead, ridiculous, impossible questions. One son's too quiet, she had to pull at him, swear at him, cussing and saying *I love you* at the same time confusing the boy, but at first he wouldn't move fast enough so she dragged him across the ground, called him sweet names, swore, back and forth, *I didn't mean to*, she said ... *I'm sorry*. She could see the outline of him - there wasn't time for this - she kept telling them, *There is no time for this* - somehow there was time to notice things she didn't care to see, like the way he held his shoulders tight, yes, even now, even when his legs were moving him so fast and he couldn't help falling, dragging him like that, *fuck, fuck, I love you*. Her words confusing the boy, herself, but how to make him ... *MOVE* ... Swearing no doubt at herself, at the shape of his back and his shoulders tight as her jaw, her son's legs too long and not in anyway used to this, how could he or anyone be, and his mouth moving but unable to say what he wanted, and his hair curled with sweat.

G., ... go on ...

The canopy of trees, sun shade sun shade, it was a classic

scene, falling, running, panting, voices carried all over, the shine of piss on ferns, the tongue dry, the lungs burn, uniformed calls, the dogs scrape their arses across the ground, drool and shit; the moss, fungi, the many shades of green; the wood remained serene regardless...

CONTINUE ...

[L. continues]

Do you remember, G. that time, she'd said ... If anyone should buy me a compass it is you my handsome man, it is you who should buy me one. And she had known that upon hearing her words he would come the next week and place a small silver compass into her hand and she would act surprised and she would turn it this way and that ... and she would laugh and she would walk with home before her, the red needle flickering and she would always want other ways ...

Ssh

When a horse is running well for god's sake don't stop and offer him a sugar cube ...

Another useless line, not hers, coming at her as she runs *When a horse ...* A LIE ... Gas and air, remember that, a half-pint of breath pushing you on; breathe hard; breath hard and sure and act like you did back then, pushing out your child, sucking on gas and air, glad of it then, tank fulls then, your teeth marks on the tube. Please don't laugh at the way I pronounce daughter, laughter, adulterer, woman, whore; woman you were a different kind of mother then ...

DON'T STOP ...
G. CONTINUE
CONTINUE ...

She stops ...

page 10. She stops.

Thinks of everything stopping, thinks only of closing her eyes, her children's eyes. A slow fall continues with the final image of her standing in the middle of the wood mimicking the trees falling, now standing as still as the tree, her feet sink with the weight, the suddenness of her halt, her feet sink with the muck of memory given over to the breeze laughing with the leaves, knees buckle and so on, quite dignified now as if all choreographed in her from some other time, allowing herself to sink into a mulch of leaves, the pine-needled floor, the children bewildered, still run turn run hesitate ... call out as they run back in confusion ...

G. speaks directly, looks up at you staring at the screen. A LIE ... it says. A lie is written.

No-one owns up.
no-one says a thing.

YOU stand on the bed gazing at the screen.

It's meant to be confusing and abrupt at the end, G. says.
That's how it feels to be in here in the room. We cannot know
how she felt. You repeat that … And then it stops.

L. runs her finger over the page. It tells her to do it. Do it. Run
your finger over the page.

If I push my eyes too close to the screen, too close, she
disappears again, dissolves into pixel [your voice unstated]

Stand back it says. Ask. Who is speaking now? No one
remembers whose turn it is. Suddenly. All three of you in the
room have no idea whose turn it is to speak.

Sit down a while, move back, L. says, It says that here. See.
Move back from the screen. You do as she says, it says, [G.
pats the bed] page unmarked. You do as she says, it says.

I had almost forgotten I was standing on the bed. I say, not
sure if I have even spoken this aloud. If anyone heard me?
Wake En, wake him, it's time he woke.

Come sit beside us, L. says, come lay back down, be careful of
En's feet. He doesn't wake up …

~~En sleeps on~~. It's written here, G. says, [page unmarked,
under-erased. Strike through]

So maybe he does wake, L. says, it's not clear, there's
hesitation. Maybe uncertainty as to whether he will wake or
not, by the end of the scene that is, that said, the room does
wake, the room begins to fill with sunlight. It's early morning,
the clock has sounded the hour again. The pigeons take flight.
People are preparing for work. Her face comes into focus again
on the screen as if every thing is about to repeat itself, except
the hour, the hour has moved on. She can't see us through the
screen, I'm sure of it. She cannot see us but you swear she is
trying to …

You pull around the sheets. You pull around the sheets. [L. and
G. will say together - as they sit on the bed beside you] Bunch
up, they say. [We'll all stare at her face on the screen - the
scene will pan out]

There'll be no more interruptions. G. says, It's clear … It's clear
that the three will sit quietly together and watch the screen.

En, we presume, will sleep on.
The room will continue to get lighter.

No-one, we presume, will eat.
<u>LISTEN. CONTINUE</u> [capitals, underlined and in bold]
Only her voice
now [repeat]
Only her voice ...
[lower case, italics]

From: Moinous@aol.com
Sent: 23rd July 2004 2.13am
To: angelamorgancutler@ntlworld.com
Subject: Re: exile in poland

excuse me angela if I am brief today
today Ron died

I feel sort of empty - it's like I don't believe it - it's like I would also like to die today
I was asked to write something for the American Book Review that
Ron founded - I don't want to write anything - I have nothing to say
yes I will write this

Rather than write about Ron's great achievement - rather than praise the great man he was - the great writer he was - the great friend he was of more than 30 years with whom I fought many battles - I decided today - July 23 - to reread all of Ron's books - one after the other - chronologically. I think Ron would like that. I think Ron would do the same for me if ...

Your Polish is improving
when are you back from Krakow - it already seems so long

love
MXXXXX

From: <angelamorgancutler@ntlworld.com>
Date: 2004/07/22 Thu PM 06:48:47 GMT
To: Moinous@aol.com
Subject: Auschwitz

Reply Reply All Forward
            Delete   Move To:

this is the second attempt I hate thezse internet czafe s and this keyvord -
I 'm sorry I can't pick up my messages - i have rmno idea if minbe are gerring through - sorry I can;t
wzasgte tinme - more tinme - be longer - say more - o0

we weent to auschwitz today

I nwanted to tell you - and I lit {as I said I womluld] i lit a candle in the gas chamber for you - otjer wise it was hard to feel any connection

76

to the plavce - well i can't procress it all yet - all I cna say is
thta I wore a tourtquoise skirt — painted my nails pink - wrote in the
prsent tense - it of coutrse left me feeling empty - not surw what we
were supposed tp feel - what we were doing there - what we were looking
for - at -with so many otehrs - all strangers- so many chewques of
people all loojking -

I rubbed my head along the gas chamnber wall and thought how unremarkable
a room it was - - -howe unremarkable - and so what did I expect - not
what i saw - the crudeness of the roomn su9rprised me - lieke some
building you might happen upon abandoned inside a wood - the stuff of
child killing and so it was - we tjhen went to berkenau and sat beside
a pond full of ashesz - waht a factory of death - rubble - enormous
expanses of nothing - did youfp go there as well? - I picked up some
small things from the grouns d - I want to send you from aush witz -
you know - bits of nothing as there is nothing - buit I want to send
them anyway and will - also sending love - we thoighty of you - - sorry
abouyt this - this oinpoossible keybporadf - and that i can't say more
- its so hit i mean hot in here - bodies all tightky packed in and
toying away - words to who knoes who - max telling me that someone in
the cornere is watchong porn on their screem - 0 i wondeered why he wsa
so quiet - write soojmn ==,i will - Axxxxxxx

From: Moinous@aol.com
Date: Thu, 22 Jul 2004 15:41:14 EDT
To: angelamorgancutler@ntlworld.com
Subject: Re: auschwitz

finally even Auschwitz has become a banality - a place where one
feels totally out of place - a space of emptiness - it has become empty
of even the smell of smoke that always lingers after a fire - it used
to be dangerous to light a candle in the gas chamber because of the lingering
traces of gas but now even that chamber is empty - yes one must bring color
to Auschwitz to defy its empty darkness - turquoise is perfect for that - and
flamboyant nails too that bring life to a dead place - excuse the rumbling -
these words are coming out of me without any control on my part - I don't feel
anger as I did when I was there back in 1981 - I feel nothing - yes bring me
back some traces just to see how they will feel - the only thing Auschwitz is
now is a word - a word that makes you feel sad each time you pronounce it
or write it - that's all it is - certain words enter our culture out of some tragedy
or comedy and they remain inscribed in our vocabulary - some make us sad
- others make us happy - when the word Godot entered into our culture and
I heard it for the first time I felt happy - the word Godot made me laugh -
maybe because I felt Godot was a joke - a fantastic joke — Auschwitz is not
a joke - it can never make you laugh - it can only make you sad - finally to
ask if one can write poetry after Auschwitz as Adorno did is a joke - of course
one can write poetry - because great poetry is always written after a tragedy
has occurred - Auschwitz may yet inspire some great poetry - but before that
poetry can be written Auschwitz must simply become a flat postcard - all the
Auschwitz poetry written since Auschwitz - was written about what happened

at Auschwitz - written about the place - great poetry is not written about places or the events that took place at these places - great poetry is written about language - about certain words that engender other words - now that Auschwitz has become just a word - maybe some great poetry will be written - and who knows the poetry will take away the sadness from Auschwitz - perhaps finally the Auschwitz poetry will make us laugh - that's the only possible solution for Auschwitz - laughter - otherwise - it seems that when one returns to the scene of the crime one is there essentially to lament one's losses - then the criminal is the victor.

sorry angela for the digression - you inspired me –

miss you but feeling good that you are there –

have you seen any happy places

where after Krakow xx

From: <angelamorgancutler@ntlworld.com>
Date: 2004/07/23 Thu PM 17:43:09
To: Moinous@aol.com
Subject: auschwitz

```
Reply Reply All Forward
         Delete          Move To:
```

```
this is the second attempt the messages keept boiuncinbg back
- I hate thezse internet czafe s and this keyvord -
I 'm sorry I can't - I'm s0 sorrry about ron - sorry abouyt this
- this
oinpoossible keybporadf keeps jumping- and that i can't say
more - havenit jmore tinme - be longer - but wanted to say - I am so
sorry abouytb ron dying - I am - but from what uooy said I I had a
feeling - thaylke more tinme - be longer - oops - say more

but I wanted to say - I am so sorry about ron - sorry abouyt this
- this
oinpoossible keybporadf - and that i can't say more
I'm not eveh sire waht is hgetting throuvjh your end - damn – I have to
go - soryt it's all in the wrong ordeer - and repeating
- have to go
thinking of yoou - A xx
```


From: Moinous@aol.com
Sent: 22nd July 2004 10.48pm
To: angelamorgancutler@ntlworld.com
Subject: Re-more on auschwitz

Angela - here I was talking with this young writer about Auschwitz - I was explaining to him that Auschwitz is now only a name that has entered our vocabulary and our culture - what's left of Auschwitz over there is just a mockery of the real Auschwitz - a Disneyland version - but totally fake - not really gas - not even the smell of smoke - human bones - not even a piece of flesh - the real Auschwitz - I was explaining - is now just a word - and when a new word appears in a culture or even a civilization then it is immediately appropriated by the poets - that's why there are so many Auschwitz poems in the world - but they don't make money those poems - and the young writer told me -

I once had a 1968 VW bug that was destroyed by a drunken driver & a series of bad mechanics. At some point, I was getting sick from carbon monoxide in the compartment & started calling it Little Auschwitz. I don't know if you'd call that humor or irreverence or both
IT'S A GOOD STEP FORWARD IN THE USE OF AUSCHWITZ AS A WORD
I take the Lenny Bruce approach: use a word so often that it loses the power of taboo.
Should we consider a mock travel guide, Auschwitz for Lovers? Or Auschwitz on $50 a day?
I HAVE A BETTER IDEA

let's make T-shirts that say I love Auschwitz

WHAT A FORTUNE ONE COULD MAKE WITH THE NEO-NAZIS THE SKINHEADS THE REVISIONISTS THE KKKs AND SO MANY MORE WHO STILL THINK THE PLANET IS FLAT AND THE SUN GOES AROUND THE EARTH AND STILL BELIEVE THAT INDIA IS WHERE AMERICA IS AND ON TOP OF THAT VOTE FOR A COWBOY TO TAKE CARE OF THEM

I TELL YOU IT WOULD MAKE A FORTUNE

this could become a great story –

love xxxxx m

Tuesday 27th July 2004 - Poland 5 a.m.

I won't send this, it's hard to keep sitting in the cellar of the internet café and fighting to put every letter and come to that, emails, in the right order. I've sent several messages but I don't know what's getting through. It's barely light. I woke early after many disturbing dreams - maybe that's why I'm writing to you - to tell you about one dream that's been recurring, and seemed again to go on for most of the night. In the scene which took place in a replica room to the one we have here in Poland, I see a woman running, being hunted down, her voice woke me again as it had the previous night, or at least that's how it seems.

The sun here is cruel; not even the evening brings relief. We've all been fighting over the one electric fan. The first Polish word I learned was *pozar*: fire. I've told you this already. The tiny fire brand of a word was written on a piece of paper with instructions to call it, surely, scream it from the window should there be a blaze. Turns out that I slipped up on the word when I wrote to you earlier so instead of using *pozar* I'd written *pozer*: meaning I am indeed a buffoon, fraud, hoax; a version of humbug, that I'd felt when we'd first arrived and climbed the seven flights to our top floor apartment, only to find that there are no fire exits, only two wide window ledges filled with pigeons, some over-complicated instructions on how to crawl onto the roof in an emergency. I find myself in advance, imagining the choice of how to exit, head or leg first, if to then stand or shuffle, feet, handstand, knees or bum, what to take with me to the sill, En and boys aside. We discover soon enough, that the apartment block looks out over the fire-station yard, below us more than seven trucks, at least four of which have huge hydraulic ladders which - when fully extended each morning, as part of their drill inspection - can easily reach our window and beyond.

Yes, as I said, the airless nights of Poland bring little relief from the heat, a woman's voice. The same scene repeats each night, a woman with her two children, a wood, dogs, men in uniform, maybe everything you'd expect from a dream post Auschwitz. And when I woke yesterday it preoccupied me. I was skipping, RIDICULOUS, I'll explain in a moment, but yes, all day yesterday we were in a wood and you could say, that the image of the woman in my dream, now haunted not just my sleep or waking hours, but now haunted the wood we were in, a wood held inside a wood. Yes, and all of it kept going round in me while I was walking with Max. Not that I'd mentioned it to him, not today, but I was quiet no doubt, far away, he said so, sensing a kind of wistfulness; my preoccupation betraying something that made him take my hand in his, Mother, he said, come on … let's skip.

Skip!

And I hadn't blushed for as long as I hadn't skipped and I felt shy at his suggestion and told him so, but he was holding my hand and smiling at me, making me explain what shy meant. He said, maybe you meant to say, embarrassed, not shy; in the end we agreed on both.

   We'd been to the Krakow zoo again, it was our second visit in a week. The zoo is surrounded by very beautiful woods on all sides. We'd found the wolf again that we'd named Gloria, collected clumps of Gloria's fur from the wire fence; stretching myself over as far as I could, Max telling me to watch out, be careful! He was holding onto my ankle as I balanced and stretched toward the inner fence that was out of bounds. And as we'd later left Gloria behind, re-enter the wood, still discuss the silver of her eyes, her hinged paws, long snout, her unusually red coat, the woman I'd seen in my sleep re-enters my thoughts ...
Skip: fail to attend to, fail to deal with, leave quickly and secretly.
Skip v.: children skipping along in the sunshine, move quickly away, pass rapidly by, flit, dart.

It was then he took my hand in his, my son, Come on, he'd said … Let's skip mother, here in the wood. And he knew he could make me do it if anyone could … It's in keeping for him to make me do things I had almost forgotten, coaxing me on, as if he somehow intuitively knew that to ask me to run with him, there in the wood, would have somehow been insulting, demeaning, as if instead we had to find another way forward that day in the Wolski Forest, and for many days after when Max turned our walks into a dance, easing me into his little bid, pulling, persuading me that having forgotten the motion, that I'd so love the motion and what I now needed was only to remember how fast you can go when you hold on this way, hands clasped tightly, when we set off like that in a wood, in the street, wherever we happened to be; knees bobbing, the little slide of the jumping foot; you go faster that way, no-one lagging. Come on mother, he'd say: over there, just to the tree, just to that next trunk - just over there, to the next and the next. A fine rhythm we made. Holding hands when trees allowed.

From: Moinous@aol.com
Sent: 28th July 2004 11.32pm
To: angelamorgancutler@ntlworld.com
Subject: Re: exile in poland

I didn't write because I didn't want to disturb you in the middle of the gefilte fish and the blintzes and the cabbage and the boiled potatoes and especially the vodka - make sure you guys bring back a couple of bottles - the best one - kosher vodka - really that's the name - it has nothing to do with being kosher - but wow is it good - you keep in the freezer - and drink it just like that very cold without mixing it with any other crap - then you go to bed and for sure you'll have fantastic polish dreams

here things drag still sad
feeling useless
George and I are rereading Ron's books
MISSING YOU LOTS - BUT DON'T RUSH - I don't want to depress
you -
xxxx

From: angelamorgancutler@ntlworld.com
Date: 1st August 2004 11.58am
To: Moinous@aol.com
Subject: Re: back from pogland

I am so sorry about your friend - about Ron - I only just read
all my mail properly and I know I said this before, that I thought that
he may have died while I was there in Poland, but I was not sure what
mail was reaching you - those Polish komputers - well the keyboards -
letters and thus my words in all the wrong order
- story of my life -

I'm sending you a big hug -

Maybe we are both already dead … ever thought that one of us is making
the other up - is a figment of an over-egged imagination - what did Ron
say - *Writing is about Language - screw imagination - and / or - Use*

for your laughingtion before someone else does -
xx

laugh Raymond - it's all that's left to do -

We travelled back from Poland through the night and so haven't
slept for 24 hours

Auschwitz -

Yes I have so much more to say on my visit there which seeped into my
dreams - in fact every dream I had in Poland - and subsequently - was
of concentration camps - in fact one dream was so profound it woke me up
and I almost yelled out - the secret of life is the words concentration
camp - it felt like a eureka moment and then I found myself laughing with
the absurdity of what I had just said to myself at 4 a.m. - wide awake
and wondering what now ...

I also had a long dream about Sam which also took place in a concentration
camp-come-psychiatric hospital - in fact I keep getting the two places
mixed up - well Auschwitz and the first huge psychiatric hospital I
worked in - Yes - when I was there so much of it reminded me of my
first impressions of those enormous institutions I worked in when I was
eighteen - the smell - no - there was no smell at Auschwitz - I take
that back - but the orderly red-brick buildings were the same - the neat
tree-lined avenues and pattern of buildings which mask so much - the
grounds - the railway line - the woods of Birkenau - so many similarities
to the Hospital - where the horrors and the cruelties of incarceration
were also covered over with a gloss of day-to-day normality as routines
kept everyone firmly in their place - in the case of Auschwitz - the
institution so strongly in focus - the tight rituals of the day to day
that almost normalised abuse - death - murder - where within that ritual
locking up - we confront the thought of being left alone in such a place
- when the loss becomes tangible as you suddenly feel the enormity of
what happened - When I was in Auschwitz - I was constantly trying to
avoid the crowds - to find moments to be alone - but I never strayed that
far - because that straying - being alone in those buildings - fields -
between trees - inside chambers - also frightened me back to find others
again - safety in numbers - the din of the crowd -

the experience of going there and finding yourself becoming the character
of your own fiction as all the real characters are missing - yes -
watching yourself going / arriving / being there - watching yourself and
others react / not showing - some kind of reaction / keep asking - how to
behave here - how to walk here - how to ... *Look* - watch the children play
on the shimmering tracks - wonder where the branch line began from - the
line of people we joined on their way to the gas chamber - the randomness
of who you share this moment with - everyone suddenly so very quiet -

will write more when I have time -
I can't go on I'll go on
- I do go on ...

Are you OK?
Always - Axxx

From: Moinous@aol.com
Sent: 2nd August 2004 8.15pm
To: angelamorgancutler@ntlworld.com
Subject: Re: fed up

I am reading a book by Ronell on Stupidity which is pretty much how I
feel - I was up half the night failing to write about the wanting to
write about Auschwitz -
I don't feel like talking

I feel exactly the same
so let's call today a blank day in the stream of the words

you know

I know

the way it all goes
some days are like that

others are different
one never knows which day
it's going to be when one
drops out of bed still full
of haunting dreams

oh last night I dreamt that we were somewhere - don't ask me where
- but it was in color - in technicolor - I mean the dream - and there was another
guy with us - tall, good-looking - but not as vibrant as I was - and then the two
of you decided to drop me - to leave me behind to manage by myself - but I
screamed because I told you two that I didn't know how to manage by myself
that I always need the others - the two of you shrugged your shoulders and left
and there I was all alone and it started raining and ... I fell out of bed

From: angelamorgancutler@ntlworld.com
Date: 3rd August 2004 11.55pm
To: Moinous@aol.com
Subject: Re: fed up -

And I wonder how do I look in technicolour - isn't it strange to imagine
how other's see you in their dreams -

my tomorrow's horror-scope says - *you can be so cute when everything
is going your way*

From: Moinous@aol.com
Sent: 3rd August 2004 9.54am
To: angelamorgancutler@ntlworld.com
Subject: Re: stupidity revisited

By the way - your second message was the transition message - with one knee still in Poland and the other at home -
It also requested a vulgar amount of flowers for your funeral as we were talking funerals - but no dice - I hate flowers - I find them useless - they make me sneeze - they fade away - and after they die the water in the vase stinks like vomit
instead of flowers I'll throw loose pages from my books on your grave - and then I'll lie in them [like the old man did in TTV in the Deutsch Marks] and ...

well you know the rest of the story
finally Auschwitz is a waste - that's all I have to say now about that word - and besides it's such a fucking nuisance to spell it correctly - I never know when I write it if the ch goes before the w or if it's the reverse - same problem with Nietzche [sic]

did I ever mention to you that I once gave a lecture about Godot explaining that it was the first play ever written about the Holocaust even though not a word is said about it in the play
Godot/Auschwitz
what a title for a doctoral dissertation

From: angelamorgancutler@ntlworld.com
Date: 3rd August 2004 10.30pm
To: Moinous@aol.com
Subject: Re: stupidity revisited

Auschwitz - I also said the same thing to En last night - I mean about the impossible spelling of it - yet - realising that when En asked me how it was spelled that I now knew off by heart - its correct order and arrangement - hear myself say it aloud - almost with pride - almost with my hands held behind my back my head straight my body swinging back and forth slightly - the way a body prepares itself when it is about to perform or get something right - yes - spelling it for him with the confidence now of someone who has written it too many times with the confidence of a child who had first learned to spell and say aloud before her class the word she so feared - yes - before the whole class where if you misspelled something you were made to stand on a chair as a punishment - and what here is the punishment for not remembering how to spell Auschwitz - what if my first class spelling had been Aus-ch-witz instead of Wed-nes-day - what then -

From: Moinous@aol.com
Sent: 3rd August 2004 10.48pm
To: angelamorgancutler@ntlworld.com
Subject: Re: stupidity revisited

I love when you talk to yourself and say shut up A

don't feel guilty
that's the only way of getting rid of Auschwitz [which rhymes with
sandwich]
is to keep writing it
until it becomes just a word
we were are still all implicated one way or another

tell everything
how you felt
how it affected you
how it disgusted you
how it infuriated you
how it excited you
how it revolted you
how it felt nothing just emptiness
etc.

that's all I've been writing all my life my resistance to writing
or rather the resistance of writing to my writing
when you say

here I am writing about my resistance to writing -
and now all these loose pages are forming themselves into 3 parts -
already a damn structure - next there'll be an orchestra

they had orchestras at oswitz [os in french mean bones]
Mahler's daughter conducted there

one should never write in anger one writes only with doubt
and it is doubt that tells us how to write and what to write

For sure A x

For sure M x

The Gas Chamber

I get up early, change this title from *The Room* to *The Gas Chamber*; tell myself I must call it by its name, have the guts to say it. I change the title and my neighbour, by coincidence, carries flowers to my door, raises a bunch of blooms with pride, with the love of the gesture, the surprise obliterating her head with a bunch of red dahlias. I ring Sarah. I say, you won't believe this: just hours after I was talking to you about flowers, or rather the lack of them at Auschwitz, my neighbour carried an enormous bunch to my door, as if she knew flowers were on my mind. How I'd imagined that on the day of our visit to Auschwitz, before our journey to the Krakow bus station, I'd walk across the road and buy a bunch of pale pink roses from the seller. I was specific about the colour. I had decided well ahead, and also from which seller I'd buy them: the woman we'd pass each day who kept a plastic bucket of blooms, steeped in a little water, tucked safely beside her feet. The roses I'd decide on would be opening a little. They'd smell as I'd remembered. It was something that I'd thought I could rely on: that the roses would smell good and that I'd carry flowers to Auschwitz. But finally, I could not make the journey on a public bus with flowers. Too unsure of what seemed proper. *Back to that*. And the gas chamber that I'd imagined would be filled with flowers was, after all, a flowerless place - empty except for one over-scented lily that had been so formally placed on a metal stand, in that room the normal gestures were not carried through; flowers could not easily be formed into language.

But of course I cannot, *do not* mention to my neighbour, all that we had talked of on the phone. How to exchange the word Auschwitz for an arm full of dahlias?

The day we were to go to Auschwitz, I had my clothes ready. I have said this before. The turquoise skirt was pressed and hanging on the door as if I were already standing ahead of myself. Like those first days of school, the uniform, all ready, waiting for your small sleeping reluctant form to open it to life, a miniature headless you swinging when the door opened and closed. When we returned from Auschwitz, I told a friend: I don't know what made me choose that colour skirt; it somehow felt important, later felt all wrong. It made me think of the choices others had made - when and if they were given time. Before the window of shoes at Auschwitz, I thought of all those shoes that had travelled across and from so many countries, that were once lined up waiting beneath clothes hung up, all those individual choices, all those night-befores. This same friend I talked to about the clothes, had said that while we were away, he'd watched his mother pick out the clothes she would wear to the mental hospital the next day. He said he'd watched her flounder over the choice, as if she didn't want to be admitted or be seen by the psychiatrist in the wrong choice of outfit. As if it mattered - but for her it did. She decided on a formal suit to explain how, since her husband's death, she had been hallucinating a chorus of men singing *Land of My Father* beside her armchair; she had begun to see small birds fluttering where the drawer handles were. She chose a navy fitted suit, a white blouse that buttoned to the neck and tied into a small bow. He had to help her fix the bow; her fear, that she would not return home again. He said that the night before, he'd sat with her, and they'd both stared at the clothes spread on the counterpane as if it was her body laid out before them.

I'm beginning again. Day four of trying to write this. Yes, last night, what nonsense: so many flowers, clothes and shoes, so many words and versions piled up, pages numbered and arranged neatly enough. En had made up the fire in the living room - it's so cold here. We visited Auschwitz in the hottest of summers, I end up writing this in the coldest of winter months. So there we were warming ourselves, and on the TV, another complete coincidence, a moment's coverage of the sixtieth anniversary of the liberation of Auschwitz by the Soviets - well, initially just four men riding in on horseback - and we were again taken inside the very room - the very gas chamber I had failed to write about thirty times over. The fire roared, and with one eye on the screen, on the room's passing, I sat forward, threw all those tired attempts onto the fire and watched them burn. A ridiculous gesture, what misplaced symbolism, but for sure an impulse that forces me to start again. Take my word for it, in that moment all those pages opening out into ash, looked more beautiful more fragile than anything I was trying to say about the gas chamber.

Stop stalling, Angela. Tell me where you are …

I'm in Auschwitz.
I'm in a room.
The far end of the gas chamber.
I tell you that I have not been here
nor seen it before - not like this.
I read about it, of course: who hasn't. I have seen virtual models of it and more than enough fictions - but none of it the looks the same. The virtual tour where the walls are so smooth, so monochrome, so sanitised, too much like flawless metal. I see now that I expected too much.
I began with a room.
A room that I refused to name for weeks. Others had named it, but now the room alone seemed too large to stay put on the page, even though the room was not as big as expected, literally. In our anticipation this room is of course, has always been, enormous, weighted down with years of wondering what it really looked like. But until now, had I wondered enough or instead relied too much on other's accounts of this room, relied too much on other people's diagrams, all those perfect pencil line drawings made with steel rulers; ink sketches; pristine white cardboard models; the abstract smearing of thick paint; all those grainy documentaries - image after image taken alongside the misplaced amateur snaps, too sharply focused but still unsure how to address: what was it like to be a family standing in this very room, years before, years later, reject in advance that

we walked into this room with any idea of what to expect. Yet in the end, this room is nothing like I'd ... What? ... *Imagined*, always back to that - you could say that one of the first things that strikes me about this room is that it seems insufficient for purpose, although it obviously was more than sufficient some sixty years back. This room becomes chamber, or was it always named thus; the word *chamber* goes round in me as if it is too grand for what I can see and experience as I enter the room, my mouth still tasting of moth balls from that other room of hair, that old moth-balled tongue trying to chew itself up trying to mutter something out ... A chamber for formal or public events [perverse enough]. Chambers of Law. The part of a gun bore that contains the charge. Contains <music> for a small group of instruments. An enclosed space or cavity. A private room, especially a bedroom: the bed-chamber, the chambers of the heart.

There's a room - I saw it. It's called a gas chamber. What was not expected. The sudden announcement of gas, no, not yet! But on entering, on hearing the word announced as we arrive, barely inside, the word again spoken, clearly repeated, emphasised, yes, the word gas, coincides with an abrupt change of light, snatched, as you walk in the direction of silence, others beside you, strangers who share this small time and room with you, meeting here by chance, congregate at a single point, through two sets of doors one inside the other, then spread out into your own way of looking. No one tells you this, it just happens, you wander in a neat line, you shuffle, you're patient, who wants to rush here, and once you cross the threshold - no one's carried, only babes in arms, toddlers exhausted from the sun - yes, once inside the room you wander off of your own accord, find your own place to stand, crouch, dare you sit here on the floor, lie out, I doubt you would. No matter how long you sleep with another in your bed, En says - in the bed you share each night - once you're asleep you are alone not even aware of the one beside you ... dreams take you into separate worlds always. But this has nothing to do with dreaming. When we enter the gas chamber, we of course know where we are ... In our case, we know well enough where we are headed, finally, already the eyes take their time adjusting to the sudden loss of sun, to the dimensions neither big nor small, it's the sudden cold and starkness, it's the catching up with the ... *this can't be it* ... It's a room made from thick walls. It's the definitive shape that's frightening if abstractions will do here but I have no inclination to run for the metaphors and I know little of geometry but it's the shape only speaking of itself, its function, low ceiling, it's the solidity of the walls that hurt, that you mistrust even now, yes, even now, once inside the darkness of the room there's a tiny splinter of doubt, the sound of yourself saying - don't be ridiculous - a tiny murmur that you cannot be sure you'll leave here.

In the adjoining room - the crematorium, cold bricks, the gone-out, the gone-by, a woman is pushing a video camera into the oven's face. The woman over there beside En, *Reconstituted*, she's saying, a man at the back of one of the ovens he's saying, *Room of skin*. He's saying ... *Nakedness fixes itself onto the eye*. Moinous telling me later ... *I never saw my mother naked, in all the time we spent*

in our one room apartment in Paris. I never saw her naked but in this room I saw
her naked for the first time and it frightened me. I saw her naked body being pushed
into the oven.

Who can stay dressed here?

The terror of the nothing-left-to-see-through - no windows not anywhere here no natural light, still somehow there's the contradiction of the open crematorium doorway joining the two rooms together, a thin white line of light crosses the floor - the way we'd chalk the floor as children - ends by forming itself into a rust-orange square on the chamber wall opposite the doorway that separates the rooms symbolic demarcation, the before and after. Clouds and sloppy daubs of new cement spread over the gas chamber walls, gestures the not-thought-out, what's passed by, what's scratched in and through; what's hidden beneath only made more visible to imagination, and again, what use imagination in this room? There's no sense pretending. There is a hatch over there, and the absurd image comes at me of gas pellets raining down inside; the doctor, who had to oversee the *procedure*, transported to the chamber in a small white van, a red cross painted on one side, resembling an ambulance; of a man, crawling across the flat roof each time, opening tin after tin up there on the roof, and the sound that made in this room.

The temptation at this point is to close my eyes. What place does description have here? Quiet now. Try to linger a while. Try to stay put when all I want to do is sleep. Get out of this room. *We all get here eventually,* she's saying ... *No liar* ... Enough weeks enough tack. This room's sealed with doors within doors, two sets at each end. One room demarcated from its crematorium with an opening that I imagine was not there before. In our case, we were on the point of leaving when we knew we had to get here to see this room, we kept saying we have to go soon, but we haven't seen *IT* yet ... We have to go now ... But we haven't found *IT* yet; we got a little lost on the way here, we had to look at the plan, we turned the map in our hands, this way and that, we were on the point of asking for directions to the gas chamber when we saw that everyone was going that way, quietly, in an orderly line, heads down but forward eager steps, the getting it done with, the getting it seen, the getting it known - *as if you could* - well, maybe then it's time to get it over with, it's next, it's inevitable, you can't come here and miss this one out, you can skip many of the other rooms but not this one ...

And in many ways it's unremarkable, a room children might come across in the woods, a room that's up to no good, that sneaks up behind you, that's at the back of you ... look ... Wander inside silence, my husband and children move to and from one another, the way we all move inside here is random. The way you move your hands and the way you move your hair over the wall here is random, hands rub on silence, on absence, my body held in attention, derailed enough, all details blur. It's the main room some would say, it's the room that will teach us not to go looking in other peoples' rooms, inside other peoples' stories. Think of a room that will put an end to all looking, a beginning to all looking that crooked inadequate way seeing thinks. *What accent do you have ...*

Be careful here the boy said ... My hands to my nose, it's the over-scented lily, just one, no, in many ways, anatomically speaking, that is, you could say that it's a colon, an anus of a room. It's time we got out of here, this room with its no care cement wiped over the walls, the eye fixed - how else, at the far end of the room where I find myself drawn to peep through a sealed door much like the entrance that only leads to another door going nowhere, my eye locked to a peep-hole so minute ... *So look inside the boy* said ... *Take a look* ... That makes me jump, in front of him my body jerks my eye back from the tiny hole, an invisible cobweb, ashamed in front of the boy, of him seeing my fear ... *What did you expect ... I wish you hadn't witnessed me jump.*

I've moved again. I need to get out of this ugly room, I need air. I wasn't asleep but I've shifted now, hardly move, and the boy's disappeared. I avoid the corners. Did I tell you that once it wouldn't have been safe to light a candle here, people say that, but I light one anyway; I move it three times, hope no-one notices my indecision, the darkness is obviously not my motivation, so I push the candle into the corner. I have such a bad feeling about the corners. Edge my way to the centre of the room, this time, press my back against the wall, when the man speaks, he's pressed into the wall directly opposite me, he's six foot three at least, he's not smiling and he's holding a curled-up newspaper in his hand, he has defiant white hair, he holds my eye and the paper tightly for a moment. He's silent for a long time, stares hard at me, blatant, asks ... *What comes next ... Nothing comes next.*

I'm left alone. There's a hole of light above my eye, smaller than a curled-up fist, an oversight for sure, that I looked up, that I even noticed at all, I could have so easily missed it, kept my eyes to the floor, the sky here of all places, surely a mistake. I wonder if I should go tell En what I've found, and what is it I've found: it's nothing, it's of no concern, it's everything. It's just - if you stand here at the far end of the room to your left, face the wall, place your palms open, flat, stretch your neck back, your belly pressed hard to the wall, you can see it. You cannot get out of this room but your eye can, look up, stand so still, so straight, arch your neck until it hurts, your eyes strain as far up as they can go, there's nowhere to go, no way to sit, not here, only the eye escapes, only a small hole of light, colour taken into each nostril, the sky turning blue as once remembered, a passing cloud whiter than remembered.

Dream #67352

You are at home, Moinous, and I am visiting. Your daughter Simone is there. You tell me that Simone is going to direct us for a while because I had written a play where we, as the characters, live in a world denied writing. A world absent of books, a world that has no real sense of time and where one's own memories are denied. In this world, the only way we are allowed memory is to beg other people to keep our memories for us, to be our readers. In the play, people stand on street corners, in search of someone who will read and remember their memories for them, to thus find some meaning and relief, to leave the limitations of a world otherwise stuck in the present tense. In the play I, as the character, agree to have one of your memories for you. In turn, you tell me that Simone will be there the whole time directing me, so that I don't get scared or worry that things will get out of hand.

I tell you.

Tell you that, I will try to remember that we are in a play about the denial of our own memories. I say that I will try not to get the I or the you of the characters of the play mixed up with the I and the you that we are. After having and reading your memory, I will try to do everything I can to write down all I have seen even though it's forbidden to do so. That I, as the character, will be allowed to keep your memory and hold it for you only for the time of the reading, or until something or someone interrupts the reading, or at best until someone else wants me to have their memory instead.

We begin.

I enter.

Enter a house that is made up of many many rooms. Expensive and plush like fancy hotel bedrooms. Yes, each room has a bed and each room is blue-grey. I see that you always remember things in blue.

I digress.

Digress inside the memory to recall a film you once saw called *The Flower of My Secret*. Not the best of titles - in fact, a really awful title. I shift to a small scene from the film where Leo [the woman] and Angel [the man] are in a square. They have just seen some flamenco; Angel is teasing Leo and mimicking the dance. Then he slips on the wet cobbles and Leo rushes to help him, asking if he is okay. *No*, he says, *I am broken everywhere, every part of me is broken.* And she helps him up. They stand very close to the other and he says …

Do you remember in Casablanca, when Bogart asks Bergman's character: Have we met before? and she says,

IB: *Let's see … the last time we met …*
HB: *Was it Bella Rue?*
IB: *How nice you remembered, but of course that was the day the Germans moved into Paris.*
HB: *Not an easy day to forget.*
IB: *NO.*
HB: *I remember every detail. The Germans wore grey, you wore blue.*
IB: *Yes, I put that dress away. When the Germans march out I'll wear it again.*

And then Angel says to Leo, *Yes, and the day you decided to come into my life you wore Azul.*

Yes, and in this memory you are thinking in blue. You are searching for your mother. And I say aloud: I can see that's what you think this memory is about, but this is not your mother. This woman that you chase through these rooms is called Violet, and I can see, as I follow the course of this memory, that Violet is actually called Viole[n]t. And she is not good for you, I say. This woman is an impostor. I can see that you are beginning to slowly realise this and that I am slightly ahead of you as I try to translate her to you.

You keep disappearing.

Disappearing into rooms with the woman you call mother and I can hear you screaming at her as you now remember that this of course is not your mother. You are shouting, Where is my mother, Viole[n]t? Where have you hidden her? The rooms keep turning into one another, replacing one another, a whole spectrum of rooms and blue. I am afraid of the screaming, the noise of you arguing and so I miss out those rooms where you fight and realise that within this memory I can move about independently of you. Inside this memory there is a whole other layer of rooms, other domains that you had not been able to see when you were originally present in this place.

I look.

Look around other rooms while you continue to fight and shout at Viole[n]t. In each of these other rooms [ones you cannot see, rooms that are lit with small bedside lamps as if it's dusk] there are tall blue-grey dogs sitting on the floor. Grey like Marina Tsvetaeva's devil, *grey skin like a great Dane - there was no fur; there was the opposite of fur, she writes, complete smoothness, even clean-shavenness, fresh-cast steeliness.* And in each of these replica rooms, one and the same, each contain a smooth blue-grey dog. And there is also a child on the floor beside the bed. Dog, child, bed, lamp. Each dog and child take up the same pose. Except sometimes the dog has its back legs wide open and the child is licking the dogs hard genitals or it is the child who has its naked legs apart and the dog's long grey tongue is lapping between the child's thighs.

And I want to tell you.

Tell you what I've seen but I do not know how to without upsetting you. So I stay silent. And still you and Viole[n]t argue, become more physical with the other, throw things around the room. I can hear china breaking apart as it hits the walls.

In the memory we are now together again.

We are together again as you come rushing out of a room saying to me ... *You must open all the drawers here, search my clothes, look at my papers, diaries, everything, pull everything open. You must help me to find mother.* We both sense the memory is soon to end and there isn't time to be coy.

You return to your fight with Viole[n]t. I find all your papers and flick through your diary and find lots of red signs I cannot decipher. I feel I am failing your memory. I can't figure it out.

There is a small cameo picture of your mother inside the book and I call you to come see. Look. I have found some-thing. I show you her picture and as I do the photograph comes alive. You are frantic to get to her and you shake the diary, the now moving photograph, and I am worried and say, *Don't shake her so hard, you'll hurt her. I must get her out of this photograph* you shout, and continue until the book breaks apart and the pages with the red signs scatter and you spill your mother onto the floor at our feet.

She unfolds and is wet.

She unfolds, glistening. She is wearing a long brown coat over a floral dress. Brown stockings and solid shoes. She unfolds and you rush to pick her up, to try and get her to her feet when my, your, memory implodes.

The memory implodes and we are outside your house. You and Simone are talking about the play and you keep expecting me to speak but all I can do is shake. I pull five pencils, one at a time, from behind my ears, and I see that you glance at each one appearing from my hair. Offer me a small notebook so I can write down what I saw. *Be quick* ... But each pencil is broken and I have already forgotten everything.

Monday 26th of July 2004 - Krakow

Moinous, I don't expect I will send this to you, not now. It's still not easy to get to the internet cafés and maybe after all I am writing to myself by the way of you, as you wrote once ... *One picks up somebody, one person, and shares his thoughts with that person, and only that person, because you know that that friend you are writing to will read the whole thing - for perhaps somewhere in the back, at the end of the letter, the writer will sneak a little in about the receiver and this is why you go on reading this crap.*

But as I always forget so much so quickly, I want to just tell you, that this evening in the rain we went to the ghetto wall in Krakow. What's left of it, a small row of what resemble Jewish headstones. On March 21st 1941 the SS moved the entire Jewish community from Kazimierz, the Jewish quarter, over the Powstancow Slakich Bridge, to an area of 329 buildings in the Podgorze suburb. In the film Spielberg made, the ghetto was filmed in Kazimierz where the buildings are still quite elegant - pretty streets and courtyards, and synagogues; many restaurants and tourists. I am sure this is now where most people think the ghetto was, as Spielberg's celluloid becomes *the real*. Maybe most people don't make it across the river to the poorer area where the houses are crumbling and oozing. Despite some attempts to renovate some areas here, it feels in some ways like a forgotten desolate place.

Yes, Podgorze still looks abandoned. I wonder where all the Polish people had been forced to move to from here, sixty years back, to make way for the ghetto. I mean, when you form an area into a ghetto I guess no-one asks the people already living there what they think, and so what happens to those people? Do they live alongside, or are they expelled, and if so, then to where?

While we take photographs next to the ghetto wall a woman walks by, stares as she waits for her dog who resists her tugs, is instead more intent on shitting against a parked bicycle. We huddle under our red umbrella, that I feel, without intention, becomes, in the gloomy monochrome of the evening, an awkward reminder of Spielberg's red coat that you'd felt had sentimentalised what should have remained a film drained of colour. We find the square where many people were gathered and shot. I recall an image of Jews clearing ice from the streets. Blood in the snow. I'm sure it was here. This square where many were killed. Now no more than a dreary bus station where locals wait for the bus to take them home. I look on, no more than an uncomfortable tourist; open to all, my symbolic red brolly made brighter by the drizzle.

En wants us to find Schindler's factory - which he came to last year with his mother Elise - which we'd failed to find yesterday morning. I want to go back to our cosy apartment; enough for one day, but I say nothing because he wants me to see what we eventually find, another dreary sight: the *Telepod* electronics factory, as it was named a year back, only when we stand in front of it at last, the sign over the gate now has Oscar Schindler's name proudly reinstalled over the entrance. It's from here, each day, the Schindler Jews walked 5 km from Plaszow camp, to and from his enamelware factory. Only a small section of the Schindler factory is now open and kept in what seems to be its original state. The steps, from the famous scene where the young woman comes to the factory to persuade Oscar to take in and save her parents. The first time she comes to the factory steps, or so it is portrayed, Oscar peers at her down the steps, it's implied that because she looks too plain, he walks away. The second time, she returns in full make-up, more seductive feminine clothes, clothes that she later confesses she has borrowed, and this time he invites her to talk.

On the way here we pass others' houses and I hear the sound of TVs. Shouting. People eating. It's evening and the lights are on. The rain makes it darker and it feels as if it makes us more conspicuous - well, the camera does, for sure. I don't want to have any more photographs taken but there are the obligatory ones outside the factory gates. We had to cross beneath a railway bridge and across tracks to reach the factory road. Young boys, my children's age, played on the lines. In the factory, the part that is not just open to the tourists, the cleaner let herself in. Opposite the factory in the tenement blocks a young woman in shorts is carrying armfuls of ribboned presents from a car. She's laughing with her mother and I see that she does not look across at us nor even seem to notice us gathered in the gateway posing for the next shot. And why should she have noticed, when each day there must be a constant collection of tourists and their cameras opposite their ground floor flat.

En waits at the bottom of the Schindler steps. The children say they do not want to come with me so they wait with him. He says he's seen it before so I should go on my own.

At the top of the Schindler steps there's a safe, open and empty. Something about the open safe, the huge chunk of weighty and waiting metal - waiting for what, for my face peering inside - frightens me. I wonder what was kept in there; if it was the obvious things that you normally keep safe, or something more sinister. I wonder why it is here at the top of the steps in such an open place. There's a black and white photograph to the right of the safe, in a small corner: a type of makeshift gallery. The glossy photograph is of Ben Kingsley from the Spielberg film. Beside him, one of the actors - or was he one of the *real* Jews playing an actor playing himself?

There were two other photographs next to this one, but they have obviously been stolen and ripped from the wall. The cardboard frame is still visible, left half-glued to the paintwork. The captions are there still, and Ben Kingsley was probably in all of them. I consider how easy it would be for me to take the final one and be done with it: a photograph of Ben and the actor who played Jakob Lewertow, the one Schindler called The Rabbi, the one who was asked to make a hinge and was timed, the one who would have been shot but for the fact that the Commandant Amon Goeth's gun refused to work. I consider taking the photograph home, but then I think what would I do with a photograph of Ben Kingsley and where would I put it and who would I show it to, because then I would have to reveal the source of my souvenir and what would that then say about me? I decide to leave it for someone else to take. Instead, I sign the visitors book, trying to find En's name from last time but it doesn't go that far back. I sign his mother's maiden name as it sounds more authentic. I hesitate over leaving a message and I have no idea what to say. Instead, I peel a large flake of olive-green paint from the wall. I think the paint looks sixty years old and must be surely be authentic. I then recall that they used these same steps in the film and so it cannot be. The paint in the film was not peeling. Unless the steps were recreated in Hollywood. I have no idea, but want to imagine that the paint is the original Schindler paint. I will add it to the Auschwitz stones and the bark and the pigeon feather and flowers pressed between my book. I will tell everyone it is the same paint and no doubt they will not think about the film and the possibilities of over-painting. Having got the paint flake home intact - no easy feat - surely then I won't be able to decide what to do with it. It will be carefully moved from envelope to box to book to window-sill to shelf to dressing table and round again until finally it begins to fracture into five or more tiny pieces that I will want to throw away but feel I cannot until finally it is no more than a pile of green dust that disappears behind a dresser along with the dried Auschwitz flowers I will keep meaning and forgetting to frame, along with the Auschwitz straw. Again, never certain if the single piece of the oldest dustiest looking straw that I place in my bag - take out from time to time, turn between my fingers, not knowing what to do with it or who to show it to, will finally also disappear without my knowing when or how I mislaid it - if this straw is original or not.

Next to the open Schindler safe there's a door that opens onto the factory corridor. I am unsure which side to take, as the corridor curves away in both directions. I decide to go right, and see only a series of doors - all of which seem to be locked, padded on the outside, the padding is unnerving and like the safe at the top of the stairs, it doesn't make sense. I don't go near or try to open these doors. I change my mind and go left, but again all I can see are more and more of the same doors. All I can hear are my footsteps and my heart and for no reason other than the sound I make in this emptiness, I frighten myself when I can no longer see the only door I want to see, the one that led into the corridor. I run back to the steps and to En waiting, smiling, at the bottom.

On the way back we wait at the bus stop in the square and read about the factory. We read that many of the people who worked here were finally sent the sixty km west from here to Auschwitz. En shows me photographs of the Plaszow camp. Old photographs show SS soldiers at Plaszow smiling, picking and holding handfuls of wild flowers. It looks like a scene from *The Sound of Music.* The small booklet reads - *Wild flowers grew abundantly here in Plaszow, in fact, it is now a nature reserve for rare flowers and herbs.* Reminding me of something I'd scribbled in the back of my notebook - a line of Sam's sent between us one day - *In the meantime who knows no more than withered flowers. No more.*

Pigeon

What is it that draws me toward a lone bird; a lone tune as yet unlocatable, always bringing on the dawn. Did I see myself rise and go to the window - not mine - walking to the window each morning at 5 a.m. It's summer. It's July and dawn comes early in a foreign city, in Krakow, the noises, smells, untranslatable to begin. I am looking for the sound of a bugle: the hejnal, in the way I had once looked for the Muezzin that had once sounded from the minaret, the call to Adham; that low voice at dawn sung to the four corners of the world, to the compass points. I listen now for the Krakow bugle in the way I had once listened out for that human voice stirring my sleep: not here, that was another unexpected city another time another call that had woken me, then as now. I was tired, I hadn't wanted to find myself awake at such an early hour, but after this first call, in the days that followed, I was waiting for this voice, I was ready to receive it. And now the bugle calls, pursing his lips over my dawn with repetition; spit finds its way into my room, under my sheets. You can fall in love like this, you can fall in love with this call; it's not my name I hear but something in this call knows me, is known by me; this same unmodulated tune free to move inside but no fixed abode or melody until he interrupts it right into the heart of my sleep here now in Krakow, the distant sound of a bugle waking me at dawn.

I tell no-one of the faint sound of this bugle coming to find me. I know nothing of its history. It will be a few days before En reads to me from the Polish guidebook. This is what will begin the afternoon rest, the sound of En's voice reading to me. The bugle call from the church of St Mary [Kosciol Mariacki]; every hour, four times on the hour to the four winds. In the past, the sound announced the opening and closing of the city gateways. The six tower watchmen who in pairs shared their watch, morning to noon to midnight from the city's highest point. B flat sounds the watch. During the war in 1297, an arrow from a Tartar soldier shot through the bugler's throat, stopping him in mid-note. To this day the bugler's call is interrupted, in remembrance of this.

Before this, for days, I am woken by the trumpet. I also catch it in the day, for a while claiming it as my own; even when half-awake I'm a romantic. To begin, never sure if I am making this bugler up, constantly trying to locate him. I think he is here and then he moves, no fool, over there, the way the chimes of the city's clock are snatched and carried to and from by the wind in a playful mood. So early she cuts time up, halves and quarters stolen away; she, the wind, laughs at my effort as I strain to hear, to count beneath the sheets without moving from my bed - but here in Krakow I do rise and go to the window, while everyone sleeps, I try to locate the sound, decide it is coming from somewhere almost in front of our building but slightly to my left, when in actual fact the sound is coming from the right, east, but I do not yet know its location, the bugler's note held through time, En's reading is still to come. There's just me, no better than a risen corpse restless in a white sheet, at the window tinged green by this first unsure light. And what hour did my child come, wasn't it also 5 a.m. - steady child who still loves his routine. Many years back, there was another window, there was that other-mother tree, the tree came to take the baby; what labour under the branches; hush, for now we are here in Poland. Here I am still at the window, not our window, but one that I make ours for three weeks. I even hang glass chimes there in front of the glass, small bluebirds, don't laugh, but it is not the chime that wakes me, rather it's the sound I locate beneath the top floor apartment just over there, six floors up: a crudely curtained window behind which there's a man no doubt and he cannot speak to me because he speaks only Polish, of course he does, and he's playing the bugle for me, not needing to know or see me but casting out the way a fisherman fishes and he's caught me, ah, what mush of a morning; he's playing from memory no doubt and his wife is long dead. That's the story I make up and it's mine for now, at least: for now I make him a widower. I kill off the wife in no more than two seconds: not elaborate, but easy. The widower does not bother to dress, he wears an old frayed gown, shorts beneath, bare feet veined by the age he has stood here and played, waited: for what is music without its destination without its persuasion without a stranger's surrender.

I think I have located him in a cluttered room, behind a curtain that's nailed unevenly to the window, between the gather and tuck at each nail, the shabby green light exposing the age of cloth and the shadows of over-stacked furniture. He's at the very top of the building just opposite mine; above him an attic room. Yes, over his head, over his apartment, there's an attic room over-filled with pigeons in and out, and one's trapped. Pigeon back and forth behind the window's glass, pigeon no longer able to remember that he'd flown into this misery this back and forth no better than an old toy bobbing not reaching water nor sky; nothing more stupid than a bird stuck behind glass cooing as if to say … Please … Please. It's behind you, no, *above you*, I want to shout - that hole to the sky; it's there if you look, it's that simple … But I do not speak and he will not look up to see that escape is just a stretch of the neck away; he, she, I mean: who can tell the gender of this bird, especially from over here. And did you know that pigeons mate for life, take turns on the egg, the female from late afternoon through night, the male from dawn to dusk, the male bird feeding the young; but in his new-found coop there is too much time for such regard, too much time to ponder on the small details of stolen routines - if ponder he can - for now there is nothing to rely on, no egg, no turn-taking, no fidelity, only one bird awaiting the other's return, one bird with only a bugler beneath him, a bugler for breath, a bugler who cannot see him; a man living below with a bird replacing a memory. In the squint of a new day I locate the room, the bugler's sound; in a yawn I find this bugler in semi-squalor with nothing but a trapped pigeon in his head.

And it is their dedication to the hour that impresses me - yes, bird and man for sure, instead of being the victim of time passing, the hour reminding them of the-nothing-to-be-done, everything has gone by - except a life, of course, still passing; instead they deprive themselves of needed sleep to stay vigilant and proud, their commitment to the hour played out, even in the blasphemous heat to come a note a song will be pursued and kissed.

I will tell him, you, as if he could hear me ... Listen:

When it was Christmas time at home - very far from here - they'd decorate the clock at the centre of our small town, the clock, with its four illuminated faces, looked more like an iron lighthouse. It was the clock where lovers met or stood each other up, where mothers waited, where deals were made, where the cars prowled and young men whistled, where the dogs fucked each other anti-clockwise: the clock which marked death. And at Christmas the guts of the clock was filled with singing and I believed them when they said there were small families living inside, don't laugh, a miniature family, my father said, not unlike the Von Traps (or is that going too far?) no doubt the children dressed in curtains, fur-trimmed for Christmas - him laughing at the time of telling - so that every hour I could run and listen and migrate with their contorted faces over the holly and the ivy, the feast of Stephen, the crib and the hay.

But for now, it's the pigeon I seek. A kind of sleepwalking toward time, all my life, clocks and tunes and birds, for now it is the bugle drawing me to the pigeon, or is it the pigeon to the bugle? I did not imagine *she*: neither pigeon nor player. Trapped dumb things. Birds one by one fill the empty roof-space, some almost kill themselves by flying round and round, hitting glass and walls; others deranged from lack of food, half-delirious with the repetition of moving back and forth behind the pane, looking across at me. Look at me! Now in the half-light - well, in the light of the apartment walls caught in the dawn fast rising, having no idea of the range of pigeon's sight - I imagine that he can see me: I wish that he could see me as I do him.

And I feel a fondness for the pigeon, admit so soon to both affection and neglect as I passively watch his tomfoolery with a mix of clemency and spectacle, find myself half-smiling, or is it a grimace I make at his tiny clown's face, absurd stance, fearful circled eyes alert and almost drunk on getting nowhere, dizzy on flapping, his wings fail again but try again, again, wings held open as if to gesture that he did have a past, indeed only hours earlier he had a whole sky in which to open those same wings he now holds up only in hesitation in indecision the way someone with amnesia ponders over a name which may have once been theirs; in the way a demented man plucks at the air, desperate and proud enough to try to seize something not quite there, not quite forgotten; my own passivity preventing me from acting to go rescue him. And I am not saying I do not consider rescue, but considering my position, the dawn, yes, my lack of Polish or, at this hour, clothing; the lack of air this night, or rather daybreak, the seven floors down and then up to his side of the building, I decide against any movement, against anything more active than the gaze, one to the other, he, staring at me, me at him; I keep so very still while he struts on feet no better than ill-fitting shoes, each of us watching the other from our equal-sized windows.

And I won't be flippant and imply that the pigeon and I are just a mirror for the other, I won't suggest the cheap psychobooboo of who was watching who die behind glass. Not that it didn't occur to me, that maybe it was he who felt sorry for me all along, he who most likely decided nothing was to be done other than to stare and wait for my inevitable fall. And what must I do ... Up Up Up most stupid of birds. I see myself point - as if to translate the hole above him, *over your head!* - whisper, so as not to wake En in the bed behind me; as if the bird can lip-read, comprehend my bobbing forefinger, my popping mouth; as if he cannot read the warning sign of pigeon shit smeared over glass; of feathers free-floating in the air; as if he cannot doubt the memory, the ferocity of the afternoon sun that will for certain return and be upon us later, that for sure will heat him into madness; the incessant coo-cooing which will force panic to blunder a different tone in him. I can tell by his expression that he is already scared and it is his eyes more than his swelling throat or his rocking that makes me almost turn away. Almost. If only he hadn't forgotten to look up.

And so there's the pigeon, every hour the fading fading sound of the lone bugler, an encumbered widower, half-dressed recluse with a pigeon still lodged in his head. I wonder, does the bugler ever wander upstairs to this small attic room over him. Does he ever make that small climb to clear away the remains, dispose of what must be the inevitable stench.

There's a better view now from the kitchen window, there's me drinking a glass of yellow tea. I have time for everything. I still haven't mentioned the bugle to En. I won't wake him, not yet; I won't mention yet that almost shy cry, so unsure of itself, listening out for those five notes soon to come again: it's almost ten to the hour.

I didn't dream of you, pigeon. I didn't see you fly in. I dream of more exotic birds. I do not dream in grey or the dirty pink of your ringed feet, nor in the black and white of your small eyes; there's only me looking at you bird with the slight smugness of the one who can walk away, seven flights down. Ah, listen to that bird: Seven *flights* ... to escape to the Krakow streets early morning, to hear all that opens beneath us: yes, soon, bird. Soon they will begin washing the pavements; we'll smell the scent of bleach and lime; they'll boil the coffee seven times; arrange the chairs especially well; the perfume of newly-washed hair will be fresh upon the air while you, my bird, are gradually waiting to die; waiting as the sun won't wait to puff you up behind heated glass that you still fail to translate.

Will you die in threes, in the three weeks I am with you? In the three weeks when I won't even notice if another bird replaces you? For sure it is cruel to say you all look the same to me, look at you all looking the same, all flying the same way in and not knowing what you did. Not even knowing how or what you did to end up so betrayed.

I pretend there are other ways out of here; like you, not always one for looking that directly up when another bird no more than a mere shadow on my eye moves between our windows, not you my bird, but another in flight this time; not even then do I realise what I also forget, Up … Up … Up … The sky's just in front of my eyes.

From: Moinous@aol.com
Sent: 9th September 2004 2.48pm
To: angelamorgancutler@ntlworld.com
Subject: Re: SORRY just thinking allowed -

this is all I could find of your Polish emails so far

From: <angelamorgancutler@ntlworld.com> Date: 2004/07/22 Thu PM
06:48:47 GMT
To: Moinous@aol.com
Subject: auschwitz

this is the second attempt I hate thezse internet czafe s and this
keyvord -
I 'm sorry I can't pick up my messages - i have rmno idea if minbe are
gerring through - sorry I can;t
wzasgte tinme - more tinme - be longer - say more - o0

we weent to auschwitz today

I nwanted to tell you - and I lit {as I said I womluld] i lit a candle in
the gas chamber for you - otjer wise it was hard to feel any connection
to the plavce - well i can't procress it all yet - all I cna say is
thta I wore a tourtquoise skirt - painted my nails pink - wrote in the
prsent tense - it of coutrse left me feeling empty- not surw what we
were supposed tp feel - what we were doing there - what were we looking
for - at - with so many otehrs - all strangers - so many chewques of
people al l loojking -

I rubbed my head along the gas chamnber wall and thought how unremarkable
a room it was - howe unremarkable - and so what did I expect - not what
i saw - the crudeness of the roomn su9rprised me - lieke some building
you might happen upon abandoned inside a wood - the stuff of child
killing and so it was - we tjhen went to berkenau and sat beside a pond
full of ashesz - waht a factory of death - rubble - enormous expanses
of nothing - did youfp go there as well? - I picked up some small things
from the grouns d - I want to send you from aush witz - you know - bits
of nothing as there is nothing - buit I want to send them anyway and
will - also sending love - we thoighty of you - sorry abouyt this - this
oinpoossible keybporadf - and that i can't say more - its so hit i mean
hot in here - bodies all tightky packed in and toying away - words to
who knoes who - max telling me that someone in the cornere is watchong
porn on their screem - 0 i wondeered why he wsa so quiet - write soojmn
==,i will - Axxxxxxx
Angela - I have to look in other corners hope it helps
late here - hot like hell - feeling l - a- z - y - washed out - impatient
to
get going
excuse the briefness but I instead of me talking today I sent you the
small book I wrote for Ron
xxxM

oh - I just found another piece - Is this what you lost -

From: angelamorgancutler@ntlworld.com
Date: 10th September 2004 5.12pm
To: Moinous@aol.com
Subject: Re: SORRY thinking allowed -

No no - you sent a right mish mash of e-mails - sorry - I have these
already - I know you are trying but I need the other e-mails that I sent
from the Polish internet cafes - if you have them - I have everything
else - well I have the ones you sent to me - but not the emails I sent
back to you - <u>I need all of them</u> - It was from the <u>16th of July - August
31st</u> but I don't know what you keep – if indeed you have them all -

It's tragicomic - don't you think - that the Polish e-mails are now
missing like the missing pages I was telling you about -
Are you with me - the whole book no more than a series of missing
missives - which then presents me with the dilemma - if to make up the
missing missives, if to give an authentic veneer of authenticity to
authenticate these missing messages -
to fabricate or not -
that is the question -

*If there is, among all words, one that is inauthentic, then surely it
is the word 'authentic'.* [Blanchot]

Today I have to go buy fish - half baked fish and words that's how it
goes some days - maybe when I get to the market the fish will also be
missing -

Thank you for the book you wrote for Ron. I will keep it safe. It is
very special
Ax

From: Moinous@aol.com
Date: Fri, 1 Oct 2004 00:18:32 EDT
To: angelamorgancutler@ntlworld.com
Subject: Re: almost 4am -

it's very late here so only a few words

I am half drunk

some of my former students took me out for a fancy dinner with fancy wine

one of them announced during dinner that he just turned 50 - and I still
think of them as my undergraduate and graduate students

finally it's a good visit here - but I wouldn't want to spend the rest of my
life in this place - the crotch of america

En has a sense of humor
he bought you a mop -

maybe the title of the book could be

Mopping Auschwitz

One aspect of the book I think should be a wiping out of that horrible place -

anyway

we'll discuss all that

a powerful and loving cutch xxx

From: angelamorgancutler@ntlworld.com
Date: Sat, 2 Oct 2004 11:23:07
To: Moinous@aol.com
Subject: Re: almost 4am -

You write well for a half drunk
hardly any visible slurring

Mopping Auschwitz

that's perfect -

A xx

The Missing Pages

The day after Auschwitz, I have the feeling that I have done something atrocious. I write to Moinous to tell him, but the message I send never gets through and I am glad of it. The final resent version, altered beyond recognition but still the feeling will return, all day it will plague me: the day after Auschwitz I feel that I have done something atrocious.

Sshh

Sometimes I don't remember that I am trying to remember what I don't want to remember, forget that I am too scared to remember that there's nothing to remember until I remember that I have done nothing wrong.

Relief reminds me to laugh at myself,
but there's no-one to hear …
I did nothing wrong …
And so the thought begins again: the day after Auschwitz, all day, I have the feeling that maybe I have done something atrocious.

But any attempt to write this is cheap, cheaper than smoking while eating soup, and here in Auschwitz, more than anywhere, they sure knew how to fuck up a good soup.

What do you want me to say? Again, with just the weight of this name to go on; with every kind of book and document and report made in its name. With all sorts of advice given in its name. Be careful he said, take care how you use that word, how you speak of it at all.

There we were in Auschwitz, I was holding my son, I have said this before, only in this version I decide to ease my notebook from my bag. To rest the open notebook on my son's back as he now sits next to me on the steps; remember, we'd been sitting in the shade of a hut, our eyes were closed. Turn around a little I tell him, let me rest the book. See my hand smooth open the page, empty, waiting, make a start, write down something: begin with the name Auschwitz, copy down the spelling from the little pamphlet they gave us with the tiny folded map. Copy down Auschwitz at the top of my page as if I were in school all those years back, when then, as now, I'd write my titles boldly because I didn't have a clue what came next; knew that I was floundering, so I trace the word and make it thick with ink and underline it hard and certain in all uncertainty beginning …

Auschwitz,
Poland,
The World,
The Universe.

And then what happens?
And then what'll happen is,
that as soon as you name:
Auschwitz,
everyone comes running,
or they'll walk away, avert their eyes,
toward or away.
Ask ...
Does it have to be an either/or situation?
A choice: if to look at the name, consider the name or are you already turning away?
Watch yourself here,
Yes, now as I say and repeat the name ad infinitum, consider,
in what direction are your eyes in relation to the floor,
where are your hands in relation to your hips or ears,
is your mouth firmly closed or are your lips
a little apart.

Yes, now that the word is spoken, they'll all come - or go - carrying their bundles of narratives, their opinions and stories, their denials and politics, or they'll go silent or maybe instead,
they'll SHOUT,
rant.
They'll almost forget silence,
comfortable, meaningful silence, in the silence of the night still, still, be quiet, hush,
they'll shout forgetting,
concealment, reticence, taciturnity,

There'll be others who invite themselves over for breakfast, sit across a table from you and they'll say: enough now,
or they'll write you notes saying: be careful,
go easy, they'll say,
Telling me this and that, mainly over the breakfast table, over the spoons and forks and the wilting flowers over the bacon and runny eggs. He's such a bad Jew they'll say, look at the amount of bacon your husband packs away. It's a joke! but he's eating up the pig all the same.

Anyway ... anyhow,
now that the word is out, they'll sit up in their wicker chair, the one kept for visitors, and the chair will make that creaking sound that indicates that they are not only sitting upright but preparing to speak, clearing their throat ...
Yes, now that the name is out,
they'll say ...

Think of all the atrocities that are happening
still, that have never stopped after Auschwitz

There is no after Auschwitz

Still stuck in the past tense

Think of all the others who go unheard-of, uncared-for, unmemorialised

Think of that! they'll say …

Think that it's a word that stopped everything, that stopped nothing

Think of all that's was claimed in its name

Think of all that's excluded in its name

Think of the other holocausts all over the world that never get a look-in

Think of my child asking, Mum, when is a holocaust a holocaust? When a genocide is a genocide? What *is* a genocide? What's the difference and who decides … Who agrees and disagrees … hands up.

Think that we now see our genocides, in colour, on our TVs, three times a day, hourly if the radio is on, with food, with the optional pod casts, listen in live, listen again, stream every evening, war-torn between putting out the garbage, turning over the channel, making ourselves another herbal tea, making love, wanting to help, kicking the dog, going to help, yelp.

And where to go
Away to go
To which atrocity should I assign myself, they'll say -
still over the breakfast table -
which one? …
Not then,
NOW.
Pass the sugar they'll say,
and the salt.
It's all there in front of us,
all of it still to come,
all of its been seen before
all comes out the same
Can never be the same
Can be compared

No.
Come on,
which is it?
Make up your mind.

Now that the word is out, they'll say,

we all know and knew
Of course ...
We all choose and chose to sit in our fat armchairs and do nothing.
Nothing changes, they'll say.
Human nature, they'll say.
Changed everything, they'll say.

There was a note in the Los Angeles Times, way back - remember?
- way back, sixty years back, *Liberty Under The Law* it said, *True Industrial Freedom* it said, Wednesday Morning, March 22nd 1944, a small news item torn out, underlined by some unknown hand, the odd sentence picked out with a fountain pen, uneven strokes, some unfinished words, what choice among 500 words of newspaper print - uneven black lines mark out *500,000 persons mostly Jews, had been put to death - concen* [not completed] *Ozwiecim; south west of Krakow. Auschwitz*, it said, *poison gas* it said [not underlined].

Yes, as soon as you mention the word,
that name
They'll all come with their banners
with their hush now
with their shouldn't say,
with their flags and their bells and horns,
Shh.
They'll all come with their
with their knowing smiles and nods
with their did you know
their anagrams
their diagrams with quotations
and quotation marks
with exclamations, declarations, with poems and philosophies,
with their piety and guilt,
and don't forget regret
Regret everything he said,
with their sadness, shame and anger
with their you've got it all wrong
with their good intentions
with their should you have mentioned this -

shouldn't have mentioned that
with their say it another way
with their play it again Sam
taking up arms, or is it alms
with their leave well alone
with their denials,
more crispy bacon,
pass the sauce
pour over
their hissing spitting noise

Auschwitz: 9 across - NO MATCHES IN DICTIONARY try again
- try instead - **Auscultation** n. the action of listening to sounds from the
heart, lungs or other organs with a stethoscope. DERIVATIVES auscultate
v. auscultatory / sknltat / adj. - ORIGIN C17: from L. *auscultatio(n-)*, from
auscultare 'listen to'.
We are where, remind me,

you were looking for a book.

A book.

One you said you'd write.

Write

One word beginning everything

Everything

One word

And then I could have cancelled all the rest

The rest of what?

All the rotten carrots of trying to go on with this.
Did I tell you that I picked the skin from the trees in woods in this heat, in
Auschwitz.
one word formed a whole book,
one word and three hundred missing pages.
One word and a book of empty sheets.
I lie easy

As if that matters
As if things won't get altered along the way.
Imaginative leaps
Parts and intentions.
Obligations.
Manipulations.
Wrong versions.
Lost versions.
Forgotten versions.
Misdirections.
Distortions.
Digressions.
Exaggerations.
Mispronunciations.
The unspoken and the unasked.
The story sawn in half
no, let's make that slaughtered,
quartered.
One part on its way.
One to come.
One not realised.
One never told.
It's more of a story cut up like one of those segmented cows in the butcher's
window, like one of those big old cows mapped out: the shank, the rump, the
knuckle, all parts of one whole moo, the milk long forgotten from the engorged
udders.

Lines coming at you in the half light in a half sleep ... ridiculous lines ...

*Tell the one he's going to be put to sleep my way, tell the one no-one's going to linger
on his looks*

For god's sake
try a little tenderness.

Who is that speaking now?

Who's the one feeding you lines in the dark

Who's the one waking you at 3.30 a.m.

The one whispering in your ear.
Be specific.

The right ear.

Who's the one running?
Because if this is to be written it needs to be 'written on the hoof, on the run.'

Tell her she's going to be killed my way, tell her no-one's going to linger on her looks ...

Ridiculous, the kind of sentence that gets you nowhere, waking you again; other people's lines coming at you in the half-light, some other's voice and arm and hand opening out your mouth rotating your eyes an arm pushed inside your head twizzling no better than an owl turned 360 degrees on the page, hooting other people's stories at you, lines coming and going, call out, the root of the word is to receive ... the root of the word is to persuade ...

Go tell them that the cheeses are dying ...

I called this from a half-sleep in Krakow, another overheated afternoon repeats itself. Remember feeling foolish when En later told me what I'd said.
     In Auschwitz, Max, my small child, had rubbed water over my hair and feet, remember, after Auschwitz, between one place and another, between dreaming and living, half-asleep between loose cool sheets, En was rubbing my feet, found me dozing via my toes ... count them all ... when a voice moved close to my ear, not En's, he's at my feet, when a voice whispered ... *Come close ...*
Go tell them that the cheeses are dying ...

J. says I wear my Judaism like a fake fur. I feel hurt by the comment but love the line so plagiarise it at every opportunity.

Maybe she's right, maybe you're right Moinous when you say that now, this place, Auschwitz, it's all Dixieland, all Hollywood. He says someone wrote to him the other day and asked would he contribute something to their Holocaust museum? A little story. A little half-life story. He said, you're sixty years too late.

Finkelstein calling it an industry. The Holocaust. The museums. The celebrations, or was that commemoration? Was that memorial?

Ron writes in *Mosaic Man* ...

How many of you have the feeling that you're from another world, not this one? That you're someone else, not the person you're supposed to be?
     That's sometimes Ron's feeling and sometimes events bear it out. That must be the way it feels to be Jewish, and even if you think you're not a Jew, if you've never felt that way you must be Jewish too. Whether Christian, Moslem, if you go back far enough. Even if you think you're not.

Personally, being Jewish [Ron says] *is just an advanced case of being human, and being human may be a terminal disease that has run its course.*

Writing this as if I am keeping a plum tucked inside my blouse like a tiny pet, like a well kept secret.

Someone saying that the Greeks entered death backwards, a line I hung onto, translates into a night where I saw body after body emaciated, plum blue. I saw a man I loved lying in his metal cot, his legs where his arms should have been, his feet sticking out from the side of his head like two small wings. He was speaking to me, not realising that each sentence he spoke was spoken backwards: he was saying good-bye in the wrong order.

That's not all, in that same scene, I saw a coat hanging from a chair, its shoulders hunched as if it were laughing, or shrugging away a question, a coat covered in small yellow stars. Covered.

The book smells of milk she said ... I could smell it on the pages.
Who was that speaking?

Despite everything, when I returned from this place - from Auschwitz. I read the books, so many books that have been written in the name of this place. I didn't know where to start. Sarah and me agree to read the same book, to begin with one book on Auschwitz - when of course there are thousands of books, *some say*, more than enough; could there ever be enough books written in the name of this place? So here we are, thousands of miles apart, as if that matters, Sarah in the States, me in Britain, and we agree on one book, Agamben's *Remnants of Auschwitz*. Agree it's a start.

At the end of the book the Muselmann speaks, the Muselmann is the name people at Auschwitz gave to the prisoners that were *husks, mummy-men, the living dead, slow, malnourished, expressionless people* - the Muselmann speaks, bears witness to the one he was, to the one that in Auschwitz could not speak. After Auschwitz the man who survives comes back from the dead and speaks of, writes of and for the Muselmann he was, bears witness to himself, agreeing that, in terms of the testimony of the Muselmanner, after Auschwitz ... it is the event of language that matters here, not what is said, nor how it is said, not the content, not the merit of the words, but that writing took place, that language shows itself trying to speak. Speaks in what ever way it can ...

Listen: we get to the end of our book, the copies we are reading, and Sarah rings me and she's saying that she cried. *I cried!* I, on the other hand, get to the end of my copy, to the point at which the Muselmann is about to speak - [at the end of the book, a beginning that opens ... *I was a Muselmann* ...] and I realise that the pages are missing. I mean, all I find at the end of my copy are these four words, this declaration, testimony: I was ...

And at first I think that the missing pages, or rather, the missing words on a series of blank pages is deliberate. I say to Sarah, How could you cry! I think that's perfect ... all that white space around those four words, attest that someone is indeed trying to speak, did speak; is speaking; a voice bears witness inside those four words ... *I was a Muselmann* ... In the way, so much is held inside those nine letters: Auschwitz.

Like the woman on TV last night, a survivor shouting across the snow of Birkenau ... *I was standing here naked as a child ... I am standing here now.*

En, on reading these pages En will scribble me a note he'll leave inside the book asking: *Why didn't you cry? Why don't you cry?*

These missing words that I'll later come to realize are not a deliberate absence, the missing pages are in fact no more than a printing error. Missing pages that Sarah copies and sends to me; insisting that I must read them, if not for the content but to see that the words are there, that something more was indeed said and written. But when the lost pages arrive over the screen, the words are so tiny so distorted they remain unreadable. I can do nothing to enlarge them, I cannot even read them with a magnifying glass, and believe me I'll try; still, everything remains elusive, illegible, beyond the eye, but none the less pleasing to the eye, nonetheless written, nonetheless *writing took place.*

Joan Rivers is interviewing me on a TV chat show - Even though she is doing most of the talking - she is telling me [in her rasping lilting voice] in front of a live audience sitting just feet away from us - that she is getting used to finding her way around London - how last week she made her way home from the studio only to find out later that three of her guests never made it home and are still probably wandering the one way systems - she said Angela - there are people in this life who are askers and then there are the losers - the best people always ask - Take Joan - she says - no - not me - well - me too - but Joan Collins - only last week she was on my show and she rang me as I was making my way home - she rang me on my car phone - she said - Joan - it's Joan - and I'm stuck in traffic and I admit I'm lost - Tell me about it - Joan I said - She said - Joan - I'm asking - talk me through it - tell me how to find my way out of here - And I talked her through it or maybe we talked each other through it and we found our way out - Joan's an asker - you see what I'm saying -

I know what you mean Joan - I say - One Christmas my ex came to stay - at the time I was living in North London and we - the friends I was with and myself - we decided it would be fun to drive into central London to see the Christmas lights - so I persuaded my ex to drive us there - at the time none of us could afford cars and so he did (reluctantly) drive us - He was nervous of the roads - he comes from a small village - he's not used to city traffic - all that - and I got him there easily enough - but once we were in Trafalgar Square I couldn't remember which exit was which because of the one way systems and the dark and the confusion of the lights and the laughter in the car and so he went round and round the square - and we were laughing more and more and I was shouting Ask – Ask someone - but he just continued going round and round the square and we continued laughing and he was shouting and I said - Oh for god's sake Lou - at least we got to see the lights and the Scandinavian Christmas tree all aglow - even if we did see it six times - He's not an asker Joan - maybe that's what did it - finally it was me who asked -

A woman in the audience - front row - is eating a Cornish pasty - Tell us about your book - she shouts over - looking at me - Yes - she says - Tell us - What book? - Joan screeches - A book - I can't believe this woman is looking at me and not telling me about this - Joan says - And I can't believe someone is asking me about something I haven't yet shown to anyone - I feel ashamed - panicky - as Joan's voice gets raspier and more uneven - louder - cracking on *book* - The book - she says - What's it called - tell us the name - don't go all shy on me now - she says - Come on - Tell us the name - for god's sake -

I realise that the woman eating a pasty is Joan's partner but also her researcher - that she's been into my house and nosed her way through my files - I know she knows the name - I know the name - *I must do* -

But the more they screech - Tell us - the more I can't think nor see it - I mean - I can't remember a damn thing about what it's called - All I know is that the name is something I don't want to announce - not here in public on live TV - all I know is that the name is shameful - and if I were to remember and utter it everyone would become silent - would turn their eyes away - that's all I know - But the woman front row is now finishing her pasty and licking her fingers - is asking me again to remember - Say it - she says - Say the name -

It's something that's big - I say in desperation - the name that is - what it stands for - maybe - well I'm not sure but I'm sure it was something enormous - devastating - something that could hurt you -

LOVE someone shouts from the audience - that's it - she's written a book called Love -

And before I can disagree - although I'm not sure - maybe it is Love - yes before I can come to my defence - before I can figure it out or admit that I'm not sure - LOVE is flashed on the screen behind Joan's head - LOVE in huge coloured flashing letters - No - I say in a pathetic voice - NO - But no-one is listening and the audience is chanting - She's written a book called Love - She's written a book called Love - love love love - All you need is love -

With that the credits roll and Joan is hugging me and saying - Got to fly honey - The one-way systems and all - And the audience disperse to catch their cars and the coaches that have brought them here -

I move to a seat at the front of the auditorium - the lights are dimmed as the last of the people leave - I notice that the researcher has left her bag on the floor - a paper *'Greggs the Bakers'* bag - inside there are pasty crumbs - I realise I am hungry and that I haven't eaten for many hours - I want to lick them up - I am salivating - but the thought of eating a stranger's crumbs and the smell of stale corned beef soon makes me feel disgusted and I cannot - I notice that the woman has left a set of small headphones beneath the pasty bag - and also an expensive black watch - the numbers are marked around the square face by black lacquered ticks - I put on the headphones - the hands on the watch move - startle me - I see it is 11 p.m. - Auschwitz - I say - suddenly remembering - wanting to cry - The name - Not Love - Not love - I shout - Auschwitz - A U S C H W I T Z

The Pond

Every summer, the children were born. There is obviously something that happens to the ovaries of the women in my family in October - in fact, on my mother's side all the women had July babies: my great-great-grandmother, my great-grandmother, my grandmother, my mother - my two sons born into the summer. There's an opening: straight for the womb, and it's only 11.30 a.m. at the time of writing, of recalling the Birkenau pond. October tracing itself back to July, when we found ourselves beside the pond, dates, weather reports; I'm starting from the point where I'd closed my eyes, where I was ready to tell you everything about the ash pond.

It was the 22nd of July when we found ourselves on a coach to Auschwitz, I've said this enough times, the 22nd of July when we found ourselves circling the Birkenau pond. A pond I knew nothing of until the day before our visit, when En takes me to meet the Jewish man from Krakow called Mr Les, who last year took En and Elise to Auschwitz by car. Inside the small book, he wants me to have, there is a small black and white photograph of the pond and beneath the image an inscription ...

Into this pond were dumped the ashes of many tens of thousands of people, mostly Jews, who were gassed at Krematorium IV, just behind and to the left. They were made to wait in the 'little wood' that can be seen behind the pond. In those days, a fence of interwoven branches blocked the waiting victims' view of what lay ahead.

Some say that for years no birds flew over this place, En tells me as we walk together, as we try to find the pond. On the way, in the little wood, our children pick up pine cones and stuff as many as they can into their pockets and into my handbag, the kids collect small pieces of thick glass, the pieces smooth and reinforced with tiny squares of now-rusted wire. They are arguing about who found the first and the best piece they want me to have; telling me these small pieces must once have made up the windows that people looked out of - And what did they see? No more than a changing sky, escaping.

The birds, En says, are only now returning, tentatively. Even the storks are nesting, grooming one another. Look, they are in love.

Every story begins in a wood, and weren't we approaching knowing that this most ancient of words, this place, is carried in us? The path to the wood always arouses curiosity; the path to the wood is what we are on our way to lose: the burden of innocence, to witness the fact that others had maintained their innocence here.

Here is the wood and what is expected. The reassurance and the vigilance of trees, like fathers lined up - I hate to be literal, but the trees are obviously the fathers lined up - between, the possibilities of flowers spread open, the day of unbending trees, of wild flowers; everything continues regardless.

It's the hole in the fence that draws me close, that fence that has been bent back by whose hands, and we snugly fit through, expecting wool caught on the wire fence like in the good old days. Forget the good old days, you'll say; there's no place for that expression here, not now. Neither is this a place to find sheep, I tell you for now the sheep have long gone - never arrived - the dumb sheep knew better, so maybe they were never really innocent, the sheep never wanting to be counted in sleep, each night, wanting to be seen as individuals, never turned their eyes blind.

Is this what we came for, these fields, this wood and trees. Not a single grazing animal in sight. These woods have been raped, En's saying, then repeating the words as if I have not heard ... *It looks as if each tree has been raped ... Come to that, as if the whole fucking forest's been raped ...*

I do not want to imagine each tree violated. I look at him, then at the trees, for as long as I can, and they are still there when I turn away, when I look for the evidence of change ... the wind still blows in the leaves and it is only my cheap imagination that gives such foliage menace.

Instead, I take a pen and draw a picture of a tree in my writing book, and another and again until I find myself sitting in a wood drawing a small wood, one held inside the other, drawing in what the trees knew and turned away from. This is where I begin, with one tree-line multiplying. And as soon as I wanted to see this place there was the path, there was the wood, there was the camp and the grass that replaced the bed, there are other people's photographs now stapled to the tree bark, photographs of the people who had once waited here sixty years back, groups of people sitting between trees with their children, just waiting; between trees there are many conversations. My child calling, Let's leg it through the woods ... Come on, mother. You wouldn't stand here alone. Mother, would you? Stand here like this at night alone, not even you. Would you do that? the child's asking.

It's 2 p.m.; the sun, that old misogynist, is at its fullest, to look to find to seek to question innocence; the sun, that old paedophile, pissed old fart sick on seeing, no doubt sick of being so damn reliable or was it unreliable, taking too long to die, sorry, I have my opinions but maybe this is no time for them as I try to picture everything that is no longer seen with the eye, the hope of dew, sickening greens, too many contrasting shades, that's to make sure the innocent eye can find all it is persuaded it wants. Blink Blink Blink look harder, pick up 3 more pine cones now, pick up 7, or was it 25 or was it 8,560 or a million; our arms overflowing and nowhere to place them so we drop them again and again. The impotence of the fingers of the arms of the day of the things I have come to read about this wood of the people waiting here.

I cannot lose my innocence, the eye said. Not here. But if not here then where; yes, much as I try, much as I vex my eye on the sun, much as I keep saying, Unbelievable, this wood, not now, much as I say, This grass, This piece of bark, This leaf, This glass scattered between the aspens; barking is that innocent, laughing howling holding hands, is that looking, Look, still trying to see, what?

- seeing nothing, seeing things that shouldn't be intact, things that crumble between fingers, things that won't give an inch, things ripped apart, snatched, dug up, snapped, cut, we graze on what a sheep would refuse to touch, bit by bit, what little is left, scattered, is taken away as mementoes inside pockets and handbags.

The pond we find by accident. I am in the little wood in Auschwitz and I am travelling, covering ground, I am a little out of breath, I can hear my breath, I can hear the sounds my children and others carry, finding water, nothing drinkable, but there's always water hidden somewhere. It is the story of a pond, that's pretty much all I find to say: a pond that we almost don't find; that we almost go home without seeing, my shoes carried in my hands. A pond where we lose our direction because here there is no direction, only the bull reeds overgrown, now the same reeds that had once been pulled out by other hands.

Others had been here before, not me. In all weathers they took aerial photographs across these fields, across a pond of ashes. Torn wild flowers thrown here, float, sink, the chafe of grass on feet where there is no longer any smell.

You could have just as easily drowned here in winter when everything was obliterated in snow, the mess all whitened over, everything looking almost beautiful again … Sshh … Nothing written down, only the almost silent movement of my son sinking into grass with his bare feet, pushing himself in. Less of a wet spot was once made into a wishing well but not here not now

now there is Max carrying water in his hands.

Max is carrying the water, he's with me, he kneeling beside me by the pond, he is carrying the water in his hands, the water's leaking through his fingers, he is carrying dribbles of water to and fro, whatever he can keep in his palm and he's washing his mother's arms. That's you, he's saying, that's you. He's telling me to keep still, he's telling me to lie back and relax … he's washing my head and neck with the water, he's repeating the gesture, he's dipping in his palm, he's carrying what he can save of the water and he's washing his mother's arms and feet and neck, my hair damp now around my forehead, he's combing my hair with his fingers, he's wetting my hair and lips, he's scraping back my hair from my face and he's asking too many unanswerable questions, he's pinching my cheeks to make them red, he is kissing my mouth as he speaks, he's asking, he won't stop talking, he won't stop washing my legs and arms and my face in the water.

If I had been here, he's saying … I would have grabbed a gun and legged it through these woods. It's the best place to hide. Seth is saying that he doesn't understand why so many people didn't just fight back, if there were so many thousands of them. I'm saying, it's complicated, it's not that simple … some did. I am trying, beginning to explain but no-one is really listening. Max is rubbing my feet, he's saying he likes the shape of my toes, the pink of my nails … He's saying, In the shower rooms, not here but like here, another camp, wasn't it written … one louse can kill.

Instead, this wood caught you running, caught you falling,

I'm starting from the point where I have closed my eyes,

little wood 1

Max, he's telling me to close my eyes. He's saying, Describe the taste of water, Mum, bet you can't, bet you can't, now close your eyes and try, try. Describe the taste of water.

I am lying next to the pond just here beneath the birch tree, just this tree, for a moment close my eyes here where I rest and trust nothing, here once you find the wood everything is allowed, once here I have no say in what takes place, the trees form patterns and small movements over me, a slight breeze changes shapes within a circle of water held inside a small wood, like so many other woods, maybe even bluebells in July, imagined; the sun in the leaves, kaleidoscopic, imagine the people that once sat here waiting, forming patterns on the ground, between the trees, behind my eyes I can rise above this scene, see a snippet of something forgotten over the surface of the pond that quivers like the flank of a horse when touched, go deep now into the heart of the pond, the frog spawn swallowed, not now, there, before, where you'd once cupped in your hands, the black dots of the small frogs open in your belly, croak, hiccup, small frogs grow inside, hatch small legs and tails in your belly, no way to kiss or wish, not here, lost in the wood on my way to water, on my way back from stagnant water, murk, sediment in the corner of your eye, to open my eyes again blinds what never arrives in the right order, only the myth of direction when there is no direction only the lie of order,
but still I have to open my eyes, still
I carry a loaded pen just in case,
handmade paper in case,
I carry what I can for four hours here, imagine;
believing I will find a quiet spot,
this is the only quiet spot
here beside the pond and still
I can't write, all I can say is
I came all this way in a summer skirt,
holding my shoes,
feet hug, sink into the ground,
feel the fullness of the pond
the oversized dragon flies hover beside me
hear myself say that the frogs know everything
My eyes open to Max's face coming into focus over me,
Tell me something, he says,
anything ... first thing that comes into your head ...

I was twelve when my friend invited me to muck out her horses. Are you listening, child? ... her father's horses. It was a hot day, a day much like this one. The horses were restless, irritable; they were sweating, one was bearing his huge yellow teeth, and the smell of dung was overpowering, so her father told the two of us to go play somewhere else. He sent us to the frog pond at the top end of the field, under the shade of the pine trees. He told us to go and cool off, to go and paddle, to go and see how long we could stay in there without shoes, without stockings. We undressed. I was a little shy and hoped he wasn't looking. He didn't seem to be. We left our things folded neatly at the edge of the pond. I was nervous, but I didn't want to show him or D., and so we waded into the pond, we felt the muck find our ankles, the smell find our noses, as we slipped up to our calves so soon, the too-distinct sucking sounds and movements of feet between frogs panicking sliding down our legs, escaping our toes, frogs everywhere. The final shudder of agreement to immerse ourselves completely beneath the water at the same time. The shame and relief of our muck-covered feet release, float there, our faces put up to the sky, everything moves under our hands.

And don't think I didn't consider wading into that Birkenau pond, that blasphemous deed, but it is the hottest of days, up to my knees in pond water, my dress hitched up and tucked into my knickers, later re-reading the angry words that someone had dared to fish here in Birkenau.

I don't believe there are fish in there, Seth says ... unless maybe they are hiding below the surface. But who would do the fishing here? Are there fish here, Mum, at Auschwitz? ... just under the surface, taking care ... And what is a pond without swans, Mum, or is that a lake?

   It is the 22nd of July - as if it matters, as if it matters that the water is hot in our bottles, my son, without realising what he did, washes my feet my arms my neck, yes, gently trickles water over my head, a kind of fake baptism,

   I try to leave the pond as I did that July day. I have tried to leave the pond many times but every time I write I find myself back there again, the only place where we were alone, the only place where somehow it felt OK to take a photograph, only one, yes, En's taking it, look, he's taking a photograph of me standing beside the birch tree, beside the pond to my left. An image that will half-conceal my face in too much shadow. You will see I am smiling out of habit, and because it's such an old command, and because since birth no doubt I recognise the almost threatening tone: Smile! And I'll look the way I did on school photographs, too aware of smiling, not sure if I should and if not here then where, this place where the simplest of things have been denied, forgotten, the simplest of smiles, kisses, laughter, always left in a state of hesitation and retreat.

   Later, I'll keep the photograph in my notebook, I'll look at it and it will tell me nothing, only that I looked embarrassed, awkward - well, in that moment, I'll recognise my mother's face in my expression.

I'll try to find more information about the pond. When I get home I'll find many photographs of the same spot taken in deep snow, in all seasons, black and white, mostly colour. Other tourists circle the pond, visitors like us, look, they hold hands, dance, chant, later the same circle of people now kneel, cry out, howl, the call of a slow horn sounds across the surface of the pond. I wonder: is redemption an option?

little wood 3

little wood 2

When I first put the words *Auschwitz-Birkenau's pond* in the search engine, it says, *no matches*. Instead of pond it gives me a list of James Bond books: *The Man With The Golden Gun*; a book by some other Bond on horse grooming.

An old image rewrites itself in front of the pond, a scene reworking itself after Auschwitz.

It was the story of a pond. It was late, it was a hot evening, the dusk had not cooled the air. It was almost dark. I was wearing a long gown. I saw Moinous running across fields toward a pond, rushing ahead, he didn't stop. I tried as hard as I could to catch up with him, to stop him. I kept tripping on the ridiculous dress. He got there before me and waded straight into the water. I called out, I ran after him, but he was saying, There's nothing to be done, nothing to be said. I called after him repeatedly, he said, It's okay, it's time for me to leave. And as I watched him walk into the pond, already up to his shoulders, he opened up his mouth and his throat fully and before disappearing beneath, he threw up a mouthful of silver words across the surface of the water. I waded in, I was frantic to try and find him but couldn't. I scooped up what I could of his words, using my dress, I held the dripping skirts to my face. The skirts read: The meaning of life is the words *concentration camp*. Up to my thighs in water, I laughed and laughed at what I had just said, at the idea that I had discovered any meaning. I even woke myself laughing, it took me only seconds to realise I understood nothing.

It's a mess,
what I've written.
Of course it is, Moinous will say.

Of course, that's the point, that place was a mess, the whole thing was a mess, how else could you write it but digress into shoes and hair and the child sitting in the earth writing 6,000 words at a time.
Keep trying. Write me something. Write it for me, Moinous says. Keep writing. Keep going until it becomes just a word. Write everything even if it comes to nothing. Tell me how you felt, how it affected you, how it disgusted you, how it infuriated you, how it excited you, how it revolted you, how it felt like nothing just emptiness.

Because of a disturbance the story is no more than a preparation for, Stein says, *because of a disturbance a continued story is always a surprise.*

Realising I'm just circling the pond, that's all I found, that's all there was. And in this heat, Max says, in this wood, you could almost forget for a moment, forget what this is. What this was. Yes, that's how it is here. For a moment, we almost look as if we are just out for the day with the children; yes, just out for the day.

Getting Out

This is the scene where they get out. The ones trying to write, trying to draw, trying to photograph, trying to capture everything with their digitals and their zoom lens: yes, they all get out, they rush ahead.

We are leaving today because we can.

I've decided we should go home at once …

Give up …

It's such a hot day …

Four hours here is more than enough …

Four,
or was it six hours ...

Mum … can we go now … I'm boiling …

Look … There are the taxi drivers waiting to take us away.
They're over there …
Look …

I hadn't expected them

Why not?

I don't know … It just seems a strange image … the taxis there in a line alongside the Birkenau arch.

Then how did you expect to get out to the train to take us back … back home?

Our temporary home

Look, Mum … I'm a train … stone sleeper stone sleeper stone … Look, Mum: I'm deporting.

To catch my eye like that took him at least three minutes …

Who …

The one waiting for us to decide if and when to exit. The taxi driver over there, look, Don't look!

Why are you taking so long to decide … when to go … if to go … Walking back and forth on the track, that infamous Birkenau track.

He's sulking, Mum ...

Shut up ...

Seth, he's over there, he's sitting on the small carriage just inside the archway ...
See him. Look ... it's where grandma sat when she came isn't it, remember in the
photograph, she sat there inside the archway on the line ...

   Look, Mum, he's got his legs apart, he's moving from his left to right foot,
moving the small undercarriage back and forth, back and forth on its tracks, hear
the line squeaking ... hear it ... that's him ... back and forth with the wheels
back and forth on the line ... squeak squeak ... squeak squeak.

Hush up, Max ... Stop it, Seth ...

That big lily flower someone placed on top of the carriage, it's falling off, mum
... MUM IT'S FALLEN OFF ...

Oh my God, Seth, put it back ...

It's not my fault ... it just keeps falling over ...

Can we go now ...

Max, stop sucking on the grass ... Take the grass out of your mouth.

They bring us here in buses ... we leave in taxis ... imagine.

The taxi drivers are smoking while they wait, look ... they're telling stories
and gossiping to one another. They're telling jokes, eating their pre-packed
sandwiches, spitting pips into the dust, whistling, chatting up the American
students, laughing with them. Look at them ...

I bet he's peeing in the grass, Mum ... He's a snake in the grass ... He's pissing
and hissing ... I heard him.

I said SHUT UP ...

And I said STOP BICKERING ...

Can we go now ...

The taxi drivers, their mouths smell of stale smoke and coffee while they quote
you a price while they wait for you to take your final look back at the entrance
or the exit depending on which way you look at that infamous arch, in fact

the whole place has a faint smell of roasted coffee on the breath, most likely an imported French blend.

Mum … shall we go, then …

Okay … okay … Let's go …

The taxi driver's driving like hell, don't you just love that, the bus drives you in slowly in a long digression and now the taxi's moving like hell …

Look, mum, he's doing a hundred … he's following the tracks … hundred at least.

In a four-door saloon, he's revving the engine, the wheels skid in the dust as if he knows we want the speed, after all that, the effect of speed and booming English pop music sung in an off-key Polish accent, the rosary dancing from the rear view mirror.

I want a car like this when I grow up … Mum, are you listening … a car just like this one … I'll turn it up loud … the music and the beads and the pink seats … just like this one.

This is the scene where we get out. Where he's offering us a beer.
The taxi driver. A cold beer.

This is the scene where we get the hell out, of course we do.

We come, we go, we turned stones over in every room, in every path and field, isn't that what you said … Whatever was left, we turned over. We rummaged for mementoes, crude enough. We stuck our fingers into cracks and cobwebs, put our heads to the doors, rubbed our hair into the walls, our hands in grass and bricks, re-lit the small tea candles we found pushed into rubble, we burnt our fingers on the matches, we broke off pieces of rusted metal, balanced on the railways tracks, picked the bark from the tree, we turned over leaves and sticks, we counted the numbers on the markers, threw wild flowers on the pond, crawled around and through wire fences, picked up straw, put our eyes to glass and photographs and faces and keyholes, took our spectacles on and off on and off, what else was there to do here but look at the small map, glad of any clue. Characters making small insignificant scenes. So many books and words written in the name of the unsayable, so many photographs and line drawings …
Wait … I have a feeling I've forgotten something, forgotten
something.

It's a word, it's a play-on-words, one word, many documentaries, films, books, cartoons, compositions; the renamed, too few syllables, gas tight, smaller, vaster than imagined.

Auschwitz

That's the problem with this place and that's the problem with trying to write this out of imagination - also smaller and vaster than imagined - and let that be a lesson, for what good is imagination here among the twisted mathematics and the rattle of the aspens, here where everything's all wrong.

Auschwitz-Birkenau

Auschwitz 1
Auschwitz 2

Little red house
Little white house

From: angelamorgancutler@ntlworld.com
Date: 9th August 2004 5.11pm
To: Moinous@aol.com
Subject: Re: Jew or Shiksa: How to tell
[on 9/8/04 5:06 pm, Moinous@aol.com wrote: Jew or Shiksa: How to

Tell]

Raymond - that's disgusting.

Anyway - shall I go on with what I was telling you -

OK

Today - just the day after we received the papers about Minsk - I also
met a woman who it turns out has a Polish ex-husband - well his dad is
Polish - from some small village - This ex is a journalist and he wrote
an article on the orphanages he visited recently in Minsk - Belarus -
and - so finally not so much gossip as a coincidence as En and me had
been looking Minsk up on the web only the night before - We were curious
- I mean following a conversation we'd had over dinner and the papers we
got yesterday - we were curious to see how Minsk looked - nothing like
we'd imagined - It is quite a sprawling city that was - like so many
places - flattened during the war and so it now has many modern rather
stark soviet buildings which give it the appearance of a *Thunder Birds*
set - remember that - the puppets - the space ship - Virgil - I think I
had a crush on him even though you could see the strings and his lips
were permanently swollen well before the days of botox -

En wrote to some Jewish organisation in Minsk- asking if there was
anything marking the sites - the graves where the victims were killed.
From what he was sent previously it seems there are two different woods
where people were shot - They used one wood for a while then for some
reason moved to another - so En is not sure which wood is which - in
terms of his grandparents - but I think you can work it out from the
dates - The woods are about 10 kilometres outside Minsk which is on
the train line from Warsaw - so En and me were thinking of going there
sometime as no one from his family has ever been to the city or to the
site of his grandparents' grave - I am not sure his mother could face
it - it's hard to know - maybe I am assuming and instead should ask
her - En said that when he read up about the camp - Minsk was one of
the first set up by the nazis - well - at a time when they were still
shooting people - before Himmler visited the site and got the blood and
brains on his coat [that famous story] and fainted - After this they
had to find other methods to *protect the morale of the soldiers* who had
to carry out the shootings - and we know the rest of the story - Minsk
is the 4th largest site - in terms of the numbers of people who were
killed there - but is relatively unknown - I don't know when or if we
will go but I feel we someday will –

From: angelamorgancutler@ntlworld.com
Date: Thu, 16 Mar 2006 23:54:21 +0000
To: Moinous@aol.com
Subject: Re: Jean Amery

Moinous -
I just did the wrong thing and I went to bed and read the chapter
Amery wrote on his being captured and tortured and now I cannot get the
pictures out of my head - the sound of his shoulders cracking - that
sound - that image of him hanging there by his arms pulled up behind
him may never leave me - I do not have any idea what I came here to say
- except to say - who thinks these things up - these ways of hurting -
these ways of dislocation - who comes up with such a thing of a night
- yes - it is not that I didn't know all this - I mean what they did to
people in Auschwitz and other camps - I have heard many times from the
mouths of others - the descriptions of torture - and don't we hear and
see more of the same each day - these days - hooded men tottering on
stools - lit up like Christmas trees - but Amery's voice somehow made
it close - real - singular - very personal - and no - I did not pick up
the book in a state of naivety - but I heard his voice and it somehow
got through the anaesthetics we have in place -

So what did I come here for - I mean now - what did I come here to say
- to tell you - that I feel upset by what I just read - obvious enough
[or is it] - surely too limp - upset - surely too much a privilege I
should not even speak of - something I will no doubt regret saying - no
need to say anything - just my usual whinnying for sure - and I do not
want to take anything away from what I read - from his words - I wish I
could talk to Jean Amery - right now - he may be the only one to talk to
at this moment - maybe that's why I came here - because I know you know
and will understand and I'll send this knowing I will try and tell you
everything I can - That reading his words took me back to block 11 in
Auschwitz where they tortured many political prisoners - yes - block 11
was the one place I found myself running out of - having found myself
alone for a while staring into a room - my forehead pressed against the
door's panel of glass - if the door hadn't been locked - I doubt I would
have had the courage or inclination to enter - the walls were marked
- daubed - ugly black walls - there was a long sink running the length
of the wall opposite the door - some discarded clothes which looked
arranged in their disarrangement - a crude pipe running the length
of the ceiling with an open end - maybe it was called the disrobing
room - I can't recall properly - I stared in and then wondered what I
was looking at - what had happened in that room – what had marked the
walls and the floors so - what was the pipe for - I decided I couldn't
stay there - I turned and found in my path that the corridor had filled
with about fifty people all rushing toward me - hemming me against the
wall - no doubt fresh-faced from some coach - armed with cameras and an
unexpected exuberance - Max and En emerging from the downstairs rooms
beckoning me to come now - Mum, come on - Max's attempted impatience
- En's insistence that I should come and see the Standing Cells - me
shouting across the crowds to tell them that I could not - had seen
enough - instead becoming momentarily pressed beside the gallows that
looked as if it had been cared for with the attention a cleaner may
give to an antique sideboard - it shone so - it looked almost proud of
itself - unblemished by what must have
repeatedly taken place within its hollow gut -

But to go back a little ... Amery's book opening with the following:

Take care, a well meaning friend advised me when he heard of my plan to speak on the intellectual in Auschwitz. He emphatically recommended that I deal as little as possible with Auschwitz and as much as possible with the intellectual problems. He said further that I should be discreet and, if at all feasible, avoid including Auschwitz in the title. The public he felt, was allergic to this geographical, historical, and political term. There were after all enough books and documents of every kind on Auschwitz already, and to report on the horrors would not be to relate anything new. I am not sure that my friend is right [Amery says] and for that reason I will hardly be able to follow his advice. I don't have the feeling that as much has been written about Auschwitz as, let's say, about electronic music or the Chamber of Deputies in Bonn. Also, I still wonder whether it perhaps would not be a good idea to introduce certain Auschwitz books into the upper classes of secondary schools as compulsory reading, and in general whether quite a few niceties must not be disregarded if one wants to pursue the history of political ideas. It is true that here I do not want to talk purely about Auschwitz, to give a documentary report, but rather I have determined to talk about confrontation of Auschwitz and intellect. In the process, however, I cannot bypass what are called the horrors, those occurrences before which, as Brecht once put it, hearts are strong but the nerves are weak. My subject is: At the mind's limits. That these limits happen to run alongside the so unpopular horrors is not my fault.

Despite his friend's caution - he did go on to use Auschwitz in the subtitle of his book.

Do you know him? I'm sure you must do - Is this where you took your title: The Necessity and Impossibility of Being A Jewish Writer?

From: <Moinous@aol.com>
Date: Thur, 16 Mar 2006 17:17:38 EST
To: <angelamorgancutler@ntlworld.com>
Subject: Re: FW: Jean amery

Angela

I have a terrible cold. All night I coughed and blew my nose away. Didn't sleep. Oh well. I'll survive

Yes of course I know the work of Jean Amery. You mean I never mentioned his books to you? Not possible. The essays At the Mind's Limit were extremely important to me, and yes of course I borrowed that title from him.

Do you know the story of Amery?

Here I'll tell you.

Born in Vienna from Jewish parents who never really made a point of telling him he was Jewish until the Nuremberg law forced him to confront his Jewishness. Amery is of course a pen name. The parents moved to Belgium where young

Jean became involved with the communist party, and was arrested as a communist before it was discovered he was Jewish. Then he was taken to various camps where he was tortured and on to Auschwitz which he survived. When he came out of there he settled in Belgium and started writing in a most beautiful German - the essays - but also other things. Especially about Israel.

One day the great German poet Helmut Keisenbuttel [sic] [whom I had the pleasure of meeting and even read with him in Heidelberg - he was in the german army on the russian front and lost one arm] who had a literary radio program in Cologne read Jean Amery and convinced him to come and give a talk on his program. Amery was reluctant but he went - gave a series of lectures [I believe texts from At the Mind's Limits] then when back to Belgium and committed suicide. So it goes. Anyway I am glad you discovered him.

Why do you think Angela such great thinkers writers poets novelists as Jean Amery, Primo Levy, Paul Celan, Tardius Borowski and so many others committed suicide after they wrote what they had to write

And why didn't I commit suicide? Tell me

OK - you see what a cold does to me -

Love
Raymond

From: <angelamorgancutler@ntlworld.com> Date: Fri, 17 Mar 2006 18:45:20 +0000
To: <Moinous@aol.com> Subject: Re: Jean amery

```
Rushing like crazy.......
Sorry about your cold - keep warm - drink soap and tea - Oops
- I mean soup!

The reason you haven't committed suicide is that we had to meet and
discourse freely and so therefore there is such little time and still
so much to say - and also you are indeed a happy cynic and therefore
have much still to write -
```

From: <Moinous@aol.com>
Date: Fri, 17 Mar 2006 11:17:10 EST
To: <angelamorgancutler@ntlworld.com>
Subject: Re: Jean amery

OK - let's invent a new mode of suicide
suicide by an excess of life

From: <Moinous@aol.com>
Date: Sat, 18 Mar 2006 08:24:52 EST
To: <angelamorgancutler@ntlworld.com>
Subject: Re: Jean amery

Moinous - Are you better - has your cold given you that great burst of
energy that often follows days of lying around -

Well I thought I was better and so yesterday I went to play golf and when I
got home my big monumental nose kept running and running - I mean not the
nose itself but the liquidy shit in it - and I was sneezing - and I was sick like a - I
was going to say dog - but that's a cliché - anyway I went to bed at 7 last night
and just got up - it's 8 now - and I may not make it through the day -

I am up and it's only 5a.m. - I woke at 4 and my head was full of Ashes
- so I decided to get up - Ashes was the piece that sort of began the
whole book and will maybe now end the book - although I am not yet sure
if to include it - I remember the night En was due back - from Poland I
mean - when he went there the first time with his mother - he got back
very late - midnight or maybe even later - I was so impatient to see
him and of course waited up - the kitchen and the table all afloat with
flowers - lights - food and readiness and I was restless - so while I
waited I began putting in the search engine - Auschwitz - I don't know
why but I became suddenly curious - I mean knowing he had been there
with his mother - I remember seeing a camp for the first time - well of
course I had seen it before many many times - but here I had a different
proximity to it - it was late - dark - just the light of the screen -
me with my bad eyesight - my nose pushed into detailed photographs of
an empty camp - I was not looking at people - bodies - smoke - rather
I was looking at empty brick buildings - open doors - ovens - open
empty rooms and open empty trees - all of it had served and finished its
purpose - and the domesticity of it startled me

As now finding that word startles me - domesticity - and makes me say
NO - I should delete that word - that is not the right word - then I
look it up and the Little Oxford says -
Domesticity - home or family - NO MATCHES in thesaurus
- instead I'm given -

Domesticate - 1. An animal, tame, house-train, train, break in, gentle
-
2. Domesticate a foreign tree -
Neutralise
Gentle standing there at the end of the first line like a waiting person
among a group of other words that are on the attack -

En came home bearing gifts, a strange collection of mementoes - one being
a stone from the railway track - a rather large crumbling brick from
Birkenau and a huge hard-covered book on Auschwitz - It had a newness
that could be smelt and heard in the slight creak of the spine - the
promise of the unknown unopened book - the high gloss of each page and
there again were the neat redbrick buildings and the tree-lined avenues

reminding me of something familiar. Reminding me of the institutions I'd worked in - those large red brick psychiatric hospitals where I was surrounded by difference, by a different language, by people who were locked inside but always outside of; both by the mix of psychotic voices and by the mix of staff who found their way there from all over the world. I had never heard of so many countries, heard so many tongues and ways of expression, as I did during my time there.

I have said this too many times now. Where am I among all this.

 I don't know if you remember that piece - Ashes I mean - I sent it to you and you read it out to yourself quietly in an aeroplane - you were sitting next to the fat snoring guy - or maybe the work made him soporific -

Yes I remember the piece you wrote and I still have this piece somewhere - and it should go in the book

Yesterday I got to a part of the book where I decided I wanted some kind of interruption - so I thought - maybe I'll put that piece there - work backwards - but it's over a year or possibly more since I wrote it and I hadn't looked at it since and when I did there were things I'd written in there that disturbed me and disgusted me -

That's because you have moved so far beyond Ashes - but that does not mean that these Ashes don't belong in the book

I have the same problem with the Sam book - I keep going back to it at the moment and there are pieces I feel should not be there - and yet they must be there

Yes - my obsessive taking apart of ash and combustion - ends up with fat and required temperatures for cremation and shoes left and all that made me think - I sound like a Nazi

but maybe that's how one should feel writing about such matters - put oneself into the nazi mindset

And then I shut the computer down - I mean I ran away from it and was quite unsettled - and then I said to Sarah that I had decided not to use that piece having worked on it all day - yes - it got to the point where I disturbed myself

the fact that the piece disturbed you that much convinces me that it should be in the book - maybe as a footnote - or a digression - what did Sarah say

So many pieces of writing that don't sit comfortably together - Sarah said - Maybe that's the point -

Yes - that's the point - how can one write a coherent book about such an incoherent subject

And what would it mean if I sanitise and take out those parts
- then what are you doing, Sarah said - cleaning up - keeping
yourself safe and nice -

Do not - I insist - do not SANITISE - that's what they did with Dachau and the
other camps like Auschwitz - they sanitised them - turned them into neat and
tidy museums so that the tourists would feel comfortable - you should not
make your reader comfortable

When one writes about dirt one must become dirty - I said it in Paris in an
interview - my books are obscene because the Holocaust was an obscene
affair

En's sister Anne was with me at the weekend - I'd asked her questions
about the family tree which Elise had begun writing down many years
back - before her memory began to deteriorate - we'd been trying to
find where her extended family ended up - people in various camps -
with names I'd never even heard of - unpronounceable names - people
separated - scattered - same old story - Elise's aunt's small daughter
- Lily - taken to Poland from her very privileged life outside Vienna
and selling posies in the ghetto - because they were suddenly so poor -
posies in a ghetto - none of it makes sense - of course - how could it -
some people from the family we couldn't locate, unsure where they ended
up - Sidi - Sam - Rosza - Karl - many others - Anne said that when they
found out Elise's cousin's parents had been put on separate transports,
they didn't tell Litzy [Elise's cousin] - because it would have upset
her to know that her parents had been separated - so she died several
years ago not knowing that fact - Anne said that maybe some things
should not be known - for instance when people were moved from their
homes - well the Jews who had money - people like En's grandfather who
had been a jeweller - were forced to hand over their businesses - were
then given different manual work to do - for instance - made to carry
heavy bags of coal up many flights of steps to peoples' apartments - one
man - a writer who lived in Germany was forced to dig graves - and so
on - and so what were the Jewish grave diggers and coal carriers given
to do - if that was the case - I mean the Jews who weren't comfortable
or academic to begin with - what were they given to do - I have no idea
why I began all this - Ah yes - it was to do with En's sister talking
about what the relatives of victims needed and didn't need to know -
to know too much of the details of what happened to their families she
said was unnecessary - cruel maybe - and then I am indirectly back to
the Amery quotation - the one I sent earlier - his friend saying - be
careful - take care when writing about Auschwitz

Bullshit - the word AUSCHWITZ has become such a powerful word one should
not shy away from it - one should throw it in people's faces
- especially those who won't admit what happened there.

But enough for now - presentation aside there is still the issue of sensitivity and how much I censor myself along the way and how much I leave in - the way my mind had wandered around the subject of ash and disposal of bodies where that piece had began - We have not yet begun to discuss the disposal of our bodies -

I think you are at a crossroad in the book - asking yourself - do I push further - or do I just close it here. I say push further - get lost in it.

These days we are becoming comfortable in our silences - sitting there in our chairs opposite the other - [virtually speaking of course] - with no need to always speak and for now that will be enough - but for now - today - I decided I had something to say to you across that space across time zones - between our chairs - and so I say it even if I just haven't got to what that IT yet is -

In fact what you just wrote could also go into the book - the book should constantly question itself if you know what I mean - the book should show the doubt you have about writing the book - you must show the tracks of the labour -

Well that's my thoughts for now - but remember I am dripping from all over right now and coughing too so I may be totally incoherent
I have to go blow my now now
I mean my nose - now

Love
mxxx

From: <angelamorgancutler@ntlworld.com>
Date: Sat, 18 Mar 2006 17:19:10 +0000
To: <Moinous@aol.com>
Subject: Last one

I went to the market and bought lemons - I was thinking that the word - the one I sent earlier was all wrong - *domesticity* -
There are no right words - not here - and so I confessed to the fruit and veg man that I wanted to give up work and become a fruit and veg seller - He said that I could come and work for him any time and he'd throw in a couple of free apples - I wondered if there were apple trees at Auschwitz - then I remembered the story of the man - a prisoner of the camp - collecting the stolen tomatoes from Hoess' garden on the edge of Auschwitz. Buckets of stolen tomatoes carried straight into the emerging figure of Hoess' wife.

He asked me, the veg man, what I'd be giving up to go work with him …
 Writing - I said …

Writing - What, a book …

Yes of sorts I said …

134

Really - What's it about he asks … What's it called …

And there I was back in my dream - broken by the veg man not Joan Rivers
after all - and me there with a split second to decide if to avoid
the question - or if to go right to it - hit him with it over the new
potatoes … Auschwitz … But I don't say it - instead I say -
I don't think I know -

Well if you don't know darlin' he says - you'd best start work with me
today …

And so maybe I did - maybe I am drinking coffee with the sellers -
wearing a small apron with a pocket for loose change - wrapping up
a cabbage - throwing a pineapple in the air - arranging the beets
especially well … Maybe the right word is grapefruit -

Ax

From: <Moinous@aol.com>
Date: Sat, 18 Mar 2006 09:33:28 EST
To: <angelamorgancutler@ntlworld.com>
Subject: Re: Last one

maybe that would do you good to sell vegetables for a while - and gradually
as you spend the day with this vegetable guy you reveal what the book is
and he will determine for you if you are writing the book that he wants to
read -
Vegetable guys are very smart you know - they are close to nature

From: <angelamorgancutler@ntlworld.com>
To: Anne <ann@yahoo.com>
Subject: From angela

Date: Tue, 21 Feb 2006 15:06:06 +0000

Hi Anne,
Just to say thanks for Sunday and all the hard work that went into the
meal which was delicious. It was especially nice to go through all the
old photographs with Elise, but I still find it hard to retain, I mean,
the family were so scattered and it is hard to orientate myself as to
who belonged to who. I have also been looking over the family tree that
your mum wrote out many years ago and that is also a little confusing.
I just wondered if you knew anything from the following questions that
I'd like to put to Elise really but I am sure it would be difficult
for her to answer now. I suppose the gaps and the contradictions will
always be inevitable. Thank you anyway, it just may help make the tree
she began have a little more clarity, in all its unclarity.
Many thanks, love Angela

You said that your grandparents before their deportation put boxes into
storage, when they were moved from their apartment, when that area

- in Vienna was designated a non-Jewish district, they packed and had stored boxes that may have contained bedding, some of their personal things, maybe even letters. You said that your mum couldn't afford to go back to Austria after the war. At that time and she was very busy working with your father on the land, looking after you children, they had very little money so she told her Uncle Andy, who was going to pick up maybe these and other boxes, to sell whatever they could. You said that Andy did this and they then bumped into one of his brothers while he was there in Austria. His brother wanted to get out of Austria and move to the States, Andy gave the money that he'd got for your mother's boxes to this brother. You said that he was never seen again. Your mother got neither the belongings nor the money. What was the name of this brother?

Ans. *Matty.*

According to the family tree your mother began to put together, Ibolika [Ibby] was your grandmother's sister. Ibby was married to Imre Braun. Ibby died in England and Imre in Shanghai. Their daughter Kitty ended up in the U.S. How and why did Ibby and Imre end up in two different places? If Ibby was here, did you ever see her? And where did she die and get buried?

Ans. *Ibby was ill with a heart condition all through the war in a hospital in Vienna, apparently. She must have been hidden by someone who protected her Jewish identity. After the war she came to London but died there and is buried in a cemetery, I think in North London. Imre I assume just tried a different route out and that's where he ended up. This was quite common, in the way Lotte's mother ended up here and her father was in Italy, then went back to Austria. Kitty was in Edgware for the duration of the war with Mum and Litzy [mum's cousin], Lotte and Ruth, [Ruth and Lotte as you know are twins - friends of mum's. They both left Vienna in similar circumstances to mum. When Mum left Vienna she was taken in by a Jewish family in London and for a while was a governess to their two young girls, Tessa was one of the little girls mum looked after when she first came to Britain. Ruth later married Freddy, Mum's brother. When Freddy came over from Vienna he was just 14 years old and was taken in by Tessa's mother], they later were all looking after children in a London nursery, and Ibby came to London after liberation to be with her daughter Kitty. I do not think Ibby survived that long and think she may have died even before Mum and Dad were married.*
There is no sign of Roszy, Karl and their small daughter Lily Schrenek on any of the Yad Vashem databases. Do you know what happened to them? Roszy was Andy's sister. One of your maternal grandmother's sisters.

Ans. *Yes, Roszy was Ella's [my grandmother's] younger sister, born on 03/12/1903 so three years older than mum's Uncle Andy. They lived in Edsdorf out near Krems with Aunty Ida's mother Regina, Karl, Ida's brother who was Roszy's husband, and their daughter Lily. They first went to Wien 6, Kostlergasse, as the outer districts were made 'Jew free' first I understand. They were all deported on 05/03/1941 to Modliborzyce which I understand to be in Poland. They lived there for some time and lived I think as peasants selling what they could to get by. You will no doubt be able to trace this further but I know a long* *time ago Mum and I read a book which gave a dreadful description of what happened to people in that area. I found some websites recently and it corresponds with the dates we had; they obviously made up the 999 people transported that day.*

In Krems is a memorial in the Jewish cemetery of which I have photos. The memorial looks like a stainless steel railway line running across the ground with all the names of the victims - the people from the village - engraved on to the line. I found it really shocking and was very angry as it was put up by people of the town, non-jews. Maybe well-meaning, but I thought such a thing should have been in the middle of their town, not hidden away in the Jewish cemetery that is out of town, difficult to find and you need a key to get into.

There is a record of a Rosza Weiss who went out on the same transport as your grandparents - she was deported with them to Minsk on the 20th of May '42 and killed on the 26th of May -
as were all the people on that transport from what I can see. The Rosza Weiss listed was born on the 24th of November 1893. She lived in Vienna, Wien 2, Novagasse 32. I doubt that this is your mother's aunt, as her maiden name was Weiss but her married name was Schranek or Schrenek according to your mother. The common spelling I found was Scherek and there was also a Therese Scherek on that same transport to Minsk, but no sign of Roszy, Karl and Lily. Maybe you know what happened to them? I am sure when your mother first told us about Lily - I remember seeing the photographs many years back - she knew what had happened to them, well, yes she did, we talked about it one day - we were standing in her spare room looking at the photograph album - but I cannot remember if she knew where they'd been killed. I remember Elise ringing me once when she had got back from Vienna, it was the year you accompanied your mother with the rest of your family. She rang me up saying that you'd all been to see the memorial at Krems, which were two railway lines hidden away in the local cemetery. She said that she had recognised and known almost every person whose name was inscribed onto the railway-line. She had then, somehow, found herself momentarily lost and she described how terrified she had felt. I think either you had all gone off to take the key to the cemetery back to its keeper or she had taken the key back, but somehow you had become separated and she kept talking about the key and how she had lost her bearings, that all the streets looked the same and she didn't know what to do. She said, she had wanted me to know how she'd felt, that she thought I would understand. She never mentioned it again.

Ans. *See above. Weiss is a very common name.*
Do you have any memories of your grandmother's father - great grandfather Alexander being here? En says he has only vague memories of him. Do you know when he came here from Vienna and how? Did Andy come later?

Ans. *Yes, I do have a vague memory of Alexander at a flat with Mum's Uncle Andy and his stepson Peter. Jane was a baby in a carrycot box - the box was wooden and green and seemed as big as a single bed to me at the time - and I was very young, maybe only 3. Dad was helping mum carry the box up the apartment steps. When we got inside I have a vague memory of my grandfather sitting in an armchair and I wandered into the bedroom where Peter's trombone was lying on the bed. It was as big as* *me and I was trying to play it. Alexander came to England before the war, possibly with Andy and Andy's wife Gerda, I think, but they went back to France as Gerda did not like it in England. Well, hindsight is a wonderful thing. Mum says that she had to give her grandfather some of her money each week to help him financially, I think it could have been as much as 5 shillings, which was a lot of money then. I seem to remember her saying it was to pay for his tobacco.*

Andy told En he'd been in Auschwitz and escaped, that camp and two others. En never really discussed this with him. Is this your understanding? I remember he had a number tattooed on his arm. He showed me once and mentioned something very briefly about his sister's death. I also understood from what I've read that the tattooed numbers were specific to Auschwitz. That Auschwitz was the only camp where people were tattooed. That meant he must have been there.

Ans. *Not as far as I know. Well, I don't know about the numbers. He did have one on his arm but as far as I know he was in Dachau, it was very early on when people did tend to go and then leave again if they had sponsors. Sometimes because they signed over things, mum thought he may have signed over his business, but I'm not really sure. Andy talked very little of his experiences.*

There are two records of Clara Wang - which was Litzy's mother, [Elise's uncle's wife.] The one, which must be her on Yad Vashem, says she was born to Esther and Naftali, that corresponds to the tree we have of the Wang family. It says she was 54 when she died and that she was taken to Riga in Latvia where she died. Does this correspond to your information? Didn't you get information about her for Litzy's son Tony when you went to Vienna a couple of years back? Tony mentioned that uncles on his father's side were killed in Minsk but he didn't mention his grandparents on his mother's side?

Ans. *They were deported to the same place our grandparents were sent in Minsk, she went with her husband Moritz Engelhart. Klara DOB 27/07/1880 Moritz DOB 03/01/1878*

How did her husband Moritz [Clara's husband and Litzy's father] escape? According to the family tree your mother wrote out, he died in Vienna, but on Yad Vashim there is a Moritz and Clara Engelhart from the same address in Vienna who were on the same list of transports from Vienna.

Ans. *see above*

When Charles [your grandfather's first son] talked to us in Chicago and told us his story, Willy taped it. Charles asked that we be left alone and he told us how he had escaped from Poland to Belgium via Casablanca. He said that on the way he had freed the Engelharts, I think it was 2 or 3 of the brothers, not his father (your grandfather) but his uncles. I am sure he mentioned Sigmund, possibly Moritz, but that doesn't add up to what you said above. I know there were more than one of them in the same camp. I cannot remember where the camp was, but it was in France. Willy later said they had lost the tape and we never received a copy. I know Charles said he had fake papers and that when he went to the camp he told the Germans that the Vichy wanted the Engelharts and that he was to take them immediately, which he did. I think they all then fled to Belgium. Or maybe they were in Casablanca then? I don't know how the Engelharts got to be in one place and one camp?

Ans. *You would do better to e-mail Gloria Schamis, as she knew a lot of the Engelharts and relatives in NY. I did meet some of them when I went in 1978. Her Mum was Hedy and her Uncle was Hans; they got out via France before the war and I think their parents slightly later, via Belgium I think, but I know nothing about the info you got from Charles.*

Your grandfather was also asked to go to Belgium but didn't because your grandmother didn't want to be in the same place as his ex-wife. Lotte mentioned something to me once, well I think she did, that Elise had told her that. Is this your understanding?

Ans. *Possibly, but what Mum used to say was that her father had always wanted to do everything by the book; when things became difficult and there was pressure for them to leave, he'd said he had always been honest and had nothing to hide, also by the time he had all their documents all borders were closed/occupied. But maybe Belgium had been an option.*

According to your Mum's tree, on your grandfather's side, Sigmund Engelhart and Rosa Sandhaus ended up in the U.S. where they died. Sam Engelhart was unmarried and died in the holocaust but we cannot find any record of where. David Engelhart also perished but we can find no record of where. He is coupled [according to what your mum wrote] with someone called Tony Scher, she says they had no children, but this doesn't make sense as David and Tony are both men's names. Unless Tony was a woman and she misspelled her name? Unless they were gay which seems not improbable but unlikely that she didn't say that if that was the case? Anyway, Tony [the partner of David Engelhart] also died in the holocaust but there is no record of where. Henry Engelhart died in the U.S. with his wife - whose name is unknown. They had a daughter called Rosalind. Regina Engelhart died in the holocaust but again we have no record of where. She was married to Haim Leib Sandhaus, who died in Vienna. They had six children. Rosa, Kathe, Adolf, Sidi, Annie and Siegfried [Fritschy]. Rosa, Kathe, Adolf, all died in the U.S., Annie died in England. Fritschy has nothing next to his name, so I have no idea where he lives/d. Sidi died in the Holocaust but again we could not find out where. I wondered if you knew what happened to him or is Sidi a woman's name?

Ans. *There was a relative who lived in Essex I think, and it could be, I have a vague recollection of her daughter coming to stay with us at Abbots Ann. En may remember that. Mum used to correspond with her. Kathe, Adolf and Fritschy and his wife, Gloria will probably be able to tell you about them, I seem to remember I met them all when I went to N.Y. with Mum and we went to Hans' workshop in Manhattan where they all worked making lovely jewellery that he designed for Cartiers commissioned by wealthy people. I remember seeing them cutting stones. Miron telling me about a piece that Hans designed and they made at the work shop for some famous person, that was a strawberry broach made out of a ruby with emerald pips on it. Toni was a woman - mum must have written the male form of the name on the family tree you have.*

When did your mother throw away the letters she received from her parents when she left Vienna? Was it around the time of the move from Andover to Cheddar? Do you know how many letters she received during that period - I mean when she was in Britain and they were still stuck in Vienna - and when did the letters stop?

Ans. *I understand she threw them away when we moved, when En was a teenager. I never saw or knew about those letters until later. They did receive letters through the Red Cross. Mum and Litzy and Kitty, etc. would also send letters back to their parents, so they must have known about some of the hardships. Tony found letters from Litzy's parents after she died and him and his cousin, Anita's daughter, read them together but he said they were all very superficial. I guess they would have wanted to shield them from too much and were more concerned with how they all were getting on. At the time, Mum was going through a difficult period as she couldn't face another move, she was off her food and probably quite depressed when she threw them away.*

Do you know how old your grandfather was when he left Poland? I remember Charles saying he was about three when his father, your grandfather Wilhelm, left Poland.

Ans. *I understood that he did not know his ex-wife was pregnant when they separated. What was Charles's date of birth, as it may give a bit of a clue? I know that Wilhelm, our grandfather, went to America to avoid the first world war and later came back.*

How long had Ella, your grandmother, been in Vienna? My understanding is that her family, including Andy, moved from Budapest when they were much younger? That your mother went to Budapest many years back, with Lotte and they found the house they lived in, your mother is not sure where the address is now.

Ans. *I don't know, but Andy was born in 1906 and I don't think he was born in Wien. I think mum has the address of her mother's old house in Budapest somewhere, and maybe some photographs, but I can't be sure where they are.*

Netty is your maternal great-grandmother. Is she buried in Vienna near Balthazar, your paternal great-grandfather? Isn't that what you said, by coincidence? When did she die?

Ans. *Yes it is almost the next row, very close. Again, I have close-up photos, so will find them for you some time.*

In a message dated: 13/11/04 1:34pm. Subject: Elise

Dear Tessa,

I hope you got back safely and were not too tired after Elise's party. I also hope you don't think it a bit strange that I am writing to you, or that it's an imposition, but En thought you wouldn't mind. I came home yesterday and felt that meeting you had been very interesting and that I had really enjoyed talking to you. I wanted to explain more about the book I am trying to write but among all the other activities over the weekend, it didn't really feel appropriate. Today I ended up writing many pages to you - well, if an E-mail can consist of pages - and I hadn't meant to get so carried away. This message does get to a point eventually: that I was interested in the time you had spent with Elise as a child, when Elise first fled Vienna and when she lived with you in London, looking after yourself and your sister as your governess. I have I suppose, spent many pages telling you my story to say I was interested in yours.

Part of me would like to be able to discuss the writing I am working on with Elise but it does feel difficult, partly because of her memory problems, and partly - how do you raise such a subject as the holocaust when she is just over for the day. Not that I ever intended to write a book that would include Elise's story. Neither did I intend to write a book about Auschwitz, if that's what this is, but the writing grew almost behind my back.

I know that Auschwitz is of course very symbolic and in many ways represents all the Nazi death camps, encapsulates all that happened. I think going there for both Elise and En was in a way an alternative to Minsk as no-one had ever suggested or talked about going to the actual place where her parents were killed.

Tessa, I am aware that I am writing lots and I hope you don't mind. I wish more than anything that I could also write this to Elise but I really don't think I could, especially now. When she took us to Vienna it was very special indeed, one trip that stands out because it meant so much to see where she was born and spent her childhood. While we were there, Elise talked a little about her experience, but not much. She did show us some shops that had been daubed with the Jewish star and been smashed on Kristallnacht; she also said that Freddy had been there at the time this had happened and then left shortly afterwards. She took us up to her apartment and we walked to the top floor and stood outside the door for sometime. It felt strange to be locked on the other side of a door she had once freely used, and I wondered who now owned it and if they'd come out to find us all standing there. She'd said that one day she'd been alone in their apartment and some soldiers had come to the door and asked her why she was not displaying the Nazi flag from their balcony. We have a photograph of her standing on that balcony, she's smiling, turned away from the camera, she must be about 17, she's carving a loaf of bread. She'd said when the men came to the door they'd asked her if she was Jewish and she'd had to say yes, she'd said they told her she had to display the Nazi flag, and she'd felt frightened. I can't remember what else she talked about; if anything, it was very little. When we came downstairs again we asked a man to take our photograph outside what had once been their front entrance, he had white hair, he took some time to take the photograph and he must have overheard our conversation. As he finished, he said to Elise, The same thing happened to me. That's all he said.

In many ways, there are just scraps of nothing, and aren't all our family histories the same collage of fictional hand-me-down tales that, over time, get added to and distorted, subtracted with our memory lapses that make every final version unreliable. *I know I had a childhood,*

Jeannette Winterson says, because my mother told me. But I guess around such a huge displacement as Elise's there seems to be a greater need to know, to ask, but no-one ever does as it always seems too intrusive, too taboo, and then too late. I also sometimes find it more difficult to probe as I am, by marriage into the family, both connected and removed. Maybe in some ways this helps, I don't know. A close friend of mine who is a playwright and lives in the States, wrote to me about a neighbour of hers who had been detained for some years in Auschwitz. He met her on the street one day and said to her, You write the story for me, as no-one Jewish can write this. But of course many Jewish writers have written of their experiences in many different and successful ways but so much goes untold and will be lost soon for sure and maybe elements of both distance and proximity are necessary. En says maybe writers will feel freer to explore this subject when this generation dies, as it will make us less self-conscious.

But to get back to the book and Elise. When she came over the other Sunday and we had lunch together, En began explaining about the information we had on Minsk. She did look through it all, and she read out some papers that were in German. She was interested, she said she would sometime like to go there, but when En began asking her about that time when she had to leave Vienna it was difficult to know what she was thinking and if we had the right to even ask. She has got a lasting memory of her father running after the train and she did naturally look upset on recalling this and after that it felt distasteful to continue. In other ways she is one of the most unsentimental people I have ever met. We were talking to Tony yesterday about it, Tony's mother and Elise were cousins, he said he also had family killed at Minsk, his father's brothers. He agreed that it is hard in terms of being torn between the wanting to know as much as you can, for this shapes your sense of self, and wanting to protect and respect his parents right to silence. Maybe it is not even a right to silence but an absence of words, of remembering, when so many stories ended on a station platform and after that all those who did know were killed and silenced; all those left behind had only questions and a life of not-ever-knowing; so what can another generation want from a story already based on the never-to-know?

And I ask myself what is the splinter in the thumb of this work. I think if anything has become evident as the writing unfolds it is that my children become more and more present at the centre of it; this was not expected. Maybe this is not that visible to anyone else, but for me they are the part that continues, the part that escapes, slips through and carries on.

I was very sure when I began that I didn't want the work to be sentimental and wanted as much as possible to avoid the obvious clichés - but that remains a challenge. I have read and re-read so many testimonies and stories in the course of researching the subject, but what exactly am I looking for as I rummage through other peoples' words. I am clear that I do not want to regurgitate the accounts I have come upon because that somehow feels crass, many are so horrific they always tightrope between sensation and voyeurism, even though they are, I'm sure, not meant to be read that way. I think I was / am more interested in the minutiae, in the tiny details of the nothing I found at Auschwitz, the small seemingly-insignificant stories to be found here in our own families. The experience of being with the boys was the thing that mattered for me: what was said and what was not said between us that day in Auschwitz. The only small account I did want to retell - but again, there is the danger of it sounding sensational - was written in the book En brought back from the Auschwitz museum and it moved me more than any other story, disturbed me more than any other because at the time of writing, coincidentally I am a mother watching her sons make that that awkward transition from childhood to adulthood [that-space-between] and they are the same age as the boys in the story. I guess you saying that Freddy - Elise's brother - was only 14 when he left his parents and Vienna touched a chord, in that way you'd said, It's the same age as Seth is … *Imagine Seth*. And so too was Raymond that same age. This somehow made the reading of this page, significant for me, I mean when I read this account not expecting what was coming next, because I felt it was the children that kept moving the words along.

It's from the manuscript of the Jewish prisoner Zalmen Lewental, the account, the writing was discovered after the war at the site of the camp:

"600 boys were led there in the middle of one bright day, 600 Jewish boys aged 12 to 18, dressed in very thin, long striped camp uniforms, with ragged boots or wooden clogs on their feet. The boys looked so beautiful and were so well built that not even old rags could make them look bad. This was in the second half of October [1944]. 25 SS men, heavily loaded down [with hand grenades] led them in. When they reached the square, the Kommandofuhrer ordered them to dis[robe] … The boys saw the smoke belching from the chimney and realized instantly that they were being led to their death. They began running around the square in wild horror, tearing out their hair, [not know]ing how to save themselves. Many of them broke down in grievous weeping, a terrible lament [went up]. The Kommandofuhrer and his helper beat the defenceless boys mercilessly to make them disrobe. His club broke from the beating. So he fetched another and kept beating them over their heads until his violence won out …"

And it goes on … and goes part of the way to answer the question both yourself and Seth raised, as to why people went so passively, or not, to death.

Maybe I know more what the book is not: it is not a book about the Auschwitz of the war, because I was not there. When I went there it was empty, it was of course 60 years on - but the thing I was not anticipating was the lack of people. I mean, when we arrived there it was in many respects too full of people all wandering and looking, all caught up in the process of searching … and what is quickly evident is that there is nothing to discover, uncover, find. And strangely or not, it's the people that you miss most within that great absence because they are not walking around: the fields are empty, the bunks, the rooms, the paths, the gas chamber is an empty disused rectangle, the ovens are empty, ashes and dust and it's all gone by. It's all over. It's too late.

Sorry, Tessa. I should get to some point.

143

I wondered what you'd feel about writing back to me with your memories of the time Elise came to you and also what happened to you when you had to leave her behind when you were evacuated, which is a story of its own.

I plan to write a similar message to Lotte, as she was also a close friend of Elise and as you know, still is. I just wanted to know a little more about how they met, etc.

It was lovely to see you again, thanks for your patience.
Love, A xx

From: angelamorgancutler@ntlworld.com
Date: Sat, 11 Sep 2004 21:45:28 +0100
To: <Moinous@aol.com>
Subject: Perec's work and the chapter on the 1.5 generation

Yes, Perec's work is interesting - did you know him - *How does one write autobiographically when one has no childhood memories … One solution is to prop up memory with fiction; another is to make the absence of memory itself the subject of the book.*

Did I tell you we are planning to go to Budapest in November on our own - well, without the boys - only for a few nights - En's Grandmother was born there and lived there until she was 11- well we think so - and so did his uncle Andor - this was Elise's Uncle Andy, the one we knew who lived in London - Elise can't really remember where the house is but she is trying to locate the address - we want to try and find it - Axxxxx

From: Moinous@aol.com
Date: Tue, 2 Nov 2004 17:04:40 EST
To: angelamorgancutler@ntlworld.com
Subject: Re: cowboy day

it's going in all directions - the writing

but fuck it
I have to stop
E and I are going to vote - if Bush gets in again - it's all over –

From: Moinous@aol.com
Date: Fri, 4 Nov 2004 17:37:55 EST
To: angelamorgancutler@ntlworld.com
Subject: Re: Bush gets in again - this is the end

Yes - it probably is the end

It's the end that is worse than the beginning than the middle in the end
- it's the end that is the worse as sam once put it

Did you see that film-maker in the Netherlands - who was shot
- A Van Gogh - you make Art you get shot

didn't see it - what is it called

No - it's not a film - it's for real -

Here - we have been taken over by jesus freaks - it's dangerous that's how
the whole thing started - back in the caves - so why should it change - the
first asshole who looked up at the sky and gave himself the lie [as sam put
it] fucked up everything for us - he should have looked at his sexual organ
instead

En says, do not despair; if we have to have our catastrophe let's get
it over with it - things have to collide, he says, or someone else did
and he's quoting - he says - that you must keep writing for the sake of
the cynics whose turn will come again … oh I can't read En's writing -
there's more but I can't read it [he wrote me a note before work - to
send to you]

I agree with that but meanwhile - I want to go down the drain in style

To finish - En says - life needs to be refreshed. I'm afraid, dear En
- for me - I just want a cup of camomile and to be able to write a few
good lines now and again -
camomile - how about arsenic - as for the good line - borrow from Sam - me I
played golf this morning - damn well in fact - to hell with the rest -

that's nothing - this morning over breakfast Max asked - Mum what's
an orgasm - and so I spent 10 minutes trying to explain - rather than
demonstrate - something inexplicable - and he was so serious and
wanting to understand over his toast and peanut butter - and why am I
telling you all this when at the moment I am not really in the mood
to write - I mean - it's not you - just me - sometimes I cannot stand
anymore of this blah blah - it presently feels like futile shit -

I think max is just going through the pains and delights of puberty

Anyway

Yes - anyway - take your courage in your hands

It all goes no where - the words - that is -
where is there to go

angela it's not the where that counts
it's the when

I have no conclusion - as if I even could -

good for you - a conclusion is a closure which is also an end which is also a
wall
which is also a final period
so skip the conclusion and go on
Axx
Mxx

From: Moinous@aol.com
Date: Thu, 4 Nov 2004 20:09:20 EST
To: angelamorgancutler@ntlworld.com
Subject: this is the end

where are you angela when I need you the most
did you see those dumb fucking americans - they re-elected that dumb
cowboy -

this is terrible

america is going to regress rapidly to the middle-ages
he's going to start world war 4 in the middle-east because he hears god
telling him to do that this is scary

if I wasn't a total cynic before, now I am what's the point

I feel like giving up writing
I feel like giving up life
I am leaving

good-bye

remember me
raymond moinous federman

From: Moinous@aol.com
Date: Tue, 9 Nov 2004 23:11:19 EST
To: angelamorgancutler@ntlworld.com
Subject: non-stop

remember me

the nice guy with the white hair and the long nose and the cynical smile whose
words are so incoherent that sometime they arrange to make sense

146

here I am

where are you

ok I'll speak
just listen
and when
you're ready
to speak
let me know

good day here working on the novel - it's still very confused and not clear
which direction it is going but I am piling up the words - for me once there is a
pile of words I can get going -

this one may turn out to be even more self-reflexive than all the others
- fuck it - I have nothing to lose any more

We can't spend our life worrying over the potential readers

Julia [wife of Ron] stayed with us last night - she came for the memorial
reading Thursday at Chapman University - then she and I are flying to Boulder
for another memorial for Ron who taught there at U. of Colorado for 25 years

I have become a memorialist

and soon - as you know - I leave for Avignon
This life is too much trouble - I may have to give it up for another life
- ha - ha -

when can you speak to me - I know you are not currently in the mood
- but the writing will have to take care of itself and all you can do is - Go
on -

so - what time shall I expect you -

miss you a lot

good round of golf today - shot an 84

I'll send you the program for Avignon more soon

much love
your best
Mxxxxx

From: <angelamorgancutler@ntlworld.com>
Date: Sat, 15 Nov 2004 20:01:06 +0000

OK thanks for your lovely mail

I am so exhausted I have to go sleep - we just came back from our
friends and I hardly slept last night as I ended up with Max squashed
next to me and the kid never stops talking even in his sleep he won't
shut up and he kept smacking me in the face every time he turned over -

I am glad all went well with Ron's memorial. Was it good to see
everyone? Did you read from the small book? Thanks for the poem and
all you sent -
Is an 84 better or worse than an 89?

Before I go - I wanted to send this to you - it's an article about the
artist who made the Auschwitz Lego - well sent via Sarah
- It's self-explanatory and had me in mind of the piece you translated
from Patrik Ourednik's book re: the Barbie Doll -

*In 1986, a Barbie doll appeared dressed in a striped concentration-
camp uniform and a striped cap too. Various ex-prisoner associations
protested and said it made a mockery of the suffering and the memory
of the victims, and the manufacturers answered back and said that on
the contrary, it was an appropriate way of acquainting the younger
generation with the suffering in the concentration camps, and that
little girls who bought the doll in the striped uniform would identify
with it and later, when they were grown up, they would more easily
comprehend what sort of suffering there was.*

Well - similar arguments below - the artist who made the Auschwitz
Lego is Polish - his name is Libera - he made the work some years
back - maybe late 90s - he also made his own Barbies with bulging
stomachs, hairy legs and armpits and what he calls unflattering thighs.
A different thing to Ourednik's but his Auschwitz Lego caused a similar
response to the one Ourednik wrote of.

I have shortened what Sarah sent below, see her message below, and I
pulled out the jpegs of the Lego images so you can have a look through
- click on a little way down on the yellow page

Also by coincidence I found a passage from an essay today by Jean Luc
Nancy called *Forbidden Representation* that made reference to Libera's
Auschwitz Lego alongside various other art works, film making, that
draw on images of the holocaust, Nancy saying in response to Libera's
Lego: *[…] although I do have certain reservations about this work […]
It seems to me, however, that one could do an analysis […] of the
unrepresentability and/or the reduction of representation to mockery.
[…] for what in each work permits or presents the deciphering of a
resistance to 'represent' (and therefore, also of a resistance to
deliver the final or definitive work). Of course, [he goes on to say] it
would never be possible to arrive at a definitive interpretation: at the
very least, however, this question of representation must be posed, and
any potential criticism of a particular work - indeed, any condemnation
as well - must resist adopting the stance of an idolatrous mysticism*

of the "ineffable." [...] The criteria of a representation of Auschwitz can only be found in this demand: that such an opening-interval or wound-not be shown as an object but rather that it be inscribed right at the level of representation, as its very texture, or the truth of its truth.

Anyway - here's sarah's message -

from: wild@sarah-wild.com

hello A. darlin'
along my travels I came across this http://users.erols.com/kennrice/lego-kz. htm missing you muchly
Sx

LEGO Auschwitz - Konzentrationslager

Named Cruel Site of the Day January 30, 1998.
WARNING! The above mentioned site has material that may be disturbing to some people.

PLEASE NOTE! Many people have written to me asking where they can buy these sets. As far as I know, Zbigniew Libera only made three copies of these sets. They were sold for $7,500.00 each in the mid-1990s. I do not know if they have since been offered for sale. If and when they are, I expect the price will be much higher.
The Jewish Museum in New York, NY, has these sets as part of a display from March 17th to June 30th, 2002. The exhibit is called: Mirroring Evil: Nazi Imagery/ Recent Art.

LEGO-KZ1.JPG (16k) - Polish artist Zbigniew Libera holding one of his kits.
LEGO-KZ2.JPG (22k) - All seven kits.
LEGO-KZ3.JPG (40k) - Main compound (from Harpers July 1997). LEGO-KZ4.JPG (60k) - Four skeletons behind the fence (from Harpers July 1997).
LEGO-KZ5.JPG (57k) - Shock treatment (from Harpers July 1997). LEGO-KZ6.JPG (59k) - Guard and skeleton (from Harpers July 1997).

Polish artist Zbigniew Libera made up lego blocks to depict Nazi death camps. He then had to make a decision if to participate at the Venice Biennale, where he was invited to show his work but on the understanding that he would not include his most recent work: the Auschwitz Lego. One curator, responsible for the Polish entries accused him of taking one of the world's most beloved playthings and using it in a way that could be seen as anti-semitic ... The images and sets include crematories, gallows, doctors administrating electric shocks to prisoners. In one scene random Lego limbs are piled up outside an Auschwitz style barracks. In another, skeleton figures haul in bodies to be incinerated.

On 15/11/04 19:25, <Moinous@aol.com> wrote:

I took a quick look at what Sarah sent and then closed it. You know I get irritated with all that stuff now.

Last night on the history channel they had a program about Auschwitz - you may have seen it.

It had to do with the discovery during the war of what was going on in Auschwitz and the discussion whether or not the allied forces should have bombed the place.

Finally they didn't bomb it - but it was all full of phoney reasons for not doing it. I got irritated and turned it off and instead watched a basketball game.

Voila.

Oh and after the Auschwitz program there was another program about a Jewish family of dwarves who managed to survive the camps - Did you ever see that program

Ok back to work -

and I didn't understand a damn word of what Luc Nancy said - did you xxxM

From: <angelamorgancutler@ntlworld.com>
Date: Tuesday, 16th Nov 2004 7:35:41 +0100
To: <Moinous@aol.com>
Subject: Re: the art work and the dwarves

Is this the dwarf story the one you mentioned, the one you saw on TV?

http://www.jewishsf.com/content/20/module/displaystory/story_
id/25024/edition_id/489/format/html/displaystory.html

I haven't seen the film or the book they wrote but I read an article about the family of dwarves who escaped Auschwitz by becoming Mengele's *pets* -

And of course you know what Nancy was saying - the untouchable Holocaust - that subject you have spent your life writing about - how to represent this *Forbidden Representation* - if or how to make the trying - the difficulty visible [as you have ALWAYS said] - representation that never reaches an object - that never reaches a completion of - an interpretation that can never say: there it is - Auschwitz - rather - to make the difficulty of the subject - its impossibility - unsayability - visible - that this IS / becomes the heart of the work - the attempt is all there is - no containing - no Voila - finally nothing is fixed nor captured - the subject always slips by and away - we end the work and what have we said - shown? But neither should our readings our

150

criticisms of such attempts close down possibilities - present the Holocaust as something too scared to be uttered - too beyond words -

And yes I agree - that there is so much that bores us to death or irritates us in the art-made gas pipes of today - a more recent carbon monoxide pumped into the synagogue while the gas-masked public wander the installation - regarding the Lego Auschwitz - which position should we adopt - That it leaves us angry, confused about what to think, what to say ... Although I will say that there are things about Libera's work I like - maybe the fact that the work played with children's toys - the normally cute reliable lego alongside a whole market of toys that are so often designed as weapons of war - action men - guns - tanks - castles - soldiers - but yes - it of course remains problematic whatever you do - as we repeatedly say and continue to watch the latest genocide with our cries of - *Isn't that terrible* - while we eat a sandwich, swig a beer, our belly still full of detachment - switch channels - go watch the sport instead - say, who can blame us - who wouldn't admit to reaching for the remote to turning over to something more palatable - more comical - more entertaining -

Anyway, on top of all this - as I was writing the above to you - I received an email from a friend of Sarah's - here's the snippet.

Forwarded Message
To: angelamorgancutler@ntlworld.com.
Subject: the holocaust

A., last night one of the girls in the national synchronised swimming competition was doing a homage to "Schindler's List" as her solo. Yes, if you have ever seen the Saturday Night Live version of the topic w/ Harry Shearer and Martin Short in very absurd outfits, it does come to mind. This is not that far from the truth. She said, "she loved to make people cry" and so there was this great silence when she took to the stage/pool. Of course she had titled this thing so all were prepped. I was roaring. I want that tape. I think about the absurdity, the naivety, "the aesthetics", the manipulativeness, the ambition, the stupidity, the goyim and I am disoriented.
D

So it goes on. Ax

On 16/11/06 08:19, <Moinous@aol.com> wrote:

Amazing this thing about synchronised swimming - that's what the holocaust is now reduced to - I can't even find the right word - to a mockery of itself

oh well
we need not get involved with this we have our own views on all that

I dreamt about my mother last night - still wondering how she must have felt when she realized she had left her stupid dumb shy scared little boy behind -

wondering I suppose why she did that
oh enough of that

Sorry angela I got you irritated with my flippant remark about all that stuff
going on around Auschwitz and the Holocaust -

But you know the more I hear about it the more I also get irritated. Maybe it's
time for me to put that matter out of my mind. As I approach my own reduction
to ashes I am beginning to feel how futile my whole existence has been. I'm
not kidding.
I know you're going to say - look at all you've have written over the
years. So what.
Well that's the mood I am in this morning. Forgive me
Love and xx's M

From: <angelamorgancutler@ntlworld.com>
Date: Tue, 16/11/04 17:44:38 +0100
To: <Moinous@aol.com>
Subject: Re: the art work

I'm sorry too … I think it's just that I am very sensitive about failing
to write this and how to sometimes respond to the mass of holocaust
images and stories I find or come across or get sent -

And maybe I am guilty of shoving you too firmly inside the
Holocaust hole when there is much more to your life than that -

As I said - it's is not that I don't agree that much of those Art
works - the gas tubes installations - the Auschwitz Lego - et al -
aren't problematic - I am not defending individual works here but more
their effort toward - otherwise - without them - we end up with what
silence - Finally - maybe we are agreeing - saying the same thing only
in different ways -

What disturbs me in all of this is the way one minute I peep through
a window and there I am reading about Elise's aunt, uncle and young
daughter for instance - those in her family - among others - who were
kept in a Polish ghetto and killed in such awful conditions - and before
I know it - I read on and am covered in hair and skin and bone density
and bloated bodies erupting from shallow graves - graphic details
uncovering the grinding of bones - the final solution: the construction
of crematoria - via the way of the first crude post vans turning into
gas vans - the Jewish office girls taken into the cute [unbeknownst to
them now-converted] post vans - the office girls gassed on their travels
around the picturesque countryside - My instinct is to turn off the
machine - to look no further but instead I continue on - find myself
pressing my nose further into the screen - opening another window on to
a singing family with dwarfism - the seven dwarves you told me of [who
- still - according to the dictionary are described as: members of the
mythical race of short, stocky human-like creatures, skilled in mining
and metal working and no doubt entertaining] keeping their own hair and
cosmetics - their little instruments and outfits at Mengele's request
- And I don't know if I should look - but look I do - Ask - how far
152

should this looking go - how far into and through how many more stories - other people's details - the effect often saturation - the effect often exposing something that I do not wish to see - something hanging in the absurdity of the story over the image of Mengele's self-satisfied lit-up face - over the dwarves' lyrical attempts to stay alive - the oscillation between one page and the next - one voice and the next - leaves me wondering about the choice of - if or how to relay - what to include or exclude - single out- make an example - highlight - summarise - circle with a pen - what to appropriate - fictionalise - make yourself into an equally reliable or unreliable narrator come character - quote or misquote - skip over - leave out - erase completely - sharpen your pencils and wits and the scissors - sharpen your powers of imagination - persuasion - take the real story and take it in a completely new and unseen innovative direction - take everything you've read and bring it in to one whole glorious conviction - Don't shy away from asking - what does each choice then say about the one writing - about the whys and ways and wherefores - about the selections made - Ask yourself - isn't this book in danger of becoming a right old scrapbook - yes - something I'd greatly enjoyed as a child - scrap collecting - which maybe informed the work back then without me even knowing - for who could have known where all this would lead - and who would have thought I'd move on from pressed flowers and feathers - beetles - tiny skulls and scraps of dried dung to this - [after all - only more of the same] small stones gathered and raked from the ash - the endless memento mori - don't forget: death was inevitable - even in escape - some said … victims still carried death everywhere with them - yet - *Dying was everywhere* Amery said … *death was denied … No bridge in Auschwitz Led to Death in Venice.*

Yes - surely enough available stories to fill thousands of volumes - to keep someone busy for the rest of their days - stories all the more plentiful and absurd or grotesque and tender and shocking and moving - all the possible stories waiting to be told - retold and told again - all the potential voices clogging up in a disorderly queue at the back of the throat - voices and
stories that will no doubt continue to bleat and call out like the stray sheep that would torment my sleep as a child - all that will be written but not ever seen - all the books that will erase themselves - all that shall not ever be spoken - all the details and versions that will be lost - between the lines - between us
- along the way and so on -
still
A X

From: <Moinous@aol.com>
Date: Tues 16th November 2006 18:50:15 EDT
To: <angelamorgancutler@ntlworld.com>
Subject: Re: dwarves and ghosts
On 16/11/06 18:50, <Moinous@aol.com> wrote:
http://www.jewishsf.com/content/2-0-/module/displaystory/story_
id/25024/edition_id/489/format/html/displaystory.html

Yes - that's it …

Beckett would have loved that story - those little Jews outsmarting the nazis
with their comic act

it's fantastic
why should you feel uncomfortable about it - to survive one can go to extremes
- and survive they did even if they were slightly smaller than normal

Personally I think that's one of the great Holocaust stories - it beats my
own closet story

I don't like ghost stories - there are too many ghosts in my life - but I
like stories that have crocodiles in them

When are you leaving for Budapest?
have a great time

I have a feeling you will
Mxx

From: <angelamorgancutler@ntlworld.com>
Date: Tues, 16 Nov 2004 20:37:39 +0100
To: <Moinous@aol.com>
Subject: concentrate

I was just printing up an E-mail from Lotte - Elise's friend - she's 79
and has lived most of her life in Canada - She fled Vienna at the same
time as Elise - Her twin sister is married to Elise's brother Freddy
- Lotte has told me that her brother died in Theresienstadt -

I then found myself looking up the camp as I had heard about it but knew
very little of it - It was not an extermination camp like Auschwitz -
rather it served as a way station to the camps and ghettos in occupied
Eastern Europe and many went on to be deported and killed at Auschwitz
from there - Despite the many atrocities and awful conditions in
Theresienstadt - the Red Cross were allowed to visit which resulted
in a huge tidy-up to give the impression that Terezin was in fact a
model Jewish town - For the visit - fake shops - money - children's
playgrounds and cafes were created - They had many orchestras and a
children's opera - bonbons and bread filled the fake shops - the rats
that normally plagued the prisoners were no doubt swept away - they
even erected various signs in the camp to give the impression that life
there was going on as normal - BOYS SCHOOL - SCHOOL CLOSED FOR THE DAY -
Finally - 80 thousand of the inmates were transported on to the death
camps and 30 thousand died of hunger and disease in Theresienstadt -
It also said that one of the goals of the Nazis was to "concentrate"
the Jewish population in controlled locations - hence the term
"concentration camp" -
Then I wondered - how the word came about - I mean is that right that
concentration camp came from wanting to concentrate the Jews and others
into certain areas - it sounds too logical - too obvious - those words
I'd written so many times - concentration camp - and I never before
thought of it origins

From: <Moinous@aol.com>
Date: Tues, 16 Nov 2004 12:45:57 EDT
To: <angelamorgancutler@ntlworld.com>
Subject: Re: concentration

I think you are right about the word concentration - yes they wanted to concentrate the jews in one place to get them out of the way
I asked E what the German word was
Konzentrationlager - which means exactly that - concentration camp

From: <angelamorgancutler@ntlworld.com>
Date: Tues, 16th Nov 2004 20:50:09 +0100
To: <Moinous@aol.com>
Subject: Re: concentration

Yes and I just looked up the origin of concentration and it means just that - and those nazis who never had an original thought - stole it ....
Hang on ....
The Oxford English Dictionary, 2nd ed. defines concentration camp as: *a camp where non-combatants of a district are accommodated, such as those instituted by Lord Kitchener during the South African war of 1899-1902; one for the internment of political prisoners, foreign nationals, etc., esp. as organized by the Nazi regime in Germany before and during the war of 1939-45. Early civilisations such as the Assyrians used forced resettlement of populations as a means of controlling territory, but it was not until much later that records exist of groups of civilians being concentrated into large prison camps. In the English-speaking world, the term "concentration camp" was first used to describe camps operated by the British in South Africa during the 1899-1902 Second Boer War. Originally conceived as a form of humanitarian aid to the families whose farms had been destroyed in the fighting, the camps were later used to confine and control large numbers of civilians in areas of Boer guerrilla activity.*
Tens of thousands of Boer civilians, and black workers from their farms, died as a result of diseases developed due to overcrowding, inadequate diets and poor sanitation. The term "concentration camp" was coined at this time to signify the "concentration" of a large number of people in one place, and was used to describe both the camps in South Africa (1899-1902) and those established by the Spanish to support a similar anti-insurgency campaign in Cuba (circa 1895-1898 [1]), although at least some Spanish sources disagree with the comparison [2]. etc..........
A xxx

From: <Moinous@aol.com>
Date: Tues, 16 Nov 2004 21:00:33 EDT
To: <angelamorgancutler@ntlworld.com>
Subject: Re: concentration
so the british were the first to use concentration camps - can you
believe that - the fucking nazis plagiarised the british

From: <angelamorgancutler@ntlworld.com>
Date: Wed, 17 Nov 2004 03:42:15 +0000
To: <Moinous@aol.com>

Subject: Re: Budapest

Yes, I'll try and get in touch from Budapest -
En says have a great time in Avignon - and he thanks you for the kind
message you sent him the other day -
Now it's almost 4 a.m. and we are late and rushing -
I'll send a card - we are in the Jewish quarter in Pest which sounds
predictable enough but a coincidence really - En's mum still can't
remember her mother's old address but it's near the synagogue and
she remembers the building had green railings and a courtyard - *they
probably all have.*

Hugs for now - and you also be safe on your travels -
Axx

Writing as she's thinking - is that stealing. Writing while she's thinking, talking - is that a small theft each time I write, and who knows what we are both taking while we talk innocently enough across the table. Elise and I. Do you know when you are writing or not, I ask myself. I mean, is there ever such a thing as a day off, when you are not collecting and composing and stealing things for the page. Is that not guilty - guilty of writing quietly to yourself while giving the impression that you are sitting opposite Elise, just quietly listening, when all the time part of you is writing while pacing, no doubt, the one who won't sit still in you, the one who fidgets and sucks on her pen until the ink bleeds into the cavities of her teeth, she's no doubt saying … Tell me everything, even what cannot be remembered, even if you make it up. There must be something to be told. I am not dressed like a thief or a liar, though there are no uniforms for liars. Sit still, sit up, sit straight, move the one listening, and tell the one pacing to remember everything, to keep her ears sharp.

And what comes of us showing Elise the documents we found about the camp in Minsk. En saying, there are so many things I never asked you, mother; so many things we don't know. Like how you felt when you left Vienna. How did you keep in contact with your parents, and after you left, how long was it before you realised that things were bad, that they wouldn't be able to leave?

All questions are sounding quite dumb but go on anyway, awkward boy.

Are you my son, she says, my first-born son? Did I give you a middle name? Yes, he says: *Nicolas without an 'h.' I like that name,* she says: *it was a good choice.* She's laughing now and he's laughing in response, trying to sound strident now … Go on, child, ask if you will, but always remember there is little to remember. There's a lot of repetition in the way he asks and in the way En looks at and then away from her face, in the way she's saying, I don't know, do you know. There's a lot of … *you know*s, ending each line … a lot of silence between words. A lot of being very still between words and smiling on hearing her name, her parents and brother's names and their old address read out in German. *My memory is not very good these days,* Elise says. Of course, of course, we say, but there's her father running. He appears and catches us before we were expecting him, we had no idea what to expect, except here he is for a moment running. Elise is on the train to London, leaving Vienna, she is eighteen. Both my parents say good-bye, she says, of course; but it was my father who was running along the platform trying to keep up with the train, probably trying to see more of me. Then he's gone as quickly as the train leaves the station, he's slowed to a stop and all that's left behind is a man standing watching the train that's outrun him into the distance and he has no choice but to listen to his breath. *I didn't know, you know: I didn't realise until then that he cared for me so much,* she says.

Before the event of leaving a kind of sleep-walking takes you across countries you've never seen, your finger running across other people's maps. There's a crossroads, En said, on the map of Minsk; there's a crossroads that leads to indecision - don't go right, or was it left, depends where you're standing, fool - there's a crossroads near a wood just five or seven kilometres away and there I am back to the wood each time I write of late ... get out of the wood, but the pen is stubborn and has its own internal compass, not ink at all: sly pen. There it goes, sleep-walking in the day, me holding the pen tightly, me in my Sunday best all day wood-dreaming, dreaming of extinguishing the sun, just like that, by licking my forefinger and thumb and pressing it hard between saliva and skin, hear it hiss, I'm hissing at sun-up, other people's stories underfoot when I swore I wasn't writing today.

We darned the socks ... Elise said. She's telling us. *We sat together, you know, in London, all of us friends and cousin Litzy, brother Freddy. We sent things home, there was little communication between Vienna and London, things were kept quiet, no-one could have imagined what came next. We heard from them - from our parents - for a while; letters, they sent us things and even when we no longer heard from them we sent them things, we sent socks.*

I didn't ask her to clarify; she's not really looking at me while she tells me, she's no doubt seeing Ruth and Lotte, Freddy and Litzy. *We got separated after that; we all got sent very far away from each other, very far indeed.*

Whose socks? No-one is asking ... Neither of us will ask, Why were they old, in need of darning, where did you sit while you darned the socks, where did they come from and go to, did I hear right, what colour were they, were they your father's socks and in which direction are we now headed, in which direction were the socks sent, ask again, no-one speaks, What colour were the socks?

There's nothing left to ask; there's her father running beside the train and there's the socks, parceled up, no doubt, in brown paper, stamped London to Vienna, a small letter enclosed. I can never quite read your handwriting, Elise. Did they check the socks, receive the socks, won't ask, Sshh, sit down beside me now and hush, there's nothing else to ask, no more to forget. Wool silk blend, several pairs. What shoe size did he have? What stitching used over the heel, the small toe, what cannot be said or asked broken off in thread, broken off with the teeth and lips near the left foot.

When I'm writing I know I'm writing - rather, I'm always trying to forget I'm writing, it's the only way, does that let me off the old fish hook? - this is a strange way to go about saying I know everything remains in a state of ... ... ellipsis ... ... All of it ... versions and versions and silence all under erasure.

Sarah may say possession is 9/10ths of the ...

Other people's words spinning that old wash cycle.

I'll take any ol' rag and bone to get a page filled, he said. Even when I'm watching my father die, some writer or other had said, even then I'm writing, I'm holding his hand and thinking, how I can use this later? How will I later write of his death?

Your intentions and intrusions were pure, B. said, whiter than white ... who said ... don't hold your hand to your heart like that?

Who said, the post offices were closed to Jews during the war, there were mail collection points run by councils, there was a central zone, a designated zone, set up by a Jewish relief committee in Switzerland; some wrote letters from the ghettos, those who got to ghettos, if mail was sent it was stamped *Judenrat - Ghetto* in red letters across the mostly unreadable handwriting. The Red Cross got the letters through when they could. As a rule, much of the mail didn't get through at all or was greatly delayed during the resettlements. Call me up on the sound listening takes one Sunday afternoon. Lunch waiting in the larder, Elise and I sitting squarely enough opposite each other, salivating at the thought of the duck to come. *We both have a love of food,* I tell her, We both have a love of food in common. En too; En to our right. For now she didn't see the wayward pen saying, She's eighty-five next year, ask more. But what? What? Only socks. Only agreeing to find something to take to Budapest, to leave near the house, if we find it. A small memento to leave from Elise to carry to her mother's first home. I'll find something, she says.

Questions for Elise that will never be put, will never get answers

When did you first become concerned that things were not safe for you in Vienna?

I know you said that when the Nazi soldiers were first marching through the streets of Vienna, people were cheering, smiling and were throwing roses, and that made you wonder what you would have done - whether you would have joined in, if you weren't Jewish. You said that you first became aware of anti-Semitism when you couldn't go to the school you wanted to attend.

When you went to London from Vienna you said you were eighteen. You previously had said you spent time in France - I guess Paris - maybe you told us this, but things there became difficult and you had to leave. You showed us photographs of your time there, you were with a group of friends, you said you thought you had good legs then and we all laughed, you were wearing a very smart suit and had on beautiful shoes. You spoke, and still speak, fluent French and you were sad you couldn't stay there. You said that you went from Vienna to London, leaving by train and so I wondered did you leave for France before that and then come back to Vienna first, or is it that you went to France on the way and then onto London?

The silver fork you gave me that you had made into a bracelet, yes, years later you gave me this fork-bracelet as a present, you said it was too heavy for you and you rarely wore it. This fork you said was one of the forks your family used at the dinner table; when you left Vienna you, or your family, prepared a picnic for your train journey and this was the fork they gave you with the food. Or maybe you took the fork as a memento, or grabbed it in haste as you packed, or maybe it was literally packed with the picnic? What I mean is, was it intentional or accidental that you took or were given this fork by your family? To me it seems a little unusual to carry such a heavy silver fork on a train journey unless it was taken or given as a memento.

I believe your father was a jeweler. Where did he work, and am I right in thinking that it was his own business and that he didn't work for someone else? When did your father give you his jewellery to take with you to England? - the jewellery that was later stolen? I believe En has a pin somewhere with two pearls and a diamond that once belonged to Wilhelm.

When did you begin to look after Tessa and Gillian, the two Jewish girls you cared for in London? Was this arranged beforehand or was it something you arranged when you got to London, maybe some organisation helped you? I forget the girls' surname; no doubt En knows. You said their father was a solicitor.

You told me once - when we were unexpectedly standing before an Epstein sculpture in a Cathedral - that you had looked after Epstein's children. There was some sort of tragedy that befell the family, but I cannot recall the rest. Does this refer to the incident in the 1920's when Epstein's wife shot his lover and wounded her in the shoulder?

Did you travel alone to England or with others? Where did you stay when you arrived in London? Who did you stay with? Did anyone meet you at the station?

When did you meet up with Lotte and her twin sister Ruth, who would later meet and marry your younger brother Fritz - Freddy? Where had they fled from? Did you know them in Vienna?

Freddy came over after Kristallnacht, you said. How long after you came to London did he arrive? Who arranged Freddy's departure? Did you correspond over these arrangements? Were you concerned for him before he arrived? Were you then concerned that your parents didn't come too? Did you meet him when he arrived? Did you talk about what was happening to your family left in Vienna? Did he work immediately and if so, what work did he do, or did he go to school?

Did you live in the house with the girls you looked after, or did you live elsewhere?

Did you manage on the money you had?

Where did you go to eat?

What did you think of British food?

What things did you most miss about Vienna?

What were your first impressions of London?

Could you speak enough English to get by or did you have to take lessons?

How often did you write home? Were you sure you'd see your family again?

Did you sometimes wish you'd stayed behind, before you knew what happened over there, or even after that?

You said you worried that your mother hadn't survived the six-day journey when she was deported from Vienna to Minsk; you said she wasn't like you and you made two fists and raised your shoulders to indicate resilience, toughness, and then you wilted to show she was not like you, but delicate. I nodded, saying that I'm sure if they were healthy ... but the sentence trailed away and was never properly finished. What use good health, I thought, when the finish is a wood? I didn't say this, as so much is taboo and unsayable, like these questions that remain unasked. It was then that En returned to the room with more documents about our forthcoming trip to try and find your mother's old house, it was then that you asked him, smiling ... *Do you remember our mother... do you remember what she was like? ...* These lapses are not easy to leave on the page.

En later gave you a piece of my writing: a small piece; it was the first time we told you of this book and I was unsure of your response. He told me to put the sheets of words into your bag to take home, so you could read them later. I didn't feel able to go into your handbag and so I put them in with your bread bag, the bread we had bought together that morning at the Sunday market, we have a love of bread in common, soda bread I think we bought that morning, round thick crust, powdered white, or was it three types of flour the man specified? I wrapped my impression of a Polish girl I'd seen at Auschwitz - I wrapped my words that made up her portrait, around your bread. When you got home, En told me that you had divided up the bread and given half to your daughter Anne. I wonder, did you divide the words too, or put them to one side, discard them without reading them? No doubt I won't mention them again. It is probable that you will never read this book.

When you first lived in London, did you dream in German or in English? What were your first dreams in English? *As if you could remember* ... But I do remember you telling me that you had recurring dreams, nightmares, about trying to find your parents, which you said, only stopped when you much much later, found it in you, to go back to visit Vienna.

What time of year was it when you arrived here? This will no doubt be on your passport, the one with the swastika on the corner of the photograph. En says he would like to have the passport one day.

What time of day was it when you arrived and what first pleased you and then concerned you about your new home?

I ask again, did anyone meet you from the train?

After the war, when did you realise what had happened to your parents?

When you saw a television programme that had a section on Minsk, you said you hadn't known what was coming next, you said you couldn't have known and what you saw left you shattered, completely shattered.

For me, the first time I saw such images, I was quite young, I'd been sitting on the bottom of our stairs as I did when I couldn't sleep, I'd wait for my brother to doze and I'd then sneak to the bottom step. The living room and staircase was divided by a thick blue plastic concertina door, a little torn where people had pulled it too vigorously. I'd fidget on the other side of this door until my mother would say, Come on, then ... This was the first time I saw piles of dead skeletal bodies on the TV, the first time I'd asked the questions, what, who, why, no doubt screwed up my face, tucked up my legs. I had never before heard the word *Jew*. I don't remember what my mother told me that evening. I clearly remember that same moment with my own children in front of the TV. You can't think about the world in the same way after that.

I cannot remember at what age I made up a story that my grandmother was a Jewess. Excuse the digression but writing all this, I mean questioning all this, made me think about my own family - or rather all the unanswered questions we all have, the family myths and stories that get distorted and passed down in different versions, so that in the end no-one knows any longer what's true and what's not. I had no intention of putting my grandmother onto the page today, and I had completely forgotten the story I made up about her, but as my grandmother has interrupted my questions with further questions - I mean, my own familial questions - I'll go on, allow myself a digression.

She was adopted, my grandmother, and I imagined her rootless past, her wandering identity. I thought a lot about the gap in our family, about how she felt about it. I never asked her. So much in families remains unsaid; we cannot find the words and the intrusion feels distasteful; instead, I created what I didn't know. When my mother had said that there'd been a synagogue near my grandmother's house, I imagined her proximity to this building or rather to this erased building. She said that the synagogue had been knocked down, both my grandmother's house and the synagogue were erased, but one well before the other: the synagogue, mother'd said, had been knocked down in the war. No, I don't think she was telling me directly but rather telling someone else, a neighbour, while I listened in, took this as a sign, and that day I filled in the gap of my grandmother's lineage by her proximity to the flattened synagogue. Mother said the synagogue had been destroyed, but I am not sure whether this destruction was because of anti-Semitism or bomb damage. I could find out; no doubt I won't. I'd never seen *a Jew* at home, in our small town. There must have been some people living there who were Jewish but no-one ever identified themselves thus - not that I ever thought of it until I heard about the synagogue and that day decided that my grandmother was a Jewess. My most important woman. I imagined the curves of her generous body, the curves of the synagogue, the loss of the building, the loss of her mother, the loss of the people with no building in which to sit, and what may have happened to them. I do find out that there were pogroms in the small mining town where we lived. Way before my time or my grandmother's birth, a week long attack took place on houses, shops were burned. Churchill ordered the Worcester Regiment to patrol the affected area and evacuate Jewish families to find *relative* safety in the city where we now live. The Jewish people were conveyed by trains. Some say that Churchill overreacted and that the colliers and their wives, who committed the attacks, were only reacting to the strikes and layoffs at the blast furnaces. That Christian businesses were also attacked. No one agrees, and there are many conflicting accounts and opinions. Some say that the attacks were premeditated, that many of the Jewish people lent the miner's money that they later realised they couldn't repay once the strikes began - even though it's also documented that the Jewish community did not trouble the miners for repayments of loans during the strike. Some say that the attacks were planned and anti-Semitic in their determination to rid the town of the Jewish community.

I had no idea of this history, when I made up a story about my grandmother's past. I can't remember what I made up and convinced myself about my grandmother's missing family but I know that I did believe quietly to myself that they were Jews. I never told anyone this. My mother later told me that my grandmother had always known her birth mother - yes, I also find out later that my grandmother's name before she was adopted was Dix. And here I am so soon by the way of my grandmother, only to find myself with my great-grandmother Elizabeth. Yes, it is Elizabeth Dix who now appears in the middle of the day, in the middle of all these unasked questions to Elise, Elizabeth Dix opens out of my grandmother, when in truth it had been the other way around, Elizabeth, the mother of Miriam, thus pushed her out into a sunny June day.

Nothing is planned: both women simply appear on the page and ask for my consideration. Via the gap … *Mind the gap* … To recap: I tell you once more, that way back I invented a new line for myself, way before I met En, way before I had any inkling that this book was on its way, I was filling in the gaps with a new language, a new Jewish line.

And so I ring my mother - not then, I mean now at the time of writing - and I say, Mother, tell me about Elizabeth. It takes me forty-four years to ask - not ask: consider, this more. And how reliable my mother's memory and imaginings when I ring and say, tell me about great-grandmother? I'm in the middle of a haircut she says, a perm, to be exact, and I can't talk now. Go look at my grandmother's birth certificate, I say. Just quickly. I can't even recall, don't think I ever properly asked the full name of my great-grandmother until the time of this call. And no coincidence that when I ask for this name she is in the middle of a perm, for that's how I remember the three women: mother, grandmother, great-grandmother, the one who adopted my grandmother, that is - all three women perming each other's hair, me between, passing the wafer-thin papers and narrow blue and pink rollers and the whiff of ammonia so soon in my eyes. Go check, I say. No, she says, you'll have to wait, two hours at least, and it's then she tells me the name, that much she remembers: Elizabeth Dix. With or without an X, I say. I can't remember, she says … can't you wait? No, go look, I want it to be an X … go check. Yes … yes. No doubt the lotion now in the earpiece of the phone. Yes … Dix with an X. Perfect, I say, same as Otto Dix, the painter. Who? … *Mind the gap* …

But I get easily bored with Elizabeth after this, I admit it. Except to note that her father was called George, but Gheorge-with-an-h. The 'h' makes the difference and these small details fascinate me, if only for moments. H h … Elizabeth has two brothers, one also called Gheorge, also with-an-h. Father, Gheorge with-an-h, was responsible for making Elizabeth give up my grandmother Miriam - a month after her birth. Four weeks is a vast time between mother and child and I wonder about that month they spent together; and how to let go of a baby after four weeks. I decide Gheorge's 'h' stands for hard, heartless, the-head-rules-the-heart Gheorge. Or was he just looking out for her, his daughter, for what's a girl to do with another baby, having already had a son [Billie] by some other man. Billie gets to stay, Miriam has to move on.

Yes, what's a girl to do when her lover marries another. This is how is goes between great-gran and Mr Russell: Mr R has a long-time girlfriend, meets great-gran on the side, side of what? Both women get pregnant at the same time, no easy feat … naughty Mr Russell. He marries the long-time girl, great-gran gets dumped at twenty, keeps Miriam [gran] for one month and then hands the baby over to a family friend, no doubt arranged by Gheorge. Annie becomes my great-grandmother; Elizabeth disappears. Not so, my mother tells me - as she no doubt pulls her fingers through her perm

Miriam remains in contact with Elizabeth and Billie and also with the two

other sons Elizabeth has after she gets married - only not to Mr Russell; he is
otherwise engaged in his own marriage, elsewhere and producing his own boys,
not Elizabeth's. Miriam [now Marion, post-adoption, post-marriage, becoming
Ma ...] still sees Elizabeth, to the upset of her adoptee mother Annie. No-
one really speaks of it. My mother is even taken to the hospital when Elizabeth
Dix dies, aged forty. My mother remembers her dark hair, thin figure, attractive
face. Billie later dies of T.B. My mother insists that he had visited us, that I
knew him, but I have no memory of that. I wonder what they talked about,
Billie and Miriam. Billie and me. I wonder where Elizabeth is buried. I'd like
to see a photograph of her. My mother tells me she knows the family, the next
generation that is, in passing, Mr Russell's too.

Another gap is the absence of Mr Russell's first name. Neither is he on the
birth certificate, a predictable blank where father should be. But it somehow
seems fitting enough that we have this formality of no first name between us,
considering his short part and swift departure in my life history; a first name
would no doubt seem too intimate a thing between us. One night with Mr
Russell informed my life, Mr R and great-granny, that is. So which comes first,
the Dix or the Russells, in terms of me chasing my foreign gene? I'm sure if we all
go far back enough we all end up Jewish, Moinous says. The irony, the rumour,
that Hitler was a Jew, of course had his own gaps. Heydrich, the man who
ordered the killing of En's grandparents, also had Jewish blood, shot his mirror
image to prove he could kill the Jew in himself. So the story goes ...

On my father's side, my great-grandmother was an inn-keeper. This satisfies
me more. My paternal great-grannie keeping control of the bar, telling a joke or
two, selling ducks over the counter. I prefer that.

Any further questions in either direction now seem futile.

~~What did you discuss while you were waiting for the train that would take you
away from Vienna?~~

~~What do you remember about the day war ended?~~

~~How did you find out that your parents were killed?~~

~~Who was with you when you received this information?~~

~~Was it a sudden knowledge or a gradual process of receiving bits
of information?~~

How old were you then?

From Lotte to Angela. Dec 4th 2004

Dear Angela,

I got your long lovely message today. I don't really know how to begin. But, here goes. When Hitler marched into Vienna, "Everyone" was thrilled. March 1938. I was 13. All the anti-semites came out of the woodwork; your classmates got hostile. One boy spat on me, and so on. Then we were sent to a 'Juden-schule'; only Jews went there. Gerty, my older sister, went to England in the fall of '38. Our cousin Lily was already in England, and helped Gerty. They both brought out some of our family, slowly.

We were told Jews could not stay in their apartments, so we gave away most of our furniture and moved in with my mother's sister and her husband: they were allowed to stay. They then went to England. My sister Gerty, before she left, was at some place to pick up her visa. A stranger asked if she, my sister, would take her son, her 4-year-old boy, and someone in London would pick him up at the train station. Imagine that. Gerty took him and kept in touch with the young mother; she in turn got her visa later and lived in Bristol. Gerty found a rich sponsor, and then my mother took us to the train station. That was June 1939. Imagine my mother putting us on a kinder transport, not knowing if she would ever see us again. In August 1939 she got a visa to come to London and worked as a housekeeper. Ruth (my twin sister) and I went to a great private school paid for by our sponsor. We did not put much importance to all the events, met wonderful people and were happy to be out of Austria.

Before that my father was put into a concentration camp in Dachau, but released after six months. He went to Italy for the duration of the war. It was not a case of escaping the camp. At first the killing machine was not perfected, so they let them go after a few months if they agreed to go abroad. My husband Terry was also in Dachau and let go because he had a friend, a sponsor in England who got him out. My brother Kurt was sent to Theresienstadt. The Red Cross informed us that he is "Presumed Dead."

Now, no-one could get me to go to one of those camps. I did see Auschwitz on the TV and that was enough for me. We were very lucky to be where we are, compared to Freddy. When he came to England, losing his parents must have traumatised him. He has always been serious and self-educated. He is a good father and husband.

No, I didn't know Elise and Freddy in Vienna. We met in London working in the wartime nursery. The mothers could bring their children in the morning and pick them up at night. Fathers would be in the forces and the mothers went to work (war work) I expect.

Freddy visited Elise at the nursery; that's how Ruth met him. He had a bad case of chickenpox and my mother said we should bring him to her house so she could look after him. I think Elise at that time had moved into the nursery and had a room there, I can't really remember. I know that Ruth and I lived with my mother.

Elise and me and all the other Jewish girls who worked with us at the nursery never really spoke about our own experiences. We coped with the bombing and that seemed enough.

I asked my daughter the other day if I had told her about my past. She said I didn't really tell them about it but I didn't really bury it either, I just didn't dwell on it. We went through it but were all lucky not to lose my mother; also knowing my Dad was in Italy after Dachau, we then met him in London later. When we realised we were going to move to Canada he wrote and said he would like to see us. By then he was back in Vienna, after the war, with a new wife, without a divorce. He made up his own rules.

Please don't think for a minute that I minded you writing to me. I was pleased to receive your message.

One thing I might add, my Aunt Ella [yes, the same name as Elise's mother] was about 10 or 15 years younger than my mother. Gerty and Lily, my sister and cousin, wanted her desperately to come to England but she did not want to leave her husband who was in complete denial about the whole persecution aspect, so staying in Vienna meant she lost her life in a concentration camp.

Yes, I knew Andy and Gerda. Andy was actually responsible for Terry and me going to Canada. Ruth and Freddy had left London and my twin-bond with Ruth was so strong, I had to go where she was.

I also heard (likely from Elise) that her mother did not want to go to Belgium, where they may have escaped what happened to them, because her husband's first wife was there.

I can only remember that Ella's house (En's grandmother and Andy's first home) in Budapest was near the Synagogue, but that's all I remember. We took photographs that day we found it, but I cannot remember where I put them. I'm sorry I can't be of any help.
Elise and I had lots of fun in London in 1944, went to movies and had meals out, and I always enjoyed her company, also lately, as you know, all the great trips we have taken together. You can imagine how sorry I am about her memory loss.

Lots of love and hugs to you all, Lotte xxx

FROM: tess2dgf@ntlworld.com : 24/11/04 writes

Dear Angela,

I have now re-read the e-mail you wrote after we were together, there is so much to think about in it. I don't really know where to start but I will, and hope that you get something from what I tell you. I have my doubts because what I relate doesn't seem very relevant but you must be the judge. This is terribly good for me (putting some memories on paper) but whether it is of any help to you is something else. This story has absolutely nothing to do with the Holocaust and yet without that I would never have met Elise and spent so much of my formative years with her. I was so fortunate. She was the maternal influence I would have missed and would probably been a different person if it wasn't for her, though I suppose genes play a part too.

I have to start by describing my background. My parents are first generation English. My grandparents were from Russia (mother) and Poland (father). My Dad was brought up in the East End of London with 3 siblings and being the eldest was the only one educated (although they were all clever, but that's how it was in those days) and became a solicitor. He was an academic and a brilliant lawyer but ended up, naturally, being the main financial support for his parents. My mother's parents got off the boat in Southampton and settled in a suburb there and brought up 3 girls. My mother was beautiful but not at all maternal and my sister and I were cared for most of the time by staff.

I had always thought my parents brought Elise from Vienna to escape the Holocaust, but have since found out that over a game of Bridge my mother heard of Elise being unhappy with the family she was with and that's when she came to us. I was 4 years old and simply remember she cared for me. I do not remember her being sad ever but remember that she and her cousins including Litzy and Lawly and Kitty all got together in our day nursery sewing, drawing (Lawly) and talking in German. I could understand quite a lot of what they said. I loved being with them and presumably because they assumed their families at home were OK they never seemed sad.

I do remember Freddy (Fritz) coming over aged 14. He was shy and couldn't speak English. He was an awkward, plain young boy who adored my mother. I remember the small room he had in our house. He was quite secretive and I believe at the time that he thought of converting to Catholicism and hid religious material up the chimney in his room. He was very clever and I think qualified as an engineer and worked for a German refugee family who lived in our road. He was sad but I now realise why and how awful for such a young boy to leave his own parents and why he so loved my mother.

I loved being with Elise. She played classical music to me and asked me to describe what the music portrayed to me. We went walking in the countryside and I remember well blackberry picking. She made gorgeous biscuits. When I was older and she worked at the nursery in Camden Town, where she looked after the children of the factory workers on war work (where Ruth and Lotte also worked) I used to leave with her on dark mornings and help with the children. I loved this. Elise was considered my governess and I therefore went to school later than my sister because she was giving me my first school lessons.

My sister and I were sent to boarding school during the war and both of us became sick (I nearly died) so we came home. Elise was on war work then but I still think she lived with us and presumably Freddy but I can't really remember him at that time. I then became ill again and remember Elise and my father travelling with me in an ambulance to the hospital in London because my mother was hysterical and couldn't cope. I spent many weeks in hospital and do not remember Elise visiting but I remember my parents visiting a lot. There was bombing and I was one evening taken to the top of University College Hospital, but being young I thought this was very exciting, particularly when they took me on to the roof after the raid and I saw parts of London in flames.

When I was well enough my sister, Mother and I went to stay in the North of England with relations, and Elise and Dad were left alone at our house in London. I know now that they had a relationship and that my father wanted to leave my mother and go to New Zealand with Elise (Elise had intimated something to me when we stayed with them, many years later, but it wasn't until her 70th birthday party that I knew for sure, when Anne told me, thinking I knew). Some weeks after her birthday I asked her in person, and she told me that she liked my mother and was also so grateful for all she had done for Freddy and her that she felt she could not go away with my Dad (I think she also felt sorry for my mother, who was not truly happy). I was quite shocked that Dad could have considered leaving my sister and I but can well understand how this happened. My mother would go to bed early evening or even late afternoon, and Dad and Elise would talk and had so much in common. Elise was very straightforward, and in spite of all she had been through, very normal and adjusted, everything my mother was not. Dad was very left-wing and wonderful to talk to (he really wanted to become a politician). When Elise married Bill and he was still in the Forces, Dad would get Bill's political literature sent to him and forward it on to him because the Army would not have taken very kindly to a member of the Forces being involved with any political party, particularly the communist party, and the consequences could have been serious if found out and affected his pension never mind losing his job.

You know, I only remember Elise crying once, and that was during the war when she was considered to be an Enemy Alien. This meant she could have been interned and sent to the Isle of Man (or some such place) but in fact she had to stay in London and I think report to the police station each week. How mad was that? I was absolutely terrified (as young as I was) and can remember crying and imagining her and Freddy would be put in a compound surrounded by wire netting and had vivid nightmares over this. I know this was the way refugees were treated and still find it hard to understand bearing in mind they had escaped from the Nazis.

There was a huge gap in years when there was no contact with Elise, and I realise now why, but I always wrote to her off and on, and this was when she had married En's father and En and Anne were born. When they were living on Salisbury Plain. We were on holiday and I suggested on the way home we called into see them. I was conscious of an atmosphere when I made the suggestion but had no idea why. But we did visit and Jane had just been born.

Later, contact became more regular, when I was married and we'd visit with the children, when En was a teenager.

Elise was so supportive to me when it came to my somewhat difficult mother, but sort of understood my mother more than I could. I thought my dad suffered terribly, and blamed my mother, but Elise was always neutral.

Over the years we have shared so much and I find it so sad that she has begun to lose her memory. She has intimated to me her confusion at times and I find it difficult to know what to say.

I hope this gives you some insight into how our lives intertwined. When I look back I am amazed how Elise was (and is) and how very straightforward she is (and was)
Love, Tess.

In a message dated 19/11/2004 2:38:18 P.M. Pacific Standard Time, Moinous@aol.com writes:

I got that message today
I love your Hungarian spelling
it not as fancy as your Polish spelling but it tells more

synagogue
opera
goulash
archives
and more
goose
cabbage
paprika
wow
enjoy

I'm all packed

this is just a preview performance - the real full-length performance will be next year

this time I am going to work with the director - to thrash out the project ok

I'll go and shave now

lousy golf this morning
but the weather is splendid

Is it cold in budapest

when we were there it was in january and wow did we freeze our asses
bon appetite

love to you both xxxxMXXX

170

In a message dated 20/11/2004 9:37:39 AM Pacific Standard Time, angelamorgancutler@ntlworld.com writes:

that's terrible - I mean that you haven't seen my hungarian mail yet and now you arer going away -

all is wonderfukl here - we went to the synagaoge yesterdayu and thery gave us a contact for En's granmother's address but have to wait until we get home as the person who runs the archive was away until mondaz so that mean we shall have to come here again some day - which is fine as we have fallen in love with the place - went to the opera last night and saw 2 modern operas both set during the war - and one had a deranged cleaning woman ansd I understood nothingh as it was in hungarian with german subtitkles but I enjoy the opera more when tyou have to make up the stories the second one was about a hypnotist with a limp and he kept putting people into trances - making them dance - the singing was delightful - and worth it all to sit in that beautiful building for two and a half hrs -

today we are going to see more things - food is incredible
- yesterdau stuffed ourselves with stiffed cabbage and starters tio die for - En had the goose -

It's so gentle here - and the people are lovely - [ok got to go this mouse and keyboatrdf are driving me nyuts 0 that hungarian for njuters -

ok have a darluing trip again again - tell me all as if i am there next to you o0 yes 0- explauin it all 0- let me see wht they do with the work - 0 love and hugs - x aA

In a message dated 21/11/2004 9:37:39 AM Pacific Standard Time, angelamorgancutler@ntlworld.com writes:

monooooooooious are you there
are you getting my messages -
write and tell me if my messages are getting to you -
rushing - - -
XAX

From: Moinous@aol.com
Date: Sun, 21 Nov 2004 18:22:33 EST
To: angelamorgancutler@ntlworld.com
Subject: Re: Budapest

NO MESSAGES YESTERDAY - JUST THIS ONE TODAY
SOMEBODY IS INTERFERING

WRITE AGAIN

I WILL WRITE LATER

XmX

From: Moinous@aol.com
Date: Thurs, 18 Nov 2004 18:22:33 EST
To: angelamorgancutler@ntlworld.com
Subject: Re: Budapest

I don't understand why some of your message don't make here - we are being censored

another crazy day - I had to go back to the car dealer - they forgot to give me a second key - then I had to go to the ear doctor - E claims that I don't hear what she says any more - I tell her that her voice is getting weak - I kept hearing a buzzing

have a great time
you will love Budapest great city
where are you staying
on which side of the Danube
in Buda
or in pest
great cafes all over
Miss you too but some days are like that - I am sure I'll be able to communicate from Avignon

and what else did you send - I didn't get it

I give up

i saw that you left at 4 am. You guys are nuts and america is for the birds

I'll send you my address in Avignon when I get there you can send the card there
love M

From: Moinous@aol.com
Date: Sat, 20 Nov 2004 17:00:23 EST
To: angelamorgancutler@ntlworld.com
Subject: Re: avignon

two messages from you just now

number one - you like me - you like everything about me

number two - you hate me - you detest everything about me

number one and two cancel each other

I await number 3

and a full report about Budapest ok

for me it's always number one

xxxm

From: <angelamorgancutler@ntlworld.com>
Date: Sun, 21 Nov 2004 17:22:53 +0000
To: <Moinous@aol.com>
Subject: Re: already back

where art you now

my eyes are so blind tonight -

just got home and now we have to take the children out - we had the
best of times except we didn't after all manage to find Ella's house
- we walked everywhere looking but finally had to give up as we really
had no idea where to look - apart from some vague directions that meant
we were in the right area - they are rebuilding a lot of the jewish
quarter - making lots of new housing so some of the old buildings are
being bulldozed to make way for new work - but there are still quite a
lot of old places standing - some very run down -

Yesterday we went to a concert the hungarian festival orchestra with
some famous composer - he thoroughly enjoyed himself - and a young guy
- a violin soloist in the middle section - fabulous - it was a sell out
and we managed to get cancelled tickets - all the fancies of buda were
there - I can be a lovey when the mood takes me -

now back to this boring country - I must have been dropped down the
wrong birth canal for sure

damn - I have to go - more soon - hope all is well with you - tell me
all - much love

Yes in Budapest it was freezing but I loved being all wrapped up -
yesterday it even snowed - I wanted to cry with happiness - maybe I
did -

xxAxx
From: <angelamorgancutler@ntlworld.com>
Date: Thu, 18 Nov 2004 10:54:41 +0000
To: Moinous@aol.com
Subject: Re: Re: Budapest

zes0 oh jere wwe go 0 I cannot write in hungarian 0 yI git your messages
but I don;t thuink you got mine - no matter - here we are and It is
so beautifuyl just aa quick meassage on the way to eat and to the
synagoghe still trying to find en's grandmother's addresss - maybe they
have records - but as she then moved to Vienna - I don't know - anyway
I sent yiou a card and you;ll get it late after you get bakc form france
- havew fun there \ and I will think of you - got to go eat - yesterday
we went everywhere

Listen to this - I arrived and realised I had left all my underwear
behind so now |I have hungarian knickers the first thing I bought - and
very confy they are 0- oh it's hard to keep going with this keyboard -
got to dash - ok xxx's and all and all Axxxxx

From: angelamorgancutler@ntlworld.com
Date: 2004/11/17 Wed PM 02:58:57 GMT
To: Moinous@aol.com
Subject: Re: non-stop

you mean you have not received all the messages I sent yesterday tell me
something definitely wrong

From: Moinous@aol.com
Date: Fri, 19 Nov 2004 10:42:24 EST
To: angelamorgancutler@ntlworld.com
Subject: Re: non-stop in BUDAPEST

finally got one of your budapest mail - everything is in the wrong order
- dates all over the place - sounds like you're having a great historical trip - I
am sure you will write about it - maybe in connection with Auschwitz

it reminded me of how E and I in Vienna searched for the street and the
apartment and the park where E spent her childhood and how when we took
a taxi to go to the cemetery to find E's grand- father's grave the taxi driver
- when he heard the number of the gate and knew it was the jewish gate
dropped us a mile away - ah the fucking Austrians

Yes we searched just like that

but I never wrote it
You wrote it for me

I am rushing [I am late] leaving [tomorrow morning very early]

I'll try to write more later this afternoon

I miss you but these peregrinations all over the world do interfere - one of

these days we'll have to sit down and tell each other everything
but we are telling each other everything already

I am so glad you and en are having this time together in this great city

I loved budapest when I was there

I think it's a much better and more beautiful city than Vienna which is too
rococo
Did i say that already -

lots of hugs

if you don't hear from me in a few days it means I could not connect but
remember that we are always connnnnnnected

love M xxx

From: Moinous@aol.com
Date: Mon, 22 Nov 2004 05:07:42 EST
To: angelamorgancutler@ntlworld.com
Subject: avignon

Angela - I am in Avignon
I could connect my laptop
it's sunny here today
you should see this place
an old medieval monastery modernized
I have a three room apartment
well furnished
warm
with a kitchen too
no television
you should see this place it's historical
it was built in the 3rd century for the pope it's outside of the city
very isolated
and there is an old medieval fortress
above the monastery
this place is called la chartreuse de st. benediction
look it up on the net

oh the s.d. chargers won yesterday
I was exhausted last night after the long flight
and the train ride
but feel great this morning
waiting for my director to pick me up so we can get to work on the play

so end of the first report

sounds like you had a great time in Budapest
I am happy for you Angela
but don't talk to me about snow
I have no memory of snow
I had enough snow in Buffalo for 35 years

beside telling me about the food
what else did you and En discover about the past
and now what
back to the writing I hope

this place is very quiet

maybe I'll become a monk

maybe I'll get sanctified here

got to rush

lots of love and to En xxxxx and hugs

Searching for Candles

this is not my story
these are not my roads
these buildings we must visit
will visit no doubt
only other people's streets
other people's stories
keep going
we are carrying flowers no doubt
most likely
we will visit her house
no doubt
most likely
a house we'll never find
obvious enough
keep going
Ella begins it
yes
there are no green railings as we'd been told
the only small clue is a forgotten address
and the archivist's away
all we have is a name
Ella Weiss
she's the grandmother
it gets confusing
but continue
the man on my arm
he's my husband
he's the grandchild of Ella
and he's all grown up
for now all we have is a string of syllables
a torn family tree half complete in an old woman's hand
and she is not back until Monday
the archivist that is
and we leave on Sunday
and so we fill in the appropriate forms
someone has to translate
we write down the translation at the top of each section
name
date of birth
siblings
place of deportation
relation to the named inquirer

they want us to pay in shekels
wrong country
wrong currency
it's all mixed up
the names
the location
the time
the way they left
the births records were kept at the synagogue
that much we know
yes
of the grandmother
of Ella
all we have is a string of siblings that begin with Ella
she's the first of the children
or so we imagine
and she was six no it was seven
seven
when she left here for Vienna
she remembers little of the place
keep going
she is the eldest
it's confusing
the countries
the names
the pronunciation
the way everyone is moving relocating hiding
all we have is a string of siblings beginning with Ella
yes
she's the grandmother of my husband
the man on my arm
and he's happy
look
here's your grandson
he's here
and he's saying the names aloud
he's repeating
Ella
he's saying
Andor
Ibolika
[Ibby]
Ibby was one of Ella's sisters and she escaped
those with a [H] next to the name are gone

well we all know what that means
he's saying
Ibby married someone called Imre Braun
had a daughter Kitty who ended up in the States
it's confusing but keep going
he's saying
Martha [Matty]
was another sister of Ella's
she married Fritzi Mellor
no children
and they went to Israel
he saying
Roszy
another sister
married Karl Schrenek
had a daughter Lily
were killed in the same way as Ella and Wilhelm
he's saying
Wilhelm
that's Ella's husband
the grandfather
they have an [H] next to their names
yes
they are the grandparents
of the man on my arm
the husband
the son
Ella's grandson
he's saying
Andor was Ella's brother
he lived in London
and we saw him all the time
he's saying
Andor escaped different camps
he married Gerda Epstein
some had children
yes
he's saying
Lily
the daughter of Roszy is Ella's sister
he's saying
remember in the photograph
Lily is wearing her white coat
Lily

he says
she has an [H] beside her name
and I didn't say that's the name we'd chosen
the one that was never used
when we didn't have the girl we'd planned for
there's just me looking at the child in the white coat
like Ella she was six or seven in the photograph
and there are so many of these images
and we've seen them all before
and how are we to respond
she is the niece of your grandmother I say
Lily
Ella's niece
it gets confusing
the names
the family lines
I only look on
and he's saying
some fled
some hid
and some perished
there's that word again
Lily
no
perished
yes
some perished twice over
and I didn't mention her name again
there are only woods broken bricks wire
clichés and ditches
countries to pick over
where I cannot pronounce the word please
where I cannot say the word thank you
I ask a woman in the market
how do I say thank you
she says
don't worry it's too long the word
forget it
don't worry
you have nothing to thank us for

instead at night we put on the fires
we are here in Budapest
we are looking for his grandmother's home

the man on my arm and it's cold
we wrap ourselves in three duvets
and we put on the fires
one in each room
I wear his socks to bed
for a while you know
and the fire ticks
we wrap ourselves in sheets
and who would come out at this hour
and pull us from our beds and into the snow I say
try not to think of it he says it's not your story
it's another time
it's gone by
they are not your dresses in the glass cases
they are not your dresses made from prayer shawls
this is too emotive
but go on
you don't know that man holding out his hands like that
wearing his hat like that
and his greatcoat
in the photograph
yes
I recognise him
I've seen him before
I'm beginning to recognise people I never knew
and he's holding out his hands
in the photograph
yes
as if he were saying thank you
his hat only removed minutes before
preparing to be hung in his best overcoat
the weight of his coat
his hands held open like that
and then there's the silver books they kept hidden
they are not my books
they are not my crowns
they are not my candles
the smell of ink where all we have is a name
drums made from words imagine
torn words made into drum skins
into music
whoever thought of that
who sewed up the dress from the prayer shawl that won't fit me
too obvious

but go on
the silver tree
where I take his photograph
yes
the man on my arm
he's under the tree now
and each leaf has a name inscribed on it
and I don't notice
I forgot to look
shame on me
nothing to be said

we take the same streets anyway
its snowing and we're glad of it
here he is saying
maybe they have knocked down Ella's house
maybe they've painted over the green railings
here I am taking his photograph in every kind of doorway
maybe it was this house
or this one
or that one he says
we'll come back then
we'll come again soon

she barely remembered anything
Ella
she was seven when she left here for Vienna
and now her great granddaughter carries her name
and we don't ask our children if they want the names of the
dead
we assume they will carry something on
no-one asks them
does my son think of his second name
does he think of the man who owned it out there in the wood
instead he tells me
my son that is
don't take me to visit the dead
can't we go to L.A. instead or New York
let's go to the beach mother
let's go snow boarding or sky scraping
I don't want to know about the dead or a place full of dead bodies
it's scary
let's buy clothes instead
the ones with labels I recognise

It's your heritage - he tells him
the husband
the grandson
all grown up and on my arm
you don't understand child
It makes me feel shame the child says
it's like I shouldn't have been born
he's only twelve I say and listen to this
listen to this
When I see the faces of dead boys he says
it's like I shouldn't be here
Eat your lamb I say
Let's go snow boarding he says
Let's go shopping for clothes
What do I want with rubble and glass and wire and hair
snow or heat it's all the same the water boiling in our bottles
Eat your lamb I say
these are not my streets
these are not my buildings
my stories
my history
my children's
of course
Eat your greens I say
He's a quarter Hungarian
the husband of my children
the grandson
the one on my arm
yes
he's made up of quarters
dissected into parts
like the map in his pocket
like the stolen land
the bled pig quartered on the butcher's tiles
and the child is making jokes at a time like this
digression
it's all a digression
and surely this comes later
but listen
listen to this
we take the child to the dr
we say
dr dr he has problems with his concentration
the child that is

yes
and the dr is concentrating well enough
but the child gets up
he walks around the room
yes and he's laughing
it's his humour dr
it's in the genes
he's a section Hungarian
a fragment of Poland
he's all mixed up
when the child says
dr dr I have trouble with my concentration
I need to go to a concentration camp
get it get it

I always light two candles
what do you expect
it's the rituals I need
always I light two candles
no I won't say this or that or say it out loud
we are here in Hungary and the candles move
in the way you would have
in the way you did
go on
digging in the ground
nothing else to put there but an old stone
obvious enough
watch yourself here
watch the mother's face
the pious face that's not me
not in anyway me
that's not me holding the baby
that's not my expression
are the candles burning your fingers yet
so they should be
that's good
that's a good girl he'll say
how many cities have we been to now
searched for and burnt the same two candles
that's good
hear the plink of foreign coins in exchange
the change we don't want pays for memory in equal parts

It's kosher here he says

later
this comes later yes
and we eat of course we do
we find the candles
we light the candles
and leave the stones
and later we eat
that's kosher schnapps
it's made from pears he says
the man on my arm
he's telling me it's kosher schnapps
he's a handsome man I say
the one over there
see him
the one over there he's watching
No
don't look he's looking
he knows something
he's not fooling me
even beneath his blue eyes
his blue eyes on me
even beneath his beard
we recognise something of the other
and I want to say to him
maybe I do say to him
there's nothing to write about
I know he says
beneath his beard
maybe
I'm sure
he's whispering to me
I know
I know
but go on anyway

instead the man with me
the grandson
he's a man now he's all grown up
he's pouring the tiny glasses of schnapps
he lights the candles
and I stay a while and watch them burn
of course I do
hear the coins drop in exchange
it's all mixed up

and I'm laughing now
I'm drinking the schnapps and I am glad of it
glad it snows
maybe I even say so
did I tell you I was glad of it of the snow
last time it was burning us
the heat
it's all comes out the same
I'll hear you say as you always say
laughter tears heat snow
all comes out the same
did I tell you I needed it to snow
it froze our asses
so you'll say,
as I hear you say
days later

and we are standing in front of the fire
Ella's grandson and me
we are here in Budapest
we light all the fires
we put on the radio
of course we do
we listen to the violin solo
and I lift my skirt high in front of him
in front of the fire with the solo continuing
and don't get the wrong idea
I was just trying to listen more effectively
to warm myself
nothing complicated or beguiling
well maybe just a little
I can't lie
I do lie
ah
I knew what I was doing

maybe I digressed my way to find her here
to bring him here
do you see
maybe
but we cannot find Ella's house
of course we won't
she's gone now she's left
she remembers nothing

but I feel her here as we walk the same streets
that's what people like to say isn't it
yes
that's the kind of thing

maybe she came here he says
and here and there
maybe she once sat here and heard this same solo
lift up your skirt he says
it's tight around your ankles
you have to learn to walk in a new way
and he likes that kind of detail

look
here's your grandson
he's here
he's here isn't he
he's all grown up
he's happy
he's on my arm
he's happy
he's sliding his hand around my calf
he's unzipping my boots
he's putting the schnapps to my lips

From: Moinous@aol.com
Date: Mon, 6 Dec 2004 18:21:51 EST
To: angelamorgancutler@ntlworld.com
Subject: Re: FW: exhibition

Angela you look lovely in the national costume of Hungary
was that thing on your head heavy
I only just got the card today

I am back need to talk
need to tell what happened in Avignon amazing things happened there
incredible the place where they put us
E and Simone (the metteur en scene) was there too
participating joyfully in the making of
LE PROJET FEDERMAN

more will be told about that in due time and more to come

write call
send smoke signals hurry
I'm going back to frogland in march and again in june

did you get my postcard did you like the stamp - the french want the statue of
liberty back

I remember us searching just like that - E and me - just like you did - i think I
said this to you already - only we were in Vienna - where E was from -
mxx

From: <angelamorgancutler@ntlworld.com>
Date: Tue, 07 Dec 2004 09:19:01 +0000
To: <Moinous@aol.com>
Subject: Re: exhibition

hello
glad all is well and all went well - tell me more about the play -

I missed you - and yes the lovely postcard arrived - thanks -

Yes move back to France then we'll be neighbours and have to hate one
another as the Brits and the frogs hate one another but maybe secretly
the Brits want to be French - well for the summer at least when they
go camping with their 4 wheel drives with their obnoxious kids and
use their little tralala holiday french and drink french wine and eat
french stinky cheeses and think they are so interesting when they come
back and tell you every gory detail - yes - go live there and I can
begin a stamp collection

me - I am in a pig's humour and so I'd best not depress you with it
mainly britain

mainly writing - which I am perpetually giving up

mainly we went all the way to London and the only exhibition I really wanted to see in relation to some of the things I have mentioned in my book was being held in a Jewish something or other and the gallery was closed for the Jewish Sabbath -

mainly when I tried yesterday to get more info from someone called Arbach a woman gave me the wrong number and the guy on the end of the phone screamed at me RING ANOTHER NUMBER and slammed down the phone

mainly when I went to the post office and so sweetly asked this woman if she'd give my parcel to the postman - as he was currently busy and I didn't want to interrupt him - she shouted in my face - I CAN'T BE BOTHERED

mainly I have no idea what to get you for christmas

mainly I hate christmas

mainly I decided to buy Sarah some gorgeous tights and she has such long legs I don't know if to get her large or extra large

mainly no news of the Poh.Dung

mainly teenagers and having to live with them

mainly the amount of washing next to my machine

mainly the kids don't make their beds

mainly christmas robbing me of all I have taken 10 weeks to earn gone in 1 hour

mainly HC is here Friday giving a reading and that will both make me happy and depressed as she writes like an angel and I should be put out with the pit ponies
mainly david blunkett

mainly that my neighbour has gone to Sri Lanka and I am here feeding her cat every day and I have such a bad memory I'm going to have to walk around with CAT written on my hand for almost three weeks

mainly writing

and mainly that I am now repeating myself

To be continued if I don't go mute ....

love to you - Ax

From: Moinous@aol.com
Date: Mon, 13 Dec 2004 15:43:21 EST
To: angelamorgancutler@ntlworld.com
Subject: Re: waiting for ...

I had a stamp collection as a boy and the Nazis stole it - what did you call me on the card your hand writing is unreadable

I can't remember but yes - the ongoing question: what do we call the other - some unnamable creature - for sure not like a brother - well no offence but you're a little old for that

brother I am not sure - we don't have the same eyes - I could be your uncle

and then that is also too incestuous considering all we tell the other each day

but what's wrong with a little incest - I hate taboos - maybe I am your step-mother

Anyway - the thing I sent you for christmas is the antithesis of a christmas gift - it will make you want to cut your throat - it's a very depressing film -

oh I love antithesis stuff - I use my electric razor to cut my throat then - you get nothing - you know what - I hate to go to the post office during christmas season it's like a bordello - all the housewives with huge packages trying to show off that their packages are bigger and better than the neighbours

hey - I also today read an article that says that one can get addicted to cheese - just as one gets addicted to cocaine

how do you like that

You're right - I adore cheese and just before I die If I have time - I am going to eat as much of it as I can - I have a list called *Things to eat before I die* - or if I can't get hold of them - things to imagine I am eating before I die - the list is getting so big I will need to have a very long lingering death and a good appetite - and hopefully some teeth -

Never tried cocaine - it really never interested me - En took some LSD once when he was in his teens or early twenties - after it took effect - he thought he had killed someone - yes - he was convinced that he had murdered someone and kept trying to get away from the body so went in and out of a ground floor window repeatedly until someone took him to hospital -

but for now -
I am tired today - the loss of a lovely weekend and that gap between -
all I do is mull and no action

same here - I am waiting for something but I don't know what

but this is not the time - not today - maybe tomorrow maybe wednesday
-maybe baba

maybe this afternoon or 22 years from now

don't worry - no rush

Mxxxx

From: <angelamorgancutler@ntlworld.com>
Date: 11/1/05 2:34 PM
To: <Moinous@aol.com>
**Subject: Re: HALF OF US HAVE NEVER HEARD OF AUSCHWITZ ... And
patience**

Dec 3 2005
Moinous - Did you see this over there -
Shock at poll findings on Nazi death factory

*NEARLY half of Britons have never heard of the Nazi death camp Auschwitz.
And among women and the under-35s, the figure is as high as 60 per cent,
according to a BBC poll. Of the 4000 adults surveyed, 45 per cent said
they had never heard of the camp in Poland where a million were killed.
The BBC commissioned the survey in advance of Holocaust Memorial Day
on January 27, which marks the 60th anniversary of the liberation of
Auschwitz.*

Yes - agreed we have written so much and somehow survived this marathon
of words and 2 actual meetings -

So what next - I am glad that E is now feeling better - take care of
her eyes. And your ears - yes - how's your buzzing or shouldn't I ask.

Today I am not writing - I am drinking camomile tea and thinking too
much - just pages of words - daydreaming and digressions that sometimes
go nowhere - currently sidetracked by Narcissus - *each one of us must
have the courage of his own narcissism* ... Isn't that what you always
say - but no not that - I realise these are all avoidance techniques
and I ask myself am I just bee-ing lazy - scared - as resistant as ever
to this subject

Today a man on the radio was reading from a work called First Tastes -
well there was more than one reader on this topic - but he had written
about bacon - the pig not the artist - and the woman who followed had
written about buckwheat pancakes -

I thought to myself - why can't I write about bacon - the food that is - why Auschwitz and not buckwheat pancakes -

Patience - I kept writing in my notebook - then found this in Blanchot's *Book to Come*

patience that persists all the way to writings most extreme passivity … to write without desire, to desire to write no longer …

from the same book -

Echo loves Narcissus by staying out of sight, we might suppose that Narcissus is summoned to encounter a voice without a body, a voice condemned to always speak the last word and nothing else - only the mimetic

and such is the fate of […] [those] who touch each other with words whose contact with each other is made of words, and who thus repeat themselves without end, marvelling at the utterly banal, because their speech is not a language but an idiom they share with no other, and because each gazes at himself in the other's gaze in a redoubling which goes from mirage to admiration.

Narcissus beside the water - waiting - looking for - what - And yes - all this somehow taking me full circle back to the pond in Birkenau - the ash-filled water that reflected nothing back - death killed death - in Auschwitz that is - Narcissus ends up as a funereal flower beside the pond in the Little Wood - but there is nothing to gaze at - nor into - the water that is clear no more - reflects only the need to keep staring and searching for …

Amery writes: *For death in its literary, philosophic, or musical form there was no place at Auschwitz … Every poetic evocation of death became intolerable, […] the death of a human being finally lost so much of its specific content … Dying was omnipresent, death vanished from sight.*

Dream #98754

Last night I was showing you how to die. I said, when dogs throw themselves into water sometimes their coats become sodden and heavy before they realise that the command 'fetch' will be the death of them. In their enthusiasm to drown in the middle of a command, in the middle of a 'please', in the middle of retraction and inside a green pond they drown with the weight of their own coats, the stick still in their mouths. Let me show you, I say, by way of example, this analogy that came from a story about my aunt's old Dulux dog, as they call them here, renowned for their over-abundant coats. It was my uncle who threw in the stick, one of many he had thrown over the dog's lifetime. This time the dog with the stick went too far. My uncle and aunt seeing their pet's distress waded in after him, but by the time they reached him he was too heavy to move and so he died in their arms, all three of them holding each other in the water, until his water-logged body began sinking. Do you see? I jump into a tank of pea-green water to demonstrate. It's very deep. You wait patiently above, peering into the green murk and the stink. I try and demonstrate what a dog would forget to remember about the weight of its coat. I submerge myself beneath the water. It's so restful here. I momentarily forget myself, you, and what's left of the light, now barely visible above. I sink further into the murk and it begins to feel good. I momentarily drift, find I am lying at an angle on the diagonal like this \ I feel so relaxed and in such a near state of bliss that I sleep. And when I wake I realise I have foolishly almost drowned by allowing myself to drift off for seconds, maybe more, and that you must be concerned that I have not resurfaced - this was only meant to be a demonstration of death. I try to resurface to get back to you but the feeling of the water is so soothing, I try half-heartedly to surface and find myself instead going in the other direction, giving over to the water, just like that dream I had, I want to tell you, remind you of that dream that took place on a lake. Do you remember ... I try and shout through the volume of water, open my mouth fully to the stench. Take in mouthfuls, but no words this time, no way of knowing if you hear me or not, and instead of rising, I sink and drink. Find myself completely content.

From: <angelamorgancutler@ntlworld.com>
Date: Fri, 26th Jan 2005 11:51:13 +0000
To: <moinous@aol.com>
Subject: this royal boo and digging in the ground

Look, here's the Harry slip. Did you get this over there? Harry [as in
Prince - we have many Princes here as you know] the young prince wore a
swastika to a fancy dress party with the theme 'Colonial and Native'.
His picture taken by a friend at the party was then splashed all over
the papers with photographs and predictable headlines: Harry the Nazi.
What princely timing, someone said, when the country is preparing
for Holocaust memorial day on the 27th of this month. Prince Charles
supposedly telling his son to make amends by visiting Auschwitz.
The final word … *Prince William was also at the party dressed as a lion.*

What a family …

I did make little steps back to writing today. I began by reading about
the things people - well, all those who were deported - had buried in
the ground when they knew they had to flee or were in danger of being
rounded up. The obvious things like money and torahs and menorahs.
This was prompted by a story a woman told me just a few days back. Her
friend is Hungarian and during the war this friend's grandfather lived
in some small Hungarian village. In 1944, the Nazis decided to annex
Hungary, which was already a German ally. They put Adolf Eichmann in
charge, who started to organise the round up of Jewish people to the
death camps. The friend's grandfather was one of the people in the
village entrusted to look after money and other valuable possessions of
the Jewish community and hold it all in trust when they got taken away.
He buried everything at the bottom of his garden and actually kept it
safe until the few returned. I'm sure this was unusual and most spent
all they were asked to keep, or am I being cynical. And yes, I had heard
similar stories before about all the stashed money and jewellery hidden
in jars in the ground along with words dug into the earth and pushed
into walls around the camps.

I then found an article about the historian Ringelblum who ended up in
the Warsaw ghetto. He got a circle of people together, they met each
sabbath to collect stories, journals, photographs, surveys, drawings,
posters, ID cards, whatever he could gather from all who were there
in the ghetto. He even ran a writing competition, without letting
the people know what he was doing with their work because it was so
dangerous to gather such stories together. Before the Warsaw ghetto
uprising, they liquidated the ghetto and took 300,000 people from there
to Treblinka between July and September '42. Ringelblum and his group
later separated the work out into 3 parts and hid it in 3 different
places and buried it under the ground, one cache was put inside a large
metal milk pail, they found this and a metal box after the war but the
3rd has not yet been found, the work was then published in a book and
is kept in various museums in Warsaw. He escaped imprisonment twice and
on the 3rd occasion they captured him, his wife and son and executed
them all.

Anyway, that's as far as I got, except many articles I found written by holocaust deniers, turning the same subject on its head. One written in response to a story about someone finding a pair of twisted spectacles, a child's ring and gold coins unearthed beside a labour camp that had held Jewish prisoners during the war - the man who wrote the article implying that the Jews must have buried these things themselves with their bare hands or possibly with a spoon, etc. etc … . and I won't bother to repeat any more as you well know the rest of this sorry tune …

Hugs to you - Axx

Dream #24233

A woman priest had turned Birkenau into a place where people could get married, in the way people go to Vegas and Graceland. She had converted one of the wooden barracks into a marriage parlour. En wanting us to get remarried, is so full of excitement. They will remarry couples who want to show each other that they are so in love they would do it all over again, he says: the lady priest is so liberal she also does gay marriages. She is smiling at us and wears a white wedding-gown and a full veil pulled up exposing her ageing face. Her grey hair is filled with white gardenias, the perfume of the flowers is beguiling, but I wander off and feel uneasy. I look out of the window at the end of the hut and see rows and rows of couples lining the fields, but they are sunk into the ground with only their heads sticking out of the earth, planted in long rows of twos like cabbages. I say to En, Look … This is what happens … It's a trick … The whole place is a bog … After you are married inside the hut, they make you walk into the fields, not knowing it's marsh land, there you sink and die with your head sticking up from the ground. But En will not listen nor look. He is so charmed by the lady priest he is already writing her a cheque and agreeing a time for our ceremony.

From: Moinous@aol.com
Date: Fri, 28 Jan 2005 01:58:26 EST
To: angelamorgancutler@ntlworld.com
Subject: Re: remembrance day

of course it was a trick
just as the hair cuts and showers were tricks
this way to the showers ladies and gentlemen … etc. [see TTV]

angela
I'll tell you - I am in a somewhat crummy mood
yes - I am fed up with all that fuss that is being made about the
celebration [yes that's what it is finally] a celebration of auschwitz
and the whole thing turning into a circus - and so commercialized
yes - why don't we all wear Auschwitz T-shirts - soon they are going to sell
concentration camp pyjamas

this morning in the San Diego newspaper there's an article telling how in
Finland the Jews were not allowed to celebrate or commemorate because
now it's been decided that Auschwitz should be de-judaized

and in other countries too - the same discussions and on and on
and so on

I don't want to hear any more of that

it hurts angela

it's not just auschwitz finally that bugs me -

it's the not so subtle way the
whole holocaust affair is turning into a joke

in the same article it was pointed out several times that 40% of people in the
world believe auschwitz never happened - as your article suggests people
have never heard of it -

and so on

I want to write a funny book about bees and birds making love let's start all
over again
excuse this mood

I am enjoying the sam book so much right now [Le Livre de Sam]

it's becoming pure fiction

Vice president mister Cheney went to the auschwitz ceremony in a
hunter costume with boots and a hunter cap - did you see that -

unbelievable

I suppose as long as all these celebrations and memorials and the visits
to the death camps by dignitaries dressed in a hunter costume [that's the
best one] to let their crocodile tears fall on the ashes of my parents continue
…

well finally it's laughable angela

I think these celebrations are the final solution to put an end to the final
solution
give me a footnote or a headnote

love and lots of xxxxxx

Dream #77015

The children and me are in a building that is falling apart. The owner says he will fix it but while he does we must wait in the basement. The basement is huge. We find it by walking through endless corridors until the room finally opens out. I look up and see that we are inside an enormous chimney. I feel sick with dizziness when I look up. The chimney is so vast. The bricks are lined with mosaic. I can't see very well as it's so dark, but I hear men howling to my right. Max comes to find me. He says, Mum, we must get you out of here. It's full of ghosts and this chimney is about to be lit. A man brings me a word. Rather he is howling it. I cannot see him. He says that the secret word is *twendlenest*. He says it is German for swishing tail, for the swish of a mop. He says, This word means hypnosis, caused by the rhythm of water or the movement of a person cleaning up. You must beware of it, he says … Of being put under by the mop, by the tail, by the tide: it's a trick to get you to sleep.

The nest has a sh sound - nesht - but is spelled nest.

From: Moinous@aol.com
Sent: Sun, 02 February 2005 9:05
To: angelamorgancutler@ntlworld.com
Subject: Re: palm springs

Raymond - what time are you going to Palm Springs

I am leaving in half an hour

It sounds fancy - I remember you going last year - we are indeed going round in circles -

very rich plush snobbish almost british in its pretentiousness but I love it it's hot - they have rattle snakes there

I just consulted my lovely electronic oxford dictionary for the *ringleted* you wrote of -
it says *a corkscrew-shaped curl of hair*
yes - PUT THAT DEFINITION IN THE BOOK -
some of the hair was ringleted -

and now in to the shower and here I go -
Oops - I didn't mean to introduce another theme for the book into the conversation -

It is amazing that there are no pictures of the shower room with the gas slowly seeping in and the bodies twisting and falling on top of each other -

isn't it strange that the SS failed to take that picture

There are pictures of the bodies going into the shower room and even picture of them standing there looking up at the shower heads - above waiting for the warm water to come down and cleanse them of their faults their sin of being Jewish or mad or whatever -

Well I want to tell you one thing - when my mother walked into the shower room she knew exactly why they were pushing her in naked - she had a little smile at the corner of her mouth - a cynical smile that said - I have hidden behind the best of me - I told him to be quiet - chut - I said - telling him that if he is quiet - if he doesn't make any noise - if he remains silent he will be safe - and only then - when he is safe will he start shouting I am alive -
And I know why my mother left me behind so I could shout because when I was a boy I was so shy I never dared say a word until I was five years old and after that it was hard to extract words out of my mouth - when I was a boy I never screamed never cried aloud -
M xx

Date: Sun, 02 February 2005 20:07:08 +0000
From: angelamorgancutler@ntlworld.com
To: <Moinous@aol.com>
Subject: Re: your mother

Yes - this reminded me of Marian Marzynski's story - remember

I told you about him - The film maker who escaped by pretending he was a Polish child - On the small film Sarah sent me online - He said that when he was four he had an eye infection and that one of his uncles was an eye doctor - he'd performed on him without anaesthetics as they had none available. He said the pain was unbearable and so was his screaming. He said his screaming was so bad they thought that he would never be able to be silent when the time came for him to have to save himself. His father telling him earlier that the only way to live was to keep his mouth shut.

When they smuggled him from the Warsaw Ghetto in a horse wagon they had to hold a hand over his screaming mouth as he wanted to go back to his mother. He finally, aged five, stood in a courtyard and decided it was time to be quiet.

A woman wrote to me recently, she had come back from Rwanda after being there for some time, and on her return had read the piece I wrote on the photographs I saw at Auschwitz. She said she had a very similar experience when she went to a genocide memorial service in Kigali on the anniversary of the massacres. She said that the relatives of the victims, most of them survivors, were there to attend the service and to bury more mortal remains that had been recently discovered. She said she'd been worried about disturbing the relatives with her presence at the memorial service so she instead returned the next day. When she entered a room with the photographs of the massacred Rwandan men, women and children, she said they were unlike the *official* Auschwitz

photographs, these photographs had not been taken as the children
arrived at the dirt roads where they were to be tortured and murdered,
they had instead been taken at their weddings, first communions, at the
schools they had attended. There was also a children's' room, she said,
where below each small photograph, information was given about each
child: name, age, hobbies. She said that after reading that the first
little boy liked chocolate and swimming, she ran away ... she said, I
couldn't look at them any more.

I do not remember why I began telling you this.

Ax

Date: Mon, 03 February 2005 16:09:02 +0000
To: <Moinous@aol.com>
From: angelamorgancutler@ntlworld.com
Subject: Re: the abc of Auschwitz - and such new year's gifts

Did you see the alphabet I was telling you about - the one that gave
various bits of information about the Holocaust but presented it as an
ABC … well I only read part of it - I found it very disturbing - maybe
the contradiction of the childlike form and the graphic content - I
added bits into the book, and then took them out, C is for ...
Couldn't make up my mind if to leave such words and examples in or out.
Finally, a friend turned up today with things - well some information
I had been discussing with her - the yellow stars that the Jews were
forced to wear - she said there were older references to the stars
being used well before the war - not stars specifically - more types of
clothing which identified Jews and sometimes Muslims - she said that
these articles of clothing were found around as far back as 807 CE when
Jews had to wear yellow belts or tall cone-like hats - After this Jews
and Muslims in every Christian province had to dress in a way that
distinguished them from others - King Henry III of England in 1217
ordered Jews to wear two tables of the ten commandments made of white
linen or parchment - In France local variations of the badge continued
until Louis XI decreed in 1269 that men and women had to wear round
pieces of yellow felt or linen a palm long and four fingers wide on the
front of their outer garments - In Germany and Austria - Jews in the
second half of 1200s had to wear Jewish or horned hats which mimicked
the ones they had traditionally worn freely and now became mandatory -
The badges were widespread throughout Europe in the 18th century - it
was Heydrich who both gave the orders to shoot the Austrian Jews who
were deported to Minsk - thus En's grandparents - and had the idea -
at a meeting he attended after Kristallnacht in 1938 - to recycle the
yellow badge - The idea wasn't put into practice until the latter part
of the following year and after war had been declared - In Sept 1941
badges were issued in Germany - beginning with armbands - and later a
yellow Star of David with the word JUDE inside worn on the left side of
the chest - The side of the heart - Posters were put up at the exits
of doors and apartments "Remember the badge." "Have you already put on
your badge?"

Anyway - maybe you already know all this and for sure you know how some people tried to hide the badge - carrying parcels or books or bags to their chest - as you wrote about in your poem - *my mother* [you said] *wept/ quietly that cold winter day/ while she sewed/ on all our clothes/ the yellow humiliation/ then she said/ her eyes dry now/ as she straightened/ on my shoulders/ the soiled coat/ I wore to school/ just let your scarf/ hang over it/ this way/ nobody will notice*

To prevent the possibility that some people tried to cover up their stars in what ever way they could - some authorities made people then wear the stars on their backs as well as on the knees of their trousers. People could be punished for wearing a creased or folded badge - for it being a centimetre out of place - or for using safety pins to attach them - Sarah also mentioned the other day that some people sold stars in the ghettos - Sold them from stalls on the side of the roads - Some wanted silk - good quality stars with even points which were more expensive - others only able to afford whatever materials and shapes they could get - Some babies had to wear them even when in their prams -

When we were in Spain one year - En tried on a coat that when buttoned tightly - we joked - made him look like a Rabbi - He wanted it for work but I said - all you need is a suitcase and a star and they'll surely pick you up - We later wondered why no one had done that - I mean bad taste and obvious PC aside - why no one had subverted the symbols - taken it back - in the way some derogatory words get claimed back - we wondered if someday someone might design a coat covered in stars - trousers with a star on the knee. Pink, blue, white triangled patterned dresses.

Yes - K. arrived for lunch with the above information - plus a set of Auschwitz 1 and 2 postcards that she gave me for a new year's present - in the past I would have received flowers.

Someone she knew - who must have been to visit Auschwitz as we had - sent them to her with no real explanation and K. never really knew what to do with them - so of course she remembered that under the present circumstances the perfect destination was moi - I know what you feel about the postcards - well the idea of postcards in the place where you lost your family and I tell you because I know you will understand when I say - those images were so seductively shot and beautifully lit they somehow even make the gas chamber - in the snow under the soft focus orange light of evening - look as inviting as a Bing Crosby Christmas scene -

I remember while in Oswiecim waiting in the railway station for a return train - there was a revolving display of Auschwitz postcards alongside the Polish landscapes - the ice-cream and souvenir stands - the usual plastic tat - I also recall seeing postcards at the camp - yes - in the shop - well there were different types of shops located at different points of Auschwitz - I'd wanted to stop and look, maybe buy one - but again wondered why and what I would do with such a card -

"They took us because they didn't have rabbits." I found this written in my notebook today - a line a survivor had written concerning Auschwitz -

I also found a small piece I had scribbled in my book sometime back: the day before we went to Auschwitz we were sitting having a beer in some outdoor bar inside the park that circles Krakow - I had read in one of the booklets that children under thirteen were not let in to Auschwitz - as visitors I mean - and we ended up trying to persuade Max that he needed to wear his glasses which Seth believed made him look older and more intelligent - as it turned out I had misread the thing and the age reference referred to children in school parties not to individual children accompanied by their families but I didn't realise this until days later and did not think about it until we were well inside Auschwitz and I saw a small baby being carried around in their father's arms -

I think I told you all this before -

Did I tell you that we have decided to make the trip to Minsk - We have discussed it enough and maybe it is time to just do it - We have to try and find out the best way to get there - if by train or to fly directly - but it's very expensive - If we go - well - I am sure we will - we will probably go in July - just En and me this time - I am not sure if the kids should come or if they'd want too - it feels so unknown - I can't imagine how it will be - not really -

A xx

In a message dated 5/23/2005 1:14:52 AM Central Daylight Time, angelamorgancutler@ntlworld.com writes:

Dear Vitali,

I'm not sure if you are able to help me. I am writing from the UK. I found your contact details on a website about the Maly Trostenets concentration camp in Minsk.

My husband's grandparents were deported to Minsk from Vienna and killed in the surrounding forests. None of our family have ever been to visit the mass graves. I don't know if the site is still marked in anyway but I was hoping to come to Minsk later this year - well, as soon as my husband En and myself can arrange it.

We will probably fly to Warsaw and hire a car to drive to Minsk from there, but I am not sure how realistic this is and we may have to fly directly from London. I have not been able to contact anyone around Minsk who can help with information about the site of the camp. Do you have any information that would help me and could you recommend a local guide?

Kind regards, Angela

From: Vitalich
**Date: Mon, 23 May 2005 10:18:30 EDT To: angelamorgancutler@ntlworld.
com**
Subject: Re: Information

Dear Angela,

I left Minsk 16 years ago. However the site at Maly Trostenets (Trostinec, etc.)
on the highway Minsk-Mogilev was always marked as memorial. I do not think
it is changed and I do expect that most of the people know where it locates.

Just as curiosity - what was last name of your husband's grandparents (if they
were local people)?

Many from my family and my wife's family were killed in Minsk ghetto and in
surrounding towns during WWII.

Info about Maly Trostenets enclosed below http://www.deathcamps.org/
occupation/maly%20trostinec.html

You need to contact Yossi Gruzman who lives in Minsk - he will know more - I
will contact him and let him know that you need more information - he can
provide a guide for the day or whatever you need - the forests are not easy to
find or get to by yourself.

Sincerely,
Vitali

on 10/7/05 3:38 pm, angelamorgancutler@ntlworld.com wrote:

Dear Yossi, we are really looking forward to our trip to Minsk on
Thursday. Everything is now sorted out with our guide Bella and I have
spoken to her today about visiting the camp, Shaskowa and the forest
in Maly Trostenets.
Just a last minute question. We had trouble getting Belarus roubles
here, do the taxi drivers take dollars from the airport? Oh, and what
is the weather like at the moment?

Thanks again for all your help.
Angela

From: JHRG of Belarus <Yogruzman>
Date: Mon, 11 Jul 2005 04:47:53 - 0700 (PDT)
To: <angelamorgancutler@ntlworld.com>
Subject: your message

Dear Angela,

To exchange dollars for Belarus roubles will be possible directly at the airport in a special exchange bureau. Cost of 1 dollar today is 2140 bel. roubles. Maybe it is necessary to you to ask Bella to meet you at the airport. If not, let her know. After this, she can come to your hotel and accompany you to the site of the concentration camp and then to the forest. You can work out what day is best when you speak with her. Weather in Byelorussia is now warmer than usual - approximately 25-28 in the afternoon and at night is 14-18. Sometimes it rains.

Best regards, Yossi Gruzman

From: <angelamorgancutler@ntlworld.com>
Date: Tues, 12 Jul 2005 13:55:08 +0100
To: moinous <moinous@aol.com>
Subject: soon away

Moinous,

Hope all is going well over there - Is the play going well - I am
disorientated as to what you are doing now? I have so much to tell
you - The Minsk arrangements have all happened so quickly - I haven't
had time to think but maybe that is for the best - Not sure if you are
picking up my messages while you are in France - don't worry if you
can't write back - we'll catch up soon enough -

We leave for Minsk the day after tomorrow - leaving at 3 a.m. - it's so
damn hot here I am roasting no better than a basted duck - I will try
and write and check my mail over there but not sure how practical that
will be - I have no idea of anything there - of what to expect - Bella
is meeting us on the 17th of July to take us to the various places -
forest et al - speak soon -

much love **A**

from: angelamorgancutler@ntlworld.com
to: Moinous@aol.com
Date: Tues 12th of July 2004 14:05:43
Subject: Belarus

Look at that - I put in to the search engine - Belarus weather

and what comes up first

<u>Marry a Sexy Foreign Girl</u>
Sexy, Honest Girls Want Your Love! Meet Them All Today. Only
$95.
www.ElenasModels.com

Also on the same afternoon - an interview on the radio by some journalist who said that while he was in Minsk in Belarus he was watching the late night weather and came to realise that the weather girl was stripping - yes - he at first thought he'd misheard - misunderstood what he was seeing until she began unpeeling with each passing cloud - apparently no one was that interested in this particular channel he was tuned into - so to boost the ratings the corporation had decided to let the woman strip her way through mostly dry with sunny spells - so by the time she reached the long range forecast and the humidity and the mosquito levels she was slipping out of her underwear –

From: <Moinous@aol.com>
Date: 13th JULY 2005 14:11:01 EST
To: <angelamorgancutler@ntlworld.com>
Subject: Re: the book

oops sorry your message went back to you before I could even answer it - I'll try again

Moinous - Thanks for all that you sent the other day and yes I went back to find that story of Bigleux and you in your Return to Manure - [or whatever it is you are now calling your book] where the story was there all the time and I hadn't remembered - Then again by coincidence - Sarah sent me an extract from a book that included a story about the writer Levinas - Levinas was detained in a concentration camp during the war and while there he befriended a dog he called Bobby - and it of course had a resonance with all you had written about Bigleux - I mean that Bigleux was your only real companion while you [the boy] were hiding out on the farm in France during the war - not quite the same but anyway - I'll send the piece on so you can read it -

Concerning that story about Levinas and the dog in a concentration camp - I am cynical enough to think that rather than becoming a friend to the dog the guy would have eaten the dog

The reason I didn't eat the dog in my novel [or at the time] is because we had plenty of food on the farm - otherwise Bigleux would have been cooked - and beside I was the dog

Also yesterday you didn't answer my question about E's story - I mean what happened to her when her family fled from Vienna to London - then while crossing from London to the States - their boat was torpedoed - I know you told me the story once before - but I cannot find it - no rush - but I wanted to remember it - the story I mean -

On a separate note - well in relation to E's story - I was thinking of a programme I saw recently about a ship full of children who were sent from London to America during the war - like E they were also sent across the Atlantic to supposedly keep them safe from the heavy bombing that was tearing London apart - but on their journey a German U-boat torpedoed the ship and it sunk and many died - They interviewed some of the survivors - one poignant story of a girl who was left floating and adrift for many hours and her mother said to her … *Let's go to sleep now shall we … Let's just get under the water and go to sleep* - To which the girl shouted *NO* and made her mother stay clinging to some flotsam that was keeping them afloat - her sister was missing but they later survived and were reunited - Another story of a small boy who was given his brother's life jacket - as in all the commotion he'd forgotten his - His brother then became separated from him in the panic and swell of people pushing to get to lifeboats and he never found his brother - Years later - at a reunion - he discovered that his brother had made it to a rescue boat but had soon died of hypothermia and they'd buried him at sea -

Yes this is E's story - more or less - there were so many stories like that - so many boats that sunk with children and so many boats with children which never left - my boat never left - remember - it's in *Return To Manure*

But these stories are soon to be forgotten - other children are dying or barely surviving in every corner of the world and maybe someday somebody will write about them -

Look how sentimental you just made me - me the happy cynic

It's amazing that you are going to Minsk -

yes - I cannot believe we are going to Minsk - that we have at last made the decision to go - It is hard to know how to feel - Trying to pack - it's going to be hot there - and the day after we visit the site in Maly Trostenets will be a year to the day we went to Poland [and of course the day you were pushed into the Closet by your mother] - that was another unplanned turn of events - a coincidence we didn't plan - En is home early - got to dash - have to dye my hair to prepare for Minsk - again I find myself considering what do you wear to a forest - what colour hair for such a journey

Ax

Yes - what colour?

Mxxx

From: Bella Rozansky <bellzansky@list.ru>
Date: TUES, 12 Jul 2005 18:41:46 +0400
To: <angelamorgancutler@ntlworld.com>
Subject: meeting on Friday in Minsk.

Dear Angela! How are you?
Hope everything is O.K. and am looking forward to meeting you on Friday morning at your hotel. I Don't know how much you know about the camp and the forest where En's grandparents died, I gather that Yossi sent the website so you should have had that information.

I am also sending you the preface to the book, well a section of it, called "On fortunes' crossroads" written by Raisa Chernoglazova, a historian.

The book is the collected stories of the former prisoners of the Minsk Ghetto and Nazi concentration camps. If I have time before you arrive I will try and translate a little more and bring some of the stories with me when I take you to the camp and the forest for the day.
O.K.?

My best regards to you and to En and I will show you everything I can. Best wishes. Bella

By Raisa Chernoglazova: Genocide ... Holocaust ... Ghetto ...

The tragedy of the Jews of Minsk started on June 28, 1941 when Germans troops occupied the city. All men from the ages of 18 to 45 were imprisoned in Camp Drozdy, a suburb of Minsk. Following the separation of the Jews from the other captives was only the starting point in the complete extermination of this nation. Those who survived became hostages in the city prison for a contribution of "thirty thousand golden rubles".

Beginning July 20th till August 1st there was the great migration in Minsk. From all parts of Minsk and its suburbs Jewish families were forced to move to a specially allocated north-west district of the city. In this way the Minsk ghetto was formed. It was created with the purpose to make it more convenient to kill its inhabitants. Eighty thousand Jews (fifty-five thousand from Minsk) became imprisoned behind the barbed wire. There they lived months, weeks, but sometimes only days. The Minsk ghetto survived five large pogroms (destructive actions). During these pogroms most of these prisoners were killed. The first pogrom happened on November 7th, 1941. And though it had been rumoured, the planned carnage took people unexpectedly. At 4 A.M. the inhabitants of Nemiga and Hlebnaya streets and some parts of Respublikanskaya and Ostrovskogo streets were thrown out of their houses by the armed Nazis' and police. These people were taken by cars to Tuchinka in the region of Opanskaya street. Seventeen thousand people were killed there. Only those who had a working certificate survived. Though it was only a temporary delay of their inevitable death. The freed houses were enclosed with barbed wire. New prisoners, the Jews deported from the German city Hamburg settled there. Thus a special ghetto called Zonderghetto appeared in Minsk. During the War more than thirty thousand Jews from Germany, Poland, Czechoslovakia were deported to the Minsk ghetto. There they had only one future, this future was death. In two weeks after the first pogrom the second pogrom took ten thousand of human lives. At daybreak on November 20th long columns of people were moving towards Tuchinka. There they were met by submachine-gunners near pits, which had been prepared in advance.

The third pogrom on March 2, 1942 reduced the number of the ghetto prisoners by six thousand people. Some of them were killed in the ghetto near Drozdy village not far from Minsk; others were killed in the Koidanovo district. The

*forth pogrom, the most bloody, lasted four days beginning the 28th of June
1942. Unprotected people were taken to Blagovshchina near Maly Trostenets
village to mobile gas chambers and put to death.
The existence of Minsk ghetto was coming to its end. Dozens, hundreds,
thousands of people were killed not only during the pogroms but also during
daily destructive actions. The fifth pogrom, which took place on October 23,
1943 put an end to the existence of Minsk ghetto. Only a few people survived
in caves and shelters.*

From: <angelamorgancutler@ntlworld.com>
Date: Tue, 12 Jul 2005 22:08:15 +0100
To: Bella Rozansky <bellzansky@list.ru>
Subject: Re: meeting on Friday in Minsk

Dear Bella,
Thank you so much. I was only thinking of you today and yes we are
also looking forward to meeting you. Thank you for all the information
you and Yossi sent, we did have some papers some time back but not as
detailed as the website Yossi sent to us. Thank you also for going to
the trouble of translating part of Rosa Chernoglazova's book for me.
Who is or was she? Well I mean do you know her? Is she / was she from
Minsk? How and when did she gather the stories? Oh listen to me - I am
ahead of myself, I will ask you all this when we meet up very soon.
Many thanks again and we will ring you when we arrive.

Best, Angela

From: <angelamorgancutler@ntlworld.com>
Date: Mon, 11 Jul 2005 10:46:21
To: Claire Hafeec <clairehafeec@yahoo.com>
CC: Sarah wild<wild@sarah-wild.com>
Subject: Who am I writing to?

Claire - Oops. I misread and see that you meant you read it 3 times not
I sent it 3 times -

I will keep re-reading your thoughts about who this absent other is
that I speak to here - outside of the players of the book as you say
- Moinous - En and Sarah and others like yourself - Claire - and your
brief appearance here - are of course named throughout this book,
clearly addressed and in dialogue with me, but outside of the obvious
e-mail correspondence addressed directly TO ... who is it that I think
I am talking to? *Who is out there?* As someone indeed asked me the other
day - *Who is it you are addressing with your befores and afters* ... And
I found myself floundering, asking ... Should I know? Could I know? ...
And yes - isn't that something we all have to trust in when we write,
believe that there is indeed someone out there listening - [posit a
listener - J said - whatever you do] - But who? - this *no one specified*
... A moment's doubt which in many ways reflected the absence I felt when
we went to Auschwitz [or for example, when we were searching for Ella's
house - the house we never found in Budapest] as it was the people I
missed at Auschwitz [without wanting to sound senti/mental here but how

to avoid this inside such a subject] and maybe the writing grew out of talking to their / that absence and at the same time saying no more than: *I came … I am here … I am looking … I found* [no/thing / no/one] *… I am inventing … attempting … writing*

Thanks for being one great friendly ear - or between you - a complete pair -

I too am the worse kind of listener -

I will write to you from Minsk or from Rusher as Max calls it.

Axxx

From: Claire Hafeec <clairehafeec@yahoo.com>
Date: Mon, 11 Jul 2005 09:21:36 - 0700 (PDT)
To: <angelamorgancutler@ntlworld.com>
Subject: Re: Who are you speaking to?

Dear A,

Yes! I meant I read the writing you sent to me three times!
And: yes!. Your question: Who am I speaking to, when I write? Who am I addressing? Yes, Who are you speaking to? And who am I speaking to? It suddenly sounds so deeply absurd that we have a lot of words, and we'll be all right just as soon as we figure out who we're speaking to. It's frightening really. And now I want to laugh. Do you want to? To hug you and to laugh at the thought that when we write we don't have a fucking clue who we are addressing really, as if that's the tricky little bit to do away with and THEN the work begins. Which is so perfect. I'd like to know, but will I ever? Isn't the whole endeavour of writing trying to figure that out?

I read an obituary in the NY Times about Claude Simon, writer, who dies at 91 and said some good things about the new form he was trying to create. First he describes himself as such: "I am a difficult, boring, unreadable, confused writer", taking a cue from his critics. He then objects to the writer's role as a "kind of decoding machine". His form of disorderly writing in an accumulation of words, descriptions, impressions and fragments, says the article, is closer to life. And he won a bloody Nobel Prize. He cites Tolstoy: "A man in good health is all the time thinking and feeling and recalling an incalculable number of things at once."

How about a woman in iffy health? How many things can she be thinking, feeling and recalling at once? One can only imagine.

Anyway, I don't mean to take up so much room, but in exchange for what you sent I will send a few short pieces I have worked on. Some memories. Why they are selected, I can't defend. I am a difficult, boring, unreadable, confused writer.

much love, Claire

Dear one,

After a really quick read through, my first thought is actually an image, and that is of Nietzsche's giant ear attached to the tiny man 'a bloated little soul' dangling from that stalk

I just grabbed a quick look at Derrida's 'ear of the other' to see if Nietzsche's ear is there and of course it is (it was Ronell that described this ear so graphically that made me think of it, it's no surprize) how the Nazi regime used Nietzsche's name in their propaganda, etc. They were listening to him, but were they the wrong listeners, the unintended with the perverse ears of mishearing.

So when you mention 'who' here, I don't even think of a name as an addressee but as a faculty, as a thing, a hole for incomings. No name but a graphic image of a ear.

But then there are different kinds of ears, they are not free floating but attached, Derrida mentions the umbilical cord that ties some kinds of ear to "the paternal belly of the state" to different institutions, agendas, where speaking and hearing and maybe writing forms a learning machine, or a propaganda machine, or your fear: a censorship machine. Chances are this is the not the ear you are writing too but they might be listening unwillingly.

So maybe what I am thinking is the question of: not whom are you talking to but what and what kind of listening is occurring, which doesn't mean they have no name but maybe many ears

yes my instinct also says go with the unnamed ears.

Maybe what and how you are saying points to ears that we can sense are differing and our struggling to sense what kind of ears those are is the lot of the living even if its a quiet life we nonchalantly prefer the proverbial 'what are you listening to'. We seem to opt for easy listening most of the time, consciously unconsciously casting out the static that maybe has more to say.

If you knew the WHO this is, would you be writing this? Such a knowledge might be not a knowing but something else.
But maybe I am confused by what you asked - sometimes my listening is so bad.
Things here are going ok, well this hour anyway, had a crazy weekend with Duchamp's urinal, ha the bathroom is back again ...

hope yours is still joyous

Yes, write to me from Minsk

lovings
Sarah
X

Maly Trostenets Camp - Minsk

I'm waiting in the hotel lobby, waiting for Bella to arrive, an old man has now settled himself beside me to my left. En has wandered off for a moment, and in his absence, an old man beckons with his crooked finger, with the dark hair on his hands, beckons me to come close. He's trying to sell me large coins with Lenin on the front. I shake my head, but still he continues, entices me to sit nearer to him. He pats the chair between us ... Come ... he says ... Come. In my oversized leather armchair, I take a handful of green leather and squish it as he is forced to say, Look, Russian money, Lenin, You interested ... He is forced to answer his own question ... I smile too much as if it's my fault that I do not want his coins and have no interest in his monumental history nor any wish to sit beside him, as if I couldn't satisfy him with the British coins he's asks for, in exchange, just a £ to make an old man happy. I try to avoid his repetition, his body moving closer, his unshaved face, his watery eyes and especially his hand held out, turning over old money, I busy myself by writing in my notebook ...

Minsk has lived up to its expectations of strangeness, ugliness, starkness. I don't know what we are doing here, except of course we are here and of course we know what our doing here is ... It's not a place we should ever fall in love with, yet is this the fault of the place ...

The furniture in every part of the hotel has small red codes painted on the side, the table between me and the man selling coins reads: FX 1210.

I find the website pages Yossi had sent us before we'd left, folded up in the back of my book with some papers that Anne, En's sister, had copied from the last trip she took with Elise to Vienna. Anne's writing is comforting in its familiarity, in its flourish and the slant of her hand beside the more official Austrian forms which read: *Engelhart Ella: Weiss. Wien 1, Fleischmarkt 20. Budapest, Urgarn. 03 02 1896 Maly Trostinec. 20.05.42. Deportationskartei IKG Amstsblatt. ID 29225. Gatte Wilhelm - dep. T. Tot mit Bestatigung. Engelhart Wilhelm. Wien 1, Fleischmarkt 20. Kolbuszowa Poland. 21.10.1885. Maly Trostenic 20.05.42. Deportationskartei IKG Amstsblatt. ID 29226. Gatte Ella geb. Weiss-dep. memo T209/61 T. Ghetto address - blank. T.* Above *Tot mit Bestatigung,* someone has translated: *Confirmed to be dead.*

The man beside me now seems suddenly resigned to our silence, to the small gap between us; he looks over with an attentiveness that begins to seem almost tender as I continue with my small notes, flicking through the papers we were given. As the man and I give ourselves over to the other's proximity, no longer wanting nor expecting anything other than this mutual sharing of a moment of waiting, of remembering now the comfort to be found in the other's steady breath, to enjoy the way our feet spread out over the floor, the way his foot randomly taps without him seeming to know the tune, the way our eyes search, follow and lose the other and the movements of all who pass before us, with nothing in particular to look at, just the attention of being together and looking. I am an attention. Clarice Lispector wrote, *I am a woman, I am a person, I am an*

attention. I am a body looking out through the window. Just as the rain is not grateful
for not being a stone. It is rain. Perhaps it is this that might be called being alive. No
more than this, but this: alive. And alive just through gentle gladness.

Before we left to come here, Anne, En's sister, was in my garden. We're in the
sun, under the vine; rather, we are together under the vine, but together on the
telephone, faces brought close via our voices and ears opening to a memory -
that she recalls dreaming of them often - Ella and Wilhelm, that is - she used
to dream that they'd appear in her parents driveway and they'd just stand there
looking at her until she'd take them inside. Always she had the job of taking
them inside, of reuniting them with Elise. Each time they'd move house - and
they did so fourteen times - she'd decide what to hide, where to hide; she says
she spent her childhood hiding things in her room, and deciding where she'd
hide *herself*. Yes, in each new house she would find a new hiding place and think
about what she would have taken in her suitcase if circumstances were different.

Do you think they would have loved me, Max'd said, before we left - he was
in the bath, his hair white with too much shampoo. His question startled me,
in, as he'd say, its randomness, in that we had only minutes before been talking
about treatment for athlete's foot! *If they would have known me - I mean, Ella and*
Wilhelm - would they have loved me as I am? I mean, would they have understood
my ways ... Maybe they'd be too old-fashioned in their thinking to love me as I am ...

I am nervous that I won't feel anything this morning, when we meet Bella -
that the day will bring nothing. How to feel anything in a wood that is so like
any other - surely a wood is a wood is a wood. I hope Bella is someone we can be
comfortable with: it feels like such a personal trip. At first there is just the heat
of arrival, of last night, the views of oppressive concrete blocks and the blackness
of the river. Somewhere in the distance the two people we have come to meet -
no, rather, pay our respects to, Ella and Wilhelm - and I had not really thought
of the words before - pay our respects. I look it up in my portable dictionary; it
says, *make a polite visit to*. Polite!

What else? says the man who drove us here, the taxi driver older than retired,
driving faster than retired, shouting, Bombs, bombs. Making explosions with his
hand leaving the wheel, making reference to all the recent terrorist explosions
at home. We have no terrorism here, he said, Like your London bus ... He
turns up the radio so we can hear the news. No boom boom here he says. No,
here is safe, nothing happens here. And I think of his words and the reason for
our being here and I smile to myself and stare across the fields and into more
woods, We are famous for our woods, he says proudly, as if reading my thoughts:
famous. And I think about telling him our reason for being here, and cannot, for
what is it to him - what could he say to such an emotive announcement, this old
man, this stranger - and what does he remember that I can't bring myself to ask
... Where are they? This wood or that wood?

And I think about getting them back, Ella and Wilhelm, that evening. Our
first evening in Minsk, I am looking across the dark river and into the forest and

I have such an urge to go find them, to go bring them back, those two; and I find myself too embarrassed to share this with En, but saying it all the same, just quietly to myself: I am coming to see you - which of course we are not; not going to find you, not really - but this is what I say quietly to them, into the distance, into the darkness. We are coming tomorrow; we are here.

And I find myself waiting in the hotel lobby, writing in my small notebook ... Bella. I am waiting for Bella ... What if, after all, she turns out to be humourless, an air-head, a bore, a ... And then a woman enters ... I'll try to describe her briefly - as brief as she is in her entrance and in her height, as there is no amount of description that ever gets close to describing anything - of people especially. Nothing of any use in me mentioning her long blonde hair tied high in a tail, her casual dress: jeans and a striped T-shirt, her possible fifty years of age, the warmth I see in her face. Nothing of this that will give anyone, including me, a clue as to why I think this must be her, why I want it to be her, Bella. But as she chats and laughs so easily with the receptionist and does not look around for anyone, I decide that it cannot be her. I feel foolish enough sitting here waiting for a stranger, for someone suitable to spend the day with, this strange enough day in the woods to come. And my pen wanders and I quickly let go of her and wait, wait and forget her, write and forget, write again, write something ...

We are waiting for Bella, who told us yesterday on the phone that the forest currently looks like a construction site, that the roads are bad, that the heat is a stinking eighty-one degrees. Again: what to wear to a grave site? ... I can't stand the thought of them lost in this ground ... Anthleme's marvellous passage about waiting at the door ... I mean, in his book he said the Nazis didn't see them - the captured - as people. They were nobodies, faceless non-beings; not-people being waited for, not-people being missed, not-people waiting to be hugged, not-people to be kissed, to be greeted, to be imagined; not-people with front doors with homes and others waiting for them behind those front doors ... Something like that, I should have to remind myself ...

Shouldn't I be writing of the river, of the fishermen with bells on their lines, the ones we saw this morning as we walked, En and I, along the riverbank at sun-up, wandering around the river of a strange country, waiting for Bella ... saying to one another, A grave is not the same as a murder site. Bella asking on the phone, How sensitive are you, what do you want to know about what happened here? We know what happened here, En says.

I try to return to my reading, to focus on the papers Yossi had sent, that we had gathered together hurriedly before we left for Minsk, reading, but not properly concentrating, reading that only ever seems to lead to more forgetting than remembering, reading more for something to do while the old man and I sit and wait a while together one beside the other ...

*In November 1941, the Minsk Security Police and the SD (Sicherheitsdienst) established a new camp at the former kolchos (collective farm, 200 hectares / 500 acres) "Karl Marx" in the village of Maly Trostinec, **12 km southeast** of **Minsk** and 1 km south of **Bolshoi Trostinec** village. The camp site had been selected in September 1941. It measured approximately 200 x 200 m / 4 hectares.*

Initially the camp was intended to supply the local Nazi forces with food. In addition, a mill, sawmill, locksmith's shop, joinery, tailoring, shoemakers, asphalt works and other workshops were built. Jews and Soviet POWs built barracks for around six hundred mainly Jewish slave labourers and their guards.

The prisoners selected for work in the camp were kept at first in a large barn and in 20 cellars, which were formerly used by the local farmers for cooling potatoes, vegetables and meat. Later, they were housed in damp barracks, where bunks were constructed from thick unshaved wooden planks in three tiers. There was no bedding or mattresses; the people slept on straw.

From March 1942, the camp was surrounded by a threefold barbed wire fence (the middle one electrified), and wooden lookout towers were erected at the corners of the perimeter, which was guarded 24 hours a day. A guardroom was located close to the entrance to the camp, and a gallows was erected. In mid-March 1942, partisans attacked the camp and killed the guards; therefore the Germans increased the total number of guards to 250, encircled each barrack with a barbed wire fence, posted additional guards around the barracks, installed runways for dogs, and placed machine-gun nests around the entire site. A subterranean bunker was built, with a tank standing atop it. Those people who were to be liquidated the next day were held in the bunker.

The 250 men of the camp staff were free to beat, shoot or hang any prisoner without any further authority.

Knowledge of the killings in the East became known as early as 18th of July 1941.

Wilhelm Kube was the head of White Ruthenia, the area under which Minsk fell.

There are photographs of Kube in his immaculate uniform, some with his wife in her fur coat. He looks more handsome with his hat on, she looks more elegant when she doesn't smile. On each photograph there's a fat man in a uniform beside Kube. He is referred to affectionately as *The Fat Man*. He has the appearance of a Daruma doll; you can almost hear the tinkling in his guts as Kube pushes him into motion with the next trite remark. Kube's wife is thin and wears pearls.

There's a photograph of Himmler's visit to Minsk, of Himmler laughing, waiting to witness an execution, the small arrangement of wooden unfolded chairs as if they were waiting for band practice; the lines of people beside them in an orderly queue, stare out, no doubt waiting their turn to be shot. There are photographs of the daily hangings that took place in Minsk during the occupation, people hang like dolls from the city trees, some as young as ten or twelve, some almost look as if they have fallen asleep, still in their clothes, one shoe on, one shoe lost to the ground; one man almost flies from the tree like a figure of Christ ascending. Some carry small signs around their neck. I almost find myself showing the papers to the old man beside me, almost instinctively want to say to him: *Look at this.* I wonder is he curious to know what I'm holding to my face. I decide against passing any more than a glance in his direction, against the effort of a text written in a language he can't read, apart from maybe the photographs and the obvious loaded Nazi insignia that would be read only too easily, and then what of the hanging children - then what would I say, with only a repertoire of well-meaning smiles, grimaces and hand gestures that would surely go nowhere near to explaining my reason for being in possession of these images.

In 1921 Byelorussia was divided, with the western area becoming part of Poland. The eastern area became a republic of the Soviet Union, with Minsk as its capital. During the ninetieth century, Minsk had become one of the most important Jewish communities in Russia. In 1926, it had a Jewish population of 53,700, increasing during 1939 to 90,000 as people fled occupied areas of Poland. In the ghetto that was later formed, the population rose to 100,000. The camp in Maly Trostinec, 12 km east of Minsk, opened in May 1942, for the purpose of extermination.

*Execution Site Blagovshchina ***

And as I stare hard into the photograph of the Blagovshchina wood, a small grainy photograph that tells me very little, that looks like nothing more than a small worn track through some uninspiring trees, there she is over me, taking my hand, her pastel-pink lipstick spread into a smile, her sharp green eyes, strands of her white blonde hair escape everywhere, and it's her, it is the one I'd wanted as soon as I saw her enter the lobby. Just as soon as she was forgotten she arrives again, with that look that strangers, who you know will become friends, always have, that look of *where have you been* about them, a flush and exuberance of greeting, an acknowledged recognition that will pull us into a hug that will violently part the stillness, a hello that will not allow for a moment's good-bye between the old man and me, and of *course* it's you, Bella.

It's maybe idleness that for now prevents me from continuing with our journey to the camp, the journey we took in Bella's small red car. All I can say is that for someone who does not believe in endings, here I am contemplating something of this end; the approach of an ending where I had begun with nothing more than an empty notebook, somehow words accumulate and pile up and there the book forms itself off the page. What was not expected - the cow, or was it cows, plural. Yes this is how it was, I set off to write about the camp and for days the cow appeared and I denied it. I said: enough of this animal behaviour. I want no metaphors, no symbolism and I crossed out the cow, beat the cow into another field, but still it ambled back, yes, when I turned it returned; when I made up my mind I wouldn't speak to or of the cow, another came by and looked at me with those *are you sure now* eyes until the words like the fields, like the woods of Maly Trostenets, were simply overrun with cows.

And prior to this, for weeks before Minsk, there was that old bovine squarely in my dreams, no denying it, when I was turning over the other cheek, there they were in my night's sleep, intoxicated, drunk cows, yes, pissed as farts, their necks extended, their legs usually set so steadfast, so earnest, now only fit for staggering the fields, heads held to the night air, damp snouts, almost vomiting on the night, baying at the moon and mooing so endlessly that I had to hold my ears to my head to shut out the din and when I woke, yes, when I woke to the urgency of what they wanted to tell me, I was wearing my hands like muffs.

All I can say is: we are under a pine tree at Maly Trostenets watching the cows. Yes, we are at the site of the concentration camp that was, where the cows keep vigil over this story. Where here at Minsk the cows present themselves especially well, in so many particular formations in the fields and I say nothing to them, I stand and stare, do nothing and they understand, they walk along the brook, the cows lead me carefully through water, gently, gentle girls, as if to say: how many more scenes can I give you before you'll begin again, how many more ways can I position myself for you to go on?

Maly Trostenets. Where I had not expected this scene, only a sun-filled vista, almost a painting, stretches of empty green fields, everything tidied away beneath the lush grass and flowers caught in sun, the elegant poplars, the small brook, almost quaint, the tiny wooden foot bridge in the distance, even a cockerel coughing up the wrong hour, but greeting us all the same as we arrive at what's left, which is to say: nothing, only fields now edging the village that surrounds this site, that stood by, before the camp after the camp that is no more, and what did I think I'd see, nothing left but cows: lying down in the heat, cows no doubt on heat; cows standing, cows by the bellyful, cows so full of milk and ready for child and meat that falls off the bone; yes, just the cows, the fields, En, Bella and me.

Here is the spot, right here, Bella says: yes, here is the spot, the chosen spot where the camp was built and since destroyed at Minsk. And who was it that passed by here and said *Yes* to this, who was it that first heard the words *Maly Trostenets* uttered from a stranger's mouth, who in turn uttered it into a stranger's ear, wrote it down, misspelled it, maybe even mispronounced it, wrote it on the back of their hand, no better than a forgetful child; whose fingers carefully traced the words *Maly Trostenets* on a map; who was it who drove here sixty years back and said *Yes* to this brook, to this pasture; who had an eye for this scene this particular time of day this light. Something of the patient cows touching something so wanting in the one looking. The cows so set in their ways they surely looked no better, no less ample and appealing sixty years ago; cows that could not be told apart by a layman's eye, the cows who for sure chewed their way through the decisions being made by the eye upon them, the cows who averted their eyes, turned their arse to the one saying YES to this exact spot, to a decision to choose this place for killing: *Maly Trostenets.*

To reach the site of the camp, now just empty fields, you have to pass by the edge of the village that was always here; you also have to pass by the villagers' graveyard; while those incarcerated here, those denied a proper burial, denied graves, found - *as if they could* - their ashes randomly scattered - *as if to rub-it-in* - beside the locals' graves housed in substantial metal cribs, little wooden stools dotted here and there where no doubt, loved ones come and sit awhile, convey their longings and dreams, leave behind their vivid recycled stories mixed always with the smell of golden chrysanthemums that filled our eyes and our entrance here: remember that the flower, so popular for the dead, begins with a cry and ends in mum, death ends in small cots that return you to birth. Death ends in ashes scattered across these fields.

Bella is telling us, When the camp was here and in use, there were different workshops. Some made shoes, others asphalt, various things. But the camp existed for the purpose of killing, after taking what possessions people had, each day they'd take five hundred people to what they called the Shed, where they would kill and cremate them. She repeats again, that the ashes from this Shed, were then brought back here and scattered. The site of the Shed, is on the other side of these fields, where Bella had taken us first thing. Through the Shaskowa forest, she's saying, over there where we began this morning with the small memorial edging the wood, but nowhere on any of the memorials is there any mention of the Jews, only of the Russians and political prisoners and the partisans that were killed. She's saying, The murders were committed by shooting, and later - but that would have been after your grandparents came here - gas vans were also used. The SS would meet the trains arriving at the goods station in Minsk. The people who'd been deported had been told they were to be re-housed in estates around Minsk, but before this took place they were to leave their suitcases that would be forwarded by trucks. They also had to leave their ID cards and money and valuables, for which they were given receipts. A small number were selected to work at the camp or in the *Sonderkommandos* - special detachments. In May 1942, when your grandparents came here, she says to En, they would have been taken in trucks directly to the execution site at the Blagovshchina forest, where we will go next. Before they were killed they would have had to undress and march to the 60m long and 3m deep pits, where they were shot by the SiPo and SD men. Special groups of Russian labour workers had to dig out the pits, which in winter were created by using dynamite. After the shootings the Russians had to cover the bodies with earth, using bulldozers or tractors to finally level the pits. To cover the shots they played music from a gramophone amplified by a loudspeaker. The shootings were done early in the morning between 4-5 a.m. on Tuesdays and Fridays. I remember reading this much before we came here, working out that their deportation took place on the 20th of May '42, which was a Wednesday; after a six-day train journey from Vienna to Minsk they were killed on the 26th, which was indeed the following Tuesday.

And I find myself repeating the name of the camp quietly to myself, wandering a little to look into the face of a cow, simple, to approach quietly now so as not to startle her, to look with the look of a cow with a question mark of a face that unsettles the one looking and being looked at, to stand on my locked legs in front of a cow with its face asking: WHAT do you want me to say or to tell you; what do you expect me to know? Questions that cause me to stare back dumbly enough; that only lead me back to the silence of the place, of her face on me; to the nothing to be found here; only questions that in turn keep undoing and repeating and turning in on themselves; questions incessantly drawn out in the cow's expression and stance and udders in each methodical chew, in the promise of milk, in my elongated head reflected back from her oversized eye twisted on me, in all that can never be known or undone here: *Maly Trostenets*.

What was not expected here: the cow shit mixed up with the human, the site scattered with used beer bottles and small groups of men half-pissed sitting in the grass playing cards. And what was not expected, had I not seen in a dream? - those very cows and men all mixed together intoxicated on their own milk, intoxicated, yes, spell it out, they were drunk, I tell you, the dream I had before my visit here came back to me while Bella is telling us that she came here yesterday, You know, with a friend, she says, to the site, this one, and to the forest where I will soon take you … I was unsure of the roads, with all the construction that is happening near the forest, I was worried for us, well, how we'd get through the roads under such conditions, so I took a friend, she says, a friend who had never been to the site before, who knew little of it and I rehearsed the whole story to her yesterday. I am touched that Bella not only did this, but that she admits to living today out twice, that ahead of us, in our absence she felt the need to rehearse, to get it right for us. That while she'd driven us to the camp this morning, to the fields of Maly Trostenets and the Blagovshchina forest, she'd told us story after story. I am trying to remember everything she says, everything she is trying to remember but there are so many details that will be lost. In her small red car on the way to these fields, there's her story, there's her mother's story, her aunt's story; her daughter's story: Bella's father was a soldier. He was captured in Italy, and her mother stayed in Minsk with their two young sons. The father was injured and couldn't get home. When the Nazis marched into Minsk, her mother fled with the children to her brother's home in Moscow. Her mother's sister, Bella's aunt, refused to go; she stayed and became a partisan, her neighbour betraying her. Her aunt and Bella's young cousin were taken and shot in the street. Bella's mother was reunited with her father in Moscow. During the war, Bella was conceived. Her mother returned to Minsk many years later, and only then found out what happened to her sister. When Bella had a daughter, she named her after her aunt's child: Eurina. There's the story of two lovers: a German soldier who fell in love with a Jew, who saved a whole village; there's the story of a distraught woman in a near by village telling Bella that she will surely go to hell for snatching the shoes of a Jewish girl [taken with her family and friends, lined up to be shot, the child undressing, preparing to die]; this woman, then a small girl herself, watches the Jewish girl undress as instructed, watches her neighbour's careful gesture of placing the shoes neatly on the ground beside her. Let's say the shoes were shiny, if not new, they'd been polished that morning; let's remember it was only a short sprint the other made toward the no-longer-needed shoes, saying, You won't be needing these any more. How it forever played on the woman's mind, Bella said. Especially her words to the girl, the shoes she kept. Can you believe it, for all those years; as much as she wanted to dispose of them, she felt too guilty to throw them away. There's the story of the Jewish orphans who were shot. Just behind your hotel, Bella says, there's a new memorial - and it turns out that the site of our hotel was the ghetto. It makes me smile that we end up, without knowing it, in what was the ghetto, that we eat our first meal, without knowing, in a building that had once been the school for rabbis: the Yeshivah - she tells us, The children were taken one day in March 1942 from the orphanage into a square and shot, including the people who cared for them. No-one knows what happened to their bodies, where they were taken and burnt. A few people escaped, and after the war seven of these survivors came back and they placed a tiny monument there for the children, and each year they would meet there on March the 2nd, the day of the shootings, the seven people would come back to the spot where the executions took place; they would gather there on that same day, and also on labour days. And they wanted to do this quietly, Bella says, but the government on labour days would play exuberant nationalistic marches through loudspeakers all through the streets and there was no place to be quiet with their thoughts, so the survivors complained about the music but only five years back did they erect a proper monument and agree to stop the noise.

Each time we move from site to site in her red car, Bella tells me to wind down the window as she has no air-conditioning, and that to close the door I have to slam it hard. After five or so goes I get confident enough, want to please her enough to slam it as forcefully as I can. I give myself over to her; allow her to parent us, even though I believe she has no obligation to us, even though En and I had agreed we'd wanted to be alone when we got to the forest, even though I think Bella is being over-cautious, and I cannot see the harm a few drunk men will do us, I see myself nodding, complying, feeling moved by her concern for us, when she says, I want you to understand that I will not be leaving you alone, it's not safe. I know you want to be alone, to be private, especially when you go to the forest, she says, it's not that I don't know that, but when we go there, you are my responsibility and you need to understand that I want nothing to happen to you, that it's not safe for two foreigners who can't speak a word of Russian to be out here wandering around on their own, with all these intoxicated men everywhere. I will make myself discreet, she insists, but I will not let you out of my sight.

Maly Trostenets: what was not expected. The cow's shit mixed up with the human shit. None of us speaks of this mix as we pick our way along a path, through the fields into the path of tall shady poplar trees. As we approach each human patch the flies scatter, so too the blue flies in their blue cow pats, knowing how to glory in the real daily business, irritated by our parting them from what they have always unashamedly called home. None of us will mention the flies as we pick our way: in we go. On the edges we were happy to say, Look Cows, Look grass, each flower named. Look at the small memorial, like the one we found this morning, each surrounded by fake and real flowers. Look at what we stand in front of, stare hard, not knowing what to say about the fading florescent petals. What we'll photograph ... The tethered goats near by. Their pleasing skin, we'll say so as we cautiously approach, try not to startle them, Look. But none of us will say, speak of, photograph, stare at, neither point at or call out, Look! - everywhere, human shit. Only months later I will ask Moinous, Shall I mention the human shit at the camp? and he'll say, Of course. What else to find there but the shit all covered in shit, the shit all covering over the shit of what took place here.

What was covered over: obvious enough - grass, and the cows acting as if everything went on as usual, the normal animal business of chewing the cud and evacuation each day. Finally it's a homeless destitute place, finally everything's been hidden beneath the earth, no sign of anything, no remnants of any buildings, no-one lingers here except the outcast; here where it is safe to sleep in the grass to drink yourself into oblivion to shit before breakfast and what is breakfast here, more liquid. Let's begin again, say again, what is any longer normal in this chosen place in this place where the men drink their morning vodka and lie half-naked in the grass with their stained hearts and kings fanned before them; where the cows keep their eyes close to the grass; where the goats bleat and are the colour - and no doubt have the feel - of the skin of my suede notebook. I touch skin, I want to touch them or did I slip up on a word and write: *punch*, to pull at their flesh and teats, to say: Take this at the end of a name, Take this body which is broken for you, Take the milk from you, Take my stare from you, as there is really nothing left to look at or to do here but approach the cows and goats who graze, gaze, to ask ... What do you know of what you touch here as you put your full weight, heart, tongue, nose, eye, even each newborn, so close to this ground; grass, weed and brook. Look ...

En has his arm in the brook. He's lying on a few planks made into a bridge. It is hard to know if this crossing has always been here, looked this way from the day someone on his knees, placed down these pieces of wood. En, now on his stomach on the half-rotten wood we'd just teetered across, lying spread out over the footbridge up to his elbow in bright green scum. Bella is shouting, What's he doing. Looking for stones, I say. She screws up her face ... A stone ... En says ... for my mother. Together we watch him move his hand around, lose his arm to the muck-filled water. Two women, we worry he will cut himself, we tell him, Come on, there's nothing in there; we tell him, That's enough; we tell him, It's filthy in there; we stand over him, watching him swill his arm this way and that, when he pulls his arm to the surface, plunges it back, we call: What … what. When he is upright again, we tend to him without agreement or discussion, we simply work together wiping his arm dry on some rags, dust down his clothes, look at each other as we take our turns to rearrange him, raise our brows as he repeats that he found nothing but thick sediment beneath the water. Nothing here but grass and trees and shit enough, goats silent bellies pressed to the ground, only the men over there, no-one else here but the men drinking, sleeping, falling. Bella calls out to one of them, a man staggering around; he's in an old crumpled suit, he's crossing a chosen path. Passing one another, we exchange looks. He says - she translates - The only woman from the village who could have talked to us, who was old enough to remember the camp, recently died just a few months back. He points out her house. *Over there.* We all turn and look along the extension of his trembling arm to the empty wooden house. The villagers, Bella says, were frightened for their lives. They were shit [look at that, shot coming out as shit, shot as shit, each time I try and write it] yes, if they came to their windows they'd be shot, Bella says, They learned to keep away from their curtains, but for sure they heard the screams.

Now, there's nothing here to mark the spot but another small memorial, the plastic flowers mixed up with the real, the marigolds mixed up with, among other things, the plastic purple and gaudy pink lilies sprouting blue stamens, all of it sticking from the ground, all of it fenced in and gated, small demarcations and borders watered in by the Council. The fat council boy who arrives on time with his big-bellied water tank, while Bella shouts at him about the mess, he pulls the hose through the cab window, refuses to leave the wheel while he gestures to her and to water the ground. He waters lethargically between smokes and turning the newspaper. A young woman arrives some minutes later, plastic bag in hand, filling it with the strewn beer bottles that litter the memorial site. She reassures Bella, who is telling her, The memorial should be cared for better than this. Clean up or these people will go home with the wrong impression … What'll they think, she says, translating everything to us while she begins to help put the beer and vodka bottles, rattling, into the sack. The young woman doesn't say too much but relieves the man of his hose and properly waters the flowers he has missed. We continue between the trees, knowing now that we are soon to leave here. The shit hidden in the path of trees; again, I write so fast that shit still keeps coming out as shot, shit-shot-shit-shot maybe shit all the same. It is hard for me to remember all that Bella is saying, especially to retain the number of people who died here, while we clean off some stones and sit awhile, while I try to hang onto the figures and the dates she keeps repeating. I feel as overwhelmed as when I was six, in class, understanding nothing but the driving hum of numbers and dates and figures and history and facts and statistics I could not connect nor retain nor calculate. I feel myself dizzy with numbers and names and places, and no matter how many times she tells me, or I read it from the papers we were given, it is hard to hold on to any of it for more than a moment, each detail obliterates the last, making me feel the same shame as I did back there at school when they'd stood me on a chair for innumeracy, for forgetfulness, for misspelling:

990 Jews arrived at Minsk from Hamburg, Bella reads.
April 1942 Heydrich orders everyone be killed on arrival.
After the first phase
November 1941:16 trains with more than 15,000 people arrived from Poland, Austria, France.
Four gas vans were in operation from June 1942, a month after En's grandparents died.
Here's a picture of a lake where the vans were cleaned.
Bella holds out the photograph, so small and indistinct, I have to wear my glasses but still can't get a sense of what I am looking at. I almost slip from my stone, causing the flies to panic, turn our air blue.

The vans were known locally as 'Soul killers'.
Trainloads from Austria, the information says,
Trainloads arrived at Minsk from
Germany,
Czech Republic,
Berlin,
Hanover,
Dortmund
Münster,
Düsseldorf
Köln,
Frankfurt am Main,
Kassel,
Stuttgart,
Nürnberg,
München,
Breslau,
Königsberg,
Wien,
Praha,
Brno,
Terezin
(Theresienstadt).

First transport left Wien for Maly Trostinec on 6 May 1942, a further 8 transports containing 7,500 Viennese Jews followed, along with several hundred Austrians taken from Terezin.

Only 17 people are known to have survived.
Almost 9,000 Austrian Jews were deported to Maly Trostinec.
Between 14 July 1942 and 22 September 1942, five transports arrived, each containing about 1,000 people, arrived at Maly Trostinec from Terezin.
One of these transports left on 4 August.
40 deportees were removed from the train in Minsk.
The remaining 960 Jews were ordered off the train, loaded into gas vans and driven into the forest.

Himmler visited Minsk to witness an execution. It states that he witnessed a small number of shootings: only 100 instead of the usual 1000 per day. Himmler complained of stomach pains, almost reeling at the sight, almost falling to the ground with the shots, arguing with the firing squad that they were not shooting accurately enough, calling out that some of the people were still alive. Himmler in that same visit, allegedly getting blood and brains on his coat, which lead him to report back to his seniors that the effect on the men being asked to carry out the killings was unbearable. That the SS needed to find more 'humane methods', for the sake of their own killing squads. A report, prepared for Himmler on 23 March 1943, summarised the number of Jews deported to Minsk, up to 31 December 1942 from the Reich and the "Protectorate" area:
Germany 100,516
Austria 47,555
"Protectorate" 69,677
Total - 217,748.

Further transports from Germany in 1943.
Many of those transported in 1942 - 1943 from these countries were destined for Maly Trostinec, and death.
In May 1943, approximately 5,000 people were held at the camp site.
500 victims were liquidated every day by use of gas vans, the vans went to and from Minsk and Maly Trostinec every day, carrying 75 people per journey.
In August 1944, it was estimated that 40,000 foreign Jews had been killed in the Minsk ghetto and its suburbs.

It is impossible to arrive at an accurate figure for the number of Jews killed at the camp.

There were about 400,000 Jews living in Eastern Beylorussia in mid-1941.
Approximately 80%, or 320,000 Eastern Byelorussian Jews, were murdered during the occupation.
Relatively few were transported to the Polish death camps; most were killed on the spot.
In addition, the Jewish pre-war population of Eastern Byelorussia had been swollen by an influx of refugees from Poland, fleeing before the German invaders.

But Jews were by no means the only victims.
Many thousands of Byelorussian civilians, Byelorussian partisans and, most of all,
Soviet POWs were murdered at Maly Trostinec.

The estimated death toll of the Maly Trostinec complex has varied enormously.
Estimates place the total number of victims at 206,000.
In 1995, following further examination of archival material, the number of those
killed was revised upwards to 546,000, although this figure may be taken to refer to
the Minsk area as a whole.
Between September 1941 and October 1943, mass shootings were carried out in
the Blagovshchina forest, 5 km from Maly Trostinec, where an estimated number of
150,000 people were killed before the executions site was moved in October 1943 to
the Shashkowa forest. Here more than 50,000 people were murdered. It is probable
that the actual number killed, either by shooting or in gas vans, was lower.
The German historian, Christian Gerlach, has calculated the total number of victims
of Maly Trostinec at 60,000.

There seems to be no agreement over the final total. I wonder if the odd 8 or 1
at the end of thousands are maybe rounded-off, minused or plused what tallied
at the end.

  Later, Bella says, when the Nazis were losing the war, Himmler ordered Paul
Blobel to get rid of all traces of the killings in the East. The Sonderkommando
1005 was formed and their job was to exhume the bodies and burn the corpses
of everyone who had been murdered and buried in the mass graves. In Treblinka,
for example, as with many other camps, once all the evidence had been cleared
away, the fields were ploughed and planted with flowers such as lupins.

  In Minsk the *clean-up* operations began in 1943 - after Himmler's famous
speech to his principal lieutenants: *Most of you know what it means when 100*
corpses lie there or when 500 corpses lie there or when 1000 corpses lie there. To have
gone through this and - apart from a few exceptions caused by human weakness - to
have remained decent, that has made us great. That is a page of glory in our history
that has never been written.

The work to exhume the bodies here, Bella says, took seven weeks, disinterment
and cremation taking place in October '43 - one year and five months after Ella
and Wilhelm were shot and buried in the forest. There were extra police, and a
hundred Jews were forced to help. When these Jews refused, they were gassed in
the gas vans. Instead, prisoners from Minsk prison were ordered to do the work,
with a promise that on completion they would be set free. They did the work
chained together at night to prevent their escape. When the work of opening
up the thirty-four mass graves - some up to 50m long in Blagovshchina forest,
containing as many as 5,000 corpses - was over, they too were gassed. 100,000
corpses were cremated, the ashes sifted for gold and then scattered as fertiliser
over these camp fields.

The cremation facility was built on the first site we've just been to, Bella says, in the Shaskowa forest, and a three metre-high wooden fence built around this site. Six parallel rails, ten metres long, were installed at the bottom of a four metre-deep pit with an iron grate placed on them. The pit was supported on three sides with iron panels. The fourth side served as a ramp where the gas vans were unloaded or where the bodies of the exhumed victims were brought.

She shows us a photograph of what is called the Kolchos Barn and what remains of the cremated victims. As the Red Army was attacking the camp in June 1944, she says, the barracks and this barn were used to kill any remaining prisoners. In the Kolchos barn the people left were shot and burned. This was done by standing them on firewood, shooting them, then covering the bodies with more firewood. The next victims were shot and so it went on until the pile reached the top of the barn. The whole thing was burnt; pyres were still visible when the Red Army arrived on the 30th of June 1944.

And here we are already walking back to Bella's car, so soon, and so quickly so much of what was said, so many facts and figures, already become muddled or forgotten - not because of lack of interest but because it is impossible to retain so much - only images plague me. As we pick our way back through the fields, toward the car, I wonder what we would have done if we had been able to come here alone as intended, if we had spent sometime here alone without the need of a guide. I see that we are already leaving when there is so much I want to tell En, there is so much I want to slow down: stand still, take more time to figure out how to be in a place like this, how to come all this way, how to make more of a moment, how to get the shit from my head and tell him this once upon a time, that impossible line; how to say PLEASE WAIT … how to linger here, how to talk here; how to approach the men who now sit some distance away and play cards in the sun as if the circle they create protects them from happened here. No matter, this place is now theirs and they know it; what they have left I am now upon leaving. What we cannot speak of or find a common voice for is found and spoken in the waste left between us, that's all we find; the waste that took place here each day, most of it forgotten, no doubt, like the statistics that won't stay with me, no matter how well each detail is clearly spoken, recorded, reiterated, all the evidence stored line by line written with authority, but still - it's not the dates or the numbers, not the list of deportations that can in anyway be grasped … it is the waste that won't leave me. When I say - rather, what I would like to say, is: can I sit down a while with you, just sit a while now here in the grass; could we just lie down a while, just En and I among the trusted cows, touch the goats with the care they deserve this time, yes, just you and I, like the men, beside the men. Hush now, Shh, not a sound … Listen. Remember. The lupins swaying in the fields …

Dream #22876

There's a line of coils, after old rags twisted into hair, trust the plaits, trust the ribbons to carry the gesture to completion, my hands brushing hair in the dark, hadn't thought of that: no more hair to brush.

Inside the suitcase the lining is pure pink silk like expensive lingerie, a silver hairbrush placed inside - Did you carry the brush all that way? I ask the women to my left to my right. Could it be I know both of them: Who? The two women who are humming. No, liar, they are silent but for the sound of them moving soil; only a few words to a passed on tune quietly repeated inside their heads, these two women who know nothing of each other. You could say that I know both of them, rather, can see both of them, one each side. They cannot see me, they cannot see each other. Each has no idea when the other arrived here. We are where? No-one wants to speak the name of this place nor are they asking any questions. The two women face in different directions, east, west, unaware that they are facing the opposite way to one another yet they recognise the mimicry of the other's movements repeated inside them from some familiar place or memory so that together they set up a sound that calls out: listen to me, forget me. They would argue in different languages or embrace in other tongues if they were to recognize each other if they could at least remember how to turn around, how to look into the other's face.

They are more or less the same height, the two women, in stockings, no, in bare feet, the stockings all torn; remember that old way of measuring with a stick held over the top of your head against a wall? Get off your toes. Measuring now of no use as the women kneel into the ground. They are more or less the same build, they are wearing the same clothes, they are both widowed or soon to be, they do not know this yet, they are more or less the same woman and know nothing of this cruel fact or of each other's loss soon to come. They do not touch in any way. A path divides them made from stolen stones, weathered in so none could tell any longer the origin of such stones.

Between them I lie on the stone path, I lie here imagining their Greek or Italian, a foreign tongue, another's accent. I could walk between them if I chose and they would not turn and look at me. With no need to sit up, I see we form a triptych. Lines of sun find me open to the faint sound of them moving soil from here to there, just feet away, nothing else to do here, back and forth with a trowel, a hoe, but for now they are using their hands and are on their knees as if in prayer.

And on opening, the skin, the tanned grain and whiff of oiled leather, the straps unbuckled expose the pure pink silk of identical suitcases, each one, back to that, small brass buckles the women had once shined, the smell that on opening has changed something, has straightened the women's aching backs, sore hands and lips washed over with a moment's relief, with an oh-so-familiar scent, the faint tang of cologne in the mouth almost making them cry; cologne they'd once shared and rubbed between their hands, over the neck and face of a loved one, the smell, that lingered on clothes, spilled inside. Now, open and close the straps, remember, open each case, inhale that old sweet smell. Take out the clothes, search for that hairbrush tucked beneath; hair unpinned, loosened, brushed out; stray strands pulled loose to the wind, make a wish; brush the soil, furrow the soil, dig out the soil with hands and brush working as if each woman is looking for someone.

The sun's on the path now, my back against the warm smooth stones and I cannot deny it's their knees I imagine as I stretch open an arm toward each of them; close my eyes to the bone and ball of women's knees pressed into soil, knees dimpled with small scars, mottled with earth's small patch taking their imprints, 5 by 7 was it, that patch of ground, that bed, that 8 by 6 racked through. Go back ...

It was their suitcases they filled to the brim, the silk hidden beneath muck bedded down with a few weeds and bloated worms, beetles drawn to the edges and corners of the pink lining; women's sounds bring back a fleeting fear of not trying hard enough, a single moment of not going fast enough, the weight of soil briefly consoles something in them, in me, as if we were one and the same when we'll later no doubt white-knuckled carry these cases, one each, the straps fit to busting; before that we'll each take our turn to sit on the case, pull closed the buckles, fingers everywhere, we'll hitch each case up, bodies stagger, balance the weight with our free arm sticking out to one side, ridiculous, no sense of direction, still no idea of where we will carry these cases to; still no-one's prepared to ask, What is our known destination, later, no-one's prepared to speak the name of this place. And where are we now? ... Unsure if I could move any further, I am still here lying out prostrate in the 2 p.m. sun, here on the stones, arms reaching out almost touch the women either side of me, just listening out for the old words, any odd word I might recognize, something she once taught me, where words there are none.

You can lose yourself in soil before it's time. You can lose yourself in the rhythm women make as they dig. Each rhythm gentle enough: spade, pitchfork, trowel, hoe: all the words we lose woke in me: mattock, riddle, barrow, twine: listen out for the tiniest of movements where you thought there was silence enough to hear two women fill an old case; enough to say loved one digging in the soil, enough to say I am hidden between them where the pen makes no sound; see myself hesitate to gather another sentence, slow to gather another sentence.

Blagovshchina Forest

First or rather last we proceed to the forest. Blagovshchina. Isn't this, after all, why we came? Here's Bella, prioritising each site for us so that the forest is kept to the last-of-all but close now, only a short drive, only some kilometres away, for sure soon, the forest that throughout the morning is promised but always deferred. And no denying there is a sense of anticipation as we drive at last along roads heavy with lorries and construction and dust and on to Blagovshchina; at last we came, we are coming, we are on our way. And I'm saying this inside yet it is so loud in me that I am sure En and Bella will hear. In Bella's small red car whose registration spells out MAP, a language map, mapping Blagovshchina: *Map of place, very distant or remote, put something on the map, or obliterate something totally, mapless, sheet of the world, represented in graphic form, schedule of operations, (a locomotive or train) marked out by lines …* map the place where thirty-four mass graves were dug and where En's grandparents were shot.

And sometimes, like now, the car drives us as if by itself, well, I know that Bella drives the car, but there are times, like now, when the car takes charge, becomes its own body, its own being; adopts the feeling of a good friend, has the dignity the commemoration of a funeral car, the occasion of a wedding car, a car of restitution; it contains us, carefully sits us on its lap, puts its arm around us and says … Do nothing, just relax, just watch the speed of the road blur upon your eye, just listen to the rhythm of the wheels become the perfect pitch of a single note held inside the colour and hum and whirl of four becoming one sure spinning-wheel bringing us closer. And however small, meaningless, invisible this moment is to others, it's as if the car knows the significance for us, is taking care; I am both inside and outside the car, the watcher, watched, watching us move, steady speed; we are being carried, we are on our way, we have nothing left to do but let ourselves arrive, hear the beat of the indicator mark the turn that cuts through and into the forest, hear the sound of dust and grit beneath the wheels change and slow the speed, see Bella turn the red car through a road of sand before it settles beside the small memorial nestled in the trees, hear the clunk of three doors close as we let ourselves step out and into looking upon, for the first time: Blagovshchina. To see it before us, at last to stand among its trees, to breathe in its deep blue air, its antiseptic half-light, pockets of sun form small holes in the dark ground, sun cuts open everything it touches; and what I'd feared may disappoint, what I'd imagined may leave me feeling nothing, what I'd thought may look no different to all the other trees and forests I'd lived beside, grown up with, played in, loved in, hidden in, frightened myself to death in, manages to arrest me completely, manages to make me erase the idea that a wood is just a wood. Instead it surpasses all expectations, as if I had such expectations, but it is not a place of ugliness, of deed, of what took place here, yes, but more than that, what was once a site of so much horror has transformed itself, put its face up to what misery and suffering occurred here, and what would not be taken was its beauty, what it manages finally, somehow, is a place of rest, of tranquillity, and standing here I can say there is for sure a tender dignity to this forest.

This is how it was, this is how it sounds …

Take a forest and for now add two paths of yellow dust, there's the contradiction here, the construction in the forest, inside this expected wild uninhabited place; the expected silence that's now accompanied by engines and the clanking of metal, the motion of oversized wheels to-ing and fro-ing, the purposeful expression that are men at work, men going about their business, going about their job of moving things from here to there. A small memorial marks out the area of forest where the graves were dug, our road diverges into two sand roads which cut through the forest, either side of the small memorial, the site of the graves forms a kind of island.

Add the trucks, three, maybe four. It's hard to tell if the ones disappearing along the roads are the same ones reappearing some ten minutes later. Check again by looking at the men driving, men's hands working ever-turning wheels, men's arms firmly *doing*; establish some kind of recognition in one of their faces, some familiarity. They all look the same. Can I say that? Can I say that the men are maybe one man playing tricks on us, playing at moving things from here to there. And we all do it, we can all accuse the other of this need, just for the hell of it, to move things around, just to keep ourselves in motion, how else to fill up the day, a life. The trucks that look like the ones my brother used to play with as a child, you know the sort, exaggerated toys, enormous chunky wheels, shiny white excepted now covered in a layer of dusty application, men at work, men not looking nor seeing us park Bella's small red car in the sand - the car we'll later get stuck in the sand, the car we will have to push out of here, for we have to get out of this wood - the men with no care nor flicker of interest in our reason for being here, if or how we get in or out of here at all, and why would they. So much sand it's like a beach here leading through the forest, two roads that pick up each print, sand in which you might be tempted to form a fragile castle; make a pattern of stones, draw as freely as you can, write your name, write thousands of names, make defiant marks and leave messages in the sand, wanting to get to the underside to what's beneath, make a mess, dig.

Take the people, five hundred people a day. Kill and cremate. Bella repeats the information about The Shed, remember, where we began today, the other side of this wood. The Shed, unexpected again, that name when I'd wanted more, some kind of final destination that reflected the horror, but The Shed is all there is: shed, *an open-sided building for shearing sheep or milking cattle, nonetheless for sheltering animals, origin variant of* SHADE, and here there is more than enough shade, more than enough trees to cover over everything. The shed in nearby Shashkowa forest; ask, who knows on top of that, who knows how many people were emptied from the trains each morning.

Yes, take the people transported here and walk them into this wood. Do this between 4 and 5 a.m. before anyone is up yet. Play loud gramophone music, amplify, possibly classical, no doubt rousing, possibly run through with a sweet voice left to some individual's taste and love of pathos, for the music of course, for what it evokes. Imagine them choosing the music, varying the music, repeating the same tune ad infinitum, carrying the music here into a wood and from where?

Take the people directly from the trains, from the branch line that runs into Maly Trostenets. You won't find it now; that was before, the branch line, it's long gone but go on, go all the way with this, with the way they walk them a short distance into the wood. Tell them to stop, Stop Here, tell them to dig, tell them they will not be harmed, tell them they are digging pits that will hold gasoline, the reassurance and the stink of gasoline, not for them - what are you thinking of. When the digging is complete tell them to undress, tell them to turn away from you, to stand near the edge of the pit.

Shoot once.

Some will say to the back of the head, some to the side of the head, some will say to the neck; you are left to make up your own mind.

Watch them fall in.

Layer the pit with bodies, then wood like this, surely continue like this for days until the pit is full, bodies, wood, repeat for weeks, over months - and here in Blagovshchina there are more than enough trees, surely all the trees cut down to make this site possible - yes, layer with freshly cut wood like this until each pit is full, cover with more wood and then finally the promised gasoline and burn.

Cover the grave with soil using a bulldozer. Level. Repeat thirty-four times. Plant more trees. Wait some sixty years for the forest to recover and hide what's beneath. Wait for the forest to produce wild berries to look seductively beautiful, for the trees to grow elegantly back, tall slim pines, ferns, wait for the forest to turn blue, to attract white butterflies and berry-pickers. Wait until Bella asks some passers-by, Do you know what this place is? Do you realise what took place here? Listen to her explain to them in another language, listen to her translate, watch her run after them along the sand road, listen to them saying, We don't know anything about that, nothing ever happened here. Listen to her while she says, Look at all the red berries that cover the floor. Bella.

Listen to her say, The berries are the blood of the Jews, I can't believe how many red drops cover the floor and catch the light here, look at them, find yourself agreeing, that the berries are extraordinary, the amount covering the ground, everywhere, on branches as well as on the forest floor, the berries that indeed look like drops of blood, find yourself writing this down even though it embarrasses you, somehow it does, seems something that maybe shouldn't be written down, find yourself conveying the story when you return home. Wait until someone, until Lotte, tells you that Wilhelm, En's grandfather, used to love to go to the Vienna woods and pick small alpine strawberries, collect tiny plants. Watch En pick a tiny berry, hold it in his fingers, here in the forest, go back to the word wood, ask, When is a wood a forest? There's a difference for sure, ask and forget the answer, obvious enough, for sure a question of trees, of numbers, of plants, destiny, density and purpose, but until now you have never thought of it. Hear Bella call out a sharp, No! to En with his lips on the strawberry, hear her say, You can't eat that. These berries grew out of peoples' graves. Watch En lower the berry, keep it awkwardly in his hand, squash it in his hand, tiny thing. Watch him collect the small plants that will die when we get them home, watch En make small temporary greenhouses from plastic bottles for the plants to transport them home, watch Bella pour in the water to refresh the soil around the seedlings.

Which came first, the garbage or the graves.

I ask Bella what that mountain is, the mountain of sand we passed on our entrance to the forest, the one being dismantled, or so it seems, by the trucks, men at work. When we'd entered Maly Trostenets camp, or what was left of it, we'd passed the locals' graveyard, another kind of refuse, only prettied-up with golden chrysanthemums. I am smiling or is it squinting up at the mountain as she uncovers its purpose, as I ask, I am not expecting Bella's answer, that here in Blagovshchina forest we enter the site of the mass graves by way of the local dump, the city's mountain of garbage. Still, no-one knows if they need to dismantle this mountain of trash, no-one knows where these men are taking it, no-one knows what is at the end of the sand roads that intersect the forest, either side of the small monument. Again, here in the forest, there's a monument made up of real and fake flowers, gaudy ribbons, black wreathes, a small iron fence enclosing all to mark the site of the thirty-four mass graves. No-one knows what's at the end of the sand roads, one end the dumped rubbish, the other end … ? Well, if they know, as they must, we not pausing to ask, the men for sure not pausing to tell, surely sand but no sea, well that would be rich, that'd teach me to go looking here in this wood if after all the sand led to a huge and secret expanse of blue water to a secret stash of fish and infinity, an emergency exit, that'd be something I might make a run for. Instead the men slowly move the mountain of garbage through the trees, back and forth, the trucks make small dents in its engorged body.

So here's the site.

An enormous trash mountain.

I should be impressed, I think I am impressed, not by their choice of location - although there's the absurdity of it, admit it, there's almost a twisted joke in here somewhere, of garbage marking the entrance to this place like a misplaced gatekeeper; and it's of a scale that cannot be ignored, both the killing that took place here and this monument to trash. Which came first? This monument to our messy attempts to tidy away, to keep ourselves neat and clean and orderly, our witness to what's hidden under the bed, and here there are more than enough beds, forget the king and queen size, here's a whole palace and families of beds hidden away. Here's testimony to our garbage days, our every Tuesdays or Thursdays, our annual spring clean. And as children did we not spend our wayfaring days in the trash and the ash and other people's rags and burnt-out trophies, poking the dead dogs back to life, rag-and-bone and any ol' iron and me the dump-keeper, the entrepreneur of the no-longer-wanted. And here we are, sixty years of trash marks our entrance - or maybe later, after the fact, after all, who can know the age of this heap, who can know what's hidden and absorbed into sand, what hidden stink. Yes, marking our entrance a monument of trash that no artist or memorial fund could better, giving the impression from a distance that it's no more than a hill caught in the morning sun, almost turns pink in this light almost covered in flowers almost somewhere you could picnic, stretch out and relax, something under other circumstances you might want to scale and reach the top of just to say you did it.

Before that a fight against forgetting that I'd scribbled down just days back, that ... *To kill someone in sleep,* Pessoa said, *is like a killing a child.* You're asleep, you have no idea what is happening, what you are doing in this wood; or was it a type of sleepwalking that brought people here so early in the day, so disorientated from their train journey to where in the confusion of shouting of music of too much shadow falling underfoot the dank wood has no time to consider the remnants of dreams, not now, no time to reflect over the sky changing colour, no pause for song nor direction nor wings and screeching only birds everywhere with the first shot birds flee the dawn.

I'm reluctant to keep repeating the word MURDER, not me, not here, there are things you don't say in this wood even if you should say, no-one's saying it, thinking it is one thing, so instead I see myself write the word backwards on my hand, no, too obvious, maybe in secret under my skirt the way I did as a child, across the top of my knee, calculations, names, questions hidden on the thigh, I have to write things down, that's how I am, that's how I get to see things, I have to write them down - REDRUM. It's from the film someone tells me later, the child who has *The Shining* he's calling out murder backwards, he's calling out redrum redrum redrum. And I'm not one for betting, for frequenting that old turf accountant, but it's a horse I recall, I have no idea why this story is becoming no better than an ark, even - or odds on favourite - in proportion, there are the cows and the pigeons and the goats walking into this tale and now a horse. Maybe the lack of people, I mean the people are long gone and so what is there to say here but horse, cow, goat, bird. Here in place of murder, of what cannot be said, here in the forest I reach for the first available horse. And what size grave would a horse require, just think of that, the size of that hole dug out for him. Yes, maybe now it's safer to proceed the way of a thoroughbred the way of a rearranged murder galloping through the trees. Instead I'll say horse, even though some may say, Let's call a spade a horse or a horse a murder and there I am back to the child ... To murder a person sleeping, a person walking half-asleep to this wood, having no idea, no damned idea where they are or where the hell they are going so early in the day before sun-up; killing a sleeping person is no better than killing a small child, no better than slaying an innocent horse.

We always aimed for the head, he said, straight into the temple, instant. There's a man on the TV, before we came here to Minsk, and he's saying he was here during the war, in this very wood. He was an officer in the SS and he is saying they shot people in the head. Bella contradicts this, she's saying again, How much do you know, want to know, you look like sensitive people. We'll, misunderstand the meaning of the word sensitive, her meaning: appearing to care, rather than getting or being prone to being easily upset. She'll clarify. Bella is saying that people were shot in the neck. I don't feel able to question this, to say, But there was a man on TV, he was here at the time, he was turning his head as he spoke as he was asked questions about what took place here, he could not look the camera in the eye. I was there, he said, I want people to know I was there and that the only rule we had was to aim well, to get it right. He repeats this clinging to the order, a tiny moment of decency within an indecent act.

There we were in the woods, way back, when we played cowboys, remember, as children, we all did this at sometime or another.

I know you did.

I know you always say - forget the good old days, better times, different days; forget those days when we were merely playing, but I cannot stop people just walking in like this - into these words and woods, I can't help looking back and through the trees. And I see one wood takes me on a detour to that other wood of childhood. Just for one moment. And I see that we were playing as all children do. Even killers begin as children begin as players. And it occurs to me that I must have been shot at least six hundred times between the ages of four and twelve. At least. Who was counting then? I think after this when we became teenagers we would have preferred other ways, shooting the kids, shooting's for kids,

imagine

how many new kids are out there now in similar woods practising their best shots, blowing the gun powder from their fingers and me all along just practising my fall,

I admit

I must have shot people too, plenty, I know all play-acting all make believe, we all did it, but shooting wasn't my chosen method of killing; I was instead the one being killed from the guns that got bigger and more sophisticated with the growing fingers and arms and imaginations and the weight of this or that stick, with all the boys [and the occasional girl] could hold to my head. Instead, there I was all those years back in the wood just practising my fall, depending on where their best shot took me, the crumple of the knee, arms, try so hard to let myself fall authentically without protecting myself by instinct, even at the risk of friction burns, bruises, twisted wrists, at worse, ankle breaks, teeth bloody lips, tongue lolls into pine needles, the fall was not to be guarded in any way.

You're dead.

You can't say this enough, not now not then in Blagovshchina, you can't keep saying ... Bang! You're dead ... and blowing the fingers of your gun hand. Not when you're dealing with such numbers.

Next.

You can't say anything, there's only work to be done.

It was a job, he said, the man on TV, the one who was here in Minsk here in this forest sixty years back, only this time he's looking at the camera, It needed to be done, he said ... The only rule was to aim well, we gave no instructions on how to fall, that was their business.

En digs the hole quickly enough. We've moved into the density of trees, down close, hiding ourselves from Bella as if we are naughty children. She's over the other side of the wood where she said it is safe to pick the fruit, telling us she'd give us some time alone, that she'd be watching out for us and that we were not to wander too far. En is digging a small hole into the forest floor with his hands, he's telling me that the soil here is good, he's handing me some so I can feel it, Smell it, he says holding a palmful too close to my nose, It's good soil ... It's good to be alone for a while. He's trying to remember the triangulation of trees the formation of trees next to the hole he's digging, a small symbolic hole of course where there is no grave to be found, beneath our feet, hands, knees, who knows how many people were laid and if, as we read, they were later exhumed, burnt to the ashes that would scatter the fields we have just left behind, alongside the cows of Maly Trostenets, then they may not even be here at all, but for now we imagine them here as you have to imagine something, want to imagine them somewhere - for a while we settle into the feel of them here beneath us, here in Blagovshchina. We settle into the reassurance of Bella picking the berries, over there, we both stand for a moment, peep across through trees to see her small shape bending to pick the fruit, comforted that she is there, also content that when we squat close to the ground again we know that she cannot see us or what we are doing. We both ask what makes the berries over there safe to eat, as if two temporary sand roads randomly mark out a beginning and end to what went on here, can identify and mark out with such accuracy the edible from the inedible fruit here in this overgrown forest.

En's making the small hole. He's trying to remember what we brought to put inside the ground, the little things we'll leave behind. While he digs the ground, he's saying that the ground is spongy and indeed it is, moves as we move, he says after all it has the feel of a graveyard, wild, beautiful at that. Someone has been here before us and dug and removed a huge clod of earth that leaves a hole deep enough to fall into. Momentarily distracted, we crawl over to peer in. Crouch low so that no-one can see us, as if we had shared a youth together and just remembered the rush of the other's connivance, as if we always knew how to be together like this here so close to the ground, so close to hiding from sight so we can dig in our secrets as if no-one has been here before disturbing the soil, crawling here along the forest floor as if we haven't seen a thing. As he's uncovering all is already covered as if he is ahead of himself, to make it look as if we haven't even been, he says, to make the stones and leaves look untouched; as if while exposing the small hole, he is already covering it back, already trying to remember where the small hole is, where he's left it, in case anyone wants to come, he says, in case we return one day, when we both know we will not come back. He's digging, his knees pressed into soil, I see that our being here just a short time has already stained our hands red, he digs as I unwrap the objects we've brought, stones mainly with small messages written on the underside. Things from the children, stones from his sister and mother wrapped in kitchen roll and plastic. I hand them to him one at a time, reminding him who each thing is from. He places in each trinket and I tell him he's not making the hole deep enough. He takes the things out again and begins to move the soil with his hands to dig deeper working without question. There's an urgency about the way his fingers dig, the way he drags at the soil, scoops it up, and the way we whisper out the messages, the way we look at the other and around as if we are about to be caught.

I unbind the tiny plastic doll he will leave here, no bigger than my thumb. To see her properly, before I pass her over I have to put on my glasses. This is how I am, kneeling now on the forest floor, fumbling for my lenses to examine what's written carefully on her doll's back before I hand her over. What is written clearly is, KLEEWARE ENGLAND TINIEST OF ALL. Her finger held to her lip, common enough in a pink naked doll mimicking a small child, her left hand touching her right hand so gently she may not even realise she's doing so, I mean if she weren't a doll and were in fact not plastic. Neither is it clear if she is opening or closing her eyes in the process of sight or sleep, well, some eyes awake are no better than asleep and some asleep see only image after image in a night where there is no rest from sight, but none of this is clear in her, neither her eyes nor her gender. This small doll En had since childhood.

I drew a sketch of her before we left with her packet in our case. Knowing we were to leave her out here in the wood and knowing how long he'd had her and knowing how quickly we forget the look and detail of things, faces especially. I drew a small detail of her, beginning with a trace around her body the way they do in murder scenes. In my haste and concerned that pencil may fade, I used a cheap pen which smeared while I tried to get some sense of accuracy some sense of proportion to what would soon disappear under the forest floor.

Tiniest Of All. Ah, the name alone could shame you, the name alone could break your heart, could make you laugh out loud or cry depending on your disposition and mood or way of telling of recalling, if you suddenly heard yourself say her name, heard it years later as if all brand-new on your tongue; if on speaking it he remembered his fifty-seven years of owning her, of keeping her safe, of moving her from home to home, country to country, drawer to drawer, suitcase to suitcase, of not even handing her over to his children, no mean feat to keep her for himself until now, he might even blush at the sound of her name, he might even doubt he should utter it, or bring her here at all.

There's En, before we leave for Minsk, we're eating dinner and he says he's been thinking over what to take, what to leave in the forest, some small token, and he wants to know what I think … about the doll, he blurts out her name between food and chewing as if food and chewing will help with the obvious embarrassment he feels, when no sooner does he say her name, there he is retracting it, a grown man changing his mind, no, more hesitation, asking me … What do you think … I mean of taking her. Him thinking … dumb question … dumb question. Of course take her, I say, who else, yes of course, now that you mention her, it's so obvious. And always go with your first thought I say, or the first inside the second or third choice will always behave like a small splinter of regret.

She went in first, into the hole, of course. When he'd finally prepared and got it to a reasonable depth, what felt right was to put her in first. Beside her he placed the stones with small messages written, an underside established, as stones of course do not come with an underside nor a face. No, an underside and a stone's face is of our making, in this way of his sister's making, his sister who'd said, Make sure you put the messages face down into the soil. Then a stone from his mother, from Elise, no message, as what would a daughter say on such a message on such a day, when it comes to it what is there to say that the stone can't say. Smell it, he says, the soil. We did that. Let's do it again. It's good soil. It's good that we came.

He takes three or four photographs of the things in the ground, from different angles, most will come out blurred as seems to be a recurring pattern under such circumstances. I then photograph him beside the small hole. He doesn't know how to look, so his expression is as strained as mine was when he'd photographed me in front of the pond in Birkenau. I am waiting for a moment's stillness, contemplation of the things left but, unannounced, En's shovels the soil back so soon, so quickly fills the hole he's only just moment's ago made, he hurries, his hands everywhere covering the ground like a frenetic dog, soil flies all over us, as we crouch over the hole and he won't stop flicking the earth, not even for a moment, won't rest even when the hole is full, even then he's patting and levelling it with both hands, gently at first, decisively enough, fingers replace leaves and sticks across to make it look as if we haven't seen a thing of what's inside, getting to that part where he wants it to look untouched as if no one's even been here and disturbed the ground, righteous secrets. And again he's trying to remember the triangulation of trees the formation of the three trees beside us in case we ever return one day, in case anyone else needs to know.

And I will tell this story many times and some will believe, may want to believe, we saw a ghost. Yes, a ghost in the Blagovshchina forest.

After the stones and the doll's small burial, we move across the sand road to our right, find ourselves bold enough to stray further from Bella, to stray deeper into the wood, Come on.

Still out of sight and agreeing that we'll to go over there for a while, cross the sand road, pull the other along further inside trees, soon up to our waist in dense ferns and shrubs, as if we remembered how to walk this way one behind the other, one guiding, the breathless rhythm of one following the other's arms holding back the branches from the other's face, hands held and parted by the scratching of sticks, the back of the head coming and going, En's brown eye caught in sun turns, checks I'm still close, an unexpected kiss, shoulders hunch duck under again, his body again, comes in and out of focus the fractured voice gives itself up to motion; the foot caught in a tangle of vine; a shoe momentarily torn from a foot, lost, WAIT.

Maybe over there. Yes. The graves Bella told us, are both behind the memorial and to the right of the memorial. Having dug our small hole in one part of the wood, we stray now, make a small ascent maybe follow a scent, leave our own, try to keep up, for seconds lose and find each other in a wilderness of foliage, our increased breath coincides with a slow rumble of thunder filling the wood, sudden enough as we move further inside as if we had a direction when we've only just begun, only just left our things in the small hole, only just wandered further from Bella, and now the thunder is already above us, behind us, no, over there, as if Bella is behind a tree in the distance, shaking some piece of old tin, as if she's calling us back the way a mother calls her children for dinner is ready and the berries have been picked. The thunder only just arriving as we move further into losing ourselves or rather play at becoming lost, for we do not stray that far, not really, and there I am laughing to En saying, This is becoming like a scene from one of those films … a drawn-out rumble, on cue, finishes my sentence. En saying, We shouldn't stay long, we should get out of here soon. Me protesting, We've only just arrived, we came all this way, we should stay awhile, it's only right. It's going to rain, he says. The trees. Look.

He turns me from the direction we were headed, to face the other way. I resist; a drowsy drawn out grumble causing us to hesitate again, no lightening precedes, no expected rain in sight, the sky the same bright blue that began the morning. Isn't that how it goes, we're here at last and now our only thought is to leave, move deeper inside this wood with leaving imprinted into any new steps toward, with each new rumble we stare at the trees, En points out the leaves of the birch trees showing their silver underside, even though there is no wind and I don't understand why the leaves move while other parts of the wood, the pines, the shrubs and ferns, our hair and clothes are all perfectly still. This forest surprising us again, as the trees suddenly recede to expose dry yellowed grass, a large clearing, an empty circle which gives us a moment's relief from walking, from the keeping up, from the density, relief from our scratched legs, from hands moving sticks and thorns, hands now free to rub stings and scratches from our skin, a moment's chatter and rest, a deep breath deliberately taken. That quick, the thunder again. Still not one mark of lightening - when she appears.

And it's her backside that stops me, for sure an undignified pose but dressed nonetheless, her back bent double just feet away from us, a woman unfurling from the ground as if she was there all the time, could not have been there at all, for sure she was not there when we entered the clearing. A look between En and I understood as: *Where the hell did she come from*; but few words follow our eyes stretched on her hands that emerge from her skirts, hands stained blue, red fingertips that fiddle with cheap plastic bags, no more at her feet now than bags of berries and a small pail of fruit gathered. All of it happens quickly, her backside, her body turning to face me, a face that does not look in any way surprised or alarmed to see us. All three of us now motionless before each other, except that way the ground has of sloping slightly in her favour, giving her the impression of height, the impression that this rather short woman is a head taller, also ahead of us in age, in the wear and tear of her weathered skin, when in truth it's impossible to tell what age she might be; her face is not that of a young woman yet there's a youth to her expression, her open gummy smile on us, as engorged as her lips that only accentuate the faded prints of her ill-matched clothes no more than washed-out rags, her thinned hair almost recedes to insignificance by the red bulb of her distorted and oversized face, the right side spilling all sense of a circle, exaggerated lumps - I do not exaggerate her disfigurement, her head - obviously not simple.

And for sure we say nothing, not to her, nor to each other, not yet, surely still trying to figure out who she is, where she came from. Yes, I am not sure I can say that I am scared, it's more the uncertainty, the fragility of what-will-happen-next, the speed at which my mind is trying to rationalise what refuses to be contained and understood, and at the same time there is a slowness to the moment as if time has been snatched, maybe an obvious rather clichéd way to say there is nothing clear about how to proceed, there is nothing certain now but the three of us facing each other wondering whether to move, where to move, how to move, if we could move, how to speak, should we try, one or both or all of us, should we try now, even at the risk that we all end up talking over the other, misunderstood, untranslatable, moving like sidewinders, zigzag, no one's listening, shout louder and use your hands to make yourself known, no one understands a thing of what is going on, but we're all headed for the other's direction, all meet up at a fixed point on this circle, feet together and apart.

If we don't get that far with each other it is for sure because we are overcome with her presence, unsure how to laugh here, shy even, because we can find no common language only the sight of her misshapen head, her smile, if you had the imagination for it, almost gluttonous, her smile too much a burden on us, too much something we are not yet sure how to trust. For sure she is pleased to see us, or you could presume that much, you could look at her and assume she's happy, that much seems clear in the sight of her exposed tongue as if teeth would have gotten in the way of the stamp of such a smile; she smiles so much I think that by now my mouth must be finding something of the semicircle it knows so well, although I admit from behind my mouth I am not sure what I am managing, if I'm mimicking or even worse, grimacing, maybe worse, dribbling. Maybe my mouth is not open at all, maybe instead only twisted with concentration into unasked questions troubled by the ease with which she manages to make a smile continue for that long, the way we manage to stare at each other far longer than is normally permissible, telling myself: she must be real, she must be just here picking fruit, what else here, this wood where I did not come looking or anticipating her, I can say that when I entered the wood I wasn't expecting anything in particular, I was not expecting to be afraid here, thunder aside, history aside, smiling aside, I was not expecting to say, Look at all the death that is under our feet, what would you expect here but a ghost? I was not thinking that way. En's quiet but steady voice returning will have little effect on my feet, his question that, Maybe we should leave, maybe we should get out of here, firm enough, gentle enough, a direction never answered nor acted on, not yet, instead I wipe my face clean of heat and I see that she is already busying herself, walking around, yet still with her grin on us. I keep telling myself that she must be an outcast. When we'll return home, some will later ask me, Was she Jewish? Hear myself answer with some surprise at the directness of the question, with my lack of hesitation, my firm enough definite *No* ... well listen to that ... *She was not,* but what a question, who can say; gypsy maybe, no, too easy, maybe with her swellings, her lumpy head too easy to say she had the appearance of someone from those Grimm tales we were fed as children, ready to eat you up, what big teeth granny, where there were no teeth, only the promise of being sucked to death inside her cavernous mouth; but then is her exaggerated head also to be turned into something mystical, mythical, am I reaching for the obvious fairytale where there is nothing obvious about her, nothing of those old nursery rhymes to say yes that's her. No, I cannot say she is this or that, I have no way of naming her.

Give up guessing.

I repeat to myself, she is happy to see us, that much I want to believe. She is not only happy to see us but wanting us to see the capacity of a smile, inviting us to smile back. Finally, what a scene, the three of us all stuck before each other, all stuck in our grins.

That she speaks both startles and reassures me, causes En and I to wonder, to ask each other in turn what language does she speak; her voice releasing ours, at last a deluge of words between us that rise and tangle but go nowhere, yes, speech quickly fades and seems of no use here, gets us no nearer to understanding anything of this other; not wondering at the time why she does not seem at all surprised by our foreign tongue - here of all places.

The kids, when we return home, will later say that maybe *She* is now at home, like us, telling and retelling, to everyone she knows, her many versions of her encounter *with us*, of our strange oversized grinning faces, our ridiculous dress and voice and language, how we appeared and disappeared like ghosts. K. will say, I'm all for ghosts. L. will suggest she was no doubt looking for the date, to establish what year she found herself appearing in that morning. Others will shrug in that way that indicates they do not believe me but allow me to go on anyway. How strange, people will say. Some will no doubt laugh, almost embarrassed at what we recall we saw in Blagovshchina, what we'll embellish no doubt, as who doesn't do their addition and subtraction when it comes to retelling their colourings, wide eyed voices and hands and inflections bring alive all that we saw, *believe-that-we-saw*, seesawing maybe over nothing. Our recycled story only inciting others to tell us their own ghosts stories. Weeks of vivid tales. The usual drafts and smoke, visions and orbs, children cry, move beds, a curtain blows in an icy room, there's more to add where there was only water, a path, an old man evaporates, later, a smell comes and goes under the boards. Either way, I still don't believe, maybe want to believe, it is just a homeless woman we see out here in the Blagovshchina forest, her hands so stained with berries. My mother saying on our return, I'm sure that's all it was, just someone local. Mother's quick uncertain smile that will be followed by the bread being buttered, by the nothing more to say. Just En beside her, who will now on our return only laugh at me each time I relay my suggesting that she wasn't of this world. Yes, time does that, between our being there and our being back, what can I remember of her face? It was weathered and brown, he'll say, Her face, as if she lived outdoors, yes, she was probably sleeping rough in that wood. No, I'll say, her face was red and bulbous, covered in lumps, swollen on one side, she hardly had any hair. Of course she had hair, I remember hair, he'll say. He'll agree that she disappeared the way she arrived, appeared, left without warning or us knowing where or how she came and went, with that same pose, backside bent over, bags full of fruit. With En saying, We must go now; with our small steps in the direction of leaving, walk again, our feet again MOVE; she vanishes and we will not say a word of it, not at the time, not to each other. We'll walk away silently, quickly, concentrating on moving forward into what now becomes the comfort of trees, the other's hand pulls, only a glance back, here and there, for fear, don't stop, stopping only when we complete the descent into sand, sand again, almost forgotten ... Bella, to call her, to find her waiting somewhere in the distance, Bella's reassuring face.

We'll for sure return hurriedly back to Bella but not utter a word of what we've seen, not that we'll agree this in our advance toward her, not that it will even occur to us to whisper or command ... Don't say anything to Bella, don't mention it; foolish to confess, but foolishness aside, it will just seem understood between us that we will not say a word, not yet, as if there will be something too personal about the moment that will make us silent, that to speak of it too soon will somehow feel distasteful, too much a betrayal of something, of what ... of her, of us, of something we don't yet have a language for.

Even later, when we are alone again, we're still in Minsk, I mean, after we'll leave Bella, hours after the forest, En and me we'll eat and talk and still not ever be sure of what we've seen. At first I'll rely on him to laugh, I'll rely on his scepticism, but it will be En who will say, Where the hell did she come from, what the hell was she? It will be he who won't stop talking, and implying what I'll feel foolish to say, it will be he who will become suddenly animated, his words uncoil all over, when I'll so tentatively mention her, much later at the restaurant, yes, over the soup with the thick cheese crust risen between us, my eyes on his food when he'll say, I felt so strongly that we had to get out of there, as if standing there before her we were entering some kind of other world, and if we didn't get out of there soon, I mean somehow it felt if we hadn't walked off when we did, we may have been stuck there, the three of us just stuck there forever grinning. And he'll startle me with the sureness with which he'll break through the crust to the soup beneath, with the sureness with which he'll insist that she must have been a ghost, his enthusiasm for both breaking bread, dunking bread inside the hole he's made in the crust and telling me, She was of course a ghost, I'm sure of it, he'll say, no doubt … And where was she taking us for those moments, after she appeared, after we saw her, where were we? he'll say. Until we return home and there'll we'll be in our kitchen, this time En's watching me eat, laughs at me between mouthfuls, over breakfast, now denying my version, denying that he ever said he saw a ghost. She touched me, he'll say, that means she must be real. He'll deny that he wasn't sure, at the time, if she touched him or not. Can a ghost touch, I mean, can we feel them I'll ask, skin on skin, did you feel HER skin on skin? Yes, she touched me, he'll insist, I should know, I should ask, can a ghost touch, skin on skin … No, he'll say, they cannot. But she DID touch me, so therefore she must have been real … Well I'm sure she touched me, and I'm entitled to remember it the way I do, that's how I remember it so that's how it is. You can't say more.

But let's to go back for a moment … Let's go back to the three of us, En, me and the woman in the wood, we're still standing there stuck in our grins, stuck in time, in a circle of empty ground, somewhere in the Blagovshchina forest. For now I can say it is she who is at ease, it is she who is in charge of what comes next, of the *what-will-be-will-be*; it is she who has no visible fear, we are the silence and the confusion and the hesitation, we are the uncertainty of movement and speech, the dumb and unsure footed on the pine needled floor, balanced on the small rocks, how and if to move at all. It is we who circle the same spot, it is we who dare not venture further toward her, it is we with no thought of what to do next, it is she who approaches us with ease, without any hesitation, it is she who now moves close beside En, shifts our positions, her subtle manoeuvre, so from where I have found myself shifted, from my current position, En before me, left, she before me, right, yes, from where I now stand, you could say and wonder if she has patterned us into a formation that almost looks as if I am about to marry them! That causes me instead to swiftly turn things on their head, not literally but forces me to quickly, as they say, think on one's feet, in this case - *without thinking at all* - the best I could come up with is to blurt out and affirm us man and wife, *it's the first thing I think of!* En and I, unexpectedly married again in seconds, here in this wood on this very spot with her now turned into our only witness with the words *My Husband* let off like the keys of an organ held firmly, setting sturdy bells off in all directions, *My Husband*, such an absurd pronouncement to the way she begins to pluck at En without self-consciousness. Not that I say or use the formal term - husband - very often, not that this title is something I often think about, our formal marital status, but as she moves close to him, close enough so I am forced to move in front of them, forced to stand idly by, forced into now witnessing her hands reaching out to touch him, the word *husband* floats over the scene, untranslated and nothing more is added, as if after that one announcement I forget how to speak as I watch her now lean over, pulling my husband's leg. Ha. It's his leg she's after without regard, with no shame, no joke, as before me she is plucking my husband's hip. Not a lie but unsure if she's touching or not, unsure where her hands really are, for sure so close to touch, to plucking at his trouser, her fingers reach for his pocket but not the nearest to her but the farthest one, the one she has to stretch and reach across for, the intimacy of a dark pocket, the top of his left thigh. Yes to reach his left thigh her arm must cross his hips, his pelvis, stretch across his genitals. Me no better than a dumb beast standing watching her, not able to find the words to ask *what is it she wants with him.* And if I find a word right now, just one, what would I say when HUSBAND is all that keeps repeating in me, what nonsense, and what could she reply to such a possession if she were to understand, how to make her understand, my dear man, standing completely still, letting her move across his body until she finds his arm, his wrist, and indicates that she wants the time.

The time! Of course.

I feel foolish. Momentarily ridiculous. Such a human construct, such familiarity restoring some sense of calm, a sudden rush of humour to the situation. What would a ghost want with time? I ask myself. What? For the first time, here it is, almost a giggle, as there is time for this, time to repeat and to say to myself: how ridiculous we are, how stupid, how wrong, what twisted imagination, when she is surely human after all. Time now for reassurance for En and I to hear the other repeat, Ah, the time! ... to nod, smile, feel our bodies ease into each other, into seeing his arm lifted up gladly, no hesitation now only the gesture of En's arm held out flexed and eager, time relaxing the moment into one long exhalation ... Is that right? No-one speaks, not now, for sure we hesitate - nothing lasts, say again ... Is this the right time to ask if you think that's what she wants? ... The time! ... Is this the right time or the wrong time to recall it's time we woke up, time remembered, time passed as it did this morning, a morning like and so unlike any other morning, the morning we came here to the wood ... Go back just for a second, go back to us waking in Minsk, unfurl, stretch, sense our own misshapen forms heavy across the bed, En's body pressed into my back, each morning the same lark, different shapes, imprints left, for now, different country, the light floods the room, the faint hum of the air conditioner flaps the blinds, the discarded clothes, kicked off shoes, a fly floats in a glass of stale water, the small number painted on the bedside table, XB679 is written in red ink, everything to come ... Still, half asleep, someone speaks first, mutters ...Where are we? Immediately searches the other out, ask, What time is it? Ask again, call out again, for fear, a reflex, you could say, habitual call, the answer exact enough, sound enough, trusted most always, What time is it? The answer. I am here.

But finally she doesn't take time, no pun intended, no I'm sure of it, there's the three of us standing motionless in a circle, absurd, En's arm held out and she no more than a glance away, but finally she doesn't take the time, time suspended, absurd, En's arm still held there in the air, that way Sarah described waving to the ex, once, yes, remember, there he was in the street, her ex-husband ... just there in the distance and coming closer, and we hadn't seen each other for some time, she said, weeks, maybe months, she couldn't remember, but there he was and he seemed, well, so familiar I guess, so fully present, she says, and with great exuberance, there I was in the street and at the sight of him, of his oh so familiar face, and without hesitation before I could think about what I was doing, there was my arm in the air, ahead of me, my hand waving like crazy and me smiling for sure until I realised of course that he wasn't waving back, neither smiling nor waving, in fact he was grimacing back, worse, passing right by and sticking up his finger, and there was my waving hand, she said, my half-limp hand now just held there with nowhere to go, with no way to take the gesture back, the gesture all confused, incomplete. A blush that I got it so wrong.

I think it is then that I lower En's arm for him as if he has forgotten how, as if he hasn't yet realised his arm is still between us, of no use, that she has composed herself beside him, seemingly satisfied with the nothing more needed, nothing taken, I lower this so-familiar so-loved arm, the warmth of it in the sun, arm and sun misjudging her direction, supposing her touch, the silver of his watch glints in the light, red in the sun the hairs on his arm, the endless dazzle and pose of us mistaking her touch, if touch she did, his wrist, or was it his hand reached for, who can say, just En and I misjudging, interjecting with minutes and the hour, reading time as a narrative of what *we* wanted, or tried to make sense of in a wood where logic has no place, lost again, Bella way off in the distance suddenly remembered, almost forgotten, look ...

Look at us getting no nearer to moving, look at us just standing here in this circle of yellowed ground the three of us shadow the ground no better than the hands on a gold watch face, hers, no doubt, the second hand, always ahead of us, freer, jaunty, playful hands, me no doubt reaching the hour where time finds me letting out a snort, for sure an exclamation of breath, *We are the time!*

We toy with the promise of laughter. No, more than that. With the returning uncertainty of who this woman is, what she is, what comes next, this comes next: the preposterousness of a moment that won't end, En's arm now held in mine like a pet he's only just remembering how to call back to his side. Yes, what comes next: the assurance that I am now smiling at her fully. My smile on her smile on his smile on mine, her smile again so ready so easily becoming an even bigger toothless grin, brown gums and tongue, our gaping mouths, here it comes: laughter. Yes a laugh so loud so exuberant it cuts the sky re-forms itself with the returning thunder, a sound that tosses the trees into motion, trees stretched to breaking where branches rock the leaves, tall elegant pines sway, the birches shimmy, all pull back their heads with our heads, pull in any slack, our six open lips now permit, force apart a sound so fierce that for a moment I cannot remember or see the changing colour of her eyes, not now, just the three O O O's of our mouths stretched open, the ground run through with giggling, the dead hiccupping, filling the Blagovshchina forest with their cachinnations, the whole wood alive again, so many mouths under the earth laugh.

From: <angelamorgancutler@ntlworld.com>
Date: Mon, 18 Jul 2005 12:41:34 +0100
To: "Bella Rozansky"
Subject: back home

Dear Bella, We made it back safely no more incidents - even though we
sneaked into Warsaw as we had a 5 hour wait for our connection and
couldn't face sitting in the airport so instead we had a wonderful
meal - lots of liver - jellied carp - salad even a bottle of Carmel
wine - fabulous -

It's a pretty place -

Got home after 2a.m. exhausted but we went immediately to the garden
and in the dark potted up all the plants En collected from the forest
- some strawberry and blueberry and three pines - they are now by our
back door and look fairly well - I hope they survive - the pine looks
the healthiest -

Thank you again for all your kindness -

As I said in the car I am in the process of writing a book and I want
to include our trip to Minsk as the final part - It will take some time
to translate - I will try and write about our [near] arrest and your
rescue - I have some photographs of us next to the police car - the
ones you took - Shall I send a few? Or maybe when you get back from
your trip to Israel -

Anyway, Bella - as I said, I may pester you for some stories and details
I have forgotten -

Speak soon - I feel like I have known you always - I know En felt the
same too - you are a very dear person -

Love and take care - Angela x

From: "Bella Rozansky"
Date: Mon, 18 Jul 2005 16:45:39 +0400
To: <angelamorgancutler@ntlworld.com>
Subject: Re: back home

My dear Cutlers!
I am so glad to know that you are home and safely!
And I am also glad that your short staying in Warsaw was with no incidents!
Otherwise who would help you there! (It's a joke)
What concerns the berries I am not a big expert but it seems you should dig
out the roots together with runners. I wish everything is O.K. with all plants.

I found out about the delivery of people to the Maly Trostenets' camp. The
Germans built a temporary branch-line that does not exist now.

Thank you very much for your nice words. I feel the same. It is so good to know that somewhere in the world there are somebody who thinks of you!

Angela, dear! It will be my pleasure to send you all stories that I know. I think that the first will be about my family. I cannot promise I'll do it fast as I am busy now with my trip to Israel, but what I know for sure - I'll do it! And yes, send the photographs when I get back. And when you write about the arrest - don't mention the bribe!

Love and kisses. Bella.

From: <angelamorgancutler@ntlworld.com>
Date: Mon, 17 Oct 2005 12:34:31 - 0500
To: <Moinous@aol.com>
Subject: From Soap to tattoos.

Dear Moinous,

I have avoided this long enough. Today. Yesterday. Since I read about the soap. The Jews turned into soap. And at first I wasn't going to look, at the soap, I mean. I was aware of the stories, way back, but I cannot recall if I was told about it, and if so by whom; in which room, part of the country or world was I sitting at the time; or did I read about it myself, and if so, where was it written. Was I even of an age when I could read. Most likely I saw something on TV but either way, what was my first reaction to this soap [no pun intended], surely shock; who would think up such a thing. Did I dwell on it.

And of course the more I now read about the soap the more questions it opens up, some almost unutterable, did the soap get made from the Jews only, was this some kind of exclusive twisted pun on the *Dirty Jew*, and what was the soap's destination.

And I wondered for some time - when I first mentioned the soap to you way back, when I said that En and me had indeed discussed the subject of the soap over dinner of all times, as if there is an appropriate time and place and way of wandering over this subject - and what I'd wondered was, why those who believed that the Jews [or otherwise, the mad, the disabled, the gay] were dirty, contaminated [whatever their terms were] why then would the Nazis want to wash in them. Do you see how naive I get. Did you think the same way, or did you understand that the destination of the soap was from the camps back to the camps, neither for the Nazis personal use nor for general consumption but for *Jewish consumption*, if soap we consume. Back to Max catching the end of our conversation, joining in, not understanding the type of soap En and me were discussing: *Mum, did you know, soap is more in our lives than apples. More in our lives than horses.*

Wash away your sins. Wash away the day's toil in the soap of your brothers.

Ridiculous lines. Ridiculous in the same way I entered what was called the Starvation Room at Auschwitz, yes. In the way I stood over the bowl of plastic soup in Auschwitz with the label beside it saying, *This was an example of the type of soup people ate, soup made from rotten vegetables*. And I hadn't imagined rotten - have I said this before? Did you know this? Would you have thought of this? The soup like the soap lead only to more dissection. I was alone for a moment, had wandered off when I found myself staring down into the shiny broth. I was then eager to find En to ask him if he knew about the vegetables, if he knew if the only available ones were rotten. Was it that the conditions at the camp somehow speeded up the rotting process. Was there an agreement that the soup was only to be made from vegetables that had rotted. Did they grow their own vegetables [to rot] or were they brought in rotten. Did the vegetables rot in or out of the earth. Who grew and tended to the Auschwitz vegetables. Where were they stored. Who sat over the vegetables and patiently waited for them to rot. How long did this rotting take in different seasons, or did the initially fresh vegetables rot in the recycled liquid.

And once someone points these things out to me, these small but crucial details, I hear myself say, Of course, it has its own internal logic I somehow missed. Of course, what a great circular feat. Think of all the millions interned that needed to be fed, needed soup. That needed to wash, needed soap. Soup. Showers. One side water. The other side nothing is wasted.

Today I was with some people, including a woman I didn't know too well - well most of them I didn't know too well but that's another story - and it was this woman in particular who'd made a point of saying that all her life she'd been in and out of psychiatric hospitals, *the bin,* she called it as if she knew that we'd laugh with remembering this acknowledged insult, as she knew that I'd worked in such *bins* for over twenty years and that most of the others with her had had similar experiences to hers; and when I brought up the subject of Auschwitz and soap, not meaning to blunder this subject out ... it was she who announced, interrupted, saying … Don't forget us. Well, in fact she called this across the room. What? I heard my voice again, wishing I could retract it, become silent, imagine my head and hands searching, looking for the subject of the soap as slippery as when you drop it in the bath. I mean, don't forget us, when you write your book, she said, Don't forget: the mad; that it was not only the Jews that were killed, it was all of us. The present tense of the collected *us*, gathered together in the room looking over and awaiting a reply, caused me to falter after an outright limp, *Of course!* replying with some additional waffle while trying my best to recollect that I had indeed thought enough, considered enough, lingered on and written enough of others.

I found a photograph of the soap. Did I tell you? There are a few examples here and there to be found, grainy enough, close-ups of soap caught at different angles, in different light. I decide the soap recipe I come across is too distasteful to replicate and write down here. It's not for me to to duplicate, perpetuate. I see I have throughout this book developed my own hierarchy of what I will and will not show. Someone saying, *Even in the camps we had our own hierarchy of taboo. Even within the nightmare of Auschwitz there were some things that*

would not be spoken of, would only be whispered, hushed tones. Some
things that went too far inside a world that had left all its senses.

The soap, yes, how to get back to that. Soap that has silenced me for
days, if you could call this din, silence. The contradiction, that so
many times I wanted to write to you about this Moinous, about how the
soap touches me to silence, what a lie, when I cannot stop talking,
stop asking …
Moinous, listen …
I wanted to speak to you about the soap, I decided to at last write to
you about it on the same day as the woman, I was telling you about,
reminded me of what I should not forget, that it wasn't just the Jews
who were turned into soap. I cannot know or answer her question, if a
question it was, more a demand, a way to look at the soap, a way to ask
if what she said about the soap is true ... and here is the question of
truth my concern especially when I had already made a deal with myself,
promised myself I would not mention the soap to anyone, apart from En
and you that is, but to even mention it to you seemed distasteful,
unpleasant, INAPPROPRIATE.

I told En that I couldn't stop thinking about the soap, since I went
looking for it, looking at it, all those images of soap alongside
trial notes, testimony, denials, disagreements, counter-argument, for
that you need an argument, conjecture, so much written down, more than
enough books and documents, but still I was unsure if I should mention
the soap to others. En agreeing, quickly enough, that is, without
hesitation, he'd said, Don't mention it. Best not. Not in public. Not
while you are going about your day to day business. Maybe it's too much
for people to talk about. To take. But a small niggle plagues my silence
... what am I censoring of the soap, in the soap.

Moinous, This is how it was …
I was at the bus stop - following the promise I'd made to En, that I
wouldn't mention the soap, unaware that I'd break this promise if not
sooner, no more than an hour later when meeting the woman who would
remind me not to forget the other potential victims involved in this
story - yes, it was earlier that day when an old man kissed my hand.
It was unusual. This was not something that happened regularly, if at
all. He said that he had no destination or intention of catching the
bus but wanted to sit awhile and wait with me. He called me lady. He
smelt of rum and his beard scratched my fingers as he kissed my hand.
He told me he used to be a Jazz musician. He sang me some tunes as
if I need confirmation - Bebop-bo-bebab-adeoo. And just as he made
himself comfortable to the side of me, there was the bus so soon in the
distance, approaching before I had time to speak to him. Promise aside,
cross my heart, despite all and everything I never got to say the soap
was in my mouth, burning to ask the old man if he had an answer to the
question of the soap and how to talk of it, if anyone would know it
would be him. Instead he kissed my hand again and that only made me
think of washing off his spit. The need to later find some of my own
soap, for now, to rub his spit from my skin and into my coat. How could
I? Discreetly enough, of course. He had no need to see this, he instead
said - Lady I love you. And I wanted to believe that love that instant
that fleeting was possible between strangers. Lady, now I'll walk a
while and think of you he said as he helped me on to the bus and there

I was lifting my skirt from my ankle to enter as if it were indeed a horse-drawn carriage he'd called my way.

On the bus there was a man who was dumb … I haven't finished yet. I searched the eyes of the dumb man but he was only making signs to the two old ladies across from him on the bus: identical twins I swear. And there was something so appealing and almost nightmarish about the ageing of these two who maintained their likeness through a whole life of different experience and wrinkles framed by the same sharp bobbed hairdo, the same pink hair clip placed into the same side of the parting each had, the clips even crooked at the same angle, their same shade of lipstick half-chewed with the same talk, the same shabby green raincoats. The arms of the dumb man waving about in the type of florescent yellow coat that you'd wear on traffic patrol with silver reflectors that hit the light as he talked with his hands. But he was well past that now, work not talk. I mean in terms of his age. And for sure I wanted to tell him of my own dumbness regarding the soap and no matter how many times I told myself that I should go and sit next to him, MOVE, speak with him, I did not.

Instead I told the woman, later, the one who'd called herself mad, the one who'd surprised me as much with her directness, with the sureness of her madness and her charge and conviction that holocaust victims WERE of course made into soap. Mad soap. Gay soap. Communist soap. I didn't ask the obvious. Didn't proceed with what was bothering me about the soap's exclusivity. In what I'd read so far. And I think I have for now read, questioned, sat in enough rooms, everything still unanswered ... Was the soap exclusively Jewish?

Yes, there I was promising myself I wouldn't mention IT when of course it came out like Turrets, like a touch of her breast, as if I'd sworn right into her face - SOAP SOAP SOAP. Finding myself adding on the usual tag - *supposedly* - like a safety net. Whereas the woman I'd burdened and blurted the soap at, was not in any way hesitating. For her there was no: *Could they have done this*, no *Did they do this*. Only her *Yes Yes Yes* ... Only her voice clear, unwavering was thrown across the room at me ... *Of course they were made into soap. Of course. Everyone knows that.*

And I think it would have been a hush I was after in that moment between us. A moment to breathe, pause, find a way to to say nothing, be still and quiet in the force and conviction of what she'd said. Instead, I heard myself take the middle ground. I heard myself adopt the voice of reason. Limp on ... Well, I read that no-one was sure ... I mean, there are so many books written so many experts, by so many authorities - as if she was not an authority - not I, especially, not I ... forget that. There were people, I said, historians who wrote fat books on the subject, who later retracted and denied all they had written. Not all. Some said that what they'd written and documented and authored regarding the soap, in fact at the time of writing, was 'Not based in reality'. In the Nuremberg trials, bars of soap were produced and held up as evidence but still, many were adamant that there was insufficient proof, claiming that the soap contained no fat of any description.

I didn't tell the woman that from what I've read, there was evidence that substantiate the rumours, for sure torture enough, rumours began by the Nazis, that the victims were told and knew that they would be turned into soap, not to mention the gloves and particularly the lampshades you wrote of Moinous, when you always insisted that after the war you spent part of your time in America, newly arrived from Paris, working in a lamp shade factory. And I'll come back to that later? For now, there were the Jews and who knows who, maybe the mad, the gay, the communists etc., all being told they would come back as soap. One woman saying, *I could be washing in my father …*

Instead I'll begin again, begin ...
Dear one,
Dear Moinous,
I will send this to you today, and what will you say. Maybe your laughterature. The laugh that laughs at the laugh. And today another coincidence while I was resisting coming here to write, managed to do just that; yes, before I set off to tell you about the soap, there's Joan Rivers - of all people - on the radio as if she's reading my thoughts. She saying, My husband killed himself some years back and I went back to work and told jokes about his suicide. Of course, she says. How else. The 9/11 jokes that they made her cut from her sketch. Not forgetting the holocaust jokes that they wouldn't let her put on air this morning. It's rather early, they'll say, Too soon after breakfast for Joan's: EVERYTHING is a joke, laughter as survival, laughter as a cynical act.

And the soap: well, yes, it's creeping into the absurd. No need to point that out. For sure that's more than obvious, along with the numbers and the rumours circulating through the ghettos, sixty years back, there are the people laughing, so they say, at the soap books, at the soap jokes. People shouting as the trains to Auschwitz went by … *Jews to Soap*. There's the child of a Nazi commander observing his classmate drawing in his schoolbook a picture of a Jew becoming soap, the child being given a star for doing so. No, not that kind of star! Yes, there's the teacher holding up the soap picture for the class to admire. *Ten out of ten,* she says. *I knew then something terrible was happening,* he said.

Yes. When it comes to the soap question I hear myself say, almost the way my grandmother would annunciate, a *No* meaning *Yes. No* asks and almost answers its own question … *You think so*. The details the gestures of the soap again held up in Nuremberg. It's not what you say, it's the way you tell it. It's the way you're holding the soap up as an exhibit. It's your hand held in the air like that, the way they pass it around like that between them. It's the one who forgets and sniffs by instinct. It's the photograph I saw of the soap; examples, there were many, but this particular one stands out in my memory. It's a block, in the old-fashioned sense, carbolic in appearance, looking no better than a house brick. The one I saw is in front of me now on the screen, as I write this down I am also staring at a block of soap. What did I expect. I'm not talking Palmolive here, I'm not talking the amber seduction of Pears, instead it's rough, grey, sharp-edged, you know the sort, it stinks and hurts, the way sugar, they say, is sweet. No, Barthes says, *Sugar to me is never sweet, it's violent*. In the way this soap doesn't clean nor soothe, it's not pure, sweet smelling, typically perfumed, no perfume at all, the soap instead dirties, sullies, makes filthy, it burns from violence through to cleanse, erase, wipe away, eradicate, no chance at all.

Why is it OK for us to talk about ashes, to even hold the ashes in our hands, let them run through our fingers, Sarah asked, *but it is not OK for us to talk about soap; because it is of course not OK, not within our thinking for bodies to die and end up as soap.*

Then there's the recipe - the one I promised I was not going to repeat …

It involves a vat. Scum ladled off. It makes me slip up again and write soup instead of soap. It's a recipe with no carrots, rotten or otherwise. The vat that Dr Spanner was accused of installing. The recipe he was accused of making. A vat producing human soap at the Danzig Anatomic Institute. The charges later dropped and denied. Evidence that in World War 1 the human soap stories were common and began even then ... Again, don't ask is it rumour or for real? Does it matter. Yes / No. Circle one, tick or cross through. There's the photograph of bodies. They specified Jewish. They specified large, fat bodies piled up in Gdansk, there's a human soap recipe that's been carefully placed onto the bodies at the forefront of the image, the recipe leads me to ask, who took this photograph and was it the same person who pinned this recipe on, made sure it was in focus - as evidence they said. WHO. No one answers.
Instead, listen ... I was telling you about the woman with whom I'd been discussing, without meaning to, the soap, she is still here with me in the room, other's are quiet, don't get involved, don't say a word, give us the once over or look at the floor, when all the time I keep telling myself that I must try and listen with more attention to what she has left to say, to the way the woman is trying hard to find other ways of talking about the grubby subject of the soap; even though I can say that I wasn't expecting the sudden appearance of such strong men arriving to her aid, such a muscular image that for sure opens my ears and eyes and finishes off what she is trying to tell me ... My only wish - not at the time voiced - that she shouldn't feel the need to defend her example, this unexpected image of gladiators cloaked with her apology: *that it is not the same at all as what you were saying about the soap, but let's continue for a moment ... Regarding the soap, it reminds me,* she said, *that it was common practice to collect gladiators' sweat, after they had been in battle. Yes, It reminds me of the gladiators who'd no doubt killed, slaughtered enough people and after battle they would be washed in soap. Sweat and soap lathered and mixed and scraped away from their skin, collected and made into a type of perfume that the women wore. Women wild with the odour of testosterone. No, it's not the same but let's face it,* she said, *we're all interested secretly in the details, even if there are always those who will say otherwise, those who will say, I don't want to know, I don't want to hear, we're all curious about the soap.*

Ask again, does it matter if the stories about soap are true or not? I mean, is it any longer possible to expel the soap myth at all. Could we. There's the letters embedded into the soap, RIF, that was translated to stand for *"Rein Jüdisches Fett"* which supposedly stood for [ah there it is - tagged again - SUPPOSEDLY -] *"Pure Jewish Fat"*. This translation ruling out the others who went to their death. Reinforcing the possible exclusiveness of the Jewish ONLY soap. *RIF: more likely* [others said] *to stand for the company "Reich Center for Industrial Fat Provisioning" ["Reichsstelle für Industrielle Fettversorgung"], a German agency responsible for wartime production and distribution of soap and washing products.* [More likely others said, that] *RIF stands for this poor quality soap. Surely,* [some repeat], *it contains no fat at all, human or otherwise.*

Yet, there are the rumours strong enough to make people believe, that cause others to gather the soap together after the war, to bury the soap despite what was denied. There's the soap wrapped in small shrouds. Some inside boxes. 20 boxes were specified. There's the soap wrapped in tiny shrouds, inside boxes, inside the ground while full funeral rites were given. There's the criticism of Weissenthal who was party to the soaps' burial. Some historians saying that he was in danger of colluding with the holocaust deniers. *If we draw attention to the soap,* [they said] *and the soap becomes suspect, if nothing can be proven, then everything becomes suspect.* Either way, you decide, either way the soap touches and leaves a stain. The soap dirties, chafes, stinks, makes me feel guilty for wanting to play with it, for going to look where I believed I would not. The more I rub away at the soap the bigger it gets. The more it spreads and lathers and lingers, the more mess it makes. The more I see that the soap is not going anywhere.

Think of all the stones we have placed here and there, I say to En. Think of the candles lit. The notes and inscriptions and the rituals made. Think of the doll that we placed under the ground at the site of your grandparents' mass grave.

Think that when I write to Sarah about the soap, when we correspond for a weekend over this inscribed bar, we both agree we are tired of metaphors, yes, here, we agree that soap closes down the metaphor, You find the soap you find your way to literalness. I find the soap and there's nowhere to go. No moving away from. No destination. No *as If*. No *like*. No jumping to safety over there with some image that can stand *in for*, the soap is IT. *It is made of …* Sarah says. *Not containing. It is made of …* and there is no longer the luxury of playing with the boxes. The hope of emptiness. Just the SOAP and the shame and the impotence of that. *If not, it still is,* she says, *for ever will be, haunted.*

From: Moinous@aol.com
Date: 12 November 2005 23:32:12
To: angelamorgancutler@ntlworld.com
Subject: Patrik Ourednik's book

Yes - as for reading Ourednik - yes I agree - it is - as all great books are - tedious at times - and even irritating - but as you progress you will see how this book becomes a work of fiction

how it could be read as a kind of sci-fi novel

imagine this being written for the martians who want to know how things

are on our planet during the 20th century
it has a shape

it moves gradually toward more horror and more banality and more stupidity

but you tell me more after you finished reading it

oh by the way I also playgiarized [sic] the barbie doll section

but don't tell anyone or I'll be put in jail

Mxx

To: Moinous@aol.com
from: angelamorgancutler@ntlworld.com
Date: 13 November 2005 9:30:09
Subject: from Ourednik's book Europeana back to the
tattooed soap.

Moinous

I hadn't realised when you mentioned Ourednik that there was so much in
this book that referred to the holocaust. Why didn't you mention this
when you sent me [let's say] the TRANSLATIONS you began of his work.
Yes, the text he presents without any reflection, has the authority and
tone of FACT, so finally you have no idea what is real and what is not.
It all sounds so absurd, his brief history of the twentieth century
that could surely be a fiction or as you say … becomes a kind of science-
fiction as the horror of what people are capable of unfolds.

And there on page 25 there's the soap piece I failed to write, the
recipe I felt I couldn't include. The implication of the soldier making
the *soap joke* - that shifts the soaps' destination to move beyond
Jewish consumption. He writes …

And the scientists discovered how to make soap for German soldiers
from the fat of gassed people. Ten litres of water was added to five
kilograms of fat and a kilo of caustic soda, the mixture was boiled in
a cauldron for three hours, a little salt was added, it was allowed to
simmer and left to cool, when a skin formed, which was removed, cut
up and allowed to simmer once more, and before it cooled down again a
special solution was added so that the soap did not smell. In Gdansk,
one German soldier went mad because before the war he had a mistress and
did not know she was Jewish and afterwards she was taken to Auschwitz,
and his friends told him as a joke that the soap he had been using for
a week was from that mistress, that they had found out about it from
the director of the Gdansk anatomical institute, where they took the
corpses to be turned into soap. And afterwards that soldier had to be
taken to a mental hospital in Germany.

Today I returned to the photograph of the block of soap I found some weeks back. The one tattooed with RIF. I stared at that grainy photograph and thought again of Barthes' distinction between the part of the photograph you understand [the Studium] which leads to speech, to writing. And the part in a photograph he says that shocks you: *a little shock* [a Punctum]. A puncture. A wound that stops everything. The detail you had not expected when you innocently looked in. The detail that stays with you and troubles you, the splinter which leaves you both silent and wanting to speak more than ever. And the thing that bothered me, that I kept returning to, was that the soap was inscribed with a five digit number, leading me back to the tattoos of Auschwitz.

I tell you Moinous, concerning the tattoos, didn't Leviticus say, in all his so-called wisdom ... *Ye shall not make any cuttings in your flesh for the dead nor print any marks upon you*. Yes - a huge STOP SIGN - a contemporary tale I found among the mass of information regarding the Holocaust tattoos: *Jews, if you are considering tattoos* **don't do it** [so just as well you missed your chance in the army, Moinous] but for those Jews who were religious doesn't that give the enforced tattoo a different gravity?

Instead this is how it begins, with tattooed soap, tattooed forearms, with the number you sent me in relation to a dream - so many dreams I've had since this book began -

when you wrote ...

Dialogue # 17893

Imagine the possibility of dialogue here - the life story each number took with them. And almost in unison each # forms a sleeper # stone sleeper stone sleeper, taking me back to Birkenau. We're on the train tracks, my children up ahead of us, they're holding out their arms to balance their feet wobbling on the tracks in the shimmering heat. It's a scene I have known and seen many times, that is eerily familiar. The tracks that take me away and back to what I was trying to say, to tell you of the connections that began to make themselves known while I read, tiny things, all tattle and trial notes; versions and voices written in the third and first person, tenses all over the place, all of it contradicting.

There's a small account I found of a young man who'd tattooed his arm with his grandmother's concentration camp number. He was far too young to have been at Auschwitz, but he wanted her number tattooed onto his arm as a way of remembering, as a kind of memorial. With his Grandmother's permission he had her number, 98288, on his arm. There followed a series of posts back to the author of the story, *Jewlicious*: yes that's the name I found, *100% kosher* it said - no joke. There's the post-back in response to the man's tattooed arm which as you can imagine ranged in reaction from, *it's sick,* to *how original; why not; snore; that's not very polite; never forget.*

There are several accounts, potted histories, of the 5-digit IBM Hollerith numbers began at Auschwitz in 1943. This tattooing of numbers began as part of a punch card system devised by IBM to track prisoners between jobs, across camps. By the summer of '43 all the prisoners were being tattooed on their forearms with the 5 digits. The problem being, the system was designed to track living prisoners not dead ones, so when people were being killed the system began to break down. On one occasion some 6,500 prisoners who were about to be gassed were held up for two days while their numbers were checked against the system in case they had missed any Aryan blood. Finally all exterminated prisoners were coded 'six' in the IBM system. The Auschwitz camp code was 001 [now the telephone code between you, Sarah, and me.]. Each tattooed number would correspond to a further code kept at a central office, so that any number would be traced and followed back to the central system. Each number classified the person's nationality and how they were categorised such as, Jew, Political Prisoner, Homosexual, Mentally Ill, etc. Later arrivals had a letter tattooed before the number, such as A, B, Z, or a triangle. Early tattoos were given using a stamp made up of many tiny needles that formed interchangeable numbers. The wound made was then filled in with ink. These early tattoos were made over the heart. Later ones, on the forearm, were often carried out by young Jewish girls who were given the task of using a single needle to inscribe the arm. This made it quicker to identify people among layers of bodies.

There are many accounts of Ilse Koch, tried at Nuremberg, the *Bitch of Buchenwald* - Buchenwald that was a labour camp - yes - the camp where Antelme was interned - the author who wrote that incredible novel of his experiences there. Ilse Koch, the commander's wife, who is said to have been very beautiful with long red hair. There's a man recounting the story, saying that *If anyone looked at the commander's wife, they would be shot*. He worked as the commandant's gardener, the man conveying the story, recalling that Ilse Koch ordered the men to congregate in the camp's *Appelplatz* and undress to the waist. Ilse Koch picking out the men with the most interesting tattoos and the rest is obvious, the rest is the charges against her at Nuremberg of having lamp shades, gloves, and photo albums made from the tattooed skin of these same men.

There are many other documents, lab reports, presented at the Nuremberg trials that specify the skin of Koch's photograph album was sueded, and that it probably originated from some large animal, *but that a specific species identification was impossible.*

But for now no conclusion - only things threading themselves haphazardly together - only the sudden feeling of discomfort at reading and writing all of this down.

Axx

Begin forwarded message:
From: Moinous@aol.com
Date: 11 November 2005 01:14:15 GMT
To: angelamorgancutler@ntlworld.com
Subject: Re: interview with Mark Thwaite

Yes I approve - it was very sensitively written - I especially loved what you said about Sam -

Mark's 2nd question seemed particularly relevant - I mean in terms of what I am trying to write - in terms of where now re: the subject of the Holocaust - How to approach it in two thousand and …

Recently - an Academic from some British University said that the poetics of say - Anne Michael's Fugitive Pieces *had been very relevant to the second generation of survivors* - of which she was one - her mother being the survivor [En hates the term Second- Generation Holocaust Survivor - feeling as he does - that he came from a privileged middle-class upbringing where he was very safe and secure and that he personally survived NOTHING] she went on to say that, *in the years to come, as the last survivors die leaving no more direct witnesses, this may in turn leave a space for writers and artists to find more postmodern ways of writing about the Shoah* - But what does this any longer mean - this tired overused postmodern expression which usually stands in for any old rag and bone - that usually exiles writing to the wastelands of experi-mental-ism - or as you said so long ago - *didn't postmodernism die along the way and we missed that too - so what next?*

Yes, regarding question 2 of your interview with Mark - I could have written an essay on this one - but then maybe less is more

yes I know but I am running out of things to say on the subject -

it's true dear angela - once - I was in full control of my faculties and senses - now my ears and eyes and mouth and even the rest of me are failing me - so I read very slowly - and hear very slowly - and see very slowly - and I even pee very slowly

Trust me to end up with your failing ears eyes and slow reading - even peeing which here [in this virtual house we inhabit] does not affect me -

how do you know my peeing does not affect you

but your mouth - I would say is still fast
Axx

my mouth is getting smaller
xxxxm

Moinous - I just cut out the parts of Mark's interview that particularly related to question 2 - How to be a Jewish writer today -

MT: You say in your wonderful and provocative essay The Necessity and Impossibility of Being a Jewish Writer *that to "be a Jewish writer today is not merely to be a good storyteller, but someone who questions and challenges the very medium of storytelling, or what I have called elsewhere 'the arrogance of storytelling.'" What do you mean, here, by "arrogance"? How do you avoid it yourself in your own writing?*

RF: There are some stories that cannot be told. Should not be told. Only those who died in the camps have a right to tell what happened. But of course they cannot. Those who were there and survived - Primo Levy, Paul Celan, Jean Amery, and so many others - have a right to tell their story. The rest of us, marginal survivors, children of the Holocaust as we have been labelled, can only appropriate these stories, and to do so is a form of arrogance. But we must do it anyway, for as I wrote at the end of Aunt Rachel's Fur ... my role as a survivor here or over there, in the cities, the countries, in the books I write or will write, my responsibility is to give back some dignity to what has been humiliated by the Unforgivable Enormity ... of the Twentieth Century.

MT: Your work is quite manic, playful and very energised; you are often called a Holocaust author: is there a contradiction here? Does the energy of your work come from the horror of the Holocaust?

RF: There is certainly a contradiction in writing about the Holocaust in sad laughter. But am I writing about the Holocaust? Not really. What I write is what it means to live in the post-Holocaust era. To live one's life with this burden, this responsibility, this ugly story, and above all with this absence in you. To live with what has been absented from your life - your family, your history. Many have lived with that, and then one day, unable to bear it any longer, they commit suicide. The three names I mentioned above did that. Instead, I chose laughter to energize me, so that I can attempt to write what refuses to be written, even if I must fail - fail better, as Beckett put it.

MT: What are you trying to achieve with your work?

RF: I am trying to invent a language appropriate for my experiences. A way of telling what I have lived without tumbling into the imposture of realism and the banality of sentimentality. The Holocaust was an obscenity. One cannot write about it with Belles-Lettres. One must invent an obscene language. A language that implicates rather than pacifies the reader.

From: <angelamorgancutler@ntlworld.com>
Date: 10 November 2005 12:54:49 GMT
To: <Moinous@aol.com>
Subject: Re: question 2

Moinous - to return to question 2 - this also seems especially relevant in light of the recent fuss here about the 14 yr-old boy who won a poetry competition and got accepted for a book with the title of *Great Minds* - the boy called it JEWS - I told you already that he wrote the poem from Hitler's point of view, by getting or trying to get, inside his head. The Jewish Chronicle described the poem as *an anti-Semitic school mag - or rag* - the published book that included his poem had been circulated to schools in the UK and his poem just happened to be on page 1 of this anthology - its position in the book caused further uproar.

En wrote a reply supporting The Guardian newspaper's article that had been written in response to the Jewish Chronicle's criticisms of the publisher, and his defence against being called - among other things - *a motherfucker* for allowing the poem to be printed.

Again, this raises all sorts of questions around how to speak of the Holocaust - with gloves on or off - by making yourself into a Jewish character - by avoiding Hitler - by demonising him - by writing something poetic for the victims - from the victims point-of-view - by remembering *correctly* or saying I remember nothing - I wasn't even there - and so is the fiddler still on the roof -
and Question 2 is crucial to the where now? Where do we go next?

How to write without it being overly-sentimental - or political - overly analytical - without it turning the Jew in one universal type - as what does it mean to say - Jew - Jewish writer - how to write without constant self-censorship - with the right tone that doesn't ease but doesn't ram it down your throat - is there a right tone - could there be -

These are delicate questions -

Begin forwarded message: From: Moinous@aol.com
Date: 14 November 2005 14:57:20
To: angelamorgancutler@ntlworld.com
Subject: Re: Hitler Poem

can you send me that poem

From: angelamorgancutler@ntlworld.com
To: Moinous@aol.com
Date: 15/11/05
Subject: Row over school boy's poem written from
Hitler's point of view

Moinous - I cannot send the poem because I cannot find the poem - I only heard it being read out on the radio - in many ways it is unremarkable - it is more the attempt he made to get inside Hitler's head - and the effect that had - that it caused such controversy here - despite the fact that when he submitted the work - he added the line - *Please understand I am not a racist - I was not trying to be* … like the warning on the cigarettes packet - or the work cordoned off by the boy's pre-empted explanation - On stepping back from the work isn't it that we all have the urge to erase - to say NO to our own words - to hear the voices of the censure and the shopkeepers of language already ringing out calls of - Danger - Rub it out - Make holes in it - And instead put what sentiments - cosiness - creature comforts - soothing language - in its place - How to penetrate Hitler's head and come out unscathed?

Axx

From: Sarah Wild <wild@sarah-wild.com>
Date: Wed, 20th July 2005 3:50:22 +0100
To: <angelamorgancutler@ntlworld.com>
Subject: Re: minsk

Yes very grisly reading about the forest in Minsk and the camp, from details to numbers. There was a documentary on the TV a few weeks ago about a man who survived the camps and went back to Germany for the first time since the war. He was looking for what he called "good guilt." He went into schools, universities, museums (particularly those that celebrated Jewish culture), met with many different people, talked with artists who were short listed for a new Jewish memorial that is now constructed in Berlin - (the final choice being a sculpture that was sorta poetic abstraction which he called a bad guilt choice).

He found very little of what he was looking for. On the one hand
I can nearly guess and want what he was asking for and then
on the other ... it is hard to imagine (like the extermination itself) what societal good guilt could be and how the hell could that become part of a cultural psyche.

What he found was that nothing had changed really, only the ugly and systematic surface gone underground. I am not so sure good guilt has any chance of living in anyone never mind in a group.

Anyway I meant to talk with you about the film and then forgot. If you have real player, you can watch the film on line, the guy has a wonderful voice, of a certain timbre that makes you listen very carefully:

http://www.pbs.org/wgbh/pages/frontline/shows/germans/view/

Hope the pies and balls are going down fab, its a gorgeous day here so hoping it is there - missing you very muchly.

XSarahX

From: <angelamorgancutler@ntlworld.com>
Date: Wed, 20th July 2005 11:06:22 +0100
To: Sarah Wild <wild@sarah-wild.com>
Subject: Re: minsk

Hi honey -

yes - as for the good or bad or ugly guilt - that's interesting - if we are still 60 years on caught up in guilt hierarchies who are we any longer blaming - looking for to say sorry - looking to make amends with - what gestures was he in pursuit of - which nation / generation should be guilty and others not -

For sure the film made me consider the whole issue of the monuments we *never really see* - I mean in what way do they move us - is it possible to be really touched - for instance - by the many different examples we saw in the killing sites of the forest around Minsk - or the photographs someone kindly sent us - before we left - of the official monument - so deemed - There was something so predictable so uninspiring in those images of this once neglected crumbling monument - newly renovated, so that the gold letters again shine. Still - to me - it seemed a real no-effort-grey-erection, with the usual eternal flame set inside what looks like one of those awful 70s stone-clad fireplaces - already re-crumbling into another era - But when we showed Elise the same photograph of that dull uninspiring column she said - *Oh, that's nice* - and then I felt a huge pang of guilt that I had written two blasphemous paragraphs about the miserable state of guilt-easing monuments and here she was - the survivor whose parents were killed there and she was saying very genuinely - *that's nice* - and I wondered why I couldn't find it in my heart to see it the way she did - and why do I only see the empty bad guilty gesture, an echo of: Let's quickly shove something up so our guilt can be put away - so we can then leg it back to who-cares-ville -

Or maybe as one of the artists said in the film you sent - *there should be no finishing touches no finished monuments only an endless discussion.*

much love & good colouring -

Axx

From: Sarah Wild <wild@sarah-wild.com>
Date: Thurs, 21st July 2005 11:09:29 - 0500
To: <angelamorgancutler@ntlworld.com>
Subject: Re: minsk

more on the film, I just got your other mail so will read it and send this anyway

The man in the film, the survivor, was not really sure what he was after, he realized that he was diffused with a lot of negative feelings and wanted to find a way to deal differently (because of his experience as a child even hearing the German language made his skin crawl) with researching the various memorials that were being built in Berlin. How to remember became one of the issues now that first-hand survivors are dying off. The film went into how 3rd generation Germans do not want to be told institutionally how and what to feel. The film initially was about his singular reaction to what happened to him and his family, a specific quest of an individual that addressed a whole country, an impossible conversation - but perhaps for some an unavoidable one, the only one to have - When he refers to good guilt he does so knowing the impossibility of it.

Yes the impossibility of good guilt, the forgiveness that this film-maker faced in all his conversations seemed to echo that other limit - society's dirty secret. The passion for harmony, isn't that what creates the desire for a group to eradicate all that supposedly threatens it - in the case of Germany it was the Jew, Gypsy, the Mad.

Wasn't it Lyotard's wandering Jew - 'nothing' in their being in terms of national belongingness that others could identify other than being Jewish, they could therefore not be trusted. It was this 'nothing' of wandering that disturbs those who stay in 'their' place.

In the documentary the guy was talking about how before the war, his family did none of the religious things and that it was the holocaust itself that made him Jewish. Yes all this talk is cringe saturated but it's hard not to speak, hard to speak.
enjoy the sunnio
hugs
SX

From: <angelamorgancutler@ntlworld.com>
Date: Thurs, 21st July 2005 19:09:22 +0100
To: Sarah Wild <wild@sarah-wild.com>
Subject: Re: Minsk

Yes - regarding what you said about the man in the film - Marian Marzynski's declaration that - *I am Jewish because we were killed* - this is what he sees as the negative perception others have - being made into a Jew by the holocaust. This was also Elise's experience - and I have said this before - but her family were not a religious family and the holocaust of course made them JEWS when in many ways they were forced into Jewishness like never before. When Elise left Vienna, and after the war, she in many ways, turned away from this imposed label, rejected to an extent, her German language and became political, a communist, in place of the prayer or identity she had been *given* -this generalised stereotype come false biography. En describes her as wanting to fit in to her new life in Britain, but I wonder could she really escape or become anonymous - just after the war - how possible was it to *blend in* -

Thinking more about the film - what touched me most of all was the way Marian had of standing so close to people he interviewed and looking right into their faces - the need he had to ALMOST touch all the people he met - if you take aside all he was saying - it was indeed his need to touch that somehow spoke most - asks - And how am I to understand you - Do you have what I am seeking - he was so obviously uncomfortable being in Germany and maybe also in trying to explore this idea he had of good guilt - and finally trying to search for his grandmother's grave - that when found - he discovered had been desecrated - And so where did he get to - back to [Marian's] grandmother's name again erased - leaving him and us with too many questions - but none the less his story is told - heard - *or not* - but still - something in that closeness - his touch in the other's direction - was like Barthes' *Punctum* - a detail in a photograph that troubles you to silence - that troubles you to want to say something - but what is that *something* and what form should that *something* take - And as I watched the film I found myself doing the same thing -unconsciously to begin with - yes - as he began moving very close to the people he was interviewing - I too found myself moving very close to his face - as you said - I also found myself drawn close to his voice - and toward the small and grainy quality of the jumpy film I was forced to watch on line - but more than just trying to catch all he was saying - I found that he was pulling me in - to almost touch - as he was - the faces and bodies of all the people he spoke to - something that Raymond also does - something I'd noticed when we met in our awkwardness away from the security of our prosthetic keyboards and our virtual world of words - in the awkwardness of having to deal with the REAL of the other before us - his proximity was always close - in the same way Marian touches where there is no way of speaking - maybe a coincidence - but that is what I was left with - as if in this search/ing - something was expressed - even when the people he met were not necessarily sympathetic to him or to what he was saying - asking or looking for - that something that could not be articulated was held in the spacing between bodies -

Axx

From: Sarah Wild <wild@sarah-wild.com>
Date: Fri, 22nd July 2005 09:50:03 - 0500
To: <angelamorgancutler@ntlworld.com>
Subject: Re: minsk

Yes, like a chicken's body that runs unknowing of its headless state (not that he is such a chicken but that understanding is, it clucks at the heels of all that feel and those that are tired of feeling) or maybe it is the chicken's head that runs around - and it is the body that's left to space its touch - perhaps some kind of reason is in this musculature, we just cannot think it, it thinks us - we ask what happens to suffering and memory when we touch an/other - that slight space of touch - if touch can be a space that isn't consumed by ideas of union or distant identities German/Jewish or otherwise - will think more

much lovings
SX

From: <angelamorgancutler@ntlworld.com>
Date: Fri, 22nd July 2005 17:18:22 +0100
To: Sarah Wild <wild@sarah-wild.com>
Subject: Re: Minsk

For me the part that also stood out was the interviewer asking Marian, What do you remember of your mother. *I remember her ear,* Marian replies. That's what touched me also. His mother comes back after the war and announces herself to him and he doesn't recognise her. He can't remember her and he is staring at her wondering, *Who is this ugly woman.* And the word ugly was incredible - almost inconceivable - I mean - it rang out when he dared say and announce what he'd thought back then.

Sense in French is ambiguous, Merleau Ponty says, *the meaning is both meaning and direction.* And recently, the way the soap touched me, or me it [I mean when I was trying to write about the *subject* of the Jews turned into soap and the guilt I felt, after all, it was me who went looking, no-one else] but this worked in a similar way, in that the direction of the writing became its meaning, each unexpected direction happens on touch.

This man, Marian, [coincidentally the same name as my grandmother] sent to me via you. The man [Marian] speaks as, listens to the voice of the small boy he was, which also touches me, makes me want to write something, but what. His children do not know his story, but for sure he decides to tell them, he says *It's time I did.* As he prepares to tell his story to his children, via the interviewer, he is worried what to wear, he frets, what to wear to tell such a story, to tell the story of his five-year-old self who escaped the Warsaw ghetto by being passed off as a non-circumcised Catholic, his father's insight to not circumcise the boy, his mother telling him to stay quiet, [like Raymond's last words from his Mother - her CHUT - Shh] for to speak now / then, could be the death of him. His children, Marian's, do not know his story but he wants to tell them and in order to tell them he must dress just right. What to wear. Casual or smart. He asks the children's advice, he asks, *Do I look OK in this.* Do I look good enough to tell you my story.

My name was Marian Kushner he says, *now Marzynski, Marys was the diminutive of Marian. I was five when I was smuggled out of the ghetto and left in a square with cardboard around my neck saying, My name is Marys, my parents are dead.* He is left pretending to be a Polish orphan. Left in the square with his sugar sandwich. And it was the sugar sandwich that touched me again. Again, what I was not expecting. Least expecting. The detail of the brown paper bag containing the sugar sandwich. There's Marian eating the sugar sandwich and waiting there for who-knows-who, for the Polish janitor who will come take him home. There's his mother reunited with him after the war and he does not recognise her until he again touches her ear. *I recognised her by touching her ear,* he says, *by the smell and feel of her body.* I recognised you, Marian, by the sugar sandwich given to appease. *To appease* you'd said. *Sugar and bread to appease me* [like Raymond's stolen bag of sugar lumps, the sugar he found in the closet where he hid while his family were taken away] *the best treat of all, to keep me quiet,* for to speak now would be the end of it. *And this time,* he says, *this time I know, this is it, I was ready to do it … to not speak, to not shout out, to not give away my identity.*

Before this, a woman is holding her hands over Marian's mouth, when he is taken from the ghetto he is screaming for his mother and a hand is held over his mouth for the journey, away to the Catholic side of the city, a hand stops him, there in a horse carriage
these details
the hand over the mouth
in the horse carriage
the child in the square now deciding to hush
to eat his sandwich
the word sugar
the word appease

the word diminutive
the proximity of Marys telling his story to others
dressing nervously to tell his story to his children
these things stay with me

I have no experience to draw on, not here, but the sandwich takes me
to my own sandwich, to my first day at school. Everyone's crying. It's
of course not comparable, it's not meant to be, hush. It's my first day
at school and everyone's crying, not me, I am beyond tears, I have no
vocabulary for tears not there. My mother - also *to appease* - makes
me a sandwich for my lunch box, she tells me I can choose any kind
of sandwich I want, anything. I tell her tomato sauce, nothing else,
something about the red and the bread, the butter and tomato sauce.
We make the sandwich together, with extra butter and sauce. She wraps
it in greaseproof paper and folds the edges securely. At lunchtime I
open the sandwich and the red has bled, it is not containable, it's
everywhere, it's her absence, it's the school, it's the way I look here
with the ridiculous sandwich, with the wrong choice of filling giving me
away, it's the way I walk the length of the playground some distance
between groups of children, through a dozen and more strangers and with
only a second's hesitation I bin the lot.

It's mainly a feeling of bodies and legs and shoes, Marian says, *of
dogs, of shouts. It's really all fragmented. And hours and hours of
waiting and waiting and fear, the feeling of running and running and
the anticipation of danger, that's what I learned,* he says, *and until
today I think it's in me.*
He's on the site of the memorial in Berlin, on the empty waste ground
awaiting a decision as to who will make their monument known here,
he's with Dani Karavan an Israeli sculptor. They are beginning to draw
out an enormous Star of David on the ground, Karavan's idea for the
space that will be filled with yellow flowers. He's ambivalent about how
it will be received, who will live here, surround this monument, the
apartment blocks and banks and commercial centres. Those looking down
or in on the one's visiting such a monument, yes, other's peer down from
their windows, those who will say, *Look at him, look at him down there,
is he crying, or not, Laughing or not. They Look through binoculars to
see how you are reacting* Marian adds.

When we were in Minsk, we discovered that our hotel was on the site of
what was the ghetto. Bella telling us we must visit the site of the
orphanage, well, the site where the orphans and the people who cared
for them were taken and shot, literally five minutes away from where
we are staying, this now, new memorial surrounded by young trees and
grass, and hidden away behind busy roads, by strings of modern hotels
offering discos and happy hours and available girls.

Here you see yourself again stand before a memorial laden with plastic
flowers and gaudy ribbons, this time gold Hebrew writing etched into
another black granite phallus. Here's En playing with the cats you
found, two wild kittens hiding in a drain, they live at the children's
feet, your feet on the newly laid cobbles where the orphans were
killed, cobbles and weeds and your feet covering over what atrocities
beneath. The cats keep watch - like the cows we found at the camp - it
is obviously the job of animals to do what we cannot, to live among

these ruined sites and keep vigil in places in which we feel unable to linger. As again, on entering we already move toward leaving; already prepare to walk away as soon as we enter this, and other sites, our gestures always flounder, incomplete, limited, only aware of our own awkward self-consciousness. Only aware then that En is standing so still, trying to entice the small cats out of the drain. One makes it and rolls over on her back to expose her stomach to him. The other more cautiously shows no more than an ear or eye. You see the man peer down from his balcony onto the circle below. The sight of the shooting took place in what was described as a pit, now cleaned up, into a circle of cobbles. We had to descend some twenty or more steps to get to it, a new bronze sculpture of the children who died here also descend the steps with you. Their skeletal anguished bodies are a now an expected image along with the fiddler at the top. Yet there's something arresting about the way the children move together, about the way the sun catches the metal where its been polished by hands randomly touching here and there. The way the figures look as if they are ablaze.

The man from the tower block is looking down at us and makes no secret that he's staring. As I look up at him, maybe 10 blocks up, he's in a grubby vest, his stomach exposed over his trousers. His hands firmly held together over the ledge of the balcony. I wonder about him in the way the man had talked to Marian about his yellow flowers and the scene with the binoculars. What is he thinking of us in his shameful watching, in our shameful gaze. What does he think of this memorial so close to his home, almost a garden beneath him. I wonder what he thinks of the ones like us who gather here, stand here in twos and all manner of patterns, be that solitaire or multiples. Who is watching whom?

A woman appears, a little way above us, not in the apartments, but just above the steps to the left of the circle. I turn away from the man's eyes, knowing he continues to look on at the scene below him. The woman is handsome enough. For sure in her seventies, but elegant, dark, straight, dignified. She watches you, and you her - yes, having momentarily lost the 'I' you now for some unknown reason begin again to reconstruct this scene in the second person while she - this other woman - passes slowly around the circumference above. She, who comes back on herself, decides to cut to the centre, to descend the steps to where you stand. You wait for her to approach. You wait as if you were expecting her, and knew she was coming. You wait beneath the chestnut tree beside the other more conventional memorial the other side of the circle. Yes, this one is more like the typical black or grey phallus we have come to expect. As she descends the steps, she slowly steadies herself on the sculpture; you watch her hand hold onto the bronze arms and hands of each child. She joins you under the tree. Just ask, you say to yourself. What. Something. Ask does she always come here alone. Surely, not often! Not that old cliché ... Ask, was she here when the children were shot. No too direct and crass! Was she here when this happened. What? Ask if she knew any of these people. Ask and she'll say nothing, because you cannot speak the other's language, you know there is no need to even try. Instead let her stand close to you. Only a tiny space separates your face from hers. Her arm from yours. You stop asking yourself all these questions. Instead try and keep yourself in the present tense. Keep the diminishing voice from growing back to childhood. To a time before both of you. Maybe instead you smile. Mimic

her sigh. Her breath. Her shake of the head. You see that she was once
beautiful, that she still is. Just the two of you, En unaware somewhere
over there with the cats, remember. Just the two of you. You and her.
Just minutes alone with no voice. The voice you thought you wanted you
didn't need after all.

From: "Caoimhe Walsh" <caoimhe@hotmail.com>
Date: Fri, 29th July 2005 11:48:50 +0000
To: angelamorgancutler@ntlworld.com
Subject: RE: books

Dear Angela,

No bother at all. As you probably gathered from my cider-fuelled waffling on
Tuesday I find the ongoing German guilt for the holocaust incredibly complex
and interesting. The book is called The Dark Room by Rachel Seiffert. It
has three separate stories or novellas and the last one was for me the most
interesting as it dealt with the guilt issue. A man married with a child in modern
day Germany travels to Belarus to discover more about his grandfather's
activities during the war. The age of the protagonist in the last novella appears
to be the same as my husband and as I think I mentioned, whilst reading it I
was wondering what it would be like for Oscar, my husband, to visit that part
of Russia where his grandfather was stationed - a stark contrast to the trip you
undertook with your husband to Auschwitz, but of course also a coincidence
that you went on to travel to Belarus.

I'm not sure whether you remember a piece I wrote about my imaginary
son (using the words hair, smell and son because I was too embarrassed
to write using the alternative list which included the word breast) I ended the
piece musing about the kids at school teasing my (half-German) son for his
"European" long blonde hair, salami sandals and Birkenstocks. I looked at that
piece last night and at the end of the page, I had jotted down "wedding photo
- Nazi uniform" a reference to my shock when I saw Oscar's grandfather in
his Nazi uniform, the grandfather who didn't speak at all when he came back
from the war. He had been shot and did recover from his injuries, but there
was no physical reason for his muteness. In fact, he did not speak at all for
the remainder of his life.

I had also jotted down "Joseph's family photograph" and thought I would share
this with you. Joseph is my sister's partner and he is Jewish. Himself and my
husband Oscar are very good friends and, as far as I am aware, they have
never discussed the historical incongruence of their friendship. We stayed
with my sister and Joseph early last year in London and for the first time saw
a black and white photo on the mantelpiece - a very old family portrait of
about 10 small people with dark hair, thick eyebrows and stern faces. They
all looked so alike that it made us smile and my sister Sadie whispered that
when Joseph's grandmother had recently given him the photo of his family,
my sister had commented to him that they looked like munchkins. Joseph

overheard her whispering to us and shouted in from the kitchen "You better not be laughing at my funny looking ancestors, they're my family and they probably died in a concentration camp." Oscar then whispered to us "Yes and my family probably killed them."

We laughed, my sister and I, holding our hands over our mouths to hold the laughs in. We laughed holding each other's arms, locking eyes wide with shock, biting our lips, snorts of guilt escaping from our noses.

Oscar smiled uncomfortably, pleased that he had made us laugh so uncontrollably but somehow embarrassed at how. We have never told Joseph and never will. We share the guilt of having laughed at his sick joke. I hope you don't think that was disgusting behaviour on our part.

I think of this moment when I wonder, as I often do, is it fair that this generation continues to feel guilty for what their grandparents did or didn't do. I wonder also will my son [to be] be expected to hold a sense of guilt for his German heritage. Your story about not rescuing the Krakow pigeon because it was dawn and you didn't speak Polish and … made me think of this again. I don't know the answer but maybe someday I will find an answer to this and all the other questions swirling in my head. Or maybe not.

Best regards, Caoimhe

From: <angelamorgancutler@ntlworld.com>
Date: Fri, 29th July 2005 14:03:51 +0100
To: <caoimhe@hotmail.com>
Subject: Re: books

Caoimhe - Thank you so much for that - I am very touched by your e-mail and all you said.

No of course it's not disgusting - the story of you laughing - I am sure Joseph would have laughed - ah - listen to me as if I know him - but don't you think if he had heard - maybe he did - surely his call from the kitchen, full of humour, was in itself an indication of the unspoken respect and understanding between him and Oscar.

Saul Bellow was both haunted and inspired by a very old photograph of his Jewish grandfather whose photograph attracted, intrigued and terrified him, the idea that he would when old, become this image.

All you said really stayed with me, the grandfather who came home mute, the piece about your son and the idea of guilt passed on and through the womb, or the sperm, and yes, where does that guilt end?

I have a friend who now lives in Spain, and her father was German and came here as a prisoner of war, he's was a dear, funny man, we met him many times and sometimes I would catch myself thinking about how he was treated when he arrived here. In fact I heard only this week, a series of interviews given by ex-german soldiers who talked about how badly they were treated when they were captured here, many tales of abuse and torture that are rarely talked about. I knew only a little of my friend's father's story - not from him directly - how he had at some point almost been killed when he became separated from his unit surrounded by the enemy, he stole a horse, made it to a barn, hid there overnight, was almost captured by a shooting squad. He was little more than a child. Yes, I was curious about his past, and for sure, sometimes, if we were in the middle of sharing a meal, or say, on those occasions when we were in the park together, the children and his dog playing together around us, I'd think of how idyllic a scene we made there in the sunny afternoon all those years on, and I'd sometimes find myself wondering how he felt about what he did or did not do during the war; what was done to him; if he ever thought about his past, if he too, like me, was sitting there contemplating how things move on and change. But those thoughts are unspoken and seem to have no place, made me feel guilty for sure. My friend's husband as it turns out is Jewish and I only found this out by accident one day when we were casually talking about something else over dinner and like your husband and your sister's boyfriend neither did any of us ever talk about the subject of guilt, good or bad, which never felt appropriate or necessary to raise, but it is somehow there maybe in its not being raised, because again, what would you say if you could ask anything at all. What is it we are looking for? What are the answers? Would any of us even have them?

Here's the film my friend sent - about the Jewish man I mentioned to you, Marian Marzynski who goes to Berlin in search of "good guilt."
http://www.pbs.org/wgbh/pages/frontline/shows/germans/view/
The first part questions the idea of monuments to the Holocaust. In the second part he goes in to German schools to ask children how they deal with their history and the question of guilt.

I hope you can open it.
Take care
Ax

From: Moinous@aol.com
Date: Tue, 12 Sept 2006 13:07:56
To: angelamorgancutler@ntlworld.com
Subject: Re: tell me when you leave Paris

As I write to you this morning - there is a woman who every day walks past my window and smiles and waves at me - she doesn't speak any english - she wears the same long cardigan each day - my other neighbour says this woman used to live in one of the flats at the end of the road until her husband died so the landlord threw her out - she now lives in some council run place and each day walks the miles back in all weathers to sit on the steps outside her old apartment to wait for her dead husband's return … so what is to be done to mend her heart -

I forgot to mention last time - I mean concerning what you said about the holocaust memorial in Berlin - when I was there earlier this week - we were driven to the reception - they had vans taking us to various places - we passed in front of the holocaust memorial - interesting - just rectangular blocks of grey stone aligned in various directions forming kinds of deep walkways like in a labyrinth - it's impressive - huge - covers a large space -

I was involved when I was in germany in a discussion with a group of young people who were part of the planning committee for the memorial - I even made a proposition - a huge deep hole in the ground painted all black - with nothing in it - just a hole suggesting absence - and if they insisted on putting something at the bottom - absolutely not a light - but maybe a lampshade - or a bar of soap - or else just a human bone - one bone only my memorial was not accepted anyway

As for the woman outside your window invite her in and ask her to tell you her story and write it down

From: Moinous@aol.com
Date: Wed, 13 Sept 2006 15: 12:45
To: angelamorgancutler@ntlworld.com
Subject: Re: tell me when you leave Paris

I didn't know that you were involved with the Berlin memorial - you never told me that before - or are you making that up - who knows with you what is real and what is not - and I know not to ask you for the TRUTH here -

Imagine the responsibility for the care and safety of that one bone -

I would ask the woman in but she doesn't speak any english -

Instead I picked the tomatoes and then spent the day in Auschwitz - sometimes the book is a strange solace - to be back there and tidying up without trying to sanitise as you say - to keep the *mess* visible - I am currently keeping all the pages in a shirt box did I tell you that already? [Ah. Look at that - as I write this message I get interrupted by my mailbox announcing - *Fly to Paris for only £18* - imagine - I could be there in an hour - or you could come for dinner tonight - I'll make meat balls] Did you remember that the Auschwitz book - in all its disorder - now lives in a shirt box - yes - the content will forever plague me with doubt and the constant feeling of having failed - but the shirt box itself has brought a whole new meaning to the work and I am so sure now that any copies should always be made available in a cream cardboard box that says SUy BALEN [just that way with a small y] on the front - with a crown over the word - On the back - puno doble 903 283 color blanco size or talla 40 €34

It helps to go back once in a while to auschwitz - I do that regularly - the other day I couldn't sleep - I took a little detour to auschwitz and looked around to see if I recognised anyone - nobody - mostly skeletons I could not recognize - when I woke up I was so hungry - I devoured all the peanuts and chocolate in the little fridge the fancy hotels have in their rooms - think I ate more than 20 euros worth of peanuts and chocolate - and that's not including the two beers I had - Don't talk to me about shirts - it's so hot here and humid - I killed three shirts today - I was particularly sweating while reading from a qui de droit - sweat was running down my face when I was reading the sad passages and everybody thought I was crying -

oh well -

as for the woman walking passed your window - tell her to tell you her story with gestures - with little laughs and with tears - I know she has a great story to tell -

I'll be there to look through the shirt box at 7p.m. - as for the meatballs - make sure they are not spicy

Yes Moinous - it occurs to me today - that soon - I will begin to join the dots of this work - of the book - you know like those children's pictures you so carefully join to see if you get a monkey or a flower or a puppy - or in my case hopefully I get my version of A.u.s.c.h.w.i.t.Z

that's the title of your book **AZ**

and then it occurs to me that someone should go up into the Hollywood hills some night and replace HOLLYWOOD with AUSCHWITZ -

It also occurs to me that Hollywood has indeed the same number of 9 letters - but like Auschwitz this word has of course become so much more than just 9 letters - listen to this - the blurb reads - *the recently face-lifted sign so in keeping in a town where everyone's face is lifted - this dazzling place … 300 gallons of paint brighter than a movie stars smile … brighter than the smile of a young starlet who one starless night threw herself to her death from the top of the H - the O found rolling down the hill -*

Originally 4,000 twenty-Watt bulbs charged the sign and were continually changed by their caretaker Albert Gothe who lived in a cabin behind the L - it isn't clear which L -

Maybe we should reinstall the bulbs and the caretaker - maybe we could spend the rest of our days living behind the S or maybe the Z caring for the word
A U S C H W I T Z -

Let's go do it - the minute you get home - bring some technicians and nine 45 ft letters - some flasks of tea - we can supervise - in the morning we can descend to watch the peoples' faces as the sun comes up over the tip of the A -

YES - Ok - forget the meatballs - I'll meet you there - LET'S DO IT -
Mxx

Crossing the Road

We're just yards from the post office where I am taking the postcards I've written for Moinous, the cards saying … *It's that historic day … July 16th and I am thinking of you. Here we are in Minsk and should I tell you of the forest, of Maly Trostenets, of the cows and the shit and the ghost … but no, not yet. All that will be saved for tomorrow, for our return home, yes, we'll arrive back tomorrow but by the time you receive these postcards, of course, weeks will have passed and for now all I will scribble down is the usual scourings of those in recess … We are eating this and that, the weather is suffocating, most of the city was demolished during the war and was rebuilt in austere soviet architecture, rows of concrete tower blocks everywhere so that it's hard to get a sense of any centre, any heart to the place. Soon we'll get arrested.*

Well no, I don't write anything of the sort, all that's to come, yet it's on the way to posting the cards, that we'll get arrested, if that's what I can call it, what else, an incident, an accident of sorts, no-one's hurt, no it's not technically an arrest in the nicked, nabbed, haulin', gotta-come-along-with-me kind of way; more seized, detained - for three hours at least on the pavement in the stinking sun - more being brought to a standstill, prevented from moving, a laying hold of, for a time, more an *at-to*, to remain, to stop, a sudden cessation of motion, RETARD, an interruption of sorts, more that the event of posting the cards - you could say - will be nipped in the bud, yes, it's the postcards that will cause us to cross the road, that will inadvertently cause everything to stop.

Simple enough that the cards are in my hand, my left hand to be precise. I know this as when I cross the road it is my right hand that is free to take En's left. Yes, there we are crossing a road, quiet enough, a large modern up-to-date road, maybe four to six lanes, but at the time of crossing there are no cars, only some stopping at lights some distance away. We cross quickly enough we're half- running, holding hands and we're laughing, there's time for this, you know that way you have of finding the other's hand spontaneously or by habit, rarely running any more, for now, running in that way brings us back to skipping again, you could say we make sprightly steps, that we are co-ordinated when we cross the road, that we reach for each other's hand by instinct; no doubt some throwback to childhood and danger and all our mothers said about the roads and insisted on the roads, all that's well-behaved and virtuous stored away in us, all held in that gesture to reach for the other now making us giggle 'cos we've learnt how to do it, to cross the road, for sure it's a breeze but lest we forget here we are reaching for each other's hand.

Yes, we are laughing, En and me, laughing and slowing back to a walk once we hit the pavement with complete synchronicity. In our twenty-odd years of being together we have learned how to negotiate a road perfectly, when to move when to run when to swerve when to pull or hold the other back, how to change speed and footwork on meeting the pavement with a little jump just for effect at the last a little flutter of steps between us, our four feet slowing.

We're almost at the corner, the pavements are wide here, and the door to the post office is just over there, yes, we're gazing up at the post office, a handsome enough building, pale grand architecture, stone leafed faces, tongues and bulging eyes, maybe even claws and winged beasts guard the entrance, several entrances, an invitation of steps that widen as they reach the dark polished doors, the swing and swish of bodies and doors, the smell of brass cleaner, an old man, spirited enough, cardiganed enough, in this heat bent on ragging the brass plaques to a gleam, this lightens my mood. Opposite there's the Hotel Minsk, the one we almost stayed in. I wasn't planning on recognising anything here but there it is, just over there, a true likeness just like in the brochure, look at that. And just think, if we'd have stayed here at the Hotel Minsk the post office would have been our main view, no scouring maps and getting lost, no trying to figure out half-broken directions from groups of eager businessmen and women with blue-rinsed hair, splays of fur even in this heat, none of them agree; instead there I would have been waking early, half-asleep, half-undressed, with no care for either, opening up our musty hotel curtains - attached to one of those nylon pulleys for sure, weighted, ugly patterned overly-coordinated drapes that match our discarded counterpane. Yes, there I would have been opening up the drapes, the wide window opens to the traffic and the bustle and the condiment of a foreign city's unfamiliarity; my contentment with the divide that will not ever let me see this place as anything but separate and distinct; wrestling with the thin curtain beneath the thicker outer ones, depending on your position, either sill side or inside the room, looking out through the thin weave of netting that clings to me in the warm breeze. Yes if we'd have stayed on that very side just over there, someone might have glanced up from the post office, innocently enough, and seen me there veiled in cheap voile, returning the gaze, each morning, each evening, watch the delivery boys come and go with eager regularity, the delivery boys who dream of other ways other times. Instead we're here at last just yards from the post office and our arrival puts a smile on me, I can say that I am beaming at the building, never have I been so pleased and captivated with a post office when behind us there's the slow realisation of a siren screaming.

Yes,

the road we cross by mistake, *carefully* I will insist. *Illegally* he'll say ... Just seconds away now, my protest ... *I didn't know, how would I know,* not yet; wait! For now all I know is that I am happy to be here - halcyon moment, and behind us there's a police car approaching all lights and sirens screaming. That fast, we find the pavement we find the post office and that quickly a policeman finds us, shouts at us through a loudspeaker. *He's behind you* ...There we are, in one movement we turn, turn again, keep in motion, however slow, sure that he must be shouting at someone else. And he's mad as hell now and screaming in Russian - obvious enough - screaming in his mother other tongue, flashing his car lights and driving like in one those films you know too well, all screeching and tire marks, all wheels and zig-zagging into the slide across the road, yes, he's leaning from his car window and screaming, causing us to slow a little more, to still look around for someone other, for something else happening over there, where. There is nothing else, except his anger looking directly at *Us*. I think maybe it's the way we look, *and how do we look*, or maybe it's because of what's happened back home, I mean the bombings in London and En wearing a black rucksack so maybe he thinks we are terrorists. No, ma'am, don't be so exaggeratory, as Max would have me say. I think this and dismiss it immediately. I think instead maybe it's my pickled fish and my puréed aubergine, no joke; maybe it is something about the way I am carrying the food we just bought and some souvenirs, the Russian doll, the wooden lacquered bowl with gold leaf, so they said, yes, something about the doll's over- eyelashed lids and dumb smile held in my green plastic sack. Maybe something's happened and he's needing to trace us. I jump from terrorism to fish to concern, I consider the children, my mother back home, that the policeman is trying to get a message to us, to help us, to save us from something, that something dreadful has happened and it is that moment just before we are told, that moment when everything will change with what he has to tell us. I can see he is still screaming and everyone else is looking at us. I see myself stop, no, more hesitation, my feet still hover on going forward, my head and stuttering feet no longer work in accord. My head still tells me it must be a mistake, no-one knows us here, no one. Hear in response En saying quietly, It's us he wants, hear me answer, What have we done? See that he cannot take his eyes off us, he can't understand why we are not listening to what he is screaming at us, that we persist in moving our feet and screw up our dumb faces in confusion, all he knows is he wants us. I also now realise that everyone else can see it's us. I can see their faces mix with a kind of pity, smug curiosity or apprehension for their own safety. In their concern for their own proximity to us, I can see that people now hesitate and won't come close, so soon they scatter themselves, change direction change their minds, pass quickly, glad to be skipping by, glad it's us and not them. I can see that he is driving now with his face almost squashed into the front window, he's screeching to a halt that way he'd trained for, perfected, for sure it's an opening scene.

It's the scene where he wants us so much that in his haste to come get us he opens his door without looking and a car approaching from behind smashes into his car door. That simple, fast and loud: the sound metal makes on impact, a second's eery stillness that follows. It's the part where En turns, a pirouette of sorts, on the pavement, elegant delivery, and he says to his wife - that's me of course - he says, We are done for. It's the part where the police man gets out of the car and looks at the huge dent in his buckled car door, now all colours and shapes and then there's the door of the other couple's car all dented and scraped through with blue police car paint scraped along the Ginger Boy's car and Ginger Boy's girlfriend pacing around all vexed and fretting and touching the trashed car wing; she wearing no more than a black baby doll negligée and matching kitten heels.

It's the scene where Police Boy screams in our faces, where he runs from our faces back to his car, where he can't decide what to do first if to shout or phone, so he does both. I didn't imagine a phone. I don't know why, well of course, a phone, what else, but not so soon, I'd imagined he'd speak to us first, get our story, communicate something directly, but instead what can we say to one another when neither of us can find a common language. He says nothing to us, except to indicate that we are to stay still, not to move, and already he's on his phone, telling on us for sure when we're joined by another policeman …

This one's older, he's on foot. He's shorter, slower and much calmer, good cop bad cop, here we go. He's trying to show us the underpass, the one we should have used. I didn't see it, I shout and repeat, shout and repeat and gesticulate in that way foreigners always shout and repeat and gesticulate as if the other has some inane hearing loss that comes with living over a border, a sky, a sea. Yes, we gab on in our own languages, strive forth and quickly come to realise we cannot speak a word of each other's tongue which rather than slow us only propels us deeper into trying as if the sheer volume of din and fracas between us will somehow make the other understand, that some reason will come of persistence, but no, almost amused, almost through habit an orderly temperament an attention to detail, the sidekick opens his case onto the flat trunk on the rear of the police car and begins to set up a small office there, for sure all he needs is a desk lamp and an easy chair, a plate of sandwiches and he'll be happily there for the day. He is maybe in his 50s, although I can say I have no time now or mind for guessing his age, but he's lived a while, the effects of people, air and love are all visible in him; the other, still pacing and phoning, is younger, not a kid but not far off, but built like a bull, all muscle and testosterone all raring to go, already fucked by his impulse to get us, by the way he tortures himself by looking and re-looking at the wrecked cars, for sure he's the one taking the lead here, taking control by being out of control. Maybe it's more that short man is happy to let him take the charge, maybe less a question of his seniority but more a display of his sheer force and panic and motion and the mess he's made or maybe that short man can't compete, can't be bothered to muster the needed energy to take any direction except to slowly, methodically, set up a kind of office on the boot of the car, to take a ring side seat and watch the rest unfold, to find out how the other is going to resolve this or not …

As short one fiddles with his paperwork, the other still clings to his phone, rushes at us, then back to tell everyone he can find in his in-built phone directory, friends and colleagues, anyone who'll listen: Look what these strangers did to me, these damn dog-fuckers, these dumb foreign overlords, these colonisers, suzerains, look what they did to my car, to my day, to my week … Say it loud, come to believe it, alleviate the rush of hormones that surely surge and release themselves with such verbosity through him that his head is visibly pulsing, his skin flushes and sweats, the chest puffed up over unsteady pacing legs, thick thighs rub and stick to cloth but keep him in motion, keep him sure of the need he has to keep shouting into the phone, into our faces, to remind us how incensed he is, to remind us of where our hearts are positioned. To remind us that it's all our fault, that we're in the wrong, mistaken, unforgiven, to remind us of our culpability, unduly, overmuch, needlessly over the top, point and pace, wave and shout, shove his fingers and his mouth and his spit and polished police badge in our eyes, his index finger stabs the badge and shine, shine your eyes then towards the road, towards the vehicle, and back again. I have to say, that his mouth and badge are more in En's face than mine. Maybe here women get the better deal, less of a finger, maybe here this is a man's thing, me no more than a tag on when it comes to it, me no more than the sidekick, no more than the short fat other cop who is filling out the forms, me no more than a handbag, faded lipstick, a moll with a doll in her sack, yes, when it comes to getting an eyeful of the large sun glinted badge being ripped almost from the pale blue of his shirt - careful, it is En more than me that gets it. This is where it gets you, the rhetorical swell and nob, the lie of - all things being equal, can never be equal, yes, when badge comes to shove, to shoving it to your face, emancipation is no more than a forced brassy kiss pressed to your nose, to your cheek; when badge comes to face it's women overboard, left through the exist that allows me to take a moment in which to open up my nose, who'd have thought there'd be time to take a whiff, a whiff of sweat, no, starch, the bad cop's a clean cop, that much I can say, a clean shirt marks the occasion as if he could have known that such an incident would cause us to meet like this, as if he could know that I'd notice the perfectly starched crease marks where he's taken extra care with the iron, a mother's work maybe, back to that, no I don't know why but I imagine him alone with his own iron, it's something in the way the short blue sleeves are pressed out and resemble little wings, surely unconsciously open and yet deliberately trying too hard to please, these perfectly pressed sleeves which make me see him as a loner, unloved for now, maybe this morning, like every other, what else to do but to steam press to the sound of the one cup coffee pot reaching its climax, the news on the radio echoes through the small apartment, I can almost smell the soap powder, the shirt is that clean, the spray on starch, the highly polished badge replaced, the number adds the finishing touch, quiet life, the number I memorise to myself until I can get to my notebook to write it down, not for reasons of complaint, I'm not thinking that way, but because I want to know something of him, I want his name where there are no names, not yet, if at all, for now all I have instead is some small sense of identification: 60295.

But,

Who cares about your badge I shout to him, Who cares how it shines. My voice finding its way out, surprises itself, forgets and knows that he cannot understand, continue anyway … Repeat the number, repeat that I can't emphasise enough how my eyesight's never good and he's not good at keeping still, the badge dazzles, rarely flops on top of all that starch, but he's close enough to allow me to memorise the number and note that it begins with: NO. Look harder at that, is that NO. short for what? - What's Russian for number - surely a coincidence - as in NO don't mess with me. NO. 60295. His arm extends from badge to road, the muscles of his body twitch in different and unexpected patterns, blonde baby soft down over the taut police muscle of his contracting and expanding arm. His incessant pace that makes me mimic his tread, my tempo, we click, the rate of progress, with the same steps and gait, same tilt of the head same inflection, gasps; accents differ, even with a matching cardigan long forgotten in all this heat, either way, opened mouthed, he speaks, he dials yet another number, NO. 60295 already known now off by heart. The short fat other, the number two come henchman' is still writing a small profile, surely by now a small essay, sometimes he's pacing too between words, between lines and rubbings out, he's trying to raise his voice but not quite making it, he tries at times to join in on the motion only slower on account of his gut and laid back temperament, at times almost a wry smile gives way all he can't be seen to say, not yet, because the other one has forgotten he has the capacity to laugh, to remember a simple smile …

Yes, pressing out number after number, NO. 60295, is going to his car and caressing the damage. He takes out his hat, puts it on as if he just realised he is not fully dressed therefore not completely in authority, as if regulations insist and he's only just remembered that to take charge you need to be in full uniform; or is the hat to simply shelter his fair shaved head, what was once an open fontanel. The hat, a form of intimidation or protection, surely in our case, a warning - this is only the start - now the hat is on, anything could happen. And I had only yesterday said to En, I want one of those police hats as a souvenir, there's something so exaggerated about the huge crown of the hat, the way it sweeps up wildly at the front, like all police hats it's a joke of a hat but it's a hat that says you will not ignore me, it's a hat that means there's work to be done, matters to attend to, duties to perform, a state of affairs to circle, the hat that he's adjusting in front of me as if I am a mirror and he's fixing it so it looks just right in front of my face and he still can't believe that he is talking to a pair of idiots who can't understand a word he's saying, so we all keep trying to make our self heard through more sheer repetition and volume, take our turns, Russian English Russian English and then a cocktail of noise as we forget whose next. En's reasoned voice here and there, telling me to calm down, and whatever you do - DO NOT laugh at him …

Laughter, could he again sense this was on its way. Never mind the ghost, or whatever we happened to see or not, back there in the forest, am I already laughing my way through a scene that loops itself around one spot, around the gun in No. 60295's belt, the stick in his pants, the dance of him back and forth while Ginger Boy in the background stares at his wrecked car, this pale boy shaken into silence, clinging to his baby doll whose black sleek hair curls in the unbearable heat, her small porcelain face peers over at the two of us, at NO. 60295 asking for our papers, the crudeness of non-verbals and hands desperate to form sentences, hands that soon and effectively take our passports, hands that slide them into his top shirt pocket. The wings stiffen as the pocket fills, the hat is neither doffed nor produces a rabbit, unless that comes later, instead, there's no exchange no room for charm nor ornament, instead, I can only attest to how our passports, taken swiftly, fit perfectly in his shirt pocket that only makes me want to touch, push my hand in and get them back; our passports creating a neat bulge over his chest, next to his heart, as if his pocket and heart were made for them, his pocket measured and sewn in place by some woman no doubt, someone he, we, will never meet, has made his shirt knowing the needed size, the potential snug fit, the convenience, no, he's not even thinking of this, not in anyway aware ...

And as always when things happen out of nowhere, a unexpected collision that for sure changes into an attention that snatches all you had taken for granted about walking and talking freely, about moving at will and posting cards - remembered now, those innocent cards curling up in the heat, yes with all that you had taken for granted about the unrestricted use of your time and limbs, snatched now, no, arrested, back to that, the next hours and steps no longer yours to hold onto, nor yours to abuse, to ignore; where there is both an arrest and no progression of arrest, just the indecision and the wait, with and without any sense of urgency, no room to act, nor insist on matters that are obstinate enough to leave you for now with only the trivial to get you by, with only the paltry details of the spot you are in and forced to turn inside until you find yourself rewinding the morning, surveying your little 4 by 4 plot, the shelter of your tree, the fateful section of road, the beloved but denied post office. So soon you find yourself daydreaming, bored rigid, fit to scream with the monotony of another hour becoming just like the last and more of the same to come. Yes, you find yourself staring at a beetle making love frantically with another beetle beneath the dust of your tree, a beetle hanging on with a determination you feel ebb, with just enough spring in one's step to kick the beetles apart just because you have the power to do anything to these two right now, to squash them with your flimsy summer sandal, to take them away right at the moment of orgasm, if orgasm beetles do, replay each scene and say to yourself ...

If only I had sipped my water more quickly, if only we hadn't walked around the supermarket and taken that 5th floor to the fishing tackle and lingerie section, if only En hadn't stopped to photograph me in front of the male mannequin with the ridiculous curly wig, crumpled blue suit with clashing tie, if only I hadn't stopped to photograph the statue of Pushkin, if only I had been able to climb onto Pushkin's lap and hadn't kept sliding off. If only we hadn't bumped into the journalist who had just found his way here after a 15-hour train journey from Warsaw, if only he hadn't been lost and asked us the way, if he hadn't tried to persuade us to eat lunch with him, if he hadn't whispered that he was here to get information, that we were not to mention that we'd seen him, nor the reason for his visit, his job ... all of us looking around as if we were being watched; surely he wasn't bugged. If only I hadn't stopped to pee in the railway station. The station En wanted to photograph; instead, when we find it, the station where his grandparents probably first entered Minsk, it's been rebuilt, modernised beyond recognition and there's nothing worth photographing. There's just me trying to squat over a simple enough hole in the ground, a hole-made-toilet in the station. I've seen them before of course, nothing remarkable, just this time I am tired and hot and we're trying unsuccessfully to find the post office, this time the toilet cubicles are on stilts and I have to climb some steps to get inside, note the absurdity of watching other women, some in their tight clothes and heels trying to climb the steps to their hole; holding my underwear like the memory of a nappy, lowering my body over a hole yellowed with others' waste, into no foothold, my thighs shake slightly with the awkward bulk of myself, of trying to hitch up my long skirt, trying to keep my weight even, to remember how to bend at the knee, only from this height a state of imbalance and no way of finding control. Instead, there I am almost flying from the cubicle half-dressed, almost slip over, trying to conceal my half-soaked underwear and shouting back at the toilet attendant who is letting the others out while I'm still stuck behind a barrier counting out hundreds of coins in my hands, 250 rubles for a pee. It's not the cost, it's that I haven't got on my glasses, it's that I can't see the change, it's the attendant demanding and everyone looking. It's the attendant and me not being able to find a common language and her voice so quickly slipping into screaming, it's hearing myself scream back and the shame of my foreign voice echoing across the tiled lavs ... I do not understand you, I do not understand. The tears outside the station, okay I admit it. I say to En, I have no idea why I am crying, I just am, so don't say a thing. I have no damn idea why or what we are doing here. Yes. If only we hadn't needed to sit a while, to write the postcards to Moinous, if it hadn't been July 16th, if I hadn't taken the time to write. If we'd sipped the coffee slower, but, post breakfast, there is no coffee, here everyone is already drinking flat lager or warm water. En and me staring into a series of stark concrete fountains, a few words written on a selection of cards and the rest of the morning trying to locate the post office. If only the cards hadn't needed to be posted, and the post office hadn't been built over that side of the road ...

For now here's NO. 60295's partner happily filling in forms, working methodically enough as if he has done this many times but will not be shaken by the potential boredom and monotony of his task. He uses a pen and a little stub of a pencil that he licks before he makes a mark. He has a ruler ...

We follow the shade of the tree, En hides inside its narrow shadow, he and the tree become one, as if it is the only thing keeping him upright, as he pushes the back of his body into its trunk, his hands behind him embrace it. I cannot say this enough. We're hungry and we discuss the way we would have walked to get our lunch, what we would have been eating by now. We plan our route out of here, even though we can't move as NO. 60295 - [well, I'll call him NO. for short, I can't keep repeating these digits, I have no memory or mercy for numbers] NO. is in his shirt sleeves exposing his strong arms. He's still pacing and phoning, can you believe that's all he does for hours, on and on, as if the movements and the repetition are somehow comforting him helping him to keep in motion to maintain his anger ...

I look at Baby Doll looking at us: we the arrested or about-to-be, I don't even know when an arrest is an arrest. I wonder how we look to her, I wonder how guilty I look standing here with my plastic bag with my aubergine dip turning to liquid. I check my small fish happily cooking, fish squish next to my Russian doll's wooden head, oblivious as the oil and the aubergine separates and is golden under her floral body. When I return my gaze at Ginger Boy, Baby Doll holds onto his thin body and I am confident that she won't outstare me. She turns her eyes as a horse passes behind her along the road, his elegant black haunches shiver out red shit, red drops all along the road. At first it alarms me, as if our staring too hard at one another has induced some kind of metaphor of blood to ooze from the horse's arse and then I of course remember the nosebags full of beets ...

In the distance three blind people negotiate the pavement, possibly mother son and daughter, I worry over the missing father; mother at the centre all three arm-in-arm all wave their sticks before them, not in unison, white thin sticks tap an irregular tune until they become caught in the chained-up bicycles they cannot manoeuvre, the spokes confuse them as they each take it in turn to untangle themselves. They do not seem to speak but make their way silently, pressed into each other's body, sway left or right to guide them into the needed direction, incline to take an oncoming bend. Would they do better alone, I wonder, as I watch them falter down the path, three blind mice, you'd do better alone.

I swear a lot because I trust that NO-one can understand me. I almost sing a little swearing song which comes back to me now here of all places, a little tune my great-grandmother once taught me when she was delirious on her death bed. I insult NO. whenever I can muster the needed words and effort, knowing he chooses to ignore us, knowing he can make me stand here for as long as he wants, drilled to our tree, whose spot is this any longer, this random area of pavement and such a mess of debris and people milling around like extras all over the road. Imagine if we could google us in or out of here, imagine the cursor come arrow flying over the spinning ball of the world growing large, beautiful the way it swells and then hones in, locates us right here inside a tiny framed cross that finds us, only to lose us again, so soon loosens our position. Instead, all I am left with are insults and mimicry to compensate for what NO. cannot translate. As NO. moves, I move in the opposite direction, his right to left turning left right, my left to right turning right left, depending on which way you look at it, depending on how much I want to mimic or do the opposite, either way ... Tell him I've had enough of this shit, I announce to En. Tell him that I'm going soon and not standing here all day. Tell him where we were yesterday. Tell him about the forest and explain to him that we are not on holiday here. Tell him about your grandparents. Are you kidding ... that's the last thing we should mention, En says, the grandparents. We just have to be quiet and wait. But what if I decide to walk off right now, not stand here any more. Have done with this ... Say again, I've done nothing wrong ... I'm off ... If I just go and post my cards, just there, what could he do, take me to a wood and shoot me! ...

Can't we ring someone, I say to En. Can't we press some buttons, can't we press something to our ear. There must be someone we can ring. Borrow NO's precious phone, ring Bella. Ring Yossi. Tell them that we are being kept here against our will made to stand here for hours in this heat with nothing to eat and no promise of anything happening and no-one making any decision. Tell him we have no phone of our own. Tell him it's in the hotel along with our photocopied papers.

Yes, instead of carrying photocopies of our passports as the guide advised, *just in case*. We have the photocopies neatly folded in the hotel drawer - the passports snug in NO.'s pocket. We have one bottle of water getting warmer, being sipped; being aware of the time I may have to keep this paltry sup I reassess the whole miserable incident in the railway station over the hole and now see that without knowing I made the right decision not then realising I would end up standing here on this pavement with no possibility of moving or relieving myself, except there's the tree. I suck on the water bottle's small plastic teat, this hard nodule against my tongue that normally irritates now becomes a comfort, to feel it open to liquid however stale however warm, mere dribbles, more a repetition I seek to show NO. I have something other to do than stand here waiting. However ridiculous it seems. NO. has his phone I have my water bottle, we have the afternoon spread out, spent following the shadow of a tree, a shadow that gets smaller as the sun peaks, the tree that becomes a kindness, a silent one on our side, for sure this tree is ours - or so we like to think. NO. edging his way to cross into what's left of our line of shade. Pushing his face close to us again except as if reading my mind, this time offering up his phone that he's placed in En's hand, indicating with great jabs of his finger, that En should speak. NO. then paces around our tree. Round and round as if binding us in with imaginary rope, or is it that he has an air of an expectant father about his smile and gait, a little anxious but pleased with himself, for all his efforts, I press my ear close to En's and imagine this an end to this nonsense, this is the call that will tell us we can now be on our way, the post office just feet away and no doubt our lunch, however late, is already being cooked just for us in that restaurant we'll return to in just about half an hour, no more. Go eat lunch, I imagine the woman on the end of the phone will say, Go sit down, laugh, forget it all … but no, instead a woman officer on the end of the line in broken English says, You crossed the road and should have used the underpass and now you must pay money to our country for all the damage you caused to our cars. She tells En, You will be taken to the police station and you must find a translator, she tells him, Crossing the road is illegal … It's illegal? I am shouting the question and repeating and En saying Shh shh. I am shouting, We won't pay a damn penny 'cos we did nothing wrong. Tell her it was his own stupid reckless driving and total overreaction that caused the accident, he smashed his car not us, and who said crossing the road is illegal - Ask her again, is it illegal?. And ask her who she is … Ask her how can we believe her, who is she, ask her. En telling me to calm down, telling me it's serious, they can do what they like, say what they like, keep us here if we don't co-operate and we're supposed to be flying home tomorrow morning, maybe they'll stop us going back. He is trying to find the number for the Embassy. We search his pockets and bag and wallet and again his pockets until he decides that the Embassy will probably be useless and will take too long, instead he finds a crumpled piece of paper with Bella's number, holds it out to NO …

And it's the crumpled piece of white paper, the way En is holding it and passing it over that makes me hush, yes, something in the gesture, of his hand outstretched, of the smallness of the paper, its torn edges, its crease marks, its faint line of blue numbers that makes the moment between the three of us suddenly quiet. That is all En can produce from his pocket, from his body, the familiarity of his handwriting, his great-uncle's ring on his right hand, the way he unfolds the small note and holds it out to NO. NO., already dialling Bella. He tries four times and I imagine she is not home, that she is at her friend's picnic, I picture her in the pine trees by the cool lake she had described yesterday, at her friend's party, already eating the barbecued meat, the charcoaled vegetables, the pickles being carried on her plate. Bella …

While NO. dials and redials Bella's number it's as if we all now find some reassurance in our proximity while we huddle and wait for the sound of Bella's voice. *Please be there,* I say to myself over and over. *Please, Bella …* There's just the sound of the phone being redialed over again, a ring tone that won't end, En saying that he'll try again in a minute or two, dial, try again, wait a while, there's nothing else now or new, just the three of us sheltering beneath what's left of an elongated shadow. Does NO. even notice the tree? I look up into the leaves and try and remember what type of tree it is, I am about to ask En but feel unable to intrude on this small moment that's allowing us to at least replenish our tired bodies, a small trough in the argument. Imagine a graph that could plot the last hours toing and froing, now stilled completely. NO.'s face looking at En, almost needing something from him, something other than the obvious return of Bella's voice, but he's not sure what. Just the small piece of paper back and forth between their muddle of fingers. NO.'s too-present flesh, his small blue eyes, his too-clean uniform, too much the soap of the morning. I think of how he might have looked on waking, how he might have looked before we all arrived here at this point, as if they could have known they were to meet in this way, this hopefully brief coming together, yes, two men shave themselves in two distinct places in this city, maybe at the same time or one a little ahead of the other, they face themselves in the mirror, this close, close shaving away the night's hair from their faces, the one I had witnessed the other I am now upon, a faint smell of unfamiliar cologne closes my nose …

With this a new man appears on the scene, rather comes back into focus worn through with waiting, no more than a silent extra. He's been here all the time but with all the toing and froing too easily forgotten. Despite his youth, a young enough face peers from black unwieldy locks, you might also say that his weathered face is not without character and colour, a face lit up by the immaculate whites of his eyes and teeth that smile more a squint from the back of NO.'s car. Yes, had I imagined that he was arrested when I no more than noticed that NO.

was not alone in the car, no more than a glance his way, forgetting in all the boohoo to take any further heed, until he joins us, reminds us that he's been there all along, so forlorn, so forgotten, no-one prompts him, no-one indicates or opens the door for him or even takes any care of his steps towards us when something in him decides it's time to re-establish himself, to punctuate more than interrupt the scene, to stand before us, not with his hands tied behind his back, not handcuffs or any such straps or restraints just his hands held behind of their own accord, his gentle hands protect a see-through bag full of edible, mouth watering, fresh butter-filled bread rolls. And for sure at the sight of these, I imagine the possible merging of our bags and the picnic we could make from the almost biblical blend of our loaves and the fishes, the multiplication of our small offerings into a whole feast right here on the pavement's edge, the doll I could offer up for Baby Doll, yes, with a sandwich, an offer of a gift for the one who hugs her pale boyfriend as if she were sinking, his red hair a beacon, his body a buoy, her hair so dark in contrast spills with her stares, her tired almost defeated body not able to pull off the needed stance and pose she now lacks, so that the short black nylon night-dress red-ribboned neckline wilting rosebud and lace, seem more than ever out of place. Her heels drag and she wobbles slightly turns her ankle while she returns to her damaged car. Yes, as Bread Boy emerges from his imprisoned back seat so Baby Doll returns to the back seat of her crumpled car, Bread Boy's bread already begins to sweat in its transparent sack.

It is the sound of Bella's voice at last coming from the phone's handset that makes me smile. The reassuring tones and lilt and fleeting break in tedium, the promise of rescue while NO. insists for now on taking back the phone, of talking to Bella himself, of not looking at us, sprung back in motion, words and dizzying circles and meaning it when he shouts the only words I understand among a barrage of Russian - IMPERIALISTS, IMPERIALISTS. That's us, En says.

Phone and languages go back and forth. NO. finally relinquishes the phone to En. NO. surprising me further by not only giving us the phone, but by giving us some privacy and distance while my ear is again squashed to En's and to Bella's reassuring voice telling us we must wait for her, telling us not to worry, that we must meet her at the police station, unless she can get to us first, telling us that the station is not far from where we are, she spells out the name of the road we are in, Yes, yes, that's it, she says, I'll be there as soon as I can, less than an hour. She tells us, yes, it is illegal to cross the road, you'll have to pay, nothing much, he wants you to pay a small fine, and on top, something towards the damage to the car. Don't worry, she says, if you get taken to the station before I arrive, he'll just needs statements and some money, but don't agree to anything or sign anything until I get there.

I am almost laughing again. I am. I can no longer stop myself. I am laughing I watch people come in and out of the side entrance of the post office just twenty paces away. I wonder how the inside of the post office will look, I wonder how the inside of a station will look, I am almost curious to go now in either direction, post office - police station, just to move from this tree, from this heat. Yes, now that I realise we have to go I am almost ready and impatient to see the station. I also think about how easy it would be to just move, to just walk away. Announce to En that I'm going to go post my letters. If you move they'll go nuts, En says. It is all nuts. I toy with the idea of taking small but sure steps, it seems so easy, to just go while everyone is busy, walking talking, still phoning, short guy, would you believe, is still drawing diagrams of the crash scene, while I make such a simple act, to walk to post my cards. To walk like a child does with her baby reigns hugging her chest, to see how far I can get before the yank back to see if in fact the straps have been dropped in a moment's distraction, aren't after all trailing the floor and I am free to move away, look, I'm already running ...

Instead, I sit on the floor no better than a cheap garden gnome, I see En slide further down the tree's trunk. I see NO. circle the tree again no better than a dog searching for the right latrine or scent. I sit on the floor, legs crossed on the hot pavement and begin writing in my note book. I write to Moinous, You won't believe this ... I tell him. As I write I wonder if my writing will only further fuel NO. to come take my book away. I write wanting NO. to see that I am writing. I write as if he can understand. I write his number several times NO. 60295. but he is not even looking any more ... I scribble that I am a coward for not making a getaway ... I feel sorry for En that he looks so shaken, that he feels responsible for our safety, and this gives me the privilege - he cannot allow himself - to rant and swear and laugh. I hate that he looks so upset ... I want to tell him I'm sorry but I don't know for what ... I want to eat ... to rip the bag out of Bread Boy's hands. I am dreaming of the onion soup En ate yesterday, the one with the cheese crust thick and golden and risen like a small pillow on top, of the promised cod's roe. I write down the name of the road but cannot pronounce it, I cannot properly replicate the symbols nor write my R's backwards because I have no idea how to pronounce these backward Belarussian words. I say to myself what else would I write ... now ... how else could this have ended, this trip that is not, how else could this have finished but being held here like this, with me sitting on the floor with other peoples' shoes back and forth in front of me, white scuffed heels, shiny boots, dusty toes, cigarette butts thrown beside me, someone spits, and a oversized mongrel sniffs at my skirt, his wet snout startles me, his grey overstretched balls full, ready and waiting, he's even denied his piss against our tree as En kicks him away.

A guy shows up in a taxi, a man with a yellow tape measure. Everyone begins measuring everything: the length of the cars, spaces between the cars, the road length and width, the pavement, distance to Baby Doll. It's like the tape they use to cordon off a murder scene. I wait to be approached but no-one comes to measure me or my distance to them. I'd like to measure our tree, my distance to the post office door, the circumference of NO.'s hat and the dog's balls, the length of Baby Doll's legs and heels and hair, the length of time we are being held.

Short guy now draws out a very careful map and new version of the taped up crime scene, he works like a diligent school boy, his pages all spread out carefully over the back end of the police car, held down with small keys and weights to stop them blowing away - as if there were any danger of a breeze. In all the measuring Bread Boy has somehow disappeared.

I return to my writing, not sure what to any longer write, just writing for the comfort of making marks on the page, of doing something, writing again, as I had the day before when in the hotel lobby … *We are waiting for Bella … we are waiting for* … and I look up and there she is again - running across the fateful road. In fact now everyone's back and forth across the road as if there is no longer any law to be broken. Yes, here's Bella appearing on cue appearing and already beginning negotiations.

An undernourished inspector turns up in a powder blue car also driving like in the movies, making a huge sweeping U-turn that causes his tires to screech across the road. Bella says he's come to assess the cost of the damage, she says it's probably about $150 for his door. Maybe. No-one's sure yet. Everyone is talking, signing forms, measuring, pacing drawing, looking at the cars, touching the cars, gesticulating, estimating, translating. Yes, Bella is talking loudly and her hands move to and fro with great speed. I do the same and trust she translates what I say. Her pink lipstick's been refreshed but is already melting with the heat and the talk. Baby Doll and her boyfriend sign forms, talk for some time, return again to their car and are allowed to drive off. That's it. They've gone …

Bella tells us that if we have to go to the station in NO.'s car, that she will follow in hers, that we are not to sign, not agree to pay anything, except the fine for not using the underpass. She warns us that at the station, they might interview us in rooms more like wooden booths, sometimes they talk to you through microphones, they'll probably separate you, it's not nice she says, but don't worry, I'll be there with you. I shout again about not seeing the damn underpass - No-one told us it was illegal to safely cross an empty road, or I WOULDN'T HAVE. I was just looking at the post office, that's all. That's not an excuse, Bella says. You can't tell him you were just looking at the post office. But I WAS!

With each exclamation I wonder how I sound to someone who cannot understand a word I say. I try and concentrate on the noise and the rhythm and the intonation I make as I watch NO.'s face listening to my defence. I try to hear myself from NO.'s point of view, but of course fail. I make every effort to exaggerate my sentences and finish with some flair, if he can't understand I want him to know I am at least passionate in my delivery. The young inspector from the blue car drives off as dramatically as he'd arrived. Again Bella keeps translating that NO. wants us to sign papers and then go write a statement at the station but there's no sign of movement, of anyone putting us into the car. I am sure he is stalling and has no intention of taking us anywhere. Bella explains that NO. is young, he's more than likely in a lot of trouble over this, he was obviously over-enthusiastic, he knows he caused the accident but he doesn't make much money, he wants you to pay something towards the cost of repairs, that way you can leave. She says, this is common practice, he needs you to pay so that he can keep this quiet from his superiors, the man in the blue car was his friend. He cannot find all the money himself. That's corruption, I say. Yes, of course it is, Bella and En are saying in unison, almost laughing at me ... but you need to get out of here and this is the simplest way out. En is already asking her - How much?

I knew it ... I cannot believe this, I say, a last sorry attempt. He drove like a lunatic, he totally overreacted, he's nuts. We did nothing wrong, we didn't know ... he's held us here for hours, he's taken our passports ... but no-one is listening any longer ...

I am ready for a ride in NO.'s car. I admit it. Let's go. I am ready to go somewhere, anywhere just to get away from this spot, from this repetition, this indecision, to see the inside of the station. Instead, we're all close to NO.'s car, we've all edged close without realising, it's almost a party. I no longer care what the sun will do. What NO. will do. Bella gives us the courage to inch closer to him to the car and so far he does nothing in response. First my hand, my elbow, the length of my arm, and even when I am laying my worn-out self over the top of NO.'s roof - the metal burning my skin is even somehow reassuring, letting myself move, flop, touch something of his, how the time, the mess, somehow, finally pulls us all together - he does nothing but watch me lay my plastic bag on his car, the aubergine dip is now completely green and liquid, the fish stinks and looks off. Short man finds a new job and is carefully copying out my name from my passport onto his forms and repeats and smiles - angels - angels - yan Kutler - angels - and he's found himself laughing. I start laughing, En is almost laughing, short man is really laughing, Bella is laughing and decides to take pictures with our camera of the crime scene. I tell her I wanted to but wasn't sure how he'd react. She tells NO., quickly translating - It's memorable for them, they can show their friends, their children, it's for their album. They've probably never been arrested before. Yes, there's still a lot of nothing happening, a lot of nodding and hand movements, a certain amount of smiling between translating, small moments of laughter to be heard. NO.'s face looks so different when he smiles, until he realises, his grin hovers between menace and giving into Bella's charm and deciding he'd best pull his teeth and tongue back to the safety of his closed mouth, readjust his hat. For now NO. and me let ourselves take each other in completely unabashed while Bella continues to make me laugh as she clicks the camera and moves around us telling us to smile as I pose for the next and the next photograph, this time laying my head on his car, putting my hand under my chin and pouting at Bella. NO. stares at my wedding ring for a long time, face and hands ring back and forth, he looks as if he wants to speak to me but doesn't know how to. When he quietly asks Bella to ask me how much would you pay in your country if this happened. He studies me carefully as I answer, NOTHING, tell him not a damn thing, we can cross any road anywhere. Not a damn penny. I make exaggerated hand gestures to indicate NADA. I feel momentarily sorry for him as his mouth makes small involuntary twitches at my reply, as we all continue to laugh and snide and circle him like a noose twined round an animal subdued or about to kick. Despite our increasing high spirits, I see that it's getting harder to keep shouting and gesticulating at NO. It's getting harder to judge what he's thinking now he's quiet and still. For sure we are sassy and laughing, relaxing some at last, poking him a little here and there but at any time he could change direction; the more frisky we become, the more I have the urge to run lawless across the law-filled road between the geometry of the yellow tape, along the white lines and around the red horse-shit to see how he'll respond, to take his hat to my head, to relieve him of his phone, take his hand and dance with him across restricted road, an old dance, an uneven rhythm, an unbroken code between us, to testify that we are here now looking right at each other, asking, Who the hell are you? But as much as I want to move, to startle him, I don't move at all, only my eyes on his face and his on mine and a moment's exuberance soon ebbs with the monotony that continues with the slowness of the day half-gone with the heat I am sick of mentioning, and the pointlessness and the hunger with the urge to move lingering in me as I play with the thought that I want to lie down in the back of the open grubby police car, that I almost do it … This time for sure I will just move myself the inches required, in through the open waiting car door, the empty seat, ready, enticing, waiting and stretched out, almost touches my knee. And does it matter any more if I lie down on the dirty flowered upholstery, Bread Boy's imprint and smell and crumbs still visible. Does it matter if I sleep awhile, drive a while around the block, ask myself where did that Bread Boy go so fast, so far away from the scene, from all our memories. Short cop looking at me, wondering if I'll make it, almost encouraging me in, while a wedding car goes by, a line of ten sleek white cars distracts me, a procession with pink and gold balloons and music screams from windows, laughter, a cloud of veil, groomed faces, torn cream petals fly into the road and settle on the red horse shit, and someone takes a video of us looking at them. A middle-aged Russian couple joins us, we all wave at the wedding party while Bella translates that the couple say the underpass is shut … they ask how are they to cross the road.

Listen to that, after all that … the underpass is SHUT!…

The forms take an age to complete and duplicate. Bella has to write our statements in Russian, then read them back to us. NO. stamps all the forms with a little portable ink and stamp kit that short man carries in his bag. NO. keeps up with the farce that we are going to the station any time now. I know for sure that we are not going anywhere. That he would have taken us by now, if instead he weren't just waiting for us to agree to pay, yes, here we are paying the tiny $10 fine for crossing the road. Finally that's it, just $10. Finally it's not the money, it's the principle, last throes. Bella translates, He wants to know how much you will pay him for the damage to his car. Tell him nothing … I shout. En and Bella roll up their eyes and I see they have quietly agreed and decided.

Everyone gesticulates wildly. Bella translates: he will take an extra $50 towards the damage to his car or you will have to go to the police station, he will make you stay there for hours, you may have to go to a magistrate's court to plead your case tomorrow and miss your flights. I don't believe it. En is already saying, We'll pay him. He's already taking out his wallet and counting the money. They are saying, It's nothing, let's get this over with. I am shouting, It's disgusting. Yes, yes, they say but let's get out of here.

I see it's over. I see Bella check the $60. I agree with them that for us the money is not so much, but for him it's a lot. I hear Bella calculate how little NO. must make in a week. I agree that it is more about NO. saving face but still I tut and say if it were up to me ... Let him do what he has to, let's see what he can do ... and I walk off a little to show my disgust because no-one any longer cares if I stray to the post office. I am tempted instead to pick a large flake of rust off NO.'s bonnet, as Bella slips into the car with him, as I hear the mangled door click shut with some force, as in the privacy of his front seat she passes him the money. The wait puts an unwanted picture in my head of Hugh Grant caught in his car receiving a blow job from an American hooker, neither picture do I want, neither of the bumbling Grant's hard-on nor of the wet relief passing over NO.'s face; my body jerks to the shouts of ... *You got off lightly* ... screamed across the road, as if the men laughing their way across the street have caught me out with those last images driven away with NO.'s car. With Bella retrieved, his car already accelerating into the distance, no good bye, no last look, no fare thee wells, no NO.

The restaurant is dark cool and empty by the time we arrive; most people have already eaten and left. It's built underground and although En keeps calling it a cellar, it reminds me more of a bunker with small passages and nooks where we hide away in a corner. A sweet young man places the linen napkin over my lap and says he'll make me a salad, Just how you want it ... Just tell me, whatever you want you can have. I order the artichokes tomatoes and lettuce and the promised cod's roe. Tell me what next, tell me everything. I tell him about the closed underpass, the arrest that didn't finally happen, I never did get to see the inside of the police station or cell, I never did get the promised ride in the car. I tell him of having freed ourselves of NO. ... Bella calling to us - Go enjoy your food, go eat and forget all about it, all is well ... only keep out of trouble, and remember to use the underpasses - as she runs freely across the same road, the three of us laughing.

You won't believe it, just a few blocks away, just minutes from here, I almost get arrested again for taking a photograph of En before an overblown statue of Stalin, yes, before what turns out to be a government building, an irate soldier confiscates my camera, interrogates me about why I wanted photographs of the building and him. And now here we are, telling you everything ... I mean I am telling the young waiter who tells us he's Jewish, that he also has a Polish grandfather. Everywhere we go people seem to find us and tell us the same thing as if this has become some kind of secret password, along the street the dispersed gather and whisper I am a Jew, I too had a Polish Grandfather. He's been to Israel, the young waiter, not much older than our sons, he wants to live there and not here. He says he hates it here in Minsk, the whole place is corrupt, he says, that maybe he will move to Israel or Spain, yes, he tells me with great happiness in his eyes that he can speak Spanish and would I like some Spanish wine. He brings me a jug of cool wine which he's pouring into a crystal glass, I tell him I am not used to such fancy wares, he tells me to drink and begins to plan out my next course of swordfish and grilled vegetables ...

En and I will begin arguing over the incident with the police, after the laughter, over the second course, we'll disagree about the way we both responded to NO. The conversation will wind and build and exaggerate into a question of survival ending up sixty years back with his grandparents' arrest. The rest will sound like the usual pattern of an argument, sentences stabbed, interrupted, unwieldy lines with no breath or too much breath, reinforced pauses, no ease, some spit between the shredding the bread, the mopping of fish oil, the passing and tasting of each other's food, the spilling of salt, salt over the shoulder, the water and wine drunk too quickly, the knife cuts the food too sharply scrapes across the delftware, all of it in no particular order ... the rest will cause the waiter to falter in the kitchen doorway which faces me, the doorway to En's back, in which the waiter will pace, catch my eye and snatches of our sentences, sometimes he'll stand there through a paragraph and then disappear, reappear like a magic trick, his nervous body half in and half out of the doorframe, his head peeps out, a leg hovers, worried if to approach as we'll fail to reign in the sound of the wrangle we'll make which surely only exaggerates our accent as it echoes across the vaulted ceilings of the cellar, ends over the now almost empty plates. Maybe it's finally that we'll talk ourselves into some plotless back road, some abandoned potato field, and I'll have no idea what I am saying any more, no idea of direction or if any of it matters any more; finally it will be the waiter that will make me stop, the way he's framed in the doorway, hunched over with indecision, the way his empty tray's balanced awkwardly on his wrist, the way the napkin is folded with perfection over his arm and his jacket is too blue and too big for him. I'll want to say, Come, it's okay. I'll want to say sorry to him, bring a pigeon for the bread, I'll want to give En a hug over the mess of the cloth between us - the way they embrace in those cheap films, I'll want to say My love; to reapply my lipstick and to ask if he knew what tree we were under today, our tree let's say, tell me the name of it. I'll say none of this matters and still we'll dig ourselves in for another round, spend the rest of the dessert with the Holocaust, En and me over the last of the fish and veal and let's say black cherries, some kind of trifle to follow, the cream En will scrape off to one side, the faint whiff of liqueur on his lips; we'll keep circling the question that Seth put to us at Auschwitz, why so many people went passively to their deaths. We'll disagree again about our different reactions, what we would have done, been prepared to do if some sixty years back we'd been forced to scrub pavements, to shovel snow,

Thomas Langner

FEB 6, 2022
12:35 PM

ROSE
SENIOR LIVING
Avon

to eat shit, to stand beneath a tree for hours, to avoid or provoke a shot ... As if you had a choice. As if we could know. It's an ugly conversation. It's beautiful here don't you think, she'll say - Bella that is, the next day, half-dreaming from the window, This city ... I love it here in Minsk, she'll say as she is driving us out of here and home, tomorrow, well after the meal, she'll be happy to see us safe, to get us safely to the airport. We'll joke about the whole incident with NO., we'll joke about the book I'm trying to finish and Bella laughing ... At least you'll have something to write about she'll say, but you are not to mention the bribe. I'll hear myself agree with her but know it is already included as I look from the window as she explains in NO.'s defence that he was young and over-eager to do his job, he probably has a young family and needs the extra money, she'll say. It happens all the time ... You should have seen the relief on his face when I gave him the money, his relief to be done with it.

I'll look hard into the forests we'll pass on the way home and hear myself agree that it's beautiful here, that Minsk is famous for its forests, so many forests everywhere. I'll think about us leaving Ella and Wilhelm, knowing we won't ever return, En's small doll buried somewhere out there under the soil, how Elise will laugh when we'll tell her what we left there. Poor doll, she'll say, laughing wickedly for some minutes until we were all laughing over her dolly plight. I'll try hard to see what Bella sees, to try and see Minsk as much more than a murder site. I'll hear myself wanting to please her. I'll hear her promise that she'll write to me, and no doubt we will from time to time. I'll ask her to send me her stories. She'll say Of course, but she'll forget, never get around to it; too worried over getting it right. I'll find myself wondering what NO. is thinking, I mean, if he is still thinking of us the way we are still talking about and thinking of him, still wondering who he was beyond the uniform, the shiny 60259 of his badge and the exaggerated brim of his hat ... Sure he's moved on to different days and people and bribes that come and go too soon.

But to go back ... For now there's only the waiter faltering in the doorway, wanting to bring me another drink, another plate of something, wanting to comfort something in us. I tell him I am full. I tell him everything was delicious. I see that En is tired and that we have said enough, I see that En was only trying to take care of us, finally we are free to go, free to ponder, free to say that it is not in any way comparable to ask why some people went passively or not to their deaths all those years back but still you find yourself wondering what you might have done ...

Everything will be all right, he says, the young waiter no more than a boy, as we leave he leaves me with his words, left to last, surprising him as much, surprising me as much, his words I didn't want. Yes I can say I didn't want his words of redemption as a final line but once spoken I'll find myself asking, what did I want to end this book, as if I had a bagful of final lines, intentions and finishings. There's just something in the way he stands before me, my smile pressing his lips together, his hands no doubt clutched there behind his back, unsure of himself, unsure of what he's saying, if he should say, but feeling he should so he does; there's something about his words held between us, simple enough, lyrical enough, his words offered up like a kiss, a wish, almost reminiscent of some old song I've heard somewhere, some old tune I might find myself humming one day, his words for now safe and sound, said enough times by others, letting me know that we have already in our own ways left Minsk behind, yes, even though we are here before the other we are already long gone and the last line's been given, been put in place, this last line again repeated out of him as if he tries to convince himself as much, *Everything will be all right* ... the words this time nodded out of him like a gentle Yid at prayer, that rocking repetitive chant more an incantation and me rocking before him. Yes, maybe I also find myself standing before him bobbing back and forth now, back and forth before the other, both of us, look at that, what a sight, the whole shebang. Enough to say it.

Berlin

It's Holocaust memorial day and when I turn on the radio everyone here is arguing, the Secretary-General of the Muslim Council is saying: We'll boycott the commemoration. We want the day replaced by a National Genocide Day that recognises the mass murder of muslims in Palestine, Chechnya, Bosnia. And don't forget Rwanda, he says. When is a Holocaust a Holocaust, someone asks. What about the Palestinians wearing orange stars, emblems written onto their forearms as a recent demonstration, someone says. It's a question of numbers, someone interrupts, of five hundred Palestinian towns and villages wiped out. If around three thousand people died in one day during 9/11 then imagine that each day this number of people were killed. Each day, seven days a week, for five years during the Nazi Holocaust. It's all a question of numbers and that it occurred in a civilised cultured white European State, all of it carried out in an industrialised manner.

The coincidence of the day, when only this morning I came to realise that on this same day, without planning to - not even realising what today was - I will complete the last part of this book. Hear Moinous say, You never finish a book, you just get tired of it. Or maybe it gets tired of you. Tired of the asking, and of the what for, what now, where next. And if today is the day when the final word is placed, then I can say that it will not necessarily be written in the order it will be read, but then how am I to know in what order it will be read. Ask myself again ... To whom am I speaking? Back to that old lark. En saying, If you do write about Berlin, make sure you write it to Moinous or to Sarah. And yes for sure the two of them have been present throughout. You could say, the two ears: my listening is so bad, S. says, M. with his ears a-buzzing. Yes, speak it out, En says. That chattering gossiping voice, the hand held to the side of the mouth ... Pssst ... Listen ... If I am after all talking to *you*, and who the hell knows who *you* might be ... I am today only sure that I will not send this along to Moinous, to Sarah. For now, it ends with no known destination for surely I have sent enough. Said enough.

When only the other day, before we'd left for Berlin, I said to Moinous. Can you re-send me that story, you know the one you told me way back ... and here my friend am I not in danger of that opening line sounding more like a joke than intended: *You know ... the one about ... the one about ...* E's boat being struck by a German U-boat when it was on its way from London to America. About the people caught up in the propeller. The gold and money sinking to the bottom of the ocean. I have it somewhere in our word larder but I can't find it ... And his reply. No. I hate to repeat stories I have already told. What a lie, I said. You have spent your whole life repeating the same stories. The boy's story, so many versions of your stories that cancel themselves out as they go along. Yes, but maybe for now that is enough. Enough asking and for now maybe even enough telling.

I made a small home-made film once with Sarah as the subject - did I tell you this before - or rather the film, you might say, was her story. A film about her tracking down her birth parents which we did surprisingly easily over several months. Her birth parents, it turns out, had married shortly after they'd had her adopted and some thirty years on and were still together. She found out that she has a sister. She discovered she is half-Italian on her mother's side. She had, at the time, living grandparents. We both came to see that she looked more like her father. When we take the camera with us, to what you might say was the climax, where Sarah meets the three of them for the first time - well, give or take those few, for her, unremembered days she had with her parents when she was first born. We film all evening, or rather, I film her as they talk all evening, as they tell their stories, as some of the gaps are filled in, others opened. I film them all, watch them, zoom in and out, make decisions about who to frame and where to sit, when to cut, what to listen in to. I finally, due to a technical fault and the late hour, leave them alone to talk. The next morning, as normal, I take out the camera and begin to film her again. She is applying her make-up. I ask her more questions. She pulls back her hair. Applies moisturiser. I like seeing her face naked like this. Tell me more, I say, now we are here and after some thirty years of absence, how does it feel to see them? What did they say when I left the room last night? Not now, she says, turning away, applying mascara to her top lash, right eye. Her hand twisted back, her mouth stretched into a gape, the other hand firmly holding the compact, her knuckles are white with the pressure she is applying to the mirror. I follow. I push the camera closer to her face. I zoom. Her lashes become huge. We are laughing for a while. This is what we had spent each day of months doing, me watching, asking, she the watched and the teller. I am laughing and she is no longer willing. The laughter tinged with irritation. She applying the red lipstick we share. She won't keep still. I won't leave her alone. Her face changes. She extends her hand toward me, obliterates my lens. *IT'S OVER.*

Last night Stephen Fry was on TV. He has a very similar history to En. His grandfather moved via Budapest to Vienna and married a woman from there. His grandparents luckily left Vienna through an offer of work in Britain, thus accidentally and randomly missing the war and all that followed. His great-grandparents were not so lucky and they were deported to Riga where they died. His mother's aunt, the aunt's husband and one of their three children were killed at Auschwitz. He said they'd always known or imagined that this was what'd happened to them. *We knew,* he said, *but not where, and now seeing the word* Auschwitz *does something to you. Seeing it written there. Auschwitz,* he says. *That fucking word.*

In contrast ... *random* becomes my children's favourite word. It seems fitting. The randomness of the day, the book's contents; made; done; happening without method; something similarly constructed with stones. More stones placed in random countries. Left on top of people we will not visit again. Random endings; great speed; gallop; the way it may end.

In Berlin we'd looked for the site of the Rosenstrasse Protest, which took place on March 1, 1943. The Nazis exempted Berlin Jews in mixed marriages from deportation until February 28, 1943. On that day, the Fabrik-Aktion took place, where between 1,500 and 2,500 Jewish men were rounded up and held in the Jewish community building on Rosenstrasse. The next day, a series of demonstration by non-Jewish wives and relatives took place at the site and continued for five days. The men, surprisingly, were released. This was not an expected response. It was imagined that the men were freed because the demonstrators, mostly women, were not protesting against the Nazi regime, but the Nazi violation of their own charge that intermarried Jews and *mischlinge* - half-Jews - should not be deported. That the regime possibly had some respect for the women and also wished to avoid a larger demonstration and violence in the centre of Berlin.

The book continues: There's now a kiosk on the Rosenstrasse which documents the events that took place there in 1943, and a monument in a nearby park is entitled *"Block der Frauen"* - Block of Women - dedicated in 1995 and carved by sculptor Ingeborg Hunzinger. The imagery is of the protesting women. The inscription on the rear reads: *"The strength of civil disobedience, the vigour of love overcomes the violence of dictatorship; Give us our men back; Women were standing here, defeating death; Jewish men were free."*

Moinous will say, A., you are in danger of becoming more Jewish than the rest of us. He'll laugh later and retract it, but maybe he's right. Gentile wives married to Jews, Bella says, at the time nodding a wink to En, are worse than the rest of us.

Gentle gentile, Bella writes. She calls me this once, and in another e-mail refers to *the Righteous Gentiles among us.* I erase these words both times. I find the terms uncomfortable, sentimental. I turn away from the name. I don't recognise it. Don't want to recognise it. And what shall we call ourselves? To what should we answer? Who should I say called? Who shall I say answered?

A dog with a name, Arendt says, *has a better chance of survival than a stray dog. Yes, it is me,* she says, *I recognise myself in your address. The first moment of being called and responding to that call is to take response-ability.* She says. *I did not know from my family that I was Jewish. My mother was completely a-religious ... the word 'Jew' never came up when I was a small child. I first met up with it through anti-semitic remarks.*

Lotte's e-mail arrives. Lotte, Elise's friend of some sixty years. Tell me your story, I'd said to Lotte. Tell me about your youth, about you and Elise and how you first met. When she writes she takes me back to March 1938. She's in school. She's in Vienna in school and she tells me that she knows she is Jewish because her classmate is spitting on her. Her message to me opens with someone else's spit held for sixty years in her mouth ... she writes: *I don't know where to begin. But, here goes. When Hitler marched into Vienna, "Everyone" was thrilled. March 1938. I was 13. All the anti-semites came out of the woodwork. Your classmates got hostile. One boy spat on me ...* & so on.

And so on ...

My instinct is not to write anything about Berlin, not to even mention that we came here. Not that there is anything wrong here: on the contrary; but in terms of this book, in terms of where it began, with Auschwitz, it wasn't expected that we'd end in Berlin. I could say I began with the end, in that the end of story for so many victims began with their final destination - Auschwitz - an end that was imagined, dreamt-up, began here in Berlin. Yet such words of imagination and dreams, jar, when you think of the end result or *final solution*. The before-and-after-the-war held here in Hitler's bunker now covered in snow, held [or so we read - and versions vary] beneath a basketball caught, I mean court, another of my children's latest obsession.

En is sure it's here: the bunker that the guide books skirt around. When they do mention it, they will say that it's not a marked spot or treated as a grave, just in case people - *Neo-nazis,* they specify - make it into a shrine. Various maps - with large red dots risen like infected boils - mark out other guesses, indicate that - *It could be here, it could be anywhere in this area,* as if they don't know. Some sites claim that the bunker is most likely leading off in many directions, that part of it is concealed; many go back to this idea that it's hidden away beneath, what's now, a children's recreation area. And if this is the place, it's fenced off and locked and opposite the Jewish memorial. The new one, the memorial that was officially inaugurated on the 10th of May 2005. Work temporarily halted in 2003 because it was revealed that the company Degussa, who were contracted to apply the anti-graffiti coating to each of the 2,711 concrete slabs, were apparently once part of the Degesch company that had delivered Zyklon-B to concentration camps. We have to think about the victims, they said, and so the work was halted while a new company was found. Within hours of its opening, the anti-graffiti coating did little to stop the vandals, as they were described, who had already scrawled a swastika onto the memorial. The security guards said, You can't be in all places at all times. The architect Eisenmann said, I don't care if people graffiti the monument, maybe it'll add to it. Someone else saying, You can get imprisoned here in Berlin for such displays. What kind of misplaced fear and censorship do you call that, a newsman argues back.

The site of the memorial is said to be the size of four football pitches, 6,500 square feet of ground close to the Brandenburg Gate. Costing some twenty-six million Euros to construct. We come across the memorial in the half-light of the evening which gives it more ... what? More character, more atmosphere, more blue light, more seduction, more authority, more mystery? We come across it and at first it disappoints, but I am not sure what I was expecting to see. I think of Marian Marzynski in his film interviewing a few of the architects whose proposals had been short-listed. I think of him standing here on the empty muddy site before the winners had yet to be announced and saying, Maybe these monuments should never be built, only ever discussed. The apartments overlooking us are lit up. People prepare supper. People return home from work. I wanted to hear a lullaby in German, Marian says. A woman takes our photograph. She pushes her baby in a pram through the narrow snow-filled paths between each slab. The baby is half-asleep and I hear Marian's request fulfilled as the woman sings to her dreaming child. The man who is maybe the baby's father says something to her in German as she agrees to take our photograph and they laugh. Maybe I should follow them, or walk in here alone and lose myself. Maybe I am rushing too much. Every so often a face, a figure, a stranger appears and disappears. Startles and smiles. The atmosphere is playful. There are teenage boys jumping across the tops of the pillars. They look committed to a few hours here, they look satisfied with what lies ahead for them. The possibilities of hide-and-seek and up-to-no-good as I notice and lower my eyes to one of the boy's peeing on the stones, maybe more out of relief than malice.

As expected, once inside, the pillars of stone lose their appearance of graves - in the snow, look more like iced slices of cake - and become taller, uneven, the scale changes and you become minute in its innards, so many possible directions I won't ever take. The ground rises and falls slightly but I have no sense of losing my balance, I can clearly see that I am not lost as I can see the edges and exits from every angle and so never feel disorientated or unsafe: this expectation - written by others, not a promise. And is that what I want? To fear that I'll lose myself in here? I look back and keep telling myself that I should be slowing down, taking it in, contemplate, reflect, but my moving body knows what I want to deny, it strides on and can't be fooled, inside this monument of all monuments it knows that I want only to get out of here, knows that it can't get passed this feeling that this is just another thing to do, to tick boxes, to tell others that we came here. Is that it? Then why come at all? The blurb reads that the building of the monument was designed to express Germany's UNIQUE REMORSE. I wonder who chose the words *unique remorse*. But does it feel like a place of remorse, back to the good guilt Marian Marzynski was searching for and didn't find. Remorse: *expressing intense 'force'... 'to bite'. 'Vex', 'shake', 'disturb'. Cause to feel 'annoyed' or 'worried'.* It's a place of awkwardness, of clutter and confusion. It looks predictable. It jars in the space. It is like a scab on the knee of the city. It says: I don't know what to do, what to say here ... try this ... a flower ... a million yellow flowers - would that have done better? The President in his speech said the memorial would express an acceptance of responsibility for our history. Alongside the road named Hannah Arendt-Strasse, beside her term: response- ability; a Jew - she is called and so becomes - marks the spot of what En tells me again is Hitler's bunker, or wasn't it beneath the children's park, near the site of the bombed and now missing Reich Chancellery. I expected children's laughter, I expected toddlers and mothers and primary colours flashing to run to the slide but see none of it ... Can we make the holocaust CUTE Sarah will later ask. Instead ... It may have been more impressive if they'd put the Jewish memorial over the top of the bunker site. Maybe they did, and don't say.

Inside the Libeskind Jewish museum there is so much information, so many interactions, there's even a fake tree whose branches are filled with pomegranates, some made from cardboard, some formed from grainy images on electronic pads flowering from material leaves, a metal set of steps to reach inside the tree if you care to climb, and some do, but to where and what? A tape of Hannah Arendt is played on a small screen, she's being interviewed by Günter Grass, it's a well-known interview but I don't recognise her at first. It is hard to know who is who here. Hannah is being interviewed and she looks hot. She fidgets a lot in her chair. She pushes her glasses up and onto her nose many times. She looks upset. Here all the tapes are looped so you get to constantly watch things in the wrong order. You get fractured sentences and broken pictures. Anne Frank's overblown face frozen between childhood and womanhood, smiles knowingly down over this section - even though at the time that image was taken you could say that she knew nothing of her fate - but I can't look back at her for long because she looks as if she is laughing and I am worried that I get the joke. I go back to Hannah. I watch her push her glasses back again. She fidgets again in her chair. She is saying, *What was decisive is the day we learned about Auschwitz ... This ought not to have happened. And I don't mean just the numbers of victims. I mean the method, the fabrication of corpses and so on - I don't need to go into that. This should never have happened. Something happened there to which we cannot reconcile ourselves. None of us ever can. About everything else that happened I have to say that it was sometimes rather difficult: we were very poor, we were hunted down, we had to flee, by hook or by crook we somehow had to get through, and whatever. That's how it was. But we were young. I even had a little fun with it - I can't deny it. But not this. This was something completely different. Personally I could accept everything else.*

En calls me over to see a glass case containing some worn boxing gloves, he begins reading out the story to me, but I am still trying to remember what Hannah had said, what she is still saying but she is out of reach so I can only now hear the tone of her voice but not its content. Here, there are so many displays of handwritten letters with sections blotted out, censored so that the blobs of ink become the focus of your eye and my wanting to know what was erased. There are wedding albums, there are windows of photographs and small stories. A brown parcel - the story reads, *this parcel was given to a woman for safe-keeping by a Jewish woman. The woman never returned to claim it back. The woman who held it for her never opened it and when her son found it after his mother's death, many years later, he opened it and found its simple contents:* mouthwash, soap, a small photograph and what looks like a small home-sewn bag. I cannot make out what it holds. The mouthwash is displayed and is in a pale blue bottle. The colour blue is pleasing.

The man at the door tells us we must see the very important installation as if realising that En is by now getting restless to find the way out, he says he's reached saturation. It's not the building, its that the building should be emptied, he says, that'd do it, one empty building with nothing in it. It's not the building, it's the content and the interactive games and the TV screens and the disneyfication and the flickering images and the fractured words and the names given to rooms and things, most of which contain the words memory and void. It's the way it makes you feel when you step into Ikea and you are forced to navigate endless arteries of laminated wood and displays before they'll let you out again, when all you wanted was to buy a corkscrew. And for sure, as we try to leave we only find ourselves deeper inside more corridors leading to more interactive games and videos and cases of photographs, tea cups and clothes. He, almost running now, En, and I keep losing him, around the corridors trying to find the exit, only more dead ends that circle us back to more displays and more pathways. He's telling me that is the point ... If this place makes you feel anything it's that you'll never be let out, he says, that's why the security is so heavy on the door, that's why two men took away my small penknife and placed it in a sealed bag - as if I will get it back. That's why they take away your bags and coats and possessions on arrival. That's why the entrance stinks of SOUP.

The guard instead appears again and reminds us that we must see the important installation and shuttles us along and into entering what is this time blatantly labelled *The Memory Void*. The Memory Void or Menasce Kadishman's *Shalechet* or *Fallen Leaves* is a space made up of 10,000 coarsely made iron faces that we are encouraged to walk on, despite the fact that I don't want to walk over them, we do what we feel we must. While we walk, the guard, with more enthusiasm than my feet, reminds us: *When you walk on the faces the movements of your boots over the metal heads create an almost industrial noise, something,* he says, *with deep meaning.* We walk across, following others, young people everywhere here. Parties and busloads of washed eager faces stand on top of the metal faces which remind me of a bed of Munch's screams. Overhear someone say that as promised, when you walk on these faces, it's like the Jew's individual memories clinking awake. En says he likes the noise. I tell him I can't stand it. It is getting in the way of anything I may have thought or felt. It shuts everything down. And as we reach the interior of the installation and look back over this floor of fallen faces we have tiptoed our way across, it embarrasses me to want to flee the screaming Jewish caricatures, faces which now give the impression that they have turned to dead leaves which is somehow more moving until the darkness we enter is killed off by the appearance of a large white fire door reinforcing that we are indeed inside a construct, inside a museum.

It's all fake, Moinous will say. Fake.

In another attempt to leave, we find ourselves manoeuvred into a room the young woman describes as *The Holocaust Tower*. Unlike the *Memory Void*, we are alone here. It is unlike the rest of the museum, in that for the first time something makes me feel unsettled, as we're unexpectedly closed inside dark unwindowed walls. My instinct is both go and to stay even though it frightens me, even though the handle that is visible on the door that has slowly closed behind us is oversized, is the promise - but, little more than a promise - of getting out. Once inside it's immediately icy cold, a coldness that you recognise so acutely because it will one day come to all of us. The corners of the room, one which is exaggerated and sharp and very black, are the most intimidating, yet I walk to this very corner to tell myself I can, to show myself there is nothing there to fear, I squeeze myself as tightly as possible into this corner until darkness disorientates, until I can no longer be sure of my feet or hands and for a moment

I feel I could disappear between the solidity of walls coming together, ending. The cold makes us shiver, the voices we hear are muffled and tease us into discussing if we are for sure hearing things. There's only a ladder on the other wall, a ladder out of reach and going nowhere, drawing our eyes still trying to decide, unable to adjust to an enormous chimney that ends either in a solid cork sealing us off - or what I'd feared of the corner's infinity that's now found over our heads, pulled back to face this black sky and nowhere to look but up. That leads me to recall Beckett's Lost Ones. *The ladders. These are the only objects … From time immemorial rumour has it or better still the notion is abroad that there exists a way out … The other dreams of a trapdoor hidden in the hub of the ceiling giving access to a flue at the end of which the sun and other stars would be shining … A kiss makes an indescribable sound.*

In the snow I will say, It hasn't touched me yet, this place. Will it, should it? Maybe all of it has and I can't yet see it. What is this touch I seek. What are we looking for here and in all the other museums and countries we've been that still lead us back to Auschwitz? You're questing, Sarah says.

Quest

1. *a long arduous search.*
2. *(in medieval romance) an expedition by a knight to accomplish a prescribed task.*
V. search for something.
One of the two main identified basic narratives. The quest. Quest narratives [Dunker says] *are fueled by the main character's desire. Often this involves an implicit longing for home. In the quest plot your characters can take to the road, and meet and shed other people. The danger is,* [she says] *that your reader will grow confused. If you fear losing your focus, devise a strong central character to hold your story together, and try reducing your structure to a simple linear plot.*

Who have I shed? Have I met and shed enough? Is it me that is confused, not a strong enough CENTRAL CHARACTER? Not enough character at all? Is it me who is LOSING MY FOCUS? Losing any sense of my simple linear plot? Plots are for dead people, I hear Moinous say, for cemeteries.

quester, questor, questing, questingly

Origin. ME: from OFr. queste (n.), quester (v.) based on L. quaerere 'ask, seek' search, pursuit, chase, hunt, purpose, quarry, prey.

This morning in Berlin I watch from our apartment window, with the privilege of someone away and free from routine, others get ready for work. A man in a powder-blue jumper paces to and from his desk. He is tense and full of purpose. I envy his concentration. His tautness. A woman behind frosted glass, surely middle-aged from the outline of her shape, repeatedly fixes her hair with her hands. She fluffs it up like a meringue and is worrying over her face and keeps toing and froing from the mirror in a way that is achingly familiar and echoes her neighbour's movements beneath. A young person, a gender I cannot identify, peels an orange with a small penknife, very carefully, their body moves in a way that indicates they are listening to music. They peel the orange in a perfect spiral of skin and my mouth fills with juice. I like the clutter of their kitchen best of all. I like the man who sits with his back to me with his newspaper opened looking freshly-ironed, both man and paper, the immaculate spread of his clothes and the pages. It is only 7.30 a.m. and already he has lit a small decorated candle just for the pure pleasure of the colour orange flickering, filling the walls of his morning where he believes himself to be alone in the moment. How many of us are being watched as we wallow in the false seduction of our early morning solitude? The school-children leave, their rucksacks bulge on their backs, their small bodies heavy and titled forward in padded fluffy clothes, tight boots pick their way through the ice. I think about our own children, who must also be getting ready for school in another country. Of their names that we found scratched into what's left of the Berlin Wall. We found the wall; the first things we saw were their names scratched - Seth and Max. Tell me mother, you'll say, didn't you know we were there, even when you couldn't see us? No-one will believe us, En says, that we didn't scratch their names into the wall in the right order, one over the other, that we didn't do that ourselves. Believe me we stopped there in front of the wall for some minutes and tried to imagine who these others with the same names were. Maybe brothers like ours, or a couple no longer together. Maybe now more together than ever, yes, I'd like to think they were devoted to one another. Maybe only one of them etched the names in the other's absence. Maybe written in longing. As a wish. As a question. Maybe a mother missing her children. Maybe I got up last night, came here, sneaked out and wrote it for you. Maybe you'll never know if I did that or not. The river with the black ducks sliding on squares of ice and no bread in our pockets. Give in, give up on looking, stop it now. Your yearnings and awnings and yawnings your questions and …

En in his black polo-neck making coffee. Studying the map. I photograph him and enjoy the angle of his face under the lamp. I photograph him three times as he plans the day out on small pieces of paper. When he knows I am watching through the lens, he smiles without looking up, then tells me to go away. I'm memorialised-out, I say. I don't think I'll write about Berlin. There's nothing to say. I should have ended with Minsk. Maybe I will. Maybe it's like that part when the film goes on for that extra ten minutes and you turn to the person with you and whisper, It should have finished back there, when he said nothing, when he pressed her and the note into the back of the lift. Maybe it should end with me drinking a Bloody Mary in the food hall in the Ka-Da-We. With Moinous saying they sell seventy-five different types of bread and you can eat mussels and cheese and crepes in that place, wait till you see it.

Instead I'm a thousand feet up, maybe more. I'm watching a woman walk across a frozen lake. She's sliding her way to the centre of a huge lake. I'm up here in the sky over Berlin and she's so completely unaware of me watching. That I'm flying over her, that I have already left another city behind. There's only her and the frozen lake. There's no-one near her, no-one for miles and miles. Only this woman determined in her direction, this woman who can't possibly know from down there how completely alone she is. Maybe she's waiting for the ice to break. Maybe I am. Maybe she's not thinking that way. Maybe she is only thinking of that moment when it will give way under her. She seems happy enough. Something about the way she walks - if not happy, she's at least resolute. She's on her way. She's nearing her destination quicker than is imaginable. I'm finished with this book, I say to En. This book that ends here with us flying out of Berlin, with a woman crossing a frozen lake. With a woman in a long white coat sweeping the ice as she walks. A long white coat which looks cream against the white of the ice. And she's smiling and steadfast. I can't see the details of her face, I can't see her face at all, but I can tell from her movements that she's unwavering. I can see from her motion, her rhythm, that there's nothing else to say, that I have no idea how her story ends, I have no idea what will soon happen to her out there on the lake, but I see her well enough. I see the marks she leaves across the ice, I see the trail her coat makes as fragile as the trail the aeroplane makes as we cross her, as we pass by and over each other, as she is both leaving my field of vision and inscribing my eye.

Top: Ella and Wilhelm Engelhart, En's grandparents.

Bottom: Passport of Elise, En's mother (the forename Sara was added to documents by the Nazis to indicate that a woman was Jewish).

Acknowledgements

A special thank you to Tessa, Lotte, Bella, Caoimhe and Anne who gave their stories openly. Thanks to Robert Hyde at Galileo for honouring the spirit of the book, for being refreshingly straightforward and committed throughout, and if the origins of 'gentleman' is, among other things, someone considerate - then Robert is a true gentle/man.

Certain longer passages in this book are taken from the titles listed below and are published here with the kind permission of the following publishers:

• *At the Mind's Limits*, by Jean Amery; Indiana University Press
• *Europeana*, by Patrik Ourednik; Dalkey Archive Press
• 'Maly Trostinec' (website about the camp), May 2006; Trustees of ARC (Aktion Reinhard Camps) website
• Mark Thwaite's literary website *www.readysteadybook. com*
• *More Loose Shoes and Smelly Socks*, by Raymond Federman, Replenishment Books
• *Mosaic Man*, by Ronald Sukenik; University of Alabama Press
• *Remnants of Auschwitz*, by Giorgio Agamben, Zone Books
• *Return to Manure*, by Raymond Federman; University of Alabama Press

Shorter passages from the following titles are also acknowledged:

• *Auschwitz: The Residence of Death*, Teresa and Henryk Ozwiebocki; Auschwitz-Birkenau State Museum, Bia_y Kruk
• *Book to Come*, by Maurice Blanchot; Stanford University Press
• *Coming to Writing and Other Essays*, by Hélène Cixous; Harvard University Press
• *A Jew Among the Germans*, film by Marian Marzynski, copyright Frontline
• *Federman, L'Infedère, an interview*. This excerpt translated from the French by Federman. First appeared in *Le Matricule des Agnes*, #68, November-December 2005
• *Forbidden Representation*, an essay by Jean Luc Nancy
• *Fugitive Pieces,* by Anne Michael; Bloomsbury
• *Here & Elsewhere*, by Raymond Federman, Six Gallery Press
• *Jacques Lacan*, by Elisabeth Roudinesco; Polity Press
• *Oxford English Dictionary* (2nd ed), Oxford University Press
• *Poetry After Auschwitz*, by Susan Guber; Indiana University Press
• *The Human Race*, by Robert Antelme; Northwestern University Press
• *The Portable Hannah Arendt*, (ed) Peter Baehr, Penguin Books
• *The Telephone Book*, by Avital Ronell; Bison Books
• *The Twofold Vibration*, by Raymond Federman; Green Integer

• Ken Rice's website for: http://users.erols.com/kennrice/lego-kz.htm
• The Artnet Worldwide Corporation for: http://www.artnet.com/magazine/features/rush/rush7-9-03.asp#6